CATHERINE COOKSON

BRITAIN'S BEST-LOVED STORYTELLER

THE

Invitation

Catherine Cookson was born in Tyne Dock, the illegitimate daughter of a poverty-stricken woman, Kate, whom she believed to be her older sister. She began work in service but eventually moved south to Hastings, where she met and married Tom Cookson, a local grammar-school master. At the age of forty she began writing about the lives of the working-class people with whom she had grown up, using the place of her birth as the background to many of her novels.

Although originally acclaimed as a regional writer – her novel *The Round Tower* won the Winifred Holtby award for the best regional novel of 1968 – her readership soon began to spread throughout the world. Her novels have been translated into more than a dozen languages and more than 50,000,000 copies of her books have been sold in Corgi alone. Fifteen of her novels have been made into successful television dramas, and more are planned.

Catherine Cookson's many bestselling novels established her as one of the most popular of contemporary women novelists. After receiving an OBE in 1985, Catherine Cookson was created a Dame of the British Empire in 1993. She was appointed an Honorary Fellow of St Hilda's College, Oxford in 1997. For many years she lived near Newcastle-upon-Tyne. She died shortly before her ninety-second birthday in June 1998.

'Catherine Cookson's novels are about hardship, the intractability of life and of individuals, the struggle first to survive and next to make sense of one's survival. Humour, toughness, resolution and generosity are Cookson virtues, in a world which she often depicts as cold and violent. Her novels are weighted and driven by her own early experiences of illegitimacy and poverty. This is what gives them power. In the specialised world of women's popular fiction, Cookson has created her own territory'
Helen Dunmore, *The Times*

BOOKS BY CATHERINE COOKSON

NOVELS

Kate Hannigan
The Fifteen Streets
Colour Blind
Maggie Rowan
Rooney
The Menagerie
Slinky Jane
Fanny McBride
Fenwick Houses
Heritage of Folly
The Garment
The Fen Tiger
The Blind Miller
House of Men
Hannah Massey
The Long Corridor
The Unbaited Trap
Katie Mulholland
The Round Tower
The Nice Bloke
The Glass Virgin
The Invitation
The Dwelling Place
Feathers in the Fire
Pure as the Lily
The Mallen Streak
The Mallen Girl
The Mallen Litter
The Invisible Cord
The Gambling Man
The Tide of Life
The Slow Awakening
The Iron Façade
The Girl

The Cinder Path
Miss Martha Mary Crawford
The Man Who Cried
Tilly Trotter
Tilly Trotter Wed
Tilly Trotter Widowed
The Whip
Hamilton
The Black Velvet Gown
Goodbye Hamilton
A Dinner of Herbs
Harold
The Moth
Bill Bailey
The Parson's Daughter
Bill Bailey's Lot
The Cultured Handmaiden
Bill Bailey's Daughter
The Harrogate Secret
The Black Candle
The Wingless Bird
The Gillyvors
My Beloved Son
The Rag Nymph
The House of Women
The Maltese Angel
The Year of the Virgins
The Golden Straw
Justice is a Woman
The Tinker's Girl
A Ruthless Need
The Obsession
The Upstart
The Branded Man

THE MARY ANN STORIES

A Grand Man
The Lord and Mary Ann
The Devil and Mary Ann
Love and Mary Ann

Life and Mary Ann
Marriage and Mary Ann
Mary Ann's Angels
Mary Ann and Bill

FOR CHILDREN

Matty Doolin
Joe and the Gladiator
The Nipper
Rory's Fortune
Our John Willie
Mrs Flannagan's Trumpet

Go Tell It To Mrs Golightly
Lanky Jones
Nancy Nuttall and the Mongrel
Bill and the Mary Ann
  Shaughnessy

AUTOBIOGRAPHY

Our Kate
Catherine Cookson Country

Let Me Make Myself Plain
Plainer Still

Catherine Cookson

The Invitation

CORGI BOOKS

THE INVITATION
A CORGI BOOK : 0 552 14090 2

Originally published in Great Britain
by Macdonald & Co (Publishers) Ltd

PRINTING HISTORY
Macdonald edition published 1970
Macdonald edition reprinted 1971
Corgi edition published 1972
Corgi edition reprinted 1973
Corgi edition reprinted 1975
Corgi edition reprinted 1976
Corgi edition reprinted 1977
Corgi edition reprinted 1978 (twice)
Corgi edition reissued 1979
Corgi edition reprinted 1980
Corgi edition reprinted 1981
Corgi edition reprinted 1983
Corgi edition reprinted 1984
Corgi edition reprinted 1986 (twice)
Corgi edition reprinted 1987
Corgi edition reprinted 1988
Corgi edition reissued 1993 (reset)
Corgi edition reprinted 1995
Corgi edition reprinted 1996 (twice)

Set in 10pt Linotype Plantin by
Chippendale Type Ltd, Otley, West Yorkshire.

Corgi Books are published by Transworld Publishers Ltd,
61–63 Uxbridge Road, London W5 5SA,
in Australia by Transworld Publishers (Australia) Pty Ltd,
15–25 Helles Avenue, Moorebank, NSW 2170,
and in New Zealand by Transworld Publishers (NZ) Ltd,
3 William Pickering Drive, Albany, Auckland.

Printed and bound in Great Britain by
Cox & Wyman Ltd, Reading, Berkshire.

Contents

Part One

Part Two

Part Three

Part Four

Part Five

Part Six

Part One

CHAPTER ONE

SAM

Maggie Gallacher stared wide-eyed at the card in her hand. It had a deckle edge, rimmed with gold. In the right hand corner of the card there was a contortion of initials which she couldn't make out, but she could make out the writing, for the words shone from the page as if they had been printed in pure gold dust, and she saw each one as an obstacle on the mountain that her Rodney had started climbing the day she married him, twenty-seven years ago. The card itself, this piece of cardboard, was the mountain peak, and they were on top of it now and not out of breath, by God no, sitting pretty as it were, in Savile House, in the best end of Felburn, which was not Brampton Hill any more but further out in the district known generally as The Rise. Sitting pretty within twelve rooms and two acres, with a stream at the bottom, the house furnished, as she put it to herself, like nobody's business. And that was not all; the name of Gallacher was ringing through the town like the church bell. Hadn't Gallacher and Sons built the new college and the Rollingdon and Morley Estates? And wasn't her family all set? At least five of them were. And this one sitting at her side now; well, there was going to be glory for her.

She put out her hand and gripped her youngest daughter's wrist, and Elizabeth, her grey eyes wide, her teeth pressed gently into her lower lip, shook her head; then nudging her mother with her elbow they fell together laughing, and they laughed as only the Gallachers could laugh, with a body-shaking, mouth-stretching infectious sound. As Maggie was wont to say, all the Gallachers did things as they should be done, they laughed from their bellies; except – she always made an exception in her mind of Paul. But then Paul, her youngest son, was like nobody but himself. Still, she liked what he was; she loved what he was.

'Shall I ring them?' With the end of her finger, Elizabeth wiped a laughter-tear from her long, black lashes, and Maggie slanted her eyes at her, the glint in them saying, 'What else?' And on this Elizabeth jumped up from the couch, ran across the room to where the telephone stood on a marble-topped reproduction Louis XV commode and she down on the gilt chair before it. But she paused as she was about to pick up the phone and, looking round at her mother, said, 'Sam and Arlette first?'

Maggie moved her head once, then said, 'Of course.'

Sam was her eldest son and so it was perhaps natural that he should be the first to hear the news, but she wasn't so much concerned with Sam's reaction to what he was going to hear as she was with his wife's. Women were supposed to be jealous of their sons' wives, particularly the wife of their first-born, but she had never been jealous of Arlette. She had always considered it strange, her feeling for Sam's wife, because between her and Arlette there was a wide gulf in upbringing, thought and attitude to life, yet in some strange way she felt close to her; she felt she understood her, while the rest of her family had varying opinions about their sister-in-law, some calling her reserve either snobbishness or condescension. But Elizabeth, with her young enthusiasm, dubbed Arlette 'It and a bit', which summed up her daughter-in-law for Maggie too.

She had never said it aloud, not even to Rod, but she had always thought that their Sam was damned lucky to get someone like Arlette. He might be big and good looking and have it up top with regards to business, but he was brash, aye, that was the word, brash. And there was something else, a something else that she had never been able to lay her finger on with regard to her eldest son . . . But Liz was speaking to him now.

'Hello. Is that you, Sam?'

'Who did you expect? Of course it's me. What's up? You sound as if you've been running.'

'You'll never believe what I'm going to tell you . . . it's about Mam and Dad.'

'Don't tell me they're going to be married.'

'Oh you, our Sam! I'll tell her, mind.'

'You do. Well, what's happened? . . . Aw no! She's not going to have another bairn.'

'OUR SAM!'

'Well, go on . . . I know. I know, she's going to take up French to please Arlette.'

'Samuel Gallacher, stop being sarcastic; she could an' all.'

'I know she could, she could do anything she wants, could our fat old mum.'

'You're in one of those moods, are you? Listen. Pin your ears back. They've had an invitation, to a sort of musical evening. Guess who from?'

'The Queen, of course.'

'No; but you're getting warm.'

There was a pause before Sam spoke again. 'You don't say! Go on, put me out of me agony.'

'Well, I am now holding in my hand a beautiful card which bears an invitation from . . . THE DUKE OF MOORSHIRE . . . Are you there? . . . Are you there, Sam?'

'Yes. Aye, I'm here. That's a fact what you're saying, the Duke of Moorshire?'

'Yes; I'm telling you.' The line seemed to go dead again. Then Sam's voice came over, flat sounding now as he said, 'Well, I'll be damned! We are going up, aren't we?'

Elizabeth glanced at her mother again. She wanted to say to Sam, 'You don't sound very excited,' but what she said was, 'Is Arlette there?'

'She's having a bath.'

'Do you think you can come round later? I'm phoning them all.'

'Yes, yes. We'll be round and have a knees-up and a Gallachers' laugh-in.'

'Oh, our Sam . . . Ta-rah then.'

'Ta-rah.'

Sam Gallacher put the phone down and stared at it; then he slewed his lower jaw to the side and gnawed at the corner of his lip, after which his head swung up and backwards and he let out a loud 'huh!'

He walked across the hall, through the long L-shaped lounge and dining-square, and into a smaller hall from which led the doors of the bathroom, lavatory, laundry and kitchen. There was the sound of the bath water running out, and slowly he put out his long arm and very gently turned the handle of the bathroom door. It was locked, as he knew it would be. He now took up a position opposite it between the kitchen and the laundry doors, and he waited, listening the while to the movements in the bathroom. He pictured her now standing before the mirror, her face cool, expressionless, until she realised he was in the house. She would have her dressing-gown on. Oh yes; she never remained naked long, not even in the bathroom. He had suggested one day she should get into the bath in her knickers; he had also suggested that she should live in there, even sleep in there as she liked bathing so much; that was the day he had stirred her to retaliation and she had told him why she bathed so much, and he had punched her in the mouth. Her aunt had been taken seriously ill that same night and she'd had to go straight down to Devonshire. She was almost as anxious to cover up as he was, and he knew the reason, and the reason made him more flaming mad. And the reason had now been invited to meet the Duke. God Almighty! Her, meeting a Duke!

The bathroom door opened and he watched his wife start. He watched the movement of her long hand pulling the dressing-gown closer about her.

'I didn't know you were in.' She went past him into the dining-space and through one of the two doors opposite. He didn't speak but followed her into the bedroom, and he watched her sit down at the dressing-table and start brushing her hair. He knew she wouldn't attempt to put her clothes on while he was there. He went and stood behind her and looked at her face in the mirror; even without make-up and her skin shiny from the bath, and her hair drawn back now tight from her forehead with the hard strokes of the brush, she was beautiful; in an unsmiling, stiff, lifeless way she was beautiful.

When he put his hand on her shoulder and felt her flesh shrink beneath his fingers, the muscles of his stomach knotted, and he warned himself, 'Careful, careful'; and so, looking into her eyes through the mirror, he said with a smile, 'I've got news for you.'

Her eyes waited, unblinking.

'You'll never guess in a thousand years the latest from the house. Didn't you hear the phone ring?'

Still she waited.

'. . . They've had an invitation from the Duke of Moorshire to a musical soirée. Can you believe it? Rod . . . and Maggie.'

He saw her eyes widen slightly and a suspicion of a smile come on her lips, and her voice now held a touch

13

of animation as she said, 'That is nice, wonderful really, I'm so glad for them.'

He reached swiftly out, pulled up a chair, placed it with its back to the dressing-table and close to her stool, and when he sat on it and leant sideways blotting out the mirror he was almost facing her, and his head moved in small nods as he said, 'Yes, you are, aren't you? Well, I can understand him getting the invitation and also being able to carry it off, but Mam . . . her passing herself with the Duke, can you see it?'

Her face only inches from his, her eyes did not waver from his look as she answered firmly now, 'Yes, yes I can. You can't see her doing anything right because of your . . . ' She gulped in her throat, drew her chin in, closed her eyes tightly now and made to rise from the stool. But his hand gripping the top of her thigh held her still, and he said quietly, 'It's funny, isn't it? I bet it doesn't happen once in ten million times the son against his mother and the daughter-in-law for her. And what a daughter-in-law, eh? And what a mother. Look! Look.' He moved his grip on her thigh. 'Tell me . . . tell me the truth. Why do you like her?'

She was swallowing rapidly now and, shaking her head from side to side as if pushing off a bad dream, she murmured, 'Stop it. Stop it. We've been through it all before. I've told you.'

'Tell me again; only don't tell me it was because your mother died when you were six and Mam welcomed you with open arms the first time she saw you, because as I've said afore there would be the same similarity between my mother and yours as there is between Kitty Malone in the office and Princess Margaret – chalk and cheese. No. The truth is, you like to condescend, and you can condescend with Mam can't you, because she's something to condescend to; you can't do it with the rest because they wouldn't stomach it, not even Nancy, and she hasn't the brains she was born with. But Mam laps it up because she's stupid.'

'She's not! Your mother is not stupid.'

Now he had stirred her; she tore at the hand on her thigh while she pushed him so violently with the other that the chair almost overturned. And her surprising action changed his own mood, and he steadied himself and got to his feet.

His face now was transformed, his full-lipped mouth was wide, his dark brown eyes held deep glimpses of amusement, and he coughed as he looked at her where she was standing near the door; her voice almost loud as she cried at him, 'Why do you hate her? Why? And don't you tell me it's because you consider her a slob, because I don't believe it. When I know why you hate her I'll have the answer to everything, everything. None of the others feel like this towards her, only you. You're . . . ' She checked herself again, and as she watched him coming slowly towards her every muscle in her body stiffened.

When he stood in front of her his tone was soft, contrite. 'I'm sorry,' he said; 'it's my fault, I know it. It's always my fault that we row. Yet things could be different, fine, if you'd only be a little understanding.' He put his hands on her shoulders and when his lower lip trembled she said swiftly, 'No! No!'

One big hand moved firmly under her shoulder blades, the other slid down on to her buttocks and as he brought her to him he muttered thickly, 'Just natural, that's all, just natural, none of the other, I promise . . . '

'No! NO! I tell you. No. I can't stand it. You can't, we've tried . . . No . . . o . . . o!'

As she had surprised him when she sprang up from the dressing-table, now she surprised him again, for her

15

body, exploding with fear, thrust itself up out of his arms, and her two hands, like claws on his face, pressed his head away from her; then as he renewed his grip on her, without uttering a word she struggled and tore at him until finally they fell to the floor.

CHAPTER TWO

WILLIE

Nancy Gallacher looked over her shoulder and shouted almost before she had put the phone down, 'Is that you, Willie?' and her husband, thrusting his head through the swing door between the kitchen and the hall, grinned at her as he replied, 'Who you expecting? The milk round finishes at twelve; the postman's last round was at four; the butcher doesn't call until the morrow . . . '

Nancy pushed him back into the kitchen with the flat of her hand, saying with a laugh, 'One of these days you'll start me on; there's a fellow on the dust cart that could give you head and shoulders . . . '

'Oh aye?'

'Listen, I've got news for you. That was Liz on the phone.'

'Don't tell me they're making her Mother Superior already. She's mad. I shouldn't say it but she's . . . '

'It's nothing to do with Liz; it's your Mam and Dad.'

'They've split up, I knew it.' He threw out his arm in a dramatic gesture, then ended seriously, 'But Dad doesn't know, I only left him half-an-hour since.'

'You're in one of your funny moods are you? Well, all right. Have your tea, have your wash, put them to bed, and then if you're interested I'll tell you the news.'

'I've had me wash, me tea, and they're in bed, come on.' He pulled her small plump figure towards him and she laughed into his round dark eyes, almost on a level with her own, and said in an undertone, 'You'll never guess, not in a month of Sundays. They've had an invitation.'

'Aye. Well, go on. They've had an invitation?'

'From the Duke of Moorshire.' Her grin widened when his hold slackened on her and his shoulders and head swayed back from her as if to get her into focus. 'Me Mam and Dad's had an invitation from the . . . ?'

'That's shaken you, hasn't it, Mr Gallacher? . . . Your Mam and Dad's going to Lea Hall.'

'Mother of God!' He moved back from her and sat down on a kitchen stool. 'This is because of the college.'

'Yes, I suppose it is. And yet I don't know; there was the opening reception to cover that, they both got an invitation. But remember Mam had the flu and couldn't go.'

'What sort of a do is it going to be, do they know?'

'Sort of musical, Liz said. The card gives the names of a well-known pianist, a violinist and a singer, all bit pots. We'll know more when we go round – they're all going round the night – that's if I can get Mrs Price to come and sit-in with them.'

'You know something?' Willie Gallacher stabbed his finger at his wife. 'I know why they've got that invitation. It's through the de Ferriers. Dad's had a lot to do with him of late. He was in on the college project right from the beginning, an' it was through his influence that Dad got it . . . I'm sure of it.'

'I thought he got it because his was the lowest tender.'

'Aye, that an' all. Oh aye, that an' all.' Willie, getting to his feet now, went and stood near the stove and began to lift the kettle lid up and down, forming the steam into smoke signals. It was a habit of his when thinking and worrying, and Nancy watched him as he now said bitterly, 'It's a wonder that damned college didn't break our back. If it hadn't been for the Morley Estate we'd have been sunk. I kept telling him, but you know Dad, reach for the sky.'

18

She came and stood close to him as she asked, 'Is anything wrong now?'

He turned his head and looked at her solemnly. 'Aw, nothing much, if it stays there. But there's complaints from the Morley houses that two walls have cracked; it might just be due to a small subsidence. Let's hope to God it is, because if it carries on from those two it will run straight down the belt between Longside Drive and Waterford Way, and there are eighty houses all told in that section. Aw, to hell!' He swung round. 'Let's go and see the bairns, I'm sick of talking. I told him. I told him when he started there, six years ago, that there was a doubt about that area. I'd been talking to old hands from the Beular Mine, but when I put it to him, what did he say? The Beular Mine was eight miles away and the galleries didn't run in this direction and he'd had the best advice on it. The best advice! Bill Teddington. Anyway, he was a surveyor, so what was my say against his, a lad of nineteen then? But as I said, to hell!' He grinned and pulled her to him; then pointing towards his coat that was lying over a chair, he ended, 'There's something for you in me case under there, tights . . . a dozen pairs, and your size this time.' He dug her in the chest.

'A dozen pairs?' She made a long laughing face, then asked, 'Billy Stoddard or Frank Atkins?'

'Frank. They fell off a lorry.' He again pushed her, his lips now tight in a suppressed grin, and she chuckled as she said, 'Eeh! our Willie. Fell off a lorry!'

She picked up the packet of tights, examined them, raised her eyebrows and said, 'Very nice, thank you. Ta.' She leaned over and kissed him, adding, 'I'll give Mam a couple of pairs, perhaps the Duke will notice them.' And to this he replied, 'You needn't bother; I've got a bundle for her.'

As they made their way once more towards the door

he stopped, and putting his head on one side, asked as if of himself, 'I wonder if she'll be able to carry it through though.'

Nancy pursed her lips. 'I don't see why not; she'll be dressed up to the eyes . . . she'll have to get dressed up for this, she's been letting herself go lately. When I first met her she seemed smart-like to me.'

'It isn't how she looks—' Willie smiled wryly at her – 'it's how she sounds when she gets going. A couple of drinks and her laugh would check Newcastle United in full swing.'

'She'll just likely have wine; they serve wine at those dos I think, like the cheese and wine parties.'

'You can get blotto on wine. But still it's not like the hard stuff, and that's her drink.'

He moved forward, opened the door, and as they went through the hall he said, musingly, 'I wonder what Dad will have to say to it.' To this Nancy made no reply because she didn't really know what her husband expected her to say.

Before they entered the sitting-room she touched his arm and said, 'By the way, Sister Martha phoned the day about Moira; she's been playing them up again. She thinks she's a bit too advanced, that's the trouble, and she finds the infants boring. Anyway, she's going to move her up next term. And she also said she's old enough to start taking instructions for her first confession. And while I'm on about that, Father Armstrong called in to ask would you give a hand with the Children of Mary's Dance. Get the lads rounded up; he said some of them are making their way into Newcastle on a Saturday night and taking the girls with them. He's got Liz helping with the refreshments. He's hoping it's going to be a big do and he's wanting everybody to pig in. He hasn't got half the amount of money he needs for the new window.'

'Aw.' Willie shook his head impatiently. 'They're always on the cadge, the three of them.'

'Not Father Armstrong.'

'Aye, Father Armstrong an' all; they're all alike. By the way.' His grin appeared again and he leant his face close to hers as he said, 'I tell you how he could get his window right away . . . Frank Atkins.' At this they fell upon each other, shaking with suppressed laughter.

CHAPTER THREE

PAUL

Paul Gallacher heard the phone ring as he inserted the key into the door of the house, and in his haste some notebooks slipped from his bulging case and fell to the hall floor, and he muttered, 'Damn!' and leaving them there, he dropped the case on to the chair and picked up the phone.

'Hello, Paul.'

'Hello, dear.'

'I've been ringing for ages, where have you been?'

'At school, of course. I suppose no-one else is in.'

'But it's near six.'

'Well, I'm a conscientious bloke. You know me, I don't leave on the bell. But I had a little business to do that held me up. You all right?'

'Yes, yes. I've got some news for you. Can you come round tonight?'

'Oh, that's going to be difficult, I planned to . . . '

'You must, Paul, they're all coming, at least I hope so. You'll never guess what's happened.'

'Not a catastrophe by the sound of you. Come on, spill it out, I'm dying for a cup of tea.'

'Well, hold on to your seat belt . . . What do you think? Mam and Dad's had an invitation to go to a party at the Duke of Moorshire's house.'

'Really!'

'Ah-ha.'

'Well, I never! That's great news. The Duke of Moorshire. Well! We're coming up in the world, aren't we? May they take any of their relations?'

Elizabeth's high laugh came over the wires; then, her voice dropping low, she said, 'Mam's tickled to death.'

'I bet she is. Where is she? Put her on.'

'Oh, she's just gone into the kitchen. She's going to get some bits and pieces ready for you all coming, you know her. And she'll have to do it single-handed tonight I fear, except for your humble servant here.'

'What's the matter? Another fracas with Annie?'

'You've said it.' Her voice dropped lower. 'Annie's threatened to quit unless Mam tells Mrs Slocombe to go. It's all to do with the wage Mrs Slocombe gets. And it is a bit thick when you think of it, because Annie's on all hours of the day and night for her six pounds. I think I would feel like her too.'

'Annie will never go.'

'I know that, and Mam knows that, and Annie knows that, but it still goes on.'

When her deep sigh came to him he said, softly, 'You'll miss it next year. Have you thought well about it, Liz, because there'll be times when you'll wish you were listening to them going at it hell for leather'; and she replied, 'Yes, I often think that too, but at the same time I'm dying to get away and make a start . . . Eeh! I'd better not let her hear me say that. I must talk with you, Paul, sometime.'

'Do that. The address is Flat 4, Marsh House, Talford Road.' They both laughed and she said, 'You'll come round later then?'

'Yes, yes, I'll manage; in fact I wouldn't miss it for all the tea in China. See you.'

'See you, Paul. Bye-bye.'

'Bye-bye.'

He put down the phone, gathered up the books and climbed the stairs to his flat. When he had closed the door behind him he stood leaning against it for a moment, staring across the room. An invitation to the Duke of Moorshire's place. Well, well. They were certainly going up in the world. Would she enjoy it? He moved from the door and threw the books on top of his case, then stopped again. Yes, she'd enjoy it. It was about time she got out and about and had some pleasure from their prosperity instead of being stuck in the house and thinking and worrying about the lot of them. She had been pushed into the background; while his Dad had gone striding away, up and up, and she had taken the procedure as a matter of course, she had seemed to accept being left behind, which was strange when you took her nature into account, fiery, bombastic, warm and lovable. They had all left her, one after the other; except Liz; and now she too was striving to get away, and not into the world, but out of it. One after the other they had sucked her dry emotionally. He himself was not without guilt in this way; in fact he had been the worst offender.

He went into the kitchen, put the kettle on the gas ring, and set a flower-printed tea tray with the tea things. He then cut three slices of bread and butter, put a jar of jam and an eccles cake on the tray, mashed the tea, and took the lot back into the room.

When he had poured out the tea he leant forward to switch on the television, then stopped and, sitting back in the chair again, he sipped at the tea while his gaze slowly covered the room.

It was barely furnished holding only a divan, which was his bed at night, a chest of drawers, a wardrobe, one easy chair, two straight-backed chairs, the round table at which he was eating, and a roll-top desk. The floor was covered with a grey mottled linoleum and there was one small rug in front of the electric fire.

There was not one attractive item in the room; it was devoid of all comfort. But that's how he wanted it. They'd all tried to get their foot inside the door and do something with it but he had remained firm, except about the curtains. He knew that they thought his austere way of living was but a sop to his guilty conscience: the brother, the son, who had walked out on his vocation, who should now be an ordained priest reflecting glory on the whole family, was but a teacher of English at a Secondary Modern School in Bog's End, and you couldn't get much lower, in any walk of life, than Bog's End.

He leant back in the chair; the tea went cold in his cup; he felt very tired. He'd be twenty-five next Wednesday. Funny, but it was near each birthday that his mind forced him back to the beginning. Was it really six years ago since he had decided against it, not six months, six days, yesterday? The hell of it had been so intense that at times it seemed like yesterday. He knew now there was no hell as the Church would have you believe, as Fathers Stillwell and Monaghan still pumped home; not Armstrong, he was too level-headed for that. Hell was the torture of the mind in the night, a deep deep well of despair in which you struggled and fought in darkness, where you vomited out your guilt and watched it rising again like a slimy, stinking bog to choke you. Hell in the day was the kindliness of pastor and priest, that kindliness that shed a veil over their condemnation; the kindliness of brothers in God who looked at you with pity that but veiled their envy, the envy of your will that had the power to turn you back on the path towards God. God, who was but a mirage in thought, a hope with which to inject despair, an imagery in your mind sucked from other minds, those minds which seemed so sure yet still chanted, 'I believe. Help thou my unbelief.'

Hell was the look in the eyes of his mother, the look that asked silently, 'Is it a girl?' And if she had put the question to him what would he have said? He would have said, 'No, it's not a girl, it is a woman,' for even then, with only a year between them, he had seen her as a woman, mature, different.

If he had never seen her, never met her, never spoken to her, would he have turned back down that road? Yes; yes, sometime or other he would have. His youth rising before him in relief, he saw each innocent step of his as keys opening channels in his parents' minds, the altar boy, the server, his love for the Church itself were all misinterpreted. But how could they know and he not know at that early age that the fascination of the ceremonial had him bewitched? The chanting of the Latin at the Mass – he rebelled violently against the mysteries being revealed in English – the apparent camaraderie of the priests, their ever-ready joking, their humanism as they tipped the bottle, drew him with the power of a first love; but most of all it was his mother's almost open adoration of him, her offspring, her son, who was to bring glory on the family by entering the Church, that had pressed his steps forward.

He was seventeen when he finally succumbed, and on that day she had kissed him and held him close and, the tears streaming down her face, she had whispered, 'You're like a penance for all me sins, for I've been a wooden Catholic all me life.' She didn't know it, and no explanation at the time could have made her understand, that she was offering him as a sacrifice.

He was nineteen on the day he told her he was leaving the seminary. Every day and every night for six months he had tried to make himself see sense, but it was no use. From when he had first set eyes on the girl – or the woman – he was lost. And it wasn't that love had come to him for the first time, for since he was fourteen, and before, he'd

26

had his little flings. In the cemetery after benediction on a Sunday night, when it was dark that was, he'd done what his brothers referred to as his homework. Never the whole hog, but enough to satisfy him. He was conceited enough at that time to think he had just to raise an eyebrow and they'd come running; and it was true. So when he first saw her she didn't appear to him one of a species about whose anatomy he knew nothing.

The first sight of her did not only touch his body, or heart, he could have conquered that, but she took possession of his mind. For weeks on end he had talked to his confessor about it. Then they had brought Father Armstrong to him. Father Armstrong had christened him; he had christened them all; he had married his mother and father; he was like one of the family. Father Armstrong probed deeper than his confessor at the seminary, and after it was all over he had put his hands on his shoulders and said, 'Well, there is one thing the Catholic Church can do without, Paul, and that is a bemused and bewildered priest.' He had even smiled at him; Father Armstrong was the only one who didn't seem to be saying one thing while thinking another, and he was the only one who knew the name of the woman who had bewitched him.

He leant forward and picked up the cup and made a face when his lips touched the cold tea. The teapot too was cold, and so, rising, he went into the kitchen and made himself a fresh brew.

CHAPTER FOUR

FRANCES

'Is that you, Frances?'

'Yes. Yes, Liz. Just a minute while I close the door, they're going mad . . . Did you hear them? Their Gran-Walton is here; she's bathing them. I don't know who enjoys it most or makes the most noise. Well, I'm sitting comfortably; now we'll begin.' She laughed. 'Fire ahead.'

'I've got some news that'll surprise you, Frances.'

'You have? Well, I'd like a surprise. I've forgotten what it feels like to be surprised, not counting the time Pauline put the cat in the washing machine.'

'Stop kidding, our Frances, you're all kidding the night. Listen. You'll never guess where Mam and Dad are going.'

'Oh, I can; at least I know what Dad's aiming for, the peerage. I saw him talking to Mrs de Ferrier yesterday, standing chatting to her opposite the club. She must have been there to lunch, in Ransome's you know. Only distinguished ladies are invited to Ransome's. Ha! ha!'

'Well, you're not far out.'

'What!'

Elizabeth's voice dropped to a sacred whisper. 'They've been invited to meet the Duke of Moorshire at Lea Hall.'

'Mam and Dad?'

'Mam and Dad.'

'You're joking.'

'No joking, Frances; I've got the card in my hand. The

28

Duke of Moorshire requests the pleasure of Mr and Mrs Gallacher at . . .'

'Mam and Dad to meet the Duke?'

'It's 1970, things are happening today.'

'My! I'll say they are.'

'But isn't it wonderful?'

'I suppose so.' There was a strong suspicion of doubt in Frances's tone: then she asked, 'Is Mam going?'

'Is she going? Of course, she's going!'

'When is it?'

'Four weeks today. It'll give her time to get clothes and things.'

'She wants to get her figure down before she thinks of clothes; she must have put on a couple of stone lately.'

'No, she hasn't, not all that; she's not fat.'

'Not fat!' Frances looked scathingly into the phone as if she could see Elizabeth, then she asked, 'Are they all going over the night?' and Elizabeth answered, 'Yes. I haven't phoned Helen yet, but she nearly always pops in on a Friday night anyway. You and Dave will come, won't you?'

'Well, it's our night for the club, but I suppose we could look in. Yes, we'll look in around eightish.'

'All right, Frances. Bye-bye.'

'Bye-bye.'

Frances Walton put the phone down and stood looking at it for a moment before she turned slowly round and walked into the sitting-room, where her husband was sprawled on the couch before the fire, his short legs thrust out, his feet resting on the edge of a chair. She went around the couch and faced him before she said, 'You know the latest?'

'What?'

'Mam and Dad's been invited to a do by the Duke of Moorshire.'

'Eh!' Dave Walton's feet came off the chair in a swing that brought his body upright on the couch. 'Say that again.'

'You heard. Me Mam and Dad's been invited to a do at the Duke of Moorshire's house, Lea Hall. You know, the place on the river about six miles out . . . '

'I know, I know.' He waved his hand at her. 'They've been invited there by him?'

'Yes, that's what Liz says. Well!' She drew in a long breath, then let it slowly out before dropping on to the couch beside him saying, 'Dad's flying high.'

'Yes; yes, he is.' Dave Walton reached out and picked up a cigarette from the ash tray on the side table, then as he lit it he said, thoughtfully, 'It'll all be good for business; it's contacts like that that count.'

'Will it affect you?'

'Can't help but, can it? I supply the materials . . . well, some of them.'

Frances pushed her fair hair back from her shoulders with an impatient movement, and her head jerked upwards as she said, 'I think it's too bad of Dad to split the order with Smith's, and I feel like telling him . . . '

'You mind your own business.' He tapped the ash from his cigarette, then wagged it at her before putting it into his mouth again. 'If there's any telling to do in that line I'm quite able to look after myself and my interests; and I think I know why he gave Smith the order.'

'You do? Why then?'

'Well, I must say at this stage I'm guessing, but Smith is full cousin to Redfern, Councillor Redfern. Do you get it?'

'No.'

'Well, if the Council pass it, that's if the ratepayers stand for it, they'll build the marina. Now up river there's a four mile stretch before you come to the shale, and since they're not loading any more in the east dock there's another six miles down river right to the sea. It could be a pleasure-cruise stretch.'

'Past all those factories?'

'Aye, past all those factories. But we're getting away from the point. Building the College will be like building with meccano compared to making that boat haven; cafés, sun lounge and dance hall and the motel thrown in. Your dad's throwing little hooks to Smith in order to land Redfern's vote. Redfern's the big fish on the Council.' His voice now took on a sarcastic note as he ended, 'I hope he doesn't get tangled up in his own lines, that's all.'

Frances looked at her husband. In the natural course of things she should have defended her father's tactics, for they had him alone to thank for their present prosperity, even though this prosperity, gauged in relation to her mother's as represented by Savile House, was still not very evident. She was ambitious, was Frances, both for herself and her small, dark and crafty husband.

'Well—' she rose from the couch – 'I suppose we'd better go and get ready to join the rejoicing.' As she went to pass him he put out his hand and caught her arm and, looking up at her, said with a half laugh, 'Well, look pleased about it, jealousy will get you nowhere.'

'Oh, you!' She flapped her hand at him and went down the room, across the narrow hall and up the steep stairs. At the top she paused and looked down. She didn't like this house, it was cramped and stifling. She hadn't realised how much she had liked her home until she had come here on her wedding day three and a half years ago. She'd never be satisfied until she had a house like the one in which she had been brought up since she was fourteen. She felt she was made for a place like Savile House; she would know how to run it, know how to entertain.

31

As it was now, the place was wasted: her father hardly ever in, Elizabeth leaving it next year for the convent, when it would be occupied almost solely by her mother, except on their occasional get-togethers. She knew her mother would be happier, more at home, in a house like this. Things were very unfair.

CHAPTER FIVE

HELEN

'Trevor! Look, turn that thing down.' Helen Gillespie rushed into the room, dived to the television and not only turned it down but switched it off. Then, bounding back from it, she fell into her chair with such a plop that she almost upset the small modern table on which reposed the evening meal of eggs on toast and, proclaiming the sign of the times, a bottle of seven and six Sauterne from the cut price shop in the market.

'Hel – en. Hel – en.' Her husband always split her name like that when he was slightly annoyed or put out. 'You nearly had the plate over me, on my suit.' He pushed his chair back and examined his trousers, then dusted them with a large orange coloured paper napkin.

'Well, I'm excited. What do you think Liz has just told me?'

'I don't know.' Stiffly and with a look on his face that said nor did he care, he picked up his knife and fork again and continued his meal, his manner of eating matching his pedantic speech and in keeping with his small thin, clean-shaven face and peevish look.

Helen's hands thrusting out across the table, went to grip his arm but stopped just in time. If she messed up his suit that would put a gloom on the evening. Her face now tight with her irritation, she said, 'Aw bust! For heaven's sake what does a spot on your suit matter; you could get it sponged in the shop ten times a day. Suits, suits, suits, that's all you think about.'

'That's what we live by.' He paused with a piece of egg wobbling on the point of his fork.

'Oh we do, we we? What about me, my share doesn't count? Look you here!' She poked her head across the table at him. 'I've been wanting to say this to you for some time. I was working before I married you, I'm still working. My wage is only three pounds a week less than yours. I've had two rises in two years; you haven't had one since we married and that's three years ago; so in future I'll thank you to pick your words.'

As his wife flounced out and into the tiny kitchen of the flat Trevor Gillespie put his knife and fork slowly down on to his plate and stared across the narrow space of the room towards the eucalyptus plant that was beginning to dwarf the frame that divided the dinette from the rest of the room, and that sickening humiliating feeling attacked him yet again, the feeling that made him want to bow his head on to his arms and cry, sob, wail out his frustration, his inadequacy – not inadequacy with regards to Helen; no, it was just in the shop he was a failure. But why was he a failure there? Simply because Pattenden didn't like him, not because of his work. Pattenden had never liked him, and he showed this by promoting others over his head . . . And what had he done about it? What could he do about it? Nothing, for he couldn't stand up to Pattenden; Pattenden who was tall and broad and overpowering, and right, always right. But he wouldn't stand it much longer, no he wouldn't, he would go to the head office . . . He wasn't aware that Helen had come back to the table and was standing near him until she put her arm around his shoulders and, bending down to him, whispered, 'I'm sorry.'

He smiled at her now and, stretching his face up to hers, he kissed her and taking her hand he pulled her down on the chair and said gently, 'What had you to tell me?'

Without enthusiasm now she said, 'Mam and Dad have been invited to meet the Duke of Moorshire at Lea Hall.'

She watched his mouth fall into a gape, his eyes widen and his eyebrows form black peaks above them, and she laughed at his expression.

'Really!'

'Ah-ha.'

'How marvellous . . . The Duke of Moorshire.' His mind lifted him into tomorrow, and he could hear Pattenden say, 'Gillespie, here a moment . . . take this gentleman's measurements.'

'Yes, Mr Pattenden. Yes, Mr Pattenden.'

'What's the matter with you, Mr Gillespie, dreaming as usual?'

'No, Mr Pattenden. It's just that I didn't have much sleep last night. We were kept late at our in-laws; they were discussing the invitation to a reception at the Duke of Moorshire's, and were considering what kind of a return they should make, a small dinner party or some such. You know what it is if you're asked out, you must return the hospitality . . . '

'Liz wants us to go round.'

'Yes, yes.' He blinked and smiled broadly at her. 'Of course. I bet your mam's excited.'

She looked at him, her head on one side, slightly puzzled. He very rarely called her mother Mam, it was nearly always your mother, sometimes only she. She had thought of late that he looked down his nose at her mother and she didn't like it because after all he didn't come from much himself; they were respectable but that's all that could be said for his people, for they had pinched and scraped all their lives.

She rose from the chair and began clearing the table, saying, 'She'll have to do something about her figure; she's let herself go lately and she's not all that old, only forty-four.' She stopped with the plates in her hand and said, 'Wait till the morrow when I can tell the doctors. Won't my status go up, especially with Doctor Blake for he's a snob of the first water? And his wife's a length ahead of him, swimming hard.'

Trevor laughed as he picked up the table mats and put them in their rack. He, too, wished it were tomorrow. Yes, how he wished it were tomorrow.

'Yes, Mr Pattenden; yes, Mr Pattenden; yes, Mr Pattenden. NO, MR PATTENDEN!'

CHAPTER SIX

THE BIG FELLOW

It was said that Collingwood Road was more of a boundary between upper and lower Felburn than the river itself, for behind one side of the road Bog's End started, while behind the other lay the market, the municipal buildings, old High Street, new High Street, both giving way to the park, and the park leading to Brampton Hill and, of course, to the now new quarter of the élite, The Rise.

Collingwood Road was lined mainly with warehouses and offices, and placed half on the road frontage and half in Collingwood Mews were the offices of Gallacher and Sons, Builders and Contractors.

The outer office faced the street. Rodney Gallacher's private office was behind this with a window and a door looking into the mews. The mews yard could hold two lorries and two cars, and when the business first started it had to hold them because they couldn't afford to garage them. Now it only held cars, three at the most. Rodney Gallacher's, Sam Gallacher's and the car belonging to the tenant of the mews flat.

The flat was the property of Rodney Gallacher and it was let furnished to a Mrs Morland at eight pounds a week. At least that's what it said on the books, and Mrs Morland's cheque came in every month to prove this. Mrs Morland left her flat every Friday night and was away all week-end, but this fact wasn't known to anyone except Rodney Gallacher and Mrs Morland's very close friend, Rosamund de Ferrier.

Mary Whitaker, Rodney Gallacher's secretary, and his typist, Kitty Malone, occasionally saw Mrs de Ferrier get out of her car and go into the mews flat to visit Mrs Morland, and they always remarked on her dress, so plain but superior like. 'If you saw her clothes hanging in a shop you wouldn't give tuppence for them. It's the way she carries them that makes her out,' Mary Whitaker stated, and Kitty Malone said, 'Aye, you're born with it or without it and all the money in Barclay's Bank—' which was the firm's bank – 'wouldn't help you if you haven't got it, if you know what I mean.'

They knew that their boss knew Mr de Ferrier for he sometimes came into the office, and neither of them cared much for him, uppish, la-di-da as he was, with a face, Kitty Malone said, like a powdered arse and though Miss Whitaker had chastised her for her language she had spluttered while doing so. His wife was quite a bit younger than him they thought. Their ages were discussed and compared. He was over fifty, while she, well, what could she be? She looked about thirty-three or thirty-five, but then she must be more than that having a nineteen year old son kicking around, unless she had started at sixteen, and her type usually didn't. Nineteen or twenty they would say, when she married; that would leave her about forty. Well, that being the case, they had to hand it to her.

One day last week when she had got out of her car the boss happened to be in the office and he watched her cross the pavement, and they watched him and they wondered what he thought of her, or if he thought about her at all, because they both agreed later he could look at a woman and never see her. The only things he saw were bricks, cement, window-frames, floor boards and the like. But now, if it had been Mr Sam, aw, with Mr Sam they would have had a laugh about her; but with his father, never. As Mary Whitaker said, and she should know because she had been with the firm since it had started, the boss was utterly, utterly wrapped up in the business, and what was more he was out and about so much seeing to this and that, she wondered his wife put up with it. But then he was lucky, because Mrs Gallacher, what she had seen of her, looked easy-going. Fat people always were.

The bedroom was decorated in French grey and dull pink. The curtains on the windows that looked on to the main yard were pink and padded and herringboned with grey thread, with a heavy bedcover made to match.

The bedcover was now rolled up towards the foot of the bed and Rodney Gallacher pushed his bare feet into it, stretched his long legs, pulled in his thickening waist and expanded his chest with a long deep breath as he flexed his arms sidewards.

When there was a slight rustle to the side of him he turned his head in the direction of the bedroom door and looked at the woman who had mesmerised him and dominated his life for the past eighteen months. He knew that if he ever lost her nothing in life would be worth its salt.

He turned on his elbow and watched her walking towards him. She was wearing a flimsy negligée that made her body more alluring than it had been when bare. When she reached the bed he fell on to his back again and, putting up his hands, pulled her down sharply beside him, so that her face hung above his, long and pale, her green eyes mocking as always.

Had Maggie looked at him like this he would have said she was sneering at him or bursting for a fight. At times he did wonder what state of mind he had reached that he should take from this woman such things. Had Maggie dared to utter them even in one of her lightning tempers, he would have busted her mouth for her.

All his life he'd had a sneaking respect for class. Behind his bombast and his left wing talk he had admired the tone of class, the look of class, the arrogance of class; if you had class you could get away with things, from insults to love on the side. If you had class you possessed a magic tongue, a magic eye, a magic manner. His feeling for class went back a long way. It must have been this feeling that stirred him when, at nineteen, he used to follow the Armitage girl from the convent right to the top of Brampton Hill, until, day of days, he got to carrying her bag. And that went on for a month until her father espied him, and he not only nearly laid him out but arranged it so that he got the sack from Stevenson's Brickyard.

Funny how things turn out. Papa Armitage, had he but known it, did him a good turn, for he had gone out and got a job on the buildings and had known immediately that this was his line.

It was about this time that Maggie had asked him to her birthday party. She was young, plump and fetching and he had eased himself on her. That is all it had been, but, begod, before he knew where he was he had been standing before Father Armstrong saying, 'I will.'

But he must be fair; it had worked out, it had worked out for years. She was a good cook and housekeeper; she'd given him bairns, she'd satisfied his needs, and his needs in those days were pretty demanding. Any hour any time, to give her her due, she had never said no.

And then he had started up on his own, and Maggie became but a shelter to return to from the blast of the business, for it was a blast. From the time that he built the first house, when he had to run here and there, hell for leather, begging for credit, it was a blast; but it blasted him upwards, and outwards, bigger and better each year. It blasted him into the company of men who previously had just been names, names that were said with hushed breath in the town. Names like Redfern, Pearce . . . and de Ferrier. Names that were in the gilt-edged book of Ransome's.

It was eight years ago that he had first met de Ferrier. He had been on the committee of the proposed new college. He knew about de Ferrier; he had done his homework on all that committee. De Ferrier was connected with all types of businesses, not only in the town and in Newcastle, but over the county. He had been very civil to Mr de Ferrier. If he looked too far back he despised himself, for then he saw his civility as fawning. Anyway, it had paid off and he had got the contract to build the college.

But it seemed strange now that he had never met de Ferrier's wife until two years ago. Perhaps it was as well, for from the moment he had touched her hand in greeting he was ensnared – and so was she, although it took her some time to admit it. If she held a fascination for him he also possessed something that she needed. She had told him frankly it was the size of him, the roughness of him, his almost elemental way of making love. He should have been upset at this, cast down, because if ever he wanted to play the gentleman to anyone it was to her. He wanted to match her tone, her air, but instinctively he knew that, were he capable of this, he would no longer attract her. Strange, when he came to work it out, that it should be his way of making love to Maggie that held this woman. His very coarseness was the magnet that drew her to him.

He looked downwards to where her hand, rather small for her size but soft and white, was pressing the black hairs on his chest away from their natural growth. When her hand moved swiftly downwards over his stomach and she stabbed his navel with her forefinger his body arched on the bed and he made a grunting, chuckling sound in his throat, then went to pull her to him, but she resisted him

41

with a playful flap of her hand, saying, 'Enough! Enough! Listen, I have something to tell you.'

'Well, fire away.' He relaxed on the bed. Whatever she had to tell him it wouldn't be that she was going to leave him. If he was sure of anything in his life he was sure of that.

'You are to meet the Duke . . .'

His deep-set brown eyes narrowed, his thick eyebrows hooded them still further, his puggish nose wrinkled and drew apart his thick, well-moulded lips until his whole face took on the shape of his chin and looked entirely square. 'What did you say?'

With her middle finger she stroked her hair back behind her ear and, her head on one side, she said, 'If you're not galloping into senility then you would have heard what I said, you are to meet the Duke.'

He was sitting up straight now, his arms pushed back into the pillows to support himself. 'The Duke of Moorshire? You mean our Duke?'

Her laugh was thin and merry. 'Our Duke, yes, the Duke of Moorshire. The invitation should be waiting for you when you get back.'

He slid back on to his elbows until he was leaning against the bed head, and after staring at her for some time he nodded slowly, saying, 'You've managed this, haven't you?'

She raised her eyebrows and smiled as she said, 'Well I won't disclaim all credit. I did suggest, when certain names of prominent citizens were being put forth, that Mr Gallacher had done a great deal for the town. Apart from the college there was the Morley and the Rollingdon Estates; moreover, for a man who was likely to – no I'd better not say likely to – I'd better say who *might* stand a chance of getting the contract for the Marina, a little appreciation should be shown him. What did they think? They thought as I did.'

'Oh, Mundy!' He was rolling with her back and forward over the bed, and when they came to rest he looked down into her face and said softly, 'God! If only I was an emperor, I would put you on a throne. You know, the older I get the more I can understand the Duke of Windsor business.'

'Ah! Ah!' She was tapping his lips with her finger. 'She lost him his throne don't forget, she lost him his throne.'

'Well, he had her and that's all that counts. Ah, Rosamund I worship you.' He was speaking through gritted teeth now. 'Do you know that? I wor-ship you?'

'Thank you, Mr Gallacher. I'm so pleased to hear it. By the way.' Her eyes stretched a little wider. 'You'll have to see that your lady is suitably attired for the occasion as it is a musical soirée.'

Slowly he lifted his body from hers. 'What! What do you mean . . . my lady? Maggie, you mean?'

'Who else?'

He was kneeling up now, to the side of her. 'You mean Maggie's been invited an' all?'

'Oh, Mr Gallacher.' She, too, was sitting up. 'The Duke is not holding a stag party, he is giving an evening's entertainment to which he is inviting his friends and a few prominent citizens of the town . . . and he could hardly invite them without inviting their wives.'

He got off the bed, pulled a bathroom robe from the back of the chair and put it on, and he kept his face averted from her as he said, 'It won't do; I'll have to refuse.'

'Don't be a fool, Rodney. Moreover, don't annoy me.' She, too, was off the bed now. 'I have worked to wangle this for you. Besides the Mayor and his wife and you, the only other two local business couples invited are the Redferns and the Pearces; but there'll be lots of county folk present, and you could make contacts, the right contacts.'

He had his head bowed as he walked past her into the bathroom and when he disappeared from her view and failed to make a reply to her statement she reached out, took a cigarette from a box, lit it and drew the smoke well down into her lungs before she said, 'The word snob doesn't fit you; you're an upstart, Rodney. You know that, don't you?' She was now at the bathroom door, and she stood watching him getting into his trousers. Again she waited for a retort, but it wasn't forthcoming. As he pulled his shirt roughly over his head, she said, 'What are you afraid of? She needn't open her mouth. If you are worried on that score, prime her. See that she's dressed suitably; that's all that will be required.'

He paused as he tucked his shirt into his trousers and cast a sidelong glance at her. She could insult him as much as she liked and her insults he took as compliments, but strangely he couldn't take it when she threw them at Maggie. Although a lightning warning told him to watch his step he was snapping at her, 'What do you think she is, a performing pig? She can pass herself if she wants to.'

Her eyes widened slightly; she made a move with her lips. 'I'm glad to hear it,' she said; 'but you must understand that I've based my opinion of her from your own description.'

'I've hardly mentioned her name to you.'

'True, but your silences have been very telling.'

When her lids drooped and she turned sharply from him he hurried after her into the room and, pulling her round by the shoulder, he stared into her face and swallowed deeply before he muttered, 'Don't you understand? I just don't want you two to meet, because . . . well . . . ' He jerked his head. 'You're everything she isn't, and I don't want you to . . . ' He stopped himself from saying, 'look down your nose at her'. Nor could he say, 'be sorry for her',

44

so he substituted, 'I don't want you to be sorry for me.'

She laughed outright now. 'Sorry for you? Oh, Rodney! you are funny. Do you know I could never be sorry for you, not if you were in the direst trouble. Odd that, isn't it? I've thought about it, and I know you could never evoke my pity no matter what happened to you. You're too big, bouncy, bustling.' She pressed her lips together, then ended, 'Boisterous and bumptious and—' she pushed the tip of her nose against his – 'you're also a bugger into the bargain.'

He was laughing now, his head back. That was another thing she could do, make him laugh. He always laughed when she swore, for her swearing was like no-one else's swearing. When she said bloody, bugger or sod, it was as if she were embroidering her speech with humour. When Maggie said bloody or bugger it was with bitterness, or venom; she never used the word sod, she considered it a dirty word equivalent to the four letter ones. Strange the difference in people. Some people's language grated on you, roused you to bitterness, even brawls, as Maggie's did; yet this one here, this fashionable piece, this lady, and she was all that by God, could come out with things that back in the house they would consider coarse, but which, coming from her lips, could be termed wit.

His thoughts touching on the house, he told himself that he must get home and squash any rising hopes Maggie had of them going to meet the Duke, for besides him not wanting Rosamund and her to meet, there was the dread of what she might get up to once she had a few glasses of wine down her gullet. She couldn't carry drink of any sort; it either made her right daft or put her in a fighting mood. He must get home.

He now pulled Rosamund into his arms and kissed her long and hard before saying, 'Thanks anyway for making the effort on my behalf. Although it can't be done, I won't forget it.'

She looked at him blankly. Then, her lips smiling at him but not her eyes, she said, 'As you wish, Milord, as you wish.'

CHAPTER SEVEN

MAGGIE

They were all around her, Sam and Arlette, Willie and Nancy, Frances and Dave, Helen and Trevor, Paul and Lizzie, and you couldn't hear yourself speak. It was a night like they hadn't had for years; not even on New Year's Eve had they been all together and laughed like this. She had laughed more the night than she had laughed for weeks, for months; aye, she had laughed more the night than she had laughed for the past two years. And why had she not laughed? Oh, forget it. Come on, she told herself; there might never be another night like this again, all in harmony, all jolly, all for once thinking of her, all for once talking of her and seeing her as somebody, not just as mam, or the old girl, or fat arse, a term of endearment from Sam, but as somebody . . . a somebody, somebody fit to have an invitation from a duke. By! She never thought she'd live to see this day. For that matter, she never thought there'd be a day in her life when a thing like this would happen to her.

She moved among them, a plate of meat sandwiches in each hand. Annie had brought in tea, and coffee for them who wanted it, looking all the while like the parson's sister, her nose trying to get away from her face. She'd have it out with her the morrow, see if she didn't. That one was getting too big for her boots, that one wanted taking down a peg . . . 'What were you saying, Trevor?'

'I was saying—' Trevor strained his face up to hers as he shouted – 'that you'll have to have a crest on your paper after this.'

Her laugh rang out and she nodded down to him as she cried, 'Aye, an' I'll have the lav rolls stamped with it an' all.'

Trevor gave a thin smile at this but Helen spluttered into her tea as she cried, 'Oh, Mam! Oh, Mam!' then turning to Frances and Nancy, she said, 'Mam's going to have the lav rolls stamped with a crest.'

'What's that? What's that?'

All around the room they were asking the reason for the hilarious laughter in the corner near the fireplace, and like the game of 'passing on the saying', they passed on Maggie's words and when a slightly distorted version reached Sam, he garbled, 'What! She's going to have her crest stamped on her chest?' and the laughter became painful, Helen and Elizabeth hanging on each other's necks in apparent agony.

'Look! look!' Sam was holding the floor again, and the laughter subsided into splutters as they all gave him their attention, for Sam was in great form the night, and when Sam was in form he could make a cat laugh.

'Now, this is what you'll do, Mam.' Sam had his arm extended towards his mother, his finger wagging at her. 'When the butler announces—' he assumed a stance and from deep in his throat cried, 'Mr and Mrs Gallacher—' then went on, 'You'll glide in like this.' He now gave an imitation of his mother gliding, rolling his hips from side to side and bringing fresh outbursts of laughter. 'And when he offers you his hand you take it like so.' He caught at his sister-in-law's hand and, bowing slightly towards her, he said, 'Good evening.' Then turning sharply around and addressing his mother again, he cried, 'Whatever you do, don't say, "Hello, lad, how's the missus?"' There was laughter again, but not so much this time, and it was strained. Willie hadn't laughed at the last joke; Paul's face was straight, he hadn't laughed at all.

The only other member of the party who hadn't been amused by Sam's antics or any of the fun was his wife. She was suffering from a headache.

And Maggie hadn't laughed at her eldest son's comical advice because she didn't think it was comical, he was going too far. She knew how to pass herself when it was necessary. Sometimes their Sam didn't know when to stop. She picked up the empty plates from the table and went into the kitchen, and looking from the long table to the Welsh dresser, she said to Annie, 'Have all the sandwiches gone?'

'Well, you should know; you've taken them in, an' I haven't eaten them.'

Maggie banged the plates down on the table and looked across the kitchen to where Annie was standing, her hand on the kettle waiting for it to boil, and said, 'Annie Fawcett, if it wasn't that they're all here I'd give you the length of me tongue, but it can wait until the morning.'

'I mightn't be here in the morning.'

'Well, that will suit me nicely.' She glared at the narrow shoulders, the thin head, the hair cut across the back of it as if it had been trimmed under a pudding basin. There hadn't been a day in her remembered life when she hadn't known Annie Fawcett. She had played with her before she had gone to school; they had gone hand in hand to school together; they had left school together; they had gone into the plastics factory together; and after Willie was born in '45 Annie had come to stay with her because she had been shaken by the time bomb that fell near their house in Bog's End, and her visit had lasted twenty-five years; not that she hadn't been glad of her company, and her help, she had, and she hadn't been mean in showing it, but this last three years, since she had started the early change, there was no living with her. Aw, but it wasn't only the change that was the matter with her,

49

it was Ralphy Holland. If her Rod had turned out like Ralphy she would have felt bitter an' all. You had to make allowances. Yes, you had to make allowances.

When she went back into the room the laughter had stopped and they were all in a heated discussion that was apparently bordering on argument; but that's how it went in this house. The evening could range from belly-bursting laughter to two of the brothers or sisters walking out declaring that they were never going to speak to each other again . . . until the next time. She was so used to it, it had no effect on her now; well, perhaps just a little, but not the effect it once had when she would bawl them all down, her lungs swelling to issue the bellow that would bring them to silence. Anyway she had them all about her; it was as it used to be, except that Rod wasn't here. A feeling that she wouldn't admit to a sadness crept into her chest but she bludgeoned it away as she bent down to Willie and asked, 'What is it this time? Parliament? Ireland?' She almost added, 'The pill?' but that would be bordering on religion and they all kept off religion in their arguments, solely because of Paul. Before Paul had shied away from his duty religion had had its share in the racket like everything else because Arlette Trevor and Nancy were Protestants, and the family was out to make them turn. So, instead of the pill, she said, 'Or what?'

Willie looked up to her, his face straight, dark with an anger that he seldom showed.

'It's that bloody fellow in the *Messenger*, that poor poet. He'd better stick to his love jingles if he knows what's good for him, else . . . he'll fall off a lorry.'

'Fall off a lorry?' She screwed her eyes up at him.

'Aye. Look, Frances; let me Mam see the paper.'

As Frances leant from the couch and handed her mother the paper, Willie said, 'He's a stirrer, that's what he is.'

'Because he's speaking the truth?'

It was the first time Paul had spoken to anybody except his mother since he came into the room, and there was a short heavy silence before Willie turned on him, crying, 'What do you mean by truth? Everybody's at it; things don't fall off lorries only on the roads. You can't tell me that there's a shop or a business in the town where somebody isn't helping himself. And you, can you say that you haven't brought paper from school and used it for yourself? Helped yourself to pencils and . . . aye, books? When you go back to the flat the night have a look round and see how many of the books you call yours have the school stamp on them.'

'It would take a lot of paper, pencils and books to total a hundred and twenty thousand pounds, and that's just a rough account of the stuff that fell off lorries in this town alone last year.'

Another heavy silence followed; then Willie again spoke, his mouth now tight as he said, 'You're for him, aren't you?'

'Yes, I could say I was for him.'

Sam, standing near the mantelpiece, his elbow resting on it, asked quietly, 'Do you know him then, Paul, this chap that writes the poetry?'

'Sort of.'

'Is his name really Lacker?'

'Well—' Paul jerked his head – 'I shouldn't think so.'

'I thought you said you knew him.'

'Well, I know of him.'

'Look, I haven't read it, what does it say?' Helen now looked at her mother, and Maggie, who had just finished reading the piece in question, said, 'Well, I think it's funny, although it doesn't rhyme much.'

'None of his stuff does; he's got the nerve to call it poetry.'

'Why are you so wild about it?' Paul's voice sounded

51

calm, aggravatingly calm, and once more there was a silence. before it could bring another outburst from Willie, Maggie laughed and thrust the paper sideways to where Arlette was sitting and said, 'Here, you read it. Meself, I think it's funny. Go on, read it out. You're a good reader, read it out.'

Arlette took the paper in her hand. She scanned the page, then raising her head she looked round the half circle of eyes fixed upon her, and her gaze came to rest on Paul. She took in the fact that there was a white line round his mouth, that his eyes had darkened to a deep brown that hid his thoughts and made his expression blank. She looked at the page again and began:

> They fell off a lorry
> Going jiggedy jag:
> Three dozen nylons,
> A bottle of scotch
> And a ham went wham!
>
> It's honest to God,
> I'm not lying,
> Why damn!
> It's the roads, love,
> They tilt on the cam.
>
> It fell off a lorry
> This hair spray, and say,
> Pass these to the priest
> On his visiting day.
> They're on the level,
> Straight, I'm making no mock,
> They fell off a lorry
> The whole box of socks.

Almost before Arlette had finished Willie was on his feet. 'You know something?' He looked from one to the other. 'That bloke could be writing about this very house.'

'Don't be silly.' The protest came from all quarters, and he shouted them down. 'How often have bits and pieces been passed on to Father Armstrong and Father Monaghan, half hams and slabs of butter, bottles of whisky at Christmas?' He was looking at his mother now, and her voice rising, she cried back at him, 'Hold your hand a minute. Hold your hand. It was very often out of the fridge, stuff you and Sam had nothing to do with.'

'Aye, but on the other hand very often it wasn't.'

'Now, look, Master Willie Gallacher; don't you bawl at me, lad . . . '

'I'm, I'm sorry, Mam.' He jerked his head and his voice dropped. 'But . . . well—' His words were cut off by Frances saying in her cold disinterested way, 'It could be about this house at that, and at this very minute.' She was leaning towards Arlette, her eyes on the paper, and she moved her finger on to a part of it and said, 'He's got another one here. Listen. Go on, read that one, Arlette.'

'No.' Arlette went to close the paper but Frances, pulling it from her and sitting up straight, said, 'Listen to this. It's called "Ties". Now just listen:

> Blood is thicker than water,
> Inanely is relationship explained.
> Then does water flow in the veins
> Of the mate from where
> Sprang the seed,
> Or of she who carried the nest
> In which to breed?

Love leaps the space to the stranger
And, entwined, they grow to age
And see their offspring hate and rage
One to the other, brother to brother.
The implication that love flows
Where blood is a tie
Is a lie.'

You couldn't call the absence of speech a silence, it was
more akin to unconsciousness brought about by shock.
It was Elizabeth who brought them to the surface again
when she began to cry, for Elizabeth laughed easily and she
cried easily. One after the other their voices rose to accuse
Frances in varying ways. 'Now look what you've done!
You're a starter, our Frances, if ever there was one.' To
which were added such comments as, 'It's all right, Liz, it's
all right. You should be used to it by now, you know us.'

Maggie went and stood by the side of her youngest
daughter; she was sitting on a pouffe, her elbows on her
knees and her face buried in her palms. Maggie put her
hand on her head and said softly, 'There now, there now,
there's nothing to frash yourself about.' But even as she
said it she knew there was a lot to frash herself about.

While Liz could give vent to the pain those lines had
caused, for Liz was a highly sensitive creature, she herself
wasn't supposed to feel things or show her pain. She hadn't
grasped the whole gist of the thing, she'd have to read it
once or twice over, but that last line – well, a blind man on a
galloping horse could have read what that meant. 'The implication that love flows where blood is a tie is a lie.' There
was bitterness there. Aye, but truth. Oh yes, yes, truth.

She looked around her family. They were all talking
now, except Willie. Willie for the moment was in disgrace;
he had started all this. But Frances was taking nothing on
herself, she was unconcerned. It was the usual pattern. You

54

knew where you were with Willie; he blurted out what he thought, but he didn't intend to hurt. Not so with others in her family, and she wasn't only thinking of Frances.

At this moment Annie came to the sitting-room door and beckoned her with a lift of her head. There was no anger on her face now. She looked as she used to be, at one with her, all for her. When she reached her, Annie put out her hand and drew her into the hall; then closing the door behind her, she whispered, 'Ralphy's here, and he's mortallious.'

'Oh, my God!' Maggie exclaimed. 'He would come the night, wouldn't he? And he's drunk you say?'

'As ten lords.'

'Where've you put him?'

'He's in the kitchen. I've tried to get rid of him but he won't go, he wants to see you; something he's got to tell you he says.'

'I know what that'll be,' said Maggie as she went towards the kitchen. 'He's broke.'

'No, he's not.' Annie's voice was a whisper, a hissed whisper. 'He's got a pocketful of notes. He says he's been working down the river on that dredging concern and he got good money 'cos they can't keep men there. It's finished now.'

When Maggie entered the kitchen she looked at the man sitting by the side of the table, his legs sprawled out. His head lolling on his shoulders, his long face with more hair on it than was on his head, she thought, as she had done many times before, that it was hard to believe he was the same age as Rod. As she and Annie had been pals all their young lives so had Ralphy and Rod, inseparable they were, and as Rod went up he had taken Ralphy with him. That is until the drink got hold of him; after that he had to sack him three times, and the third time was final. Night watchman's job he had then at the warehouse and had set fire to the whole place. Two-thirds of the window frames went up that night, thousands of pounds worth of timber. That was the finish of Rod and Ralphy; but every now and again when he was on his uppers he would come round to cadge. She didn't mind that, she always gave him a square meal and something in his pocket. But she got him out of the house before Rod came in, for Rod couldn't forgive him the business of the warehouse. He'd had the place over-stacked and the insurance on it hadn't covered his losses. He would have murdered Ralphy if he'd got his hands on him after that night, but he never gave him away to the police as being the instigator of the fire. Still there was one person glad to see him, although she would have denied it with her dying breath.

'Hello, Maggie me love.'

'Hello, Ralphy. You've been a bad lad again I see.'

'I'm always a bad . . . bad lad, Maggie. In some ways that is. To meself I'm a bad lad, Maggie, but I would never be a bad lad to you. If I'd got you, Maggie, I would never 've been a bad lad, not like some . . . Here. Here, Maggie.' He grabbed her hand and as he pulled her towards him he almost fell off the chair and she had to steady him. 'I've . . . I've got somethin' to tell you, somethin' you should know. 'Sprivate. 'Sprivate. Get yourself out, Annie; it's private.'

'Get out yourself, you drunken lout.'

'Aw! misery. Your face's like a dose of jollop. She always was a misery, wasn't she, Maggie? Send her packin', Maggie, send her packin'. I've got somethin' to tell you, Maggie. It's . . . private, 'sprivate like, just for the family. You should know, Maggie, I'm not goin' to stand by and see you made a bloody monkey of, Maggie . . . not me, not Ralphy Holland. By God, no!'

At this moment the door opened and Sam came into the kitchen. He was about to speak, but when he saw the visitor he stood still and, raising his eyebrows and pursing his lips, nodded towards him as he said slowly, 'Hello, Ralphy. You just dropped in?'

'Aye, Sam, just dropped in. Have some news, news for your ma.'

Sam looked at his mother and, jerking his head backwards, said, 'The big exodus is getting under way; you'd better go in.' He jerked his head again and muttered, 'I'll see to him.'

Maggie tugged her hand from Ralphy's and said, 'Annie'll give you a cup of coffee, strong and black.' She smiled. 'I've got to go; I've got all the family in. You understand, Ralphy? Come the morrow an' you can tell me all about it.'

'Aw, it won't take a minute, Maggie. I had to push meself, fight with meself. Wait. Wait. I had to push meself to come I tell you; won't come again. Look, come outside, just a minute. I'm . . . I'm not after anythin'; honest to God I'm not after anythin'.'

He stumbled to his feet and Maggie said placatingly, 'I know you're not, Ralphy; but it's the family you see. Slip down again some time. Bye-bye, Ralphy. Take care of yourself.' She backed a few steps away from him, signalled to Annie to leave him too, then hurried out of the kitchen. Poor Ralphy; there was no hope for him. He always wanted to tell her something, some great scheme he had got for making a comeback and showing up Rod. Poor Ralphy.

Back in the kitchen, Ralphy, his face dark, his jaws moving from side to side, turned about and shambled to the door, and pulling it open, staggered outside. There he turned and looked at Sam who had followed him and, wagging a dirty finger at him, said, 'You know somethin'? Your faather's a nowt, a bloody nowt, and I'm not goin' to stand by and see Maggie being made a monkey of.'

Taking Ralphy by the arm, Sam led him down the long path towards the back gate, saying, 'How do you make out Mam's being made a monkey of, Ralphy? You can tell me.'

'I know what I know.'

'Well, if anybody's making a monkey out of Mam I should know an' all, shouldn't I? I'm the eldest.'

'Aye, you are that.' Ralphy stopped and, placing his hands on Sam's shoulders, supported his swaying body for a moment before he repeated, 'Aye, you are. You are the eldest, aye, and you should know an' all. Well then, here's something for your ears. Well now, you listen to me an' every word I say's true, gospel truth, so help me God. It's your dad, he's running another woman, a swell, been at it for months . : . months and months. Love nest behind the office. Friday night's their night; sometimes Saturday but always Friday. An' I know who she is an' all. Aye, I know who she is. He's picked high. Oh, he was always a bloody upstart, your dad. De Ferrier . . . de Ferrier's wife. You know—' he now pushed Sam in the chest three times '—the big de Ferrier, his lady wife. True as I'm standin' here.'

Ralphy now straightened himself and began to walk on again with Sam at his side. When they reached the gate he said, 'Well, I couldn't keep it, but had to get bloody well plastered afore I could spill it. Still, nobody's goin' to make a monkey out of Maggie. I'd never 've made a monkey out of Maggie if I'd got her. By God no . . . Night, night Sam.' He had staggered through the gate and was some way down the road before Sam answered, 'Night' in reply, but so softly that it couldn't have reached his hearing.

He stood near the gate for some time staring over the evergreen hedge into the sky. His emotions were too mixed to sort out; he couldn't say which he was experiencing more, hate, or that peculiar soothing feeling of joy that power gives a man.

As he made his way up to the back door again he looked over the circle of ornamental shrubbery and saw someone on the point of leaving. He went into the kitchen. It was empty, and he stood with his back to the stove still looking upwards, still thinking, still savouring his emotions.

When finally he crossed the hall towards the drawing-room he saw Arlette and his mother mounting the stairs; only Paul and Elizabeth were in the drawing-room and they were talking quietly, or at least Lizzie was, about that fellow Lacker and his poetry. She was even quoting it. She was saying, 'The week before last he wrote a beautiful one about frost. It began, "The morning is bright, frost glinting on glass, trees silent of rustle, and stiff the grass." I can't recall the rest but it ended something like, "If one wish could be granted when I pass, there will go with me a morning as now, frost glinting on glass, trees silent of rustle, and stiff the grass." '

Poetry! Poetry! That was another thing he'd sort out, who this fellow Lacker was, because their Willie was right, that bit about things falling off lorries and being passed to the priest could be hitting at them, Willie and him in particular. And if it was someone in the know, someone who came to the house, well, when you were forewarned you were forearmed.

Upstairs Maggie held Arlette's coat for her as she said, 'It's been a funny night, hasn't it, starting on a high note and going flat.' She laughed now. 'You know, towards the end nobody remembered why they had come; the Duke wasn't mentioned.' Her laugh became louder then ceased abruptly as she stood before Arlette, her hands joined in front of her stomach, her blue eyes soft, her face sad as she said, 'But seriously, Arlette, I'm really scared to death now that I think about it for I won't know how to go on, what to do, or what to wear.'

'Oh, Mam.' Arlette impulsively caught hold of the plump hands and, squeezing them, said, 'There's nothing to worry about, nothing at all. I tell you what,

59

we'll get together and have a talk about it, have a rehearsal. Not that you need one.'

'Ah, will you now? You know, it's funny.' She shook her head. 'I wouldn't let our Frances, or Nellie, or even Lizzie tell me anything, yet I'd let you.'

'Thank you, Mam.' Arlette fell against her for a moment and when Maggie put her arms about her and squeezed her tightly she gave a slight moan and her body jerked.

'What is it?' Maggie looked at her.

'Nothing; it's . . . it's only a touch of fibrositis, I get it in the shoulder.'

'Have you had it rubbed?'

'No, no it just comes and goes.'

'You want to get Sam to rub it.'

Arlette turned away now, saying, 'Yes, yes, I'll do that.'

Maggie stood still for a moment watching her daughter-in-law walk out on to the landing. There was something she would like to ask her, only she didn't want to pry, but she had the feeling that things weren't as they should be between her and Sam. Yet Sam seemed the same. Sam was always the same, merry and bright. But with Sam you could never tell what the brightness was hiding; Sam was close. She didn't know who he took after; not herself 'cos she was as open as the day, too open for her own good; and Rod, Rod wasn't close, a bit tight lipped about things at times, like when the business wasn't going too well, but you couldn't say he was close. No, wherever Sam had got his secretive traits from, it wasn't from either his dad or her.

A few minutes later, when she had closed the door on him and Arlette she paused a moment, and a strange idea came into her head. 'Now wouldn't you think,' she said to herself, 'he knew what was in me mind about him, the way he looked at me when I came into the room. And to go off like that without saying anything, just nodding his head at me, then laughing. There was something funny in the way he did it.' Aw, she tossed her head. What was the matter with her, she was full of fancies. Where was Liz?

She found Elizabeth in the sitting-room, tidying up, putting the cushions straight, each with a corner upwards. She was always tidying, but she generally did it with a gaiety, often singing. Now her face was straight, her eyes still red from crying.

Maggie went up to her, put her arms around her and said softly, 'What's the matter with your face, has it slipped? Aw, come now, don't take things so hard, it's part of life.'

Elizabeth turned and looked at her mother. She loved her mother, she loved her best in the whole world, and therefore she worried about her most. She nipped at her lower lip before looking downwards and saying, 'Mam, when I go in – you know – well, will you promise me something?'

'Aye, lass; if I can keep it I'll promise you anything you ask.' Maggie's voice was soft and serious now.

'Well, from that day will you—' she swallowed '—will you promise not to take anything more from Willie or Sam? You know what I mean.' She was looking pleadingly into her mother's eyes now, and Maggie said, 'An' all this because that daft fellow wrote that poem in the paper?'

'No, no; it wasn't only that, Mam. It just brought it to a head and gave me the courage to ask. It . . . it worries me; it always has worried me, this stealing . . . '

'Aw, Liz, it isn't stealing.' Maggie's voice held a strong note of protest.

'Well, what would you call it, Mam? Willie brought you a packet of nylons tonight, didn't he? And he hadn't bought them.'

'He had. Well, what I mean is, he could have; they sell them all round the place at half-price.'

61

'Yes; at half the price, they didn't pay for them at the beginning; our Willie and Sam rarely pay anything for the stuff they get . . . Oh, I know, I know, Mam.' She closed her eyes tightly and wagged her hand towards Maggie. 'Don't try to whitewash them. They give stuff in return, stuff that . . . that's fallen off a lorry, another lorry. It's a racket, and it's wrong.'

'But what can one body do that can make any difference, lass?'

'One body and one body and one body make three people, Mam, and if people said, "No, I don't want them, they're stolen," there would soon be no market, and then the things would stop falling off lorries.'

Maggie walked away towards the fireplace and drew her hand over her mouth and up to her brow as she said, 'Aw, lass. I've always said it, you're too good for this world.' She swung round now, her expression contrite, and added quickly, 'I'm not being sarky or anything, I mean that. The world is a tough place, lass; most people would skin a louse for its hide. Ninety-nine out of every hundred are out for what they can get. If you raise your voice against them and go your own way you're sunk, you're dubbed a mug.'

'Then Jesus was a mug.'

'Aw, Liz.'

'Will you do as I ask, Mam?'

There was a considerable pause before Maggie said, 'Yes, lass; the day you go in that'll be the end of it, I promise. There, I'll cross meself on it.' At this she made the sign of the cross, and Liz, her eyes blinking, her mouth trembling, came slowly forward and kissed her gently on the cheek, then said, 'I'll go up, Mam.'

'Good night, hinny.'

'Good night, Mam.'

Left alone, Maggie sat down close to the fire and a shudder passed over her body, although she didn't feel

62

cold. It was odd the mixture you reared; Sam and Willie, and at the opposite pole, Paul and Lizzie, and hovering somewhere in between, Frances and Helen. Willie would kick up a stink when she told him she was taking nothing more, because let's face it, he was making quite a bit on the side out of her. She never took anything for nothing.

It had been a funny evening, an odd evening. It had started so hilariously, them all coming in laughing and joking and exclaiming in wonder at the Duke's invitation. Then they had gone on to the argument; and Ralphy had come, and after that the evening had somehow petered out.

She wished Rod was in. She wished he had come in when they were all here and she could have watched the pride ooze out of him, although, being Rod, he would have acted offhandedly about the whole affair.

She looked at the clock. Half-past ten. He was usually late on a Friday night; after his business in Newcastle in the afternoon he nearly always ended up at Ransome's. She still couldn't get used to the idea of her man being a member of Ransome's. She never went for him when he came in late. She sometimes chipped him by saying things like, 'Why didn't you phone me and I'd have sent your bed along?' because a man in his position had to get around and meet people, it was part of his business. As he used to say, the day he was elected to Ransome's, the names on that club book would be rungs on his ladder. Yet there were times when she longed for a night out like they had years ago at their club, The Working Men's Club. They were grand nights; good turns, plenty to laugh at, a drink, then home to bed . . . and loving.

At eleven o'clock she went upstairs and she was in bed when she heard him come in, but it was a full fifteen minutes later when he entered the bedroom.

She gave him a twisted smile as she said, 'Oh, hello. I

didn't expect you; I thought you were staying for bed and breakfast.'

He stopped in the middle of the room and stared over the foot of the bed at her. She was wearing a pink nightdress with a lace-type yoke; the hair at each side of her temples was in two long rollers, her round, unlined face was free of night cream. His eyes moved down to her breasts. They were rising like full moons out of the top of her nightdress, and at one time this sight alone would have excited him, causing him almost to jump out of his clothes and into bed with her. But now the sight of her flesh slightly sickened him, and while this reaction filled him with a sensation of guilt he told himself he was only doing what ninety-nine men out of a hundred did; and besides, in his case, no-one was being hurt – ignorance was bliss, at least for her.

'What's the matter?'

She was bending over the counterpane towards him.

'Matter? What should be the matter? I'm tired, that's all.' He turned his back on her and walked into the dressing-room. This was a fad of his of late that she couldn't understand, him undressing in there. He was funny in some ways her Rod. She explained this latest fad to herself with slight amusement, he was aping the gentlemen; they always did the necessary in the dressing-room. Aw, he would get places would her Rod; there was no stopping him. And good luck to him. But what about her? Oh, come off it, she warned herself; Rod would always see to her. What more did she want anyway, she had everything?

'I've got a surprise for you.' She raised her voice.

'Oh? Aye.'

'You'll never guess.'

'Well, you'd better tell me, hadn't you?' His voice was flat, showing no interest.

She pressed her lips together, clamping down on a laugh,

and she let a short silence elapse before she said, 'You've had an invitation.'

'Yes?'

She drew the breath deep into her chest as she imagined the result of her next words, for he would come scooting out of that room as if he'd had a dose of salts.

'Pin your ears back and wait for it . . . We've had an invitation . . . from the Duke of Moorshire.'

Her eyes were fast on the open doorway, but he did not come scooting out. It was almost thirty seconds before he appeared. He was in his shirt sleeves, pulling the bands down from them. 'What did you say, an invitation from the Duke of Moorshire?'

'Yes, yes, that's what I said. Flabbergasted you?'

He wrinkled his nose. 'No, not really. What's the date?'

'The twenty-fourth of June.'

He went slowly back into the dressing-room and when he appeared at the door again he had a diary in his hands, and after flicking the pages he said, 'It's no go; I've got an important business meeting in Doncaster that day.'

She stared at him across the room. Then in two movements she had flung the clothes back and swung her legs on to the floor and was standing facing him. 'Look, Rod!' She thrust her arm out and picked up the invitation card from the side table and held it out towards him. 'You don't seem to have taken in what I said. This is an invitation from the Duke of Moorshire. The Duke mind, the Duke!'

'I heard what you said and you heard what I said, we won't be able to go.' He went back into the dressing-room again and she walked slowly towards the open door, saying, 'Now look you here. I've never asked you for much in me life, you've gone your own way, but this is one time you're going to do this for me. We're accepting this invitation.'

His heavy body swung towards her now, his face was

dark with an unwarranted anger. 'I said we are not going and that's that!'

She stared at him unbelieving. His ferocity meant that he had dug his heels in, but by God, this was one time when she was going to pull them out.

'What's come over you? I thought you would have been over the moon about such an invitation; the top rung of the ladder you would have said. I would have sworn that the only thing which would have stopped you from accepting this—' she flapped the card in his face '—would have been if the Queen herself had asked you up. Half the town will know now that we're going, so what you going to do about it?'

'Half the town?' His face puckered.

'Aye, that's what I said, half the town. They've all been here the night, everyone of them; they left about ten and I'd like to bet their phones have been ringing ever since. There were six people alone that our Frances was going to tell, her very, very dear friends, the ones she thinks look down their noses at her.'

His shoulders slumped, his eyes closed, and his head drooped. He hadn't thought about her telling the lot of them, but it was the first thing he should have thought of – the family must know, the family must know every damned thing. Well, that settled it. But it didn't settle the anger in him. His head jerking up, he yelled at her, 'You, and your bloody big mouth!'

For a moment she was silent under his attack; then, as of old, she let him have it. 'Bloody big mouth is it? Well, I might have at that, but I haven't got a bloody big head; nor am I getting so big for me boots that I can turn me nose up at an invitation like this. The big fella. Big Gallacher picking and choosing now. A few years back you'd have been on your knees grovelling to him for recognising you were alive. And another thing when I'm on, you've never

66

taken me anywhere for years, not since we've come into this house . . . ' Her mouth was open on a word when it became transfixed and gaping as a strange thought intruded into her tirade. Her lids blinked and narrowed as she asked in a quieter, but more deadly tone now, 'Could it be, Rodney Gallacher, that you've got so high up that you think I can't follow you, that you're ashamed to be seen with me?'

If he had bawled at her, 'It could be just that. You've put your finger on it, you've just said it,' she would have known there wasn't a word of truth in it. It would have been like the old days when they cut each other to pieces with their tongues, and the more lacerations they caused the more joy there was in the healing afterwards. But now he didn't turn on her. He turned away and, sweeping up his coat and tie and his pyjamas, he thrust himself past her, stamped across the room and out, and not even when she heard the door bang across the landing and knew he had gone into Willie's old room did she move.

They'd had dos in the past that could have come under the heading of tiffs, quarrels, and battles, but never before had he left the bedroom. At one time they had lain side by side for a week and never touched or spoken to one another, but they had lain there, in their bed.

She felt sick as she had done often when as a child her mother had threatened to wallop her. It wasn't the actual walloping that had made her feel sick but the waiting. Her mother would shove her into the dark cupboard under the stairs and keep her there, sometimes as long as three hours. She used to long for the walloping for then the fear of the dark and the loneliness would be past. She had thoughts and feelings in her that she could never tell anyone, not even Rod, because they were difficult to describe. If she had told Rod that she often felt a great sense of loneliness or aloneness he would have laughed at her and said she had been reading one of those articles in the women's magazines, they were full of psychology these days. But nothing in the articles had explained this feeling that had been with her since her earliest days. She was always one for a joke and a laugh; fat people were supposed to be merry, but she hadn't always been fat. She was only nine stone when she married and that was about right for her height of five foot six, but now she tipped the scales at thirteen stone.

But fat or thin, laughing or singing in the midst of her family, there had always been with her that strange feeling of aloneness. It flooded her now and tears sprang from her eyes, but she made no sound. Her hand tightly across her mouth, she walked to the bed and sat on its edge. She was back in the cupboard under the stairs and she wouldn't get her whacking until tomorrow morning when she looked at his face . . . downstairs, for she wouldn't go into the room where he was. No. No. His walking out of their room had stripped her of everything but a shred of pride, and she must hang on to that; at all costs she must hang on to that.

She didn't see him the following morning, for he left the house very early. But he came back into the bedroom that night; then after banging about for a while he turned on her and cried, 'Well, have it your own way then. But see you get dressed properly for it.' Then he got into bed but didn't touch her; nor did she turn to him.

See that you get dressed properly for it. It was like an insult. If it wasn't for the fact that the phone had been ringing all day she would have yelled at him, 'To hell with you! And the invitation an' all.' But she was committed; the family had committed her.

68

Part Two

Part Two

CHAPTER ONE

GOD VERSUS A WOMAN

Sam got up early on the Saturday morning and went straight out. This was unusual, for his routine on a Saturday morning was to lie late, clean the car, have his lunch, then go to the football match. But this morning he had left the house by nine o'clock and he did not say where he was going; and Arlette did not ask him, but she allowed ten minutes to elapse before locking up and taking her car from the garage. Three minutes' drive from the house she stopped opposite a telephone kiosk; then having gone in, she rang a number, and when a voice answered she said, 'Hello, John; it's me.'

'Oh, hello, Arlette. How's things?'

'There's been a hitch. I want you to hold everything for a month, till the end of June.'

'Do you think that's wise?'

'Well, I can't tell them now, something's happened. It's . . . it's his mother.'

'What's she got to do with it?'

'She's had an invitation to meet the Duke of Moorshire.'

'But you're not going to let that . . . ?'

'You don't understand, John. I've told you how sweet she is, a real dear person. As . . . as I said, I would have finished the whole thing long before this if it hadn't been for upsetting her, breaking with her; I've told you I'm very fond of her.'

'Yes, you may be, but it's your life; and I mean that literally. How's he been?'

'Pretty much the same. There was a new phase last night. He had been to his mother's – all celebrating the invitation you know – and when we came back he acted like a lunatic. He was still laughing at three o'clock this morning. You know something, John; I've suspected this for a long time, but he hates her. I don't know why, or how anyone could, but he's got something against her.'

'A man like that has always got something against someone.'

'But this is particular, a special kind of hate.'

'Have you been to the doctor recently?'

'I . . . I am going this afternoon.'

'More evidence?'

She remained silent and gnawed at her lip and the voice came to her, saying, 'It's damnable. If I had my way he'd go along the line. He might even yet.'

She said now, 'How is Moira?' and he answered, 'Oh, she's got hay fever, as usual. Time of year. Where you phoning from?'

'A call box.'

'Arlette.'

'Yes, John?'

'You must do as I advised before. Don't tell him in person, just leave a letter and clear out. Moira would love you to come here, but for my part I don't think it would be safe. You must get right away, go to London, or down to the West Coast.'

'It's a pity, isn't it, we haven't any relatives to fly to in times of trouble? Still I've always had you, and I'm so thankful for it.'

'And I'm so glad I'm here for you to fly to. I may as well tell you I'm more than a little worried about the position you're in. And I repeat that I think you've been mad to put up with it for so long. Anyway, when we do start proceedings there'll be no hitch, I'll see to that. I had a word with Whicken the other day. He's the barrister I was telling you about, very clever fellow, and when I told him the facts he said it would be one of those that went straight through. But I hate to think of you lasting out another month; and sweet mother or no sweet mother, I think you should make the break now.'

'There's the pips, John, and I haven't any more change, I must go. I'll pop in one day next week.'

'Very well. Goodbye, Arlette.'

'Goodbye, John.'

She put the receiver down and stood looking in the small dirty mirror on her eye level. 'Make the break,' he had said, 'as soon as possible.' And he was right. It couldn't be too soon, not a split second too soon. Yet in making the break from Sam she was making the break with the only family she had ever known and from the woman who had welcomed her with a warmth that couldn't have been exceeded had that woman been her real mother.

She didn't remember her own mother. She had died when she was three, and her mother's sister, John's mother, had died when John was eight, and strangely both their fathers had died in Korea. More strangely still, their fathers had been only children and their mothers had no other children. Both of them had been brought up mainly in boarding schools. John who had gone in for law was now a junior partner in a firm of solicitors in the town and was doing very well. It was odd but it was at John's wedding to Moira that she had met Sam. He had been a friend, or perhaps it was truer to say a fellow rugby player with Moira's brother.

She sat in the car, her hands on the wheel, staring ahead of her. There was something else she must do this morning but it was going to be difficult, delicate in fact, but she must do it because if Sam started probing in this particular

73

direction, and she was sure that he meant to, there would be trouble, grave trouble in the house.

She started the car and drove by side roads and streets until she came to Talford Road. She did not drive the car down to Marsh House but left it on a piece of spare ground adjoining the main road, then walked down the street of nondescript high terraced houses, pushed upon the iron gate of number seventeen, looked at the four names in their little sockets, and then rang the bell for Mr Paul Gallacher.

She reached the second landing as Paul opened the door. He was in his pyjamas and dressing-gown and he gaped at her as if she was an apparition.

She smiled tentatively at him, saying, 'I'm sorry if I got you up, I know it's early and Saturday, but . . . but I wanted to see you for a moment.'

He stepped back into the room and held the door wide for her, and she passed him and glanced quickly about her. He had evidently just jumped out of bed, but she hadn't woken him because on the top of the divan were spread papers and books, and two pillows rested lengthwise against the bed head. There were the remains of a meal on the table, a parcel of unopened laundry was on a chair and two drip-dry shirts on wire hangers were suspended from a line above the sink at the far end of the room. The place looked so muddled, so cold, so devoid of any comfort that it pained her; she compared it with all the things that Sam demanded for his comfort, things that, up to two years ago, his own money would not have run to, though he had never had any compunction about enjoying the fruits of her private income. The fact of her money being tied up until she was thirty had irked her when she was first married, but now she blessed her father's foresight.

Paul hadn't opened his mouth, not even to say hello. He was backing from her towards the bathroom, and now she

74

was forced to say, 'I'm . . . I'm sorry, Paul; perhaps I can call later.'

'No! No!' His voice cracked on the second no, like that of a young treble singer. 'I won't be a minute. Sit . . . sit down. Please sit down.'

She sat down on the only empty seat, which was opposite his desk. There was silence for a while; then she heard the sound of a splintered bang coming from the bathroom and she guessed he had broken a glass, perhaps dropped it into the bath. She moved her head slowly. She shouldn't have come, not . . . not so early in the morning, she had embarrassed him. She looked down at the desk. It was covered with sheets of paper, lined paper like they used at school. She put her elbow on the desk next to a page covered with italic script, the writing black and bold, each word standing out, and the title at the top of the page read, 'My love is beautiful'. Her eyes, like quicksilver, scanned the lines:

My love is beautiful;
She hangs over me
Like grapes on the vine,
But her bloom will not fade
Or be crushed
By this hand of mine;
My love is beautiful.

My love is beautiful;
Her voice plays on my heart,
But the theme is mine;
I make her whisper,
We shall never part.
Hold me fast, I am thine.
My love is beautiful.

My love is beautiful;
And so will remain;
I will not besmirch
Her body or her brain
With fumbling hands
Or senseless chatter.
Oh, but that I could;
I would, if she were mine,
My love is beautiful.

Her eyes lifted to the title again. 'My love is beautiful.'
Oh, Paul. Poor Paul. There was a woman. He was in
love with a woman. Mam had been right; she had said
she thought there was a woman who had put an end to
him going in for the priesthood. Yet the years since he
had left seemed to have proved her wrong because he had
never been known to associate with any woman other than
those in the family. But these words were the words of a
man who loved.

She gave a loud gasp and bowed her head as his hand
came across her shoulder and, picking up the sheet of
paper, turned it face downwards. She remained seated,
her head low. She couldn't bear to look at him as she
muttered, 'I'm . . . I'm sorry, Paul; I . . . I had no intention of prying, but—' slowly now she raised her eyes
to his '—it's about this I came.'

'What!'

She watched his eyes widen, his thin lips part; she
followed his hand as it slowly went up and the fingers
spread out as they combed his coarse tousled red hair back
from his brow.

She stood up facing him now, saying, 'Please, Paul,
don't mind. I . . . I would never tell anyone, but it's
Sam. After last night, and that piece that hit directly
home—' she smiled wryly '—It fell off a lorry. I know

76

that Sam's going to probe, and when he starts, well you know Sam, he's just got to get an inkling and like a bull terrier he holds on.'

'Oh.' His chin fell on to his chest and he laughed shakily as his body slumped. When finally he lifted his eyes to hers they had a merry glint in them, and his change of attitude puzzled her for it expressed relief. He was now giving the impression that he didn't care two hoots who knew that he was Lacker of the *Messenger*. Then, the smile sliding from his face, he asked, 'How did you twig, and not the others?'

'It was when Liz and I came to put your curtains up. There was a piece of torn paper lying by the side of the desk—' she pointed '—near the wall, and I picked it up.' She smiled. 'I'm like Liz. I'm always tidying; it's a finicky habit of mine. There were some words written on the paper. They were unusual but I recognised them; I had read them the previous week: "Applauded and lauded, name breathed in awe; a poet, a poet, as never before." '

'Oh, that.' His chin jerked. 'I was showing my spleen in that one. I had just read a fulsome review of a so-called modern poet. I don't mind praise where it's due, but that was a bit too much. It may have read like sour grapes, but it wasn't, for I don't consider myself a poet. I'm just a rhymer, but nevertheless I get over what I mean, and you don't have to have a committee to dissect it before you get the gist of it.'

She stared at him. There was a bitterness in him that she had never detected before and she thought, he may not be a good poet but he takes this seriously. He's like a pamphleteer of old, putting his ideas, but mostly his objections, before the public. She remembered she had been startled by the last lines of the poem: 'It's very obscure as is all that is great, so let us with whores and urine debate.' She hadn't been able to connect this way of thinking and expression with Paul. With Sam yes, oh yes, or Willie . . .

He broke into her thoughts with his characteristic short laugh and shook his head as he said, 'I prided myself on burning all the evidence that time when I knew you and Liz were coming . . . Sit down.' He turned the seat round, then swept the laundry from the other chair on to the corner of the desk. When he was seated opposite to her he looked into her eyes for a moment before saying, 'So Sam is going to probe?'

'Yes. I . . . I've got a feeling he's gone down to the offices of the *Messenger*; he went out early.'

'Did he now?' He tapped his teeth with his fingernail. 'You know, but for one thing I don't really give a damn if Sam finds out or not, or Willie either, because I was hitting at them both. It was an underhand way I suppose, but their fiddling has got on my nerves for years. I'm . . . I'm sorry to say this about Sam . . . '

'You needn't be; it's got on my nerves too, especially when, in his case, there was not the least necessity for it. It has just become a habit.'

'Yes.' He nodded at her. 'A habit.'

He rose to his feet now and stood looking down at the desk and, slowly putting out his hand, began to move the papers around, saying as if to himself, 'If he succeeds in his probing I'll lose the source of my inspiration, because all this—' he scattered the papers with his hand '—comes from the family. Each week I milk them.' He was gnawing on his lip, and he looked at her sideways as he said, 'I would say, "Aw! to the devil. Let him find out," but it's Mam; she'll be upset about this, won't she?'

'I'm afraid so.'

He bobbed his head down at her, took three quick strides towards the door, then turned to her, saying, 'I won't be a minute. There's a phone downstairs; I can check his gallop.' He now cast his eyes quickly between the desk and the bed and gave her a twisted grin as he ended, 'I needn't ask you not to read further.' Then before she could answer he exclaimed on a high note, 'But why not? Why not? Here!' He hurried towards the bed, sorted among the loose sheets, then picked out one and handed it to her, saying, 'That's my conscience speaking; you would have read it next week. I won't be a minute.'

She did not look at the sheet in her hand until he had closed the door behind him; then she read the title 'Retaliation', and she noted that both the metre and the length were the same as always. His work, as he had said, was not that of a poet but a rhymer, yet she knew that his rhyming would reach the hearts of more people than if his words had been so clever as to be obscure to the majority of ordinary folk. She read:

> Do not tempt me to slay;
> In thought, in dreams
> Keep my mind at bay.
> Do not tempt me to slay
> With my tongue, or my eye,
> For by such weapons
> I too shall die.
>
> Let them say what they say,
> My neighbour and my friend.
> Day runs into day,
> My world will sometime end;
> The hurts and the pains
> Forever cannot stay.
> Do not tempt me to slay.

Do not tempt me to slay
My loved ones with a laugh,
Listening to their fancies,
Their foibles, their chaff.
The point of laughter
Is a deadly ray;
Do not tempt me to slay.

Yet he did slay. Every week he had slain, and his own. As he said, he got his inspiration from the family. She put the sheet of paper down on the desk beside the one he had turned over, 'My love is beautiful'. Would he publish that? She liked Paul, she'd always liked him, but . . . but she was a little afraid of him, perhaps because she saw him as not quite an ordinary man. Any man who had harboured thoughts of the priesthood seemed slightly extraordinary to her. Indeed it was this very fact which had prevented her from talking to him as much as she would have liked for she had the feeling that they could be in agreement on so many things. There was a lot of his mother in Paul, yet of all of them he looked least like her, he was the only one in the family with reddish hair. She had read somewhere that red-headed men rarely became priests because their glands were too active. Perhaps there was some truth in it.

He came back into the room, his face straight, his mouth tight. 'You were right,' he said, 'he's been . . . Arthur Dalton, he's the sub-editor, recognised him and was just going to ring me.'

'Did he tell him?'

'No; he said he wasn't at liberty to give names. He asked him why he wanted to know the name of the author, and you know what Sam said?'

She shook her head.

'He was interested in poetry.' He laughed derisively. 'Sam interested in poetry! Sam! Huh!' Again his head went down and, his voice contrite now, he said, 'I'm sorry. You must guess now, if you haven't before, that let alone not loving my neighbour as myself I don't even love my brother.'

'. . . I don't either!'

His head jerked upwards, and they were staring at each other. What, she asked herself in some panic, had made her say that? But she had said it, and to the only one in the family to whom she could say it. It was strange but she realised now that she had wanted to tell Paul this for a long time, but having said it she saw that her words had come as a shock to him. The colour had seeped from his face; all that was left of his fresh complexion were two spots high on his cheekbones. His eyes, curtains always to his thoughts, seemed to have disappeared into the back of his head and were shadowed still further by his drooped lids. But his reaction did not deter her from spilling out her trouble to him.

'I'm going to get a divorce.'

His eyelids rose again, his gaze, tight and deep, fixed on her face. She saw now tiny beads of sweat on the faint line of stubble on his upper lip. She wished he would say something. His Adam's apple jerked up under his chin and fell again, and then he said softly, 'Does he know?'

She shook her head.

'He'll never let you go, never. Not on any grounds, but mostly he'll say on religious.'

'That doesn't affect me, religion. As you know, I'm not a Catholic.'

She had been married in a Catholic church but she hadn't turned. She knew that, before they were married, Sam had promised Father Stillwell to work on her. He had laughingly told her this; but he himself was no true Catholic. Last year he had attended his Easter duties, and Midnight Mass. That was the sum total of him practising his religion. He called his Easter duties keeping up his Union dues. 'As long as your card's stamped,' he had once told her laughingly, 'you're all right.' And she knew he believed this; the stamping of his card at Easter with confession and Holy Communion was a passport to a happy death and the pleasures thereafter. Sometimes her mind grappled with the problem of this man whom she knew to be almost inhuman in his bodily desires but who could yet be so naïve in his religious beliefs.

'On what grounds will you get it?'

She swallowed deeply before she said, 'Cruelty.'

'Cruelty! Mental?'

'Pa . . . partly, but mostly—' she swallowed again and her voice sank to a murmur as she ended, '—physical.'

His eyes were lost again, his face screwed up pulling his lips from his teeth. 'Sam,' he said slowly. 'Sam. But he's mad about you.'

'Yes,' she closed her eyes as she nodded her head, 'that is the correct word, mad, about me.'

'But . . . but how?' He still wasn't believing.

She turned from him now. 'I can't tell you Paul; you'll . . . you'll know soon enough.' She put her hand to her head.

'Does he know, I mean, what you intend?'

'No, not yet. It . . . it was to begin this week, but after last night—' she turned slowly towards him '—it . . . it would spoil things for Mam and the invitation, so I put it off until the function's over.'

'He'll . . . he'll not let you do it, not Sam. Sam is . . . ' He couldn't say to her 'dangerous', but he'd always known Sam was dangerous. There were so many instances he could recall that had proved him dangerous. The first time he became aware of what lay behind his brother's laughing face happened when he was ten and Sam twelve. Sam had been badly beaten in the school yard by Peter

Morrell, and later Father Armstrong had made them shake hands. Later still, when they were outside, Peter, in his magnanimous way had punched Sam in the chest while he grinned at him, and Sam had punched him back, while he too grinned widely. That week-end Peter Morrell's bike had been stolen. They found it broken up on the waste land, but the bell of the bike and the saddle bag they found in Ronnie Dale's shed. Ronnie Dale was one of the lads who had cheered Peter Morrell on; Sam had never liked Ronnie Dale. Ronnie Dale was taken to court; it was his third offence and he was sent to a remand home. He himself always felt guilty when he thought of Ronnie Dale because he knew he had not been guilty. It had been late on the Friday night when he had seen their Sam creeping out of the Dales' backyard. Ronnie Dale's mother and father went to the club every Friday night and Father Monaghan held his boxing class. He had just come from the boxing class himself and left Ronnie Dale there. He should have split on their Sam there and then, but he was afraid of him. He slept in the same room as him and he knew what he could do, such as sticking his knuckles into a nerve in your arm until you nearly fainted.

But that Sam should be cruel to Arlette seemed impossible, because he loved her. As he said, he was mad about her. When first he knew her and was chasing her hard and she didn't show much interest Sam had said to him, 'I'll get her, and God help anybody who tries to stop me.' Yes, God help anybody who tried to stop him. Besides being six foot two and heavy with it, his brother was cunningly intelligent. And there was something else he knew about his brother and had been aware of for quite a while now: in spite of his cunning and his strength their Sam had nothing; there was a great emptiness in him, a great want. There was something wrong with their

Sam. What it was he didn't know, only that there was something radically wrong inside him.

And now Arlette was saying she was going to break with him, finish with him, divorce him. He was pulling himself round from the shock of her words; he still couldn't believe them. But she had said them and she meant to carry them out, and again he thought, He'll never let her, never, never, never. He'll do something to her first.

He took a step towards her, his hands wavering in front of him as if he were about to grasp hers; then dropping them to his sides he said thickly, 'You . . . you mustn't tell Sam; I mean you should let it be done legally by—' He tossed his head. 'What I mean is . . . '

'I know what you mean, Paul. I'm not going to tell him. When the time comes I'm going away. My cousin, you know, John, well, he's seeing to everything for me.'

'You're going away?'

'Yes.'

'Where?'

She shook her head. 'I don't know yet.' Quite suddenly she walked back to the chair and sat down again, and when she looked up at him her eyes were blurred and, her voice breaking, she said, 'That's been the trouble, that's what's made me put up with it and kept me from doing anything about it, the family. All of you, but especially Mam. It's . . . it's this business of having been brought up alone, adrift. When . . . when I came into the family, at first it was wonderful. You . . . you could never understand because you were brought up with a family, and the thought of breaking all ties with them and being thrust out and on my own again was more unbearable than, well, living with Sam; until . . . until recently.'

'Aw, Arlette.' He wasn't really aware that he had dropped on to his knees and that he was holding her hands tightly to his breast, that his face was bowed over

84

them and that his lips were on them, but the awareness returned to him in seconds and he was on his feet again, one hand running through his hair, the other rubbing the front of his shirt. And now he was muttering almost incoherently, 'I'm sorry. It . . . it was your feelings for the family; I . . . I . . . we all feel like that about you too.'

She was gazing up at his averted face now. There was a light creeping into her mind. It seemed to be coming from the far end of a long tunnel, but becoming brighter every moment, until it shone full in her eyes and dazzled her. She blinked and got hastily to her feet, and then her thoughts dimmed it; it was just as he said, the family all liked her, except perhaps Frances.

'I must be going now, Paul.'

He turned to her. His face, the whiteness of lint, accentuated the darkness of his eyes and the redness of his hair. Even his lips looked bloodless; and as she stared at him she recalled an instance before he went to college when she surprised him looking at her. She had thought then he was weighing her up, wondering if she would be a good enough wife for his brother. Even though he was a year younger than herself, she had seen him as someone much older, for she then had the idea that priests, even young ones, were men out of the ordinary, men who had been given an insight into something closed to ordinary human beings, men of high intellect, men enveloped in spirit. She had learned differently since. The three priests at the church had been an education to her. The Rector, Father Stillwell, she knew to be a narrow-minded, ignorant man, while Father Monaghan she saw as a big, brain-washed Irish bumpkin. Only Father Armstrong held her respect, and then he had his flaws, for he was the priest to whom Paul had referred in 'It Fell Off A Lorry'. She had recognised him instantly.

She did not now glance towards his desk but in her

mind's eyes she was seeing the heading 'My love is beautiful' on the turned down sheet, and linking it to his actions
of a moment ago. She thought, It's too awful. And yet,
what was awful about it? She liked him, she had always
liked him, in fact she had at times . . . She must get away
because this was really dreadful; she didn't want any more
complications, couldn't stand any more complications.

'Goodbye, Paul.'

'Goodbye, Arlette.' He didn't move, not even to open
the door for her, only his eyes followed her.

She stood in the dim lobby and drew in several deep
breaths, then opened the door and walked into the street
and down the road. As she turned the corner she saw her
car, and next to it, bumper to bumper, Sam's car.

She halted in her stride, her mind racing. Why was he
here? Had he followed her? What excuse could she give
him for going to Paul's?

He must have watched her coming towards him in
his mirror because just as she was abreast of him he
flung open the door and she had to jump back to save
herself from being knocked down.

'Sorry. Sorry.' He was standing facing her now. 'I was
going to pop along to Paul's. Came to park, and found
yours.' He thumbed towards her car. 'You've been along
there?'

'Yes.' She looked him straight in the face.

'Early aren't you?' He brought his wrist round and
looked at his watch. 'Just gone ten, and Saturday; he'd
hardly be up. Likes his bed, does Paul. What you go for?'

'I . . . I wanted to ask him something.'

'Ask him something? Why couldn't you ask him last
night? You saw plenty of him last night.'

'I couldn't with everybody there.'

He raised his eyebrows at her and grinned a one-sided
grin. 'Oh, really! So very important?'

'No, not all that important, except to me.'

'Well, spill it; I'd like to know, as well as Paul that is.'

'I'm . . . I'm going to take a university course, external, in languages. I . . . I wanted to ask him how to go about it.'

He brought his head towards her but didn't speak for a moment; then he said, 'My! My! A university course in languages. First I've heard of it.'

'I've been thinking about it for some time.' And this was true, she had; but she would have no need to go to Paul about it, she could have gone and had a talk with the Principal of the new college, or she could have obtained her information through correspondence.

'Want to fill your time up, do you? Haven't got enough to occupy you? You should let Mrs Bell go; a bit of extra housework wouldn't do you any harm. Mam will tell you that. It's a wonder she hasn't. Does she know about the new idea?'

'Of course not.' She started to move away from him. 'I told you, I just put it to Paul.'

'Oh, you just put it to Paul. Well, I'm sure Paul will feel honoured.' The smile went from his face leaving his eyes as they had been all the while, greeny blue, like a cold sea, and his voice came from deep down in his broad chest as he muttered, 'And Paul now will have more cause to look down his bloody nose at me.'

She turned now and looked at him, less fearfully than she had done for a long time, and her voice had a chill sound as she said, 'That's your trouble, isn't it, the fear of people looking down their noses at you?' She paused before adding, 'And it says in the Bible that the things they feared came upon them.'

She felt him close behind her as she went to her car door. She wouldn't have been surprised if his hands had come on her neck. Yet she would have; Sam did nothing in public that would cause anyone to point a finger at him. But his voice came at her in a low growl now, saying, 'I'll Bible you one of these days. My God, see if I don't.'

She got into the car and drove straight back home. Hurrying to the hall, she picked up the phone. There was a window to the side of her that looked on to the drive. If he was following her she'd be able to see him coming. She phoned Felburn 1212. It was strange but she hadn't known the number of the telephone in Paul's house; it was as she had paused for those few moments in his hall that her eye had been taken by the number, 1212. It was the old Whitehall number so often heard on the wireless: phone Whitehall 1212.

A woman's voice said, 'Hello,' and she answered. 'Do you think I could speak to Mr Paul Gallacher, he's in Flat 4?'

'Oh aye. Wait a minute, I'll get him.'

She kept her eyes on the window while she waited. It seemed a long time; then Paul's voice came to her. 'Hello?'

'This is Arlette. Is Sam with you?'

'Yes.'

'Has he asked you why I came?'

'No, not yet; he's toying with it, playing cat and mouse.'

'Listen, Paul. He was round the corner waiting. He wanted to know why I had been to see you. I . . . I told him I wanted advice on a university course. Do you hear?'

'Yes, yes, I hear.'

'I said I was thinking about taking it up, in languages. I thought . . . I thought I'd better tell you.'

'Yes, thanks.' His words were terse. Then he added in a whisper, 'Don't worry. Don't worry, Arlette,' and when he spoke her name it was as if there was a link between them, a secret.

She put the phone down; then slowly she took off

her things and went into the kitchen and made herself some coffee, and as she sipped at it she tried to recall the look on his face as he knelt before her, her hands gripped tightly in his, his lips pressed to her knuckles. But she couldn't get his features to materialise; they were all running into a white blur, only his eyes were distinct. She felt she was going to faint. She put down her cup and leant back in the chair. A few minutes later, the full significance of the situation came to her and she murmured, 'Oh, Paul. Oh, Paul.' Then another name was added to her murmuring; and this name brought her sitting up straight. If Mam ever got wind of this it would shatter the precious thing that was between them, because her son Paul, while being the apple of her eye, had also been the greatest disappointment in her life.

It was up to her; she should leave now; it would hurt Mam less in the long run.

CHAPTER TWO

THE PREPARATION

'Aw, I wish it had never happened; I wish I'd never seen the bloody invitation. Do you know, Arlette, I've walked more miles in this town with our Frances this week than I've done since I was born. And what have I got? Nothing; only a frayed temper and half an inch lost off me tongue. I left it with her this morning. You see—' Maggie bent towards Arlette where she sat in the button-studded pink velvet bedroom chair. '—Our Frances thinks she's got taste, but, Arlette lass, she doesn't know the first thing about it. She was all for me getting a three-quarter cocktail affair in taffeta, grey taffeta. Why! I would have looked like Nanny-cum-canny in it. I walked out of the shop, and that finished her. She exploded in the street. Well, not really in the street. She waited until we got into the car, 'cos you know Frances, all for the proper thing.' Maggie smiled. 'But I exploded an' all. I said to hell with her and her ideas and the proper thing. Etcetera. Etcetera.' She put her hand over her face now and laughed. 'She nearly threw me out on to the drive when we got back.' She nodded towards the window; then flopping down on the side of the bed she ended, 'Aw, she means well. But Frances could always rattle me, she's so damned prim. Eeh!' She flapped her hand at Arlette. 'I'm a nasty piece of work, Arlette; I'm always criticising me bairns. But you know—' again she poked her head forward '—it's a funny thing but I only do it to you, nobody else, I never talk about one to the other. No,' she moved her head from side to side, 'I've never done that. I've hardly spoken against them to Rod, even when they were little devils, especially the lads, but to you . . . ' She dropped her hands into her lap and her whole body relaxed. And looking at the slim form of Arlette she said, 'I don't know why but you do me good, lass, you always have. Funny, isn't it? And I keep on tellin' you. I must bore the pants off you.'

Arlette was smiling. 'You could never bore me, Mam. I feel the same way; I could tell you anything. Well . . . ' The smile slid from her face. That was a lie, for she was the last person in the world she could tell everything to because she was the one person in the world she wouldn't want to hurt. She, too, had thought often and often of the strange affinity between this fat middle-aged woman and herself. They had come from different strata of society, they talked differently, their intelligences were on different levels, yet beneath the skin in a realm that could not be explained or defined, they were akin, closer than mother and daughter. There was a love between them that had no sex, that was so ethereal in its substance as to vaporise when brushed by thought.

Maggie was now saying, 'Why didn't I take a pull at meself long before this? I've lost three pounds this week because I haven't eaten any tatties, and no cakes, and hardly any bread. But what's three pounds? If only the rest of me was like me legs.' She thrust them out towards Arlette. 'Isn't it funny? They've never got fat. They're not bad are they?'

'They're wonderful legs, very smart.' Arlette brought herself to the edge of the chair, then asked tentatively, 'Would you let me see to you, Mam; I mean get you dressed?'

'Would I!' Maggie gazed at her daughter-in-law; then

exclaimed with a high laugh, 'Why, lass, I'll be putty in your hands . . . I won't say fat.' Her mouth was wide, her head back.

'It'll cost something.'

'Well, what does that matter; Rod'll come round to it. How much?'

Arlette considered for a moment. 'About a hundred and fifty I should say.'

'WH-AT! A hundred and fifty pounds to rig me out! . . . Aw, lass.'

'I'm afraid so.' Arlette was smiling broadly now. 'You see you'd have to have a good foundation; that's the main thing. There's a rather exclusive shop in Newcastle, Madam Hevell's. You know it?'

'Never heard of it.'

'It's very small. It's in a side street, but she's very exclusive and very pricey. She starts with the foundation and works outwards. She'll fit you out for an occasion right down to the shoes; she's expert at this.'

'But a hundred and fifty pounds, lass.'

'It might be more; it could go to two hundred. This—' she pointed to the French-grey suit with the narrow pink stripe running through it that she was wearing '—This was forty-eight guineas.'

'Never! Never, lass.'

'Yes, it was.'

'But I thought you got most of your things at the big stores, like . . . '

'I do; but now and again I treat myself, about once a year. I've had this three years. They last for ever and never lose their shape. The dress I wore at Christmas, that was from Madam Hevell's; it was sixty guineas.'

'Arlette, you're mad. That little thing, it was almost a mini, and nothing to it, as plain as a pikestaff.'

'It's that what you pay for; it was a model, and if the

fashions don't go out too much somebody will be wearing that same dress twenty years from now.'

'Aye, lass.' Maggie considered for a moment. 'It sounds marvellous but—' she let her body flop on to the bed '—I doubt if Rod will stand for anything near two hundred pounds to rig me out. A new car, furniture, the house decorated, yes; but lass, I've never had a coat over twenty pounds in me life. Nineteen guineas I paid for my brown one.' She nodded towards the wardrobe. 'And this is the third winter I've had that. You see, I don't go out a lot so it seems a waste; and it's still as good as new . . . Two hundred pounds! I'd never have the face to ask him.'

'Well, let me buy it for you?'

'What! You buy me outfit? Not on your life.' Indignant now, Maggie rose from the bed. 'And me man rolling in money? What you thinking of? But,' her face spread into its usual smile and putting out her hand she patted Arlette's shoulder, 'it's nice of you; it's like what you would do.' Then she straightened her back and wagged her head as she said, 'He'll buy it. What time is it?' She looked at the antique gilt travelling clock on the mantelpiece and said, 'Quarter to four. Now if I'm lucky I might catch him at the office. I'll strike while the iron's hot, eh?' She hurried to the side-table, her step like a young girl's, because for all her weight she was light on her feet, and as she dialled the number Arlette said, 'Tell him it's Madam Hevell's you want to go to; tell him Mrs de Ferrier gets her clothes there, that should impress him.'

Maggie pulled a face towards Arlette. 'By! Aye, that should impress him, an' all. Does she get everything there?'

'I should think so. About everything.'

'Hello. Is . . . is Mr Gallacher in? Tell him it's Mrs Gallacher . . .

'Hello there, Rod.'

'Hello.'

'Hello.'

'I know it's you. What's the matter, what do you want?'

'Two hundred pounds.' She slanted her eyes and twisted her nose towards Arlette.

'What!'

'You heard. Two hundred pounds. I want to get rigged out.'

'Two hundred pounds! It won't take two hundred pounds to rig you out.'

'That's all you know. I've travelled the town all this week with our Frances looking for something to wear. We parted on fighting terms. But Arlette's here and she's promised to have me done properly . . . done I said.' She was laughing now. 'She said it will take two hundred pounds.'

'Nonsense!'

'Well, that's what she says and she should know.'

'There's shops in Newcastle that'll fix you up for a quarter of that.'

'So you think. But I've tried some of them. There's a lot of me to fix up; perhaps you haven't noticed.' Again she pulled a face at Arlette. 'Anyway, this shop is very classy and I don't see why I shouldn't go and get fixed up there, Mrs de Ferrier gets all her things there . . . Hello. Are you there? . . . Rod . . . Rod, are you there?'

Maggie now turned a blank face towards Arlette. 'He's rung off, or been cut off.' She put the phone down. 'I'll try again in a minute or so, but I'm sure it'll be all right; he stopped bawling me out when I mentioned your name.' She sat on the edge of the bed again and, joining her plump hands on her lap, she said, 'I feel excited, like a young lass, Arlette. Do you think she'll take inches off me?'

'More than inches. But stick to your diet; if you could lose another eight or nine pounds in the next three weeks it would be marvellous.'

'I will, lass, I will. But what about me face?' She jumped up from the bed and leant over the dressing table and looked into the mirror. 'I haven't any lines, have I, and no grey in me hair? It's a funny thing—' she half turned towards Arlette '—that Mrs Burrows-Thompson, you know, who lives in the second house down towards the end of the road, must be sixty if she's a day because she's got a daughter over forty, and her face is a mass of lines. But, you know, I always envy her because in a way she looks younger than me; it's her figure I suppose and the way she dresses. Well!' She stood up straight and gave her stomach a resounding blow with the flat of her hand and laughed as she said, 'Get ye gone Satan and leave Maggie Gallacher slim and alluring.' Then, the laughter dropping from her like a cloak and leaving her face straight, her voice flat and serious, she looked down at Arlette and said, 'I want to do Rod credit. That's all I want to do, ever want to do, do him credit.'

CHAPTER THREE

THE TAXI DRIVER

The dance was at its height. The Felburn Corkers were
blasting out the latest pop hit. Elizabeth was in the café at
the coffee end of the long table, and her arms were aching
and her head was buzzing. Where did they put it all? She
must have poured out thousands of cups of coffee. And she
said so to Father Armstrong as he bent over the counter
towards her and asked, 'How's it going, Nippy?'

'Aw, Father—' she closed her eyes and wiped the sweat,
which wasn't imaginary, from her brow with the back of
her hand '—where do they put it? I've taken nearly five
pounds in coffee alone.'

'Good. Good. It'll be ten before the night's out, at least
I hope so, so don't let your pins give way yet awhile.'
He nodded his grizzled head at her, then went on, 'Ah,
but you want a break; I'll get Mary to come. Mary!' He
bellowed across the room to where two girls were standing
near the dance room door, and as the shorter of the two
turned towards him he said in an aside to Elizabeth, 'It's
a kindness putting her out of her misery anyway; she'll
never get a partner with those feet.'

'Oh, Father!'

'Well, it's the truth. Poor girl, she was born with two
left ones.' His voice trailed away and he turned abruptly
and said, 'Ah, there you are, Mary. Now here's Elizabeth
done a two-hour stint, what about giving her a break,
fifteen minutes or so? And it's a slack time. Go on now,
get behind that counter.' He pushed the far from willing

girl, saying, 'It's kind of you,' and when she turned to him, about to speak, he said, 'I know, I know; you did your stint last time and at the Children of Mary's on Thursday night. I know, I know all about it. But go on, be a good child. Just fifteen minutes; that's all you want isn't it, Elizabeth?' He didn't wait for her answer; pulling her around the table, he led her across the room, out into the corridor and through another door into a games room that was empty now and, looking about him, said, 'Ah, this is nice. I could do with a breather meself. Let's sit down and have a crack.'

Elizabeth flopped down into a plastic-covered easy chair and stretched out her legs, letting her arms dangle limply over the sides. Anything less like a prospective nun would be hard to imagine. Her dress wasn't a mini but it rose above her knees. Her legs were long and thin, her body equally long and thin; she was tall for her age, but her breasts hardly made shadows in her dress; her face was happy, relaxed and guileless. And so thought Father Armstrong as he looked at her. She looked to him like something that had been dropped from another world and unaware that she was a stranger in this one. He was afraid for her, he had been afraid for her for some time now. Perhaps it was because he remembered Paul. Paul had been like this, unaware, walking in realms of ideas and ideals, out to please, to make people happy, and unconscious of self and the needs of self. Paul had thought of the priesthood not as the further glorification of God and his work on earth, but of the glorification of his family, of his mother in particular; yes, his mother in particular. Maggie had been to blame with regards to Paul, from the very beginning. If the boy hadn't been awakened when he was he'd have likely gone down to his grave never realising that he had become a priest solely because of his parents. Or perhaps he would have, only then it would have been too late. But as with many others, some better, before him, this very awakening could have brought him nearer to Christ than ever a vocation in the first place would have done, because in such a situation a man had great need of Christ, need of his understanding and compassion.

He turned to Elizabeth and said to her gently, 'Do you think you'll miss all this next year, I mean the dancing and the frivolity?'

'No, Father; of course not.'

'Don't you like dancing?'

'Yes, of course; but I've always been able to take it or leave it.'

'Elizabeth.'

'Yes, Father?' She pulled herself up in the chair and turned to him, her grey eyes laughing at him.

'You're sure of yourself and your intentions?'

The eyes widened, her mouth remained open for a moment as if in surprise, then she declared firmly, 'Of course, of course. Yes. I've told you. I feel I've got the vocation.'

He stared at her. He had christened her – he had christened all Maggie's and Rod's children – he had married them and they had turned out a decent enough family, except that they were lapsing here and there. But there were only really two of them he had taken to, Paul and this one here, and he hoped to God, indeed he did, that she knew what she was about. He said to her now, 'Stay where you are and rest your feet a minute, I'm going to look in on the madhouse; you never know, they might start throwing bottles.' He said the latter as if that was the most improbable thing that could happen. But when he reached the door he turned. 'There's a Bog's End element here the night but so far they're behaving like Christians. I hope their good intentions last till twelve.' He put his head back, then ended, 'They've swelled the coffers anyway; we've nearly reached five hundred.'

'Really, Father?'

He smiled at her. 'Nearly five hundred.'

'Good for us,' she said.

'Yes, good for us,' he repeated; 'we'll have that window before the year's out.'

When he had gone she sat thinking about the window. She had never been able to see why he wanted a new window in the Lady Chapel. There was a nice one there already showing the Holy Family, but apparently he had always wanted a great, long window to light up the corner, and now it had become a sort of thing with him, a thing that he wanted to accomplish before he retired in two years' time. Oh well, he had done so much for the parish he deserved his window. Dear Father Armstrong. Retired or no, he had promised to say Mass the day she took her vows.

She rubbed her hands together. She felt hot and sticky and the distant beat of the band was making her head ache slightly; she'd go out and get a breath of air. But she'd better keep away from the car park though for they'd be necking round there like mad. She smiled to herself tolerantly . . . no regret, no desire, no jealousy in her thoughts.

As she passed through the dusty lobby which was the front section of the middle of three Nissen huts she glanced to the right of her to the wide opening that led into the dance section. A tall youth in the latest style of flared trousers and a cord velvet jacket of equal modernity stopped and glanced at her, then moved out into the lobby and watched her as she went through the door on to the narrow flagged terrace fronting the asphalt drive.

Elizabeth was half across the drive walking slowly in the direction of the gates when the youth caught up with her. 'Taking the air?' he asked.

She turned her head quickly towards him and smiled. 'Yes.' She didn't know him, she had never seen him before. He was, she surmised, one of the Bog's End crowd to whom Father Armstrong had referred. She was inwardly amused at the cut of his clothes, and her glancing over them didn't escape him.

He flicked the lapel of the jacket and strutted in almost peacock fashion as he said, 'They're new. I'm in the latest; there's not another rig in Felburn like this.'

She hoped not; she kept her face quite straight as she said, 'Oh.'

He matched his step with hers and walked closer to her. 'You one of Father Armstrong's babies?'

Her face was stiff now and her voice matched it as she said, 'I don't know about Father Armstrong's babies, I'm in his parish.'

'Well, that's what I meant. Not much to choose from in there.' He jerked his head back towards the Nissen huts.

'Then why did you come? And why are you staying?'

'Two questions at once. First, 'cos I thought I might get some kicks; and second, I'm not staying. I'm on me way out. Give you the gripes that lot. And the band, where did they dig it up?'

She didn't answer, and when she reached the gate she turned immediately and began to walk back the way she had come, but he turned with her and said, 'I didn't see you on the floor.'

'You weren't likely to, I wasn't dancing.'

'Don't you dance?'

'No.'

'You mean you don't dance? You can't? Where've you been? Come on.' He took her hand. 'I'll show you.'

She pressed her heels to the ground and tried to tug her hand from his, saying, 'I don't want to dance. Leave go. Do you hear, leave go!'

'What's up with you?' He still held her hand. 'You frigid or something?'

'Leave go of me.'

'I will when I'm ready.'

'I'll call, mind.'

'Go on, call. I can deal with any pasty-faced pup that comes out of there. You're a big girl not to dance.' His other hand moved up her bare arm, and now she beat at him with her fists and cried, 'Stop it! Do you hear? Stop it! Let go of me.'

But his arms went about her and when one hand slid on to her buttocks she kicked at his shin and yelled, 'Father! Father!' When her voice was checked by his mouth covering hers she became like a wild thing tearing at him. Then suddenly, as if lightning had come between them and thrown him from her, she saw him going head over heels on to his back, where he lay perfectly still for a moment with the man who had put him there standing over him. She didn't know what age the man was for he had his back to her, but one thing she took in was that he was smallish, a head less than the boy he had thrown. She became aware of a car standing on the drive where there had been no car before, and as she saw Father Armstrong running down the steps, two of the boys with him, she gave a great shudder and the tears burst from her.

'What is it? What is it, my child? What's happened?' Father Armstrong had his arm round her shoulder while he looked to where a young fellow was turning on to his hands and knees and pulling himself up from the ground. When he reached his feet he staggered, and the man standing in front of him, said, 'Do you want some more?'

'What is it?' Father Armstrong asked again, and the stranger turned to him and said, 'This bloke, he was getting fresh with her and she didn't want any of it. She was screaming.'

Father Armstrong looked from the short young man to the tall one and he wondered to himself how the little one had managed to get the other on the ground for he had never seen anyone lying flatter. The tall fellow was from the dance – he had noticed him – but he wasn't of his parish. As he watched him turn to go back into the hall, he cried at him, 'Not that way! Don't you go in there again. Get going now, while your luck holds. Get going.'

His face twisted in a sneer, the youth dusted down his fancy jacket and his trousers, and making a movement with his shoulders as if hitching on his coat he walked slowly away. Then he turned and, looking at his assailant, shouted, 'You could have broken my back.'

'Aye I could, couldn't I?' the small man called back to him. He then turned towards the priest who was saying, 'There now, there now, give over.' Father Armstrong patted Elizabeth's back and she drew in a shuddering breath, then blew her nose. And now she looked into the eyes of the man who had rescued her. They were on a level with her own but he was shorter than her; he had fair hair, a long face, and his shoulders were very broad and his body stocky. He was a man, she thought, about the age of their Sam, twenty-six or seven. She said softly, 'Thank you. Thank you very much.'

He nodded at her and smiled. 'That's all right. Glad I was in time.'

'Were you coming to the dance?' asked Father Armstrong, and the man laughed, and it had a deep humorous sound.

'No, I was bringing a couple. Picked them up near the park. I run a taxi service, Portman's in Fowler Street.'

'Oh yes, yes.' The priest nodded. 'Portman's. I know it. And you are Mr Portman?'

'Yes, I'm Peter Portman.'

'Well, thank you very much Mr Portman; you came in at an opportune time, you did that.' He looked at Elizabeth and pressed her gently to him, then said, 'How are you feeling?'

'All right, Father.'

'Well, I wouldn't say you were all right. I think you've had enough for one night. What time are they coming for you?'

'I . . . I told Dad not to come until half-past eleven.'

'Oh.' Father Armstrong shook his head. 'That's some way off; would you like to go home now? Would you like Mr Portman to run you back?'

She looked from the priest to the taxi driver, then said, 'Yes; yes, I think so, Father.'

'Go along then and get your things . . . Will that be all right with you, Mr Portman?'

'Yes, sir; that'll be all right with me.'

The use of 'sir' told the priest the young fellow was not of the faith, but he appeared a decent man for all that. He said to him, 'Tell me what happened exactly.' And Peter Portman said, 'Well, when I drove in the gate there I picked them up in me lights. He was holding her and she was struggling, and then he started to kiss her. But I didn't think it was anything serious – you see it all the time in this business – so I turned round, got my fare from the couple, and they got out and ran towards the car park that way.' He nodded in the direction of the dark area at the end of the Nissen huts. 'When I turned to the wheel again she was still struggling, and then she yelled, and that was enough for me.'

'May I ask how you managed to knock him down, flat out like that? He was a big fellow.'

His thin chin moved from side to side before he replied, 'I practise judo. I'm a blue belt.'

'Well, glory be; you are?' The priest's head and shoulders pushed backwards as if to get the small young fellow into better focus. There was deep admiration in his tone as he went on, 'A blue belt indeed! Well, well now. Aw, I wish I'd seen it; I bet that lout didn't know what had hit him.' He chuckled deeply. 'Oh, wait till I tell Father Monaghan about this. He's our curate, young and very keen on the boxing; but I could swear he knows nothing about judo . . . What's your church?'

'Church? Oh.' Peter Portman gave a self-conscious laugh now. 'I'm afraid I haven't one. I'm . . . I'm a heathen. Respectable one you know, but nevertheless a heathen. I'm afraid I've got views about denominations.'

'You have?'

'Yes; yes, sir.'

They both laughed together now.

'I'd like to hear them sometime. I don't suppose with your views you'd like to show some of our boys how to knock big fellows on their backs, now would you?'

'Aw.' Peter Portman laughed again and shook his head. 'Most of me time is taken up with me business; I'm running four cars and have to do the night work. Nobody likes to be on call at night, and my slogan is "Peter Portman will get you there night or day, ring Felburn 60328. Trust Portman, he's never late." '

The priest's head went back again and his laugh rang out. Then he turned and said, 'Ah, here's Elizabeth.' As she came up to them he went on, 'There you are then. I've been trying to do business with Mr Portman here, trying to inveigle him into coming to show the lads how to knock big fellows on to their backs, but he's not having any. You may have better luck; you tell him just how good for the soul self-denial and charitable works are. By the way—' his voice dropped '—how you feeling now?'

'I'm all right, Father, really.' She smiled at him.

'That's it. I'll call round tomorrow, tell your mam. And thanks for your help.'

'I haven't been much of a help, Father.' She bowed her head.

'Go on with you.' He pushed her towards the car where

Peter Portman was standing now with the door open, and when they came up to him he said, 'Do you prefer the back or the front?'

She looked into his eyes again for a fleeting second, and then said, 'I'll sit in the front.'

'Goodbye now,' said Father Armstrong, bending down to the window. Then looking across Elizabeth, he said, 'And drive carefully, mind.'

'Safety is me second name. I've got a slogan about that an' all.' Again they laughed, and then he was backing the car and driving out of the gate.

They drove for some minutes along the main road in silence before Peter Portman said on a deep chuckle, 'I don't know where I'm going; where do you live?'

'Oh, silly of me. We live on The Rise.'

'The Rise!'

'I hope I'm not taking you out of your way . . .'

He said now, 'That's what I'm for, to be taken out of me way. The more I'm taken out of me way the better the business . . . Have you always lived in Felburn?'

'Yes, I was born here, but—' she looked towards him '—not on The Rise. We used to live in Weir Street, just off the Market.'

He glanced swiftly at her before turning his attention back to the road. She was a nice kid, no side. She hadn't had any need to tell him that she had once lived in Weir Street; Weir Street was no cop.

She was asking him now if he belonged to Felburn and he replied, 'No, I hail from Shields, but . . . but my wife was a Felburn lass.'

He had a wife. She had felt at ease with him, but more so now he had a wife. Yet he had said was, not is.

'Have you a family?' she asked.

'No.' He turned a corner, then another, before he ended, 'She died.'

'Oh, I'm sorry.' She glanced at him again. He was a man, but still to her he looked too young to have had a wife who had died.

'Your priest seems a decent old fellow,' he said.

'Oh, Father Armstrong. Yes, he's a decent . . . old fellow.' She laughed. 'But more than that, he's a wonderful man.'

'Aye, there are good and bad in all walks of life.'

She was puzzled by this reply but didn't take it further. He was likely one of those people who held animosity against all Catholics. Yet not all, because he seemed to like Father Armstrong. But there, who wouldn't like Father Armstrong?

As they were going up Brampton Hill and about to turn into the road that led to The Rise she said, 'It's the third turning on the left.' Then when he had turned into this road she added, 'The second gate along.'

The second gate was some distance along the road. He drove slowly through it, then skirted the lawn and drew the car to a stop behind another car, out of which a man was stepping. Before he had time to get out and open the door for her she was on the drive and running towards the man. A minute later they came towards him and she said, 'This is my father. This is Mr Portman, Dad.'

Rodney held out his hand. His face was grim. 'I understand you've been of great assistance to my daughter; I'm grateful, very grateful.'

'Oh, that's all right. I just happened to be there.' He smiled, and Rodney said, 'I wish to God I could get my hands on that lout.'

Elizabeth now put in with a shaky laugh, 'I don't think, Dad, you'd be able to do what Mr Portman did.'

'No?' Rodney looked from her to Peter Portman again, and when he didn't speak Elizabeth said, 'He treated him to some judo; Mr Portman's an expert.'

Rodney stared at the young man before him. Five foot five he would say at the most. He couldn't imagine him throwing another fellow on to his back, yet he knew it could be done, he'd seen it on television. He said now to Elizabeth, 'Have you settled up?'

'Oh no, no. I'm sorry. How much is it?'

'Eleven and six.'

Rodney took out his wallet and, extracting a pound note, handed it to Peter Portman, saying, 'That'll cover it.'

'Oh thanks. Thank you, sir. Well—' he took a step alongside the bonnet '—I'd better be making a move; you never know—' he jerked his head '—there might be more damsels in distress.'

When he was seated behind the wheel and had started up the car Elizabeth ran to the window and said, 'Thanks. Thank you again.'

'Any time.' Again he jerked his head, and she laughed now and stood back, while he drove away.

When she rejoined her father and walked up the steps he did not commiserate with her in any way. Instead he asked rather stiffly, 'How did you manage to get into a scrape like that?'

She went before him into the hall and turned and looked at him, her face straight as she said, 'I didn't manage it, it just happened. I was outside taking the air.'

'On your own?'

'Yes, on my own, Dad. What's the matter with you?'

He closed his eyes for a moment and turned his head to the side. 'What I mean to say is, why couldn't you take one of the girls with you?'

'I didn't want to take one of the girls with me.'

'What is it? What is it?' Maggie came from the drawing-room and looked from one to the other. Then, her eyes coming to rest on Elizabeth, she said, 'You're back early, what's happened?'

'Oh.' Elizabeth made an impatient movement, then pushed past her mother into the room; and Rodney following her said, 'Some fellow got fresh with her and a taxi driver apparently knocked him down and brought her home.'

Pausing a moment, Maggie looked down the room to where Elizabeth was now standing tapping her finger on the edge of a small table; then she hurried towards her, put her arm around her shoulder and said, 'You all right, honey?'

'Yes, yes, I'm all right, Mam.' There was an impatient note in her voice.

'Sure?'

'Yes, only—' She turned and looked past her mother to where her father was picking up the evening paper and she said, '—only Dad seems to think it's my fault.'

Rodney crumpled the paper angrily and dashed it against his knee. 'That's a nice thing to say.'

'Well, it was your attitude, Dad.'

'My attitude? What did you expect my attitude to be, gay? I said you shouldn't have let yourself in for that kind of thing, and I mean it, especially you in your position. And what, may I ask, were Father Monaghan and Father Armstrong doing when this was happening?'

'They were in the hall seeing to things.'

'While louts were crawling around outside! And you like a lamb took a walk among them.'

Elizabeth now bent her head and screwed up her eyes to hold in the tears; then turning, she dashed down the room and through the door.

Maggie didn't follow her but remained where she was, looking towards Rodney. Then in a voice which she tried not to raise, she demanded, 'There's something I want to ask you, an' it's just this, what's eating you? There's something up with you and I've got a right to know, so spit it out.'

When he didn't answer her or look towards her, her voice suddenly spiralled to a shout and she cried at him, 'I'm not putting up with any more of your mute protests; whatever you're protesting about, I want to know what's wrong. If you don't tell me I'll damn well make it my business to find out.'

She was to remember afterwards the quick turn of his head, the look he gave her, then the deep intake of breath as he said, 'Aw, it's one thing after another. Things are going wrong on the Morley Estate. That underground crack is spreading; four walls got it yesterday. And there's bloody union agitators at it on the Rollingdon site.'

Her anger was swept away, she was all contrition. She came and sat before him, her knees touching his, her hands gripped on her lap. 'Is it bad?' she asked, her voice just above a whisper.

'It isn't good.'

'I mean is it dangerous? Will the houses sink?'

'Oh no.' He shook his head. 'Not as bad as that. It's a minute settling really but it's enough to crack the walls and the windows in its path.'

'How are they reacting to it, the people?'

'Oh, need you ask? You know people.' He rose and went to a table, opened a cigarette box and took one out. Then went on, 'Yelling their heads off, demanding compensation. I'm going to see my solicitor, one tells the other, and it becomes like a parrot cry.'

'How long has this been going on?' she asked.

He glanced in her direction still without looking at her; then after a pause he said, 'Oh, some time.'

'Why couldn't you tell me?' She too had got to her feet now, but she didn't go towards him. 'At one time if a fellow put a brick out of place, or the cement wasn't running well, you told me. Why not now?'

He inhaled the smoke of the cigarette, then strained his

neck out of his collar before saying, 'It's big business now, nothing like the early days. Anyway, I have Sam and Willie to unburden to; that's what they're paid for.'

He moved from the table and walked slowly down the room, and when he reached the door he paused a moment and said, 'I'm away up.'

When she was left alone, it came to her that he hadn't looked at her once since he had entered the room. She sat down, telling herself to wait a moment before going up to Elizabeth. She wasn't satisfied with his explanation; there was something wrong between her and Rod. Was it because she had insisted on accepting the Duke's invitation? No, it had blown in well before that, this last chill wind. When then? How many weeks ago? How many months? How many years?

Deep within her she was aware that she had always loved him more than he had loved her; all she needed in life was him; but his needs were greater, more varied. One night a while back as she lay wide-eyed and thinking it had come to her that he was in love with his business, he had always been in love with his business. He had courted success like a man courts a mistress, but she had never been jealous of the attention he gave to his work. A man had to have something outside the house and what better or safer thing than work. No, she had never been jealous of his work; but now she was jealous of something. She didn't know what, she only knew she was jealous. She got heavily to her feet. She was tired, weary, life wasn't running right; and now this latest business concerning Elizabeth. She must go and find out all about it.

Part Three

CHAPTER ONE

THE DUKE

'Oh, Arlette, I can't believe it, I can't.' Maggie surveyed the reflection in the mirror. There was nothing about it she recognised, not even the face. 'Eeh!' She shook her head. 'It's just as you said. Mind you—' she turned towards Arlette '—although you kept tellin' me what she could do I didn't believe it, I really didn't. She's a miracle worker if ever there was one.' She flapped her hand towards Arlette, her mouth full of laughter. 'I bet the Pope could do with her because she's achieved more on a hundred and seventy-five pounds than all me forty years of praying.'

'Oh, Mam!' Arlette's eyes were bright, partly with pleasure, and partly because of a film of tears oozing up out of the sadness that was weighing on her.

Her time of waiting was almost up, the time she had given to this woman to keep her trouble-free until this great event, the event of her life, was over. She would also let the week-end pass, because on Sunday they would all be here basking in reflected glory, and she mustn't spoil that. But on Monday morning early, as soon as he had gone out, she would leave. She had everything arranged, at least about where she was going. She would take with her only a couple of cases, a few necessary things, for the slightest hint of packing would put him on his guard. He was quick was Sam. She looked at Maggie, who was looking at her. She was going to miss her so much, the comfort of her, the common-sense of her, the reality of her. She'd miss all the others too. But there was one other she would miss especially. A month ago he had just been one of the rest. Yet that wasn't true; he had never been just one of the rest; but now he was one apart. He had become the materialised essence of a dream, a dream that had grown with her adolescence and had not ceased to grow after she had married Sam. In fact the dream had expanded as the days of her marriage mounted; its vagueness hardening into longing and the longing threaded with regret, and the regret in turn full of recrimination for standards lowered, for being so weak as to be led by the desire of the flesh alone. And she had paid for her weakness, only God and herself knew how she had paid. Ask and ye shall receive. Her body had demanded that its needs be fulfilled, and it got what it had asked for, with a measure running over. Dear, dear God, and how it had run over.

'You look as mesmerised as me, dear.' Maggie put out her hand and touched Arlette's cheek, and Arlette said with a catch in her voice, 'I'm so happy for you, Maggie. Oh!' She put her hand to her mouth and closed her eyes; and then they both fell together and laughed and Maggie said, 'Aw, that was good to hear; you called me Maggie. I prefer it to Mam. You call me that in future, lass.'

'And have the rest of them after me?' Arlette pulled a face, then added, 'I'm in Frances's bad books already but I hope she'll forgive me when she sees you.' She held Maggie at arm's length, saying now, 'When Madam Hevell suggested midnight blue velvet I thought, I'm not sure, but she was right because it brings out the depths in your eyes. And the cut; it's beautiful, isn't it?'

Maggie turned to the mirror again and after staring at herself she said, 'I tell you, lass, I just can't believe it.' She gazed at her face made up as it had never been before, and she thought in surprise, I could be good looking at that. She looked from the square neck of the dress that showed the upper part of her breasts lying like moulds of smooth deep cream, down the fitted bodice to where the velvet dropped in two folds from the right side of her waist to the top of her left hip, then flowed away loosely down the side of the wide skirt, which almost touched the top of her pale pink shoes. It was on these her eyes rested as she said, 'I hope me feet don't swell; there's no room for expansion.' She laughed. 'And me corn's giving me gyp already.'

'Didn't you have it attended to? I thought you were going to the chiropodist last week?'

'Oh.' Maggie made a guilty movement. 'I . . . I couldn't fit it in so I just pared the top off.' She wagged her foot around. 'They're just a bit tight but they'll ease off. I should have worn them afore to get used to them . . . But that's not the only place I'm tight.' She patted her flat stomach. 'Yet it's worth it. You wouldn't believe it; I only lost ten pounds, but I don't look much over twelve stone, do I?'

'You don't look even that. There now, here's your bag.' Arlette handed her an embroidered bag, of the same tone as her shoes, then looking into her face she said softly, 'Now make up your mind you're going to enjoy it all. There's nothing to worry about, just do as I said and remember that after all the Duke is only a man, and . . . and rather a nice man into the bargain.'

'It should be you who's going in place of me.' Maggie's face was unsmiling now. 'You could carry it off, especially since you've met him.' And now she bit on her lip and said, 'And fancy that, fancy keeping it to yourself, even if it did happen afore you were married. If I'd met a duke the whole damn town would know, an' they will an' all after this.' She gurgled deep in her throat. Then striking a pose, she walked across the room towards the long mirror again, her head held high, her back straight, and she extended her hand and said to her reflection,

'How . . . do . . . you . . . do?' and turning swiftly to Arlette, she said, 'Are you sure that's all?'

'Yes, your names will be announced; you'll go in together, but you'll be introduced to the Duke first. He will shake hands with you and say "How-do-you-do?" and all you answer is "How-do-you-do?" '

'I don't say Your Grace?'

'No, there will be no need; you'll just walk on into the room and be given a drink. You'll stand chatting . . . '

'Oh my goodness . . . stand chatting.' She put her hand to her head. 'With them lot!'

'Half of them lot are dim . . . you'll chat. Of course you will, you're the biggest chatterer in Felburn.'

'Aw lass, I'll be so tongue-tied they'll think I'm a deaf mute.'

'Not you. Come on now, let's go down.'

'What's the time?'

'Six o'clock.'

'SIX O'CLOCK!' Maggie's face screwed up in surprise. 'And he's not in yet? He's got to get shaved and changed, and we're supposed to leave at half-past.'

'He may be downstairs.'

'He shouldn't be downstairs, he should be up here, and ready.' She laughed now and said, 'Aw, that voice doesn't go with this rig-out. I'll never get rid of Maggie Gallacher.'

'Don't try,' said Arlette, 'and stop worrying, it won't take him long once he's in.'

'It'll take him more than a half-hour. Oh, my God! if he's late and we don't arrive . . . '

'Now don't get agitated,' Arlette said soothingly. 'It's all right. Come on downstairs. I'll bring your coat.' She lifted the matching blue velvet, collarless cape-sleeved coat from the bed, then followed Maggie out on to the landing.

When they reached the top of the stairs Maggie cast a glance over her shoulder towards Arlette; then, as if going into battle, she lifted her chin and sailed down the stairs, to be brought to a halt on the last stair by Annie entering the hall from the kitchen to stop dead in her tracks and exclaiming, 'Good God!'

Maggie felt the colour flowing over her face. Annie, naturally, had seen the dress before and her verdict had been, 'It's a plain piece; you've been done if you ask me.'

'Well?' The syllable was a demand for approval, and Annie, walking slowly across the hall, stopped before the woman who was not only her mistress but her life-long friend and now she smiled generously at her and said, 'If it keeps dark you'll pass.'

'Aw, you!' Maggie thrust her aside but grinned at her as she did so, then went into the drawing-room where, waiting for her were Nancy, Paul, Frances, Helen and Elizabeth. Sam and Willy, Dave Walton and Trevor Gillespie weren't expected until later; they had all arranged to be here for the return. But now the eyes of her female family were on her, and also those of her daughter-in-law, Nancy, and her best loved son and she knew that she had astounded each and every one of them. In a way this was disturbing knowledge, for it emphasised the fact that she had been letting herself go these last few years. But that was all over. These past weeks had taught her something; she had learnt that people like Madam Hevell could make an old bag of hay look like a million dollars. Not that she had been an old bag of hay, and her million dollars' look had cost a hundred and seventy-five pounds. But it was money well spent, and she was going to spend more of it in the future, yes she was. She realised now she'd never had a decent rag on her back in her life worth bragging about. If Rod could pay over two thousand pounds for a new Rover then she was entitled to a few hundred a year to keep up with him. She had been too soft, too easygoing; you could be sat on. By! you could that.

'Well I never!'

'Oh! Mam. Mam.'

'You look wonderful. Wonderful. I can't believe it's you.'

'It's me all right.' Maggie put her hand out and slapped Elizabeth's cheek playfully. 'I have only to open me mouth. Now don't, don't rumple me. Me hair's all set and everything; it's so stiff with lacquer that if I fell on me head I'd bounce.' Maggie now turned and looked from Frances to Paul. They hadn't spoken and again she uttered the demanding 'Well?' commanding their approbation, and Frances, her head wagging, said grudgingly, 'Yes, yes, it's very nice. Bit full on the hips I think, but very nice.'

'Thank you.'

Paul came to her now, and taking her hands, he bent forward and kissed her and, his eyes bright and laughing into hers, he broke into song, 'There's nothing like a dame,' he sang; and now they were all laughing, their heads bobbing, their mouths wide.

'Aw, you, our Paul!' Maggie pushed him on the shoulder, and he stopped in the middle of a line and said, 'It's true, there isn't anything like a dame, and I've never seen a better looking one than you, Mam . . . Mame, that's who you're like, Mame.' Again he kissed her and she grabbed at him and held him to her for a moment before pushing him roughly away, saying, 'What's up with you? Look, you've crushed me frock. What's up with you all anyway? You'd think you'd never seen me without me pinny on in me life.'

'Dad's in for a shock.'

'Oh, thank you!' Maggie nodded at Frances, who had the grace to blush and say, 'Well what I mean is . . .' but Maggie interrupted her. 'I know what you mean, lass. Anyway, speaking of your Dad, where is he? Turned five past six and not a sign of him.'

'Yes, he should be here now; he won't have much time to change.' This was said in different ways by them all.

Nancy and Frances went to the window and looked out, Lizzie ran into the hall and to the front door. Arlette said, 'Shall I phone the office?' and Maggie replied, 'Aye, yes. But I hope he's left the office afore now, or we're going to be in the cart.' Then turning and catching Paul's eyes still on her, she moved over to him and hissed in mock menace. 'Don't you stand there looking at me as if you'd never seen me afore else I'll box your ears for you'; and he, smiling tenderly back at her, said, 'It's a lovely evening, Mrs Gallacher, and it's a full moon, everything's set fair.'

'Aye.' She still kept her voice low. 'Except your Dad isn't here . . .'

It was turned ten past and Maggie was standing with hands gripped tightly before her. A sick agitation was adding to the deep nervousness that was already filling her when Elizabeth shouted from the hall, 'Here he is! And Sam's with him.'

Maggie tried to compose herself as she watched the door, to force a smile to her lips to ease the tension that had stiffened her jaws. She heard Rodney answer Elizabeth, saying, 'There's plenty of time, there's plenty of time.' Then he was standing within the open doorway with Sam just behind him, and he was staring at her. His look held surprise and a sort of alarm.

There was a silence in the room while they waited for his reaction, and he must have felt this for his eyes flickered round them before coming to rest on Maggie again. Then he moved forward, not right up to her, just to the other end of the couch and on an embarrassed laugh said, 'It just shows you what money can do, doesn't it?'

At one time she would have taken this remark as a compliment. She would have laughed and pushed him and said, 'Aye, lad, it does, doesn't it? And I'm going to keep on showing you what it can do.' But although he was surprised, even a bit flabbergasted by her changed appearance, she knew he wasn't pleased; for some reason or other he wasn't pleased. Perhaps his attitude was like this because he was still worried about the business. But on a night like this, surely to God he could have put it aside, for although she hadn't talked much about the do to him, she had talked enough to let him know it was going to be the night of her life.

In reply to his words she said, unsmiling, 'Isn't it about time you made a move?' He looked into her eyes made a deeper blue by the reflection of the velvet and larger by the effect of her eye shadow, and in this moment altogether beautiful, and then dropped his gaze from hers and turned and went out of the room.

They all looked after him in silence. Then Frances, turning to Sam, who was now standing behind Arlette with his hand on her shoulder, asked, 'What's up with him?' In answer Sam raised his eyebrows, gave a shrug and said, 'Nothing more than usual, why?'

'He seems worried.'

'Perhaps he has things to worry over. Don't we all?' He looked across to Paul now, and Paul returned the look, straight and unblinking; then Elizabeth, who was standing by Maggie's side, said, 'Well, you haven't said what you think of her?'

'Oh.' Sam took his hand from Arlette's shoulder and walked slowly across the room towards his mother. He stopped within an arm's length from her and, like a farmer surveying the points of a heifer which he might or might not purchase, he looked her over, before giving his verdict with a smile on his face. 'A rose by any other name,' he said.

Paul had said there's nothing like a dame, and he had spoken from his heart. Her man had said it just shows you what money can do, and she hadn't known whether it was meant as a compliment or not. But now her eldest son, smiling at her, his mouth wide, his eyes cold – she hadn't noticed how cold Sam's eyes were until recently – meant her no compliment with his quotation. In this moment, and for the first time in her life, she became really aware of this son, aware of him as he really was; someone frightening. He wasn't the man he appeared to be on the surface, and it came to her with sickening realisation as she looked back into the eyes of her firstborn, that he didn't like her. 'Our Sam doesn't like me.' 'Don't be barmy, woman.' A private conversation was going on in her head. 'I'm not barmy; I know what he meant by a rose by any other name. He was telling me that fine clothes won't make much difference to me, that I'll still be the same old two pennorth of copper in his eyes. He's got on and he's got too big for his boots; he's like his dad in a way. What's the matter with you? Stop it. Smile. Give him as much as he sends.' But, if she were to behave like that she'd have to raise her voice and shout; she always shouted when she was angry or annoyed.

She made herself smile broadly, and she looked past him to Arlette as she said, 'That's the one I've got to thank for the transformation.'

'Nonsense!' Arlette went towards the couch and sat down. 'All I did was to give you the name of a shop.'

'Oh no. Oh no.' It was Sam speaking again, and leaning over the couch, over Arlette's shoulder, his face close to hers, he said, 'Give honour where it's due; you're the girl that can cause transformations. I should know.' When, with a swift movement, he went to kiss her cheek she was swifter still in moving away from him down the couch, and her repulse was like a slap across the mouth. Straightening up and for the moment unable to bring his smile back to his face, he looked about him, from Frances to Helen, from Helen to Nancy, from Nancy to Elizabeth, from Elizabeth to Paul. Elizabeth and Paul were standing near his mother. They seemed linked, bound together in their affection, mother love and child love. But as he stared at them a swift surge of power rose in him and helped to placate his ego. He knew things about them that would blow their little complacent worlds sky high, and he intended to do just that, with each of them.

His mother's face was made up like he had never seen it before, but one sentence from him could wipe the make-up and the grin off it, and leave it stark, and not only for the night, but for ever. But the time wasn't ripe for that yet, she wasn't at her peak. Let her come back with the pollen of the Duke dripping from her, then he would tell her. 'It's a bloody shame,' he would say, 'but you've got a right to know. Dad's got another woman. Not some flossie either but one of the nobs; he's flown high.'

His attitude towards Paul would be different. Aye, by God it would. He'd take him by the throat and say, 'You white livered pup you! So that's why you jumped the church, lusting after your brother's wife.' And there was another thing he had found out about his brother. When he went through his room yesterday his search had not only disclosed a picture of Arlette on her wedding day, cut off from him, oh yes cut off so that no part of him remained in the picture, just her, in her virginal white looking like the Madonna, blast her, it had also disclosed the identity of Lacker. All those writings and potty little poems locked away in the bureau, hundreds and hundreds of them. By God, when he'd finished with his brother he'd wish he'd never been born. And there he was standing smiling at their mam; her blue-eyed boy, whom, although he nearly broke her heart when he became a spoilt priest, she still loved better than either himself or Willie, or any of them, except of course her youngest, whom she was now betting on to restore holy glory to the family. But, that was another thing, wasn't she in for a shock with her dear innocent little Liz? Damned little sneaking hypocrite.

Well, Liz was one bomb he needn't wait to explode; he would drop it gently into his mother's hands now before she went out, and that would stop her being so bloody pleased with herself. Should he start the ball rolling by chipping Liz? Or should he take his mam aside and tip her off?

Elizabeth deprived him of the first outlet for his venom when Maggie said to her, 'Go and tell your Dad to get a move on, he'll be less likely to bawl at you than at the rest of us.' She pushed Elizabeth gently away from her and Elizabeth went from the room, saying, 'I don't know so much.'

Sam looked towards the door through which Elizabeth had just disappeared, then he turned to Maggie and said, 'What's she up to, do you know?'

'What do you mean? Liz?'

'Yes.'

'What do you mean, what's she up to?'

'Are you in the dark about it?'

Maggie narrowed her eyes at Sam, and when Frances repeated, 'In the dark, our Sam? What do you mean?' Sam turned to her. Then he cast his glance round the others, and when his eyes met those of Paul again he shrugged his shoulders, looked down and turned away, saying, 'Oh well, it doesn't matter. Sorry I spoke.'

'Look here.' Maggie had taken three rapid steps towards him and caught him by the arm. 'You're getting at something; spit it out.'

'Oh, later, later, not now and you about to go out.'

'Never mind about me and going out; if you know something that I should know then let me have it, and quick.'

Again Sam cast a swift glance at the rest of them. They were all looking intently at him now, Arlette too, and he said, 'Well, it's this fellow! I've seen her with a fellow, the same one, a few times lately.'

'Our Liz with a fellow? Who?'

'Oh, well now, from the looks of him and the car I think he's the taxi driver that brought her home that night Dad told me about.'

'And you've seen them together since?'

'Aye. The first time was when I was passing the school just at the bottom of the road, and I saw her standing on the pavement with him, near the car. She was pointing along the street and naturally I thought he was a taxi driver and had been asking her some address or other, I didn't think until after that it could be the same fellow. And then it came to me that there's no houses along there except the school and the convent house.' When he shrugged and said no more, Maggie put in quickly, 'Well, that's all it could have been, she could have been showing him the way.'

'Well, yes, as I said that's what I thought, until I saw them in the car together.'

'When was this?'

'The first time you mean?'

'Yes, yes.'

'Oh about three days after that.'

'You've seen them since?'

'Aye.'

'My God!' Maggie put her hands to her mouth and began to tap her lips; then her voice rising, she demanded, 'Why didn't you tell me?'

He stepped back from her. 'Well, it's evident, isn't it? Look at the way you're taking it now. And anyway, I didn't think anything of it until yesterday. Even then I thought she would have told you; she tells you everything, doesn't she?'

She tells her everything. Yes, yes, Liz told her every-thing, at least she used to; but she hadn't told her about meeting this man. By God no, because she would have put a stop to her gallop. But wait; she had said she had seen him once since that night. It was on the Saturday morning and she had met him in the Market. He was shopping and she said she had felt sorry for him. She said his wife had died after they were married only three months, she'd had leukemia. But she had said nothing about seeing him after that. Yet she remembered now that she had been very quiet these past three weeks, and she herself had been so occupied with transforming herself that she hadn't taken much notice of it. In her daft blindness she had thought her quietness was a form of meditation. Meditation, be damned! My God! If there was anything in this and she renegaded like Paul had done she wouldn't be able to bear it, she would die.

But Liz wasn't underhand, Liz was as open as the day, like a child. Yet the child had been meeting this man on the quiet. If Sam had seen them four times how many times hadn't he seen them? Oh dear, dear God, there was always something to rub the shine off her happiness. Now she would have this at the back of her mind all the night, and not so far back either.

She moved towards a chair and sat down, for her corn was already beginning to sting and her legs felt weak. Then her eyes were drawn towards Arlette who had made a strange sound, like a growl. She was looking at Sam and her face was tight, hard in fact; she had never seen Arlette look hard before.

The room held a chilled silence; no-one spoke until Sam ground out, 'I should have kept me bloody mouth shut.' Then all of them were startled by Arlette's response to this. 'Yes, you should have but you didn't, did you?'

Not one of them had heard Arlette speak to Sam in this way, ever. They watched him stare at her and she at him. There was bare hatred gleaming from her eyes. They were amazed, even shocked. She looked as if she loathed the sight of him. The look disturbed Maggie so much that she forgot about Liz and the man for a moment, and said quickly and placatingly, 'There, there now, there'll be an explanation for this, quite a simple one; I'll get it in the morning. Say no more the night. Shut up all of you; here they come.'

When Rodney and Elizabeth entered the room, they all looked at them but none of them remarked on their father's appearance. The novelty of seeing him in a dinner jacket had worn off years ago.

Helen attempted to lighten the atmosphere when, looking at her father, she exclaimed, 'Quick change artist; I've never known anybody able to get ready as quick as you. Trevor takes longer than me, I can never get into the bathroom.'

Her father made no remark in reply to this pleasantry but, glancing at Maggie, he said, 'Well, are you ready?' and her reply was, 'Well, if I'm not now I never will be, I've only been waiting down here half-an-hour.'

Turning quickly about, he went into the hall, and Arlette came towards Maggie, holding up her coat for her to put on, and as Maggie went to get into it she noticed that Arlette's hands were trembling. This was a new side to Arlette. She had never seen her like this; she was always composed and controlled. She had always envied her these qualities, but now she could see she was in a temper, no, more of a rage. Dear, dear. Liz on her mind, and now Arlette; well, let her get outside before anything else happened.

They all came to the door, and they laughed as they called to her while Paul helped her into the car.

'Mind your manners, Mam.' This from Frances.

'Ask him if he's looking for a saucy secretary, or a receptive receptionist.' This from Helen.

'Keep your eyes and ears open for all the scandal, Mam.' This from Nancy.

'You'll outshine them all, Mam.' From Elizabeth.

And Paul, just before he closed the door, bent towards her and said, 'Enjoy it, Mam; make it the night of your life,' and she put her hand up and patted his cheek.

There were two who had made no comment; one was Sam who was standing on the top step looking over the heads of the others, the expression on his face unguarded for the moment because no-one was looking at him. The other was Annie. Annie had made no parting comment because she was too full, for behind her hard-bitten exterior, her snappy, crabby front, which was the only defence against the emptiness in her life, she was repeating over and over again to herself, 'Like a fairy-tale it is. Like a fairy-tale.'

And some similar thought was passing through Maggie's mind as they drove away. Here she was, Maggie Gallacher, sitting in a most luxurious car, dressed up to the nines in velvet and silk going to meet a duke. It was really unbelievable. Yet in a way the event was stripped of its happy phantasy because the man beside her, this man with the short cropped hair, this handsome man, for her Rod was handsome in a peculiar sort of way, was silent, sitting like a stuffed dummy. There was something wrong, something radically wrong with him and she didn't believe now it was wholly the business. No, no, he'd had tough times before but they had never caused him to be like this.

As the car left the town and made for the open country her nervousness increased. She had told herself that if he wasn't going to open his mouth, then she wouldn't, but now she thought they couldn't go on like this because she would arrive there all het up, more than she was already. She looked at his profile and asked, 'You nervous?'

' . . . What?'

'I said are you nervous?'

'No . . . well, perhaps just a trifle.'

Was he nervous? Yes, he'd say he was nervous, but not for the reasons she thought. God, if only this night was over. But why was he so bothered? Rosamund would carry things off; that was her line, carrying things off. Maggie here, she wouldn't notice anything. How could she? Then what was the matter with him? This kind of thing happened almost every day of the week to most men, their wives and their mistresses meeting, and the end of the world didn't come about because of it. Yet it was just this, the thought of seeing Maggie and her together that made him sick to the depths of his innards.

Was it, he asked himself, that he didn't consider himself competent enough to play this kind of game? No! No! He was as competent as the next. He had kept it going for eighteen months, hadn't he, and not a flicker had appeared on the surface. It was just that there was something in him that couldn't bear the contrast between the two of them. That was it. Rosamund showing all she was, and Maggie showing all she wasn't, in spite of her rig-out. Yet that had been a surprise he had never expected, her being turned out like this, even at the cost of a hundred and seventy-five pounds. But still it wasn't clothes that made the woman; clothes might make a man but not a woman. She had only to open her mouth and start jabbering about her family; her Paul, a school teacher; Sam and Willie in the business; her two elder daughters very comfortably married; and then there was Elizabeth, Elizabeth who was going to be a nun. And this, no matter whom she talked to, would be the extent of her conversation. Oh, if only a man had his wits about him when he was young, if he could have seen where the right values lay. Aye, and if he weren't a bloody ass and allowed himself to get trapped . . . Aye, trapped . . .

'How long do you think it will last?'

'About three hours I suppose . . . Maggie?'

'Aye, Rod?'

'Don't you drink much, mind.'

'What do you mean, don't drink much? I never drink much; what do you mean?'

'No, I know that, but on the other hand it doesn't take much to get you going, does it?'

'Oh my God! That's a good start to the evening.'

'Well, I'm just warning you.'

'Well, you've no need. And there's something else I'll say while I'm on. You needn't worry your head, I can pass meself. I won't start doing cart-wheels up and down the baronial hall, nor knees-up-Mother-Brown either. I'll talk their language if that's what's needed, from Bach to Liszt, Beethoven to Berlioz, so . . .'

His head turned towards her so swiftly in astonishment that he swung the car over the middle line of the road. If she had come out with a verse in Greek it wouldn't have astounded him more.

And he wasn't the only one who was astounded; Maggie had astounded herself. She didn't think she would remember what Arlette said the other night about the music that might be played, but now she was glad she had remembered for it had put her stock up. She'd let him see.

When the car turned off the main road and into the drive they became one of a number going in the same direction. The car in front of them was a low, red open sports car in which were a young man and woman. It didn't seem quite right to Maggie that people should arrive for a function like this in a sports car. The car in front of the sports car was a battered looking Wolseley. But when Rodney was directed by an attendant to the side of the drive Maggie found they were lined up between two posh cars. She didn't recognise them as a Rolls and a Bentley, but she thought, with cars like people, there were all types.

Rodney opened the door for her but he didn't help her out and her emergence was a little clumsy to say the least; but there was no-one looking, so she smoothed her gloved hands over her coat and stretched her neck upwards. This was a trick Arlette had shown her and it worked like magic. You hadn't to pull your tummy in one way and your buttocks in the other, you just had to stretch your neck as far as it would go, keeping your chin in, until, like Val Doonican, you walked tall.

She walked tall across the gravel drive and up the stone steps, green at the sides, she was quick to notice, with moss; then through a wide high door into a hall. She hadn't time to take in the hall before a manservant, bowing his head slightly towards Rodney, said, 'This way, Sir,' and a maid, using the same action to Maggie, only adding a smile to the proceedings, said, 'The powder room is this way, Madam.'

And Maggie thought, as she followed the girl across the bare marquetry-patterned floor, a guide would be needed in this place. They'd traversed two corridors before the maid, standing aside and still smiling, opened the door for her, and she, smiling at her in return, said, 'Thanks,' then went into the room.

Inside were a couch, some chairs and two dressing tables, and a long mirror standing in a corner between them. At the dressing tables were seated two women in animated conversation. They turned their heads expectantly towards her; then not recognising her, they smiled weakly and continued attending to their faces and talking to each other.

'The Duchess won't be here then?'

'No; they went up on Friday. I understand it's his brother. Archer said he'll be back in time for this evening but the Duchess won't be returning with him.'

'That's a pity; she always sets the tone I think.'

'Yes, yes; but she doesn't follow the arts like he does. Quite candidly I think she gets a bit bored with the musical dos. You weren't at the last one?'

'No; we were in Switzerland.' The speaker rose from her seat now and, turning to Maggie, where she was standing in front of the long mirror nervously patting her hair, said pleasantly, 'Lovely evening, isn't it?'

'Yes; yes, it is.'

The woman turned to her companion again, waited for her to close her vanity bag, then went on, 'There will be a full moon later; it should be very pleasant in the gardens. The walk in the gardens always finishes it off so nicely, I think.' Her voice trailed away as she went out.

Left alone Maggie took off her coat and again surveyed herself in the mirror. Well, there was one thing, she was better dressed than either of them. You'd think that fair one had slept in her frock, and the other one was dressed in a three-quarter length dress and she looked odd and old-fashioned somehow. She touched her cheek with her hand. She was going to do nothing to herself. She'd better get back; Rodney would be waiting for her.

As she walked towards the door she stopped. She felt a little sick, and her blooming corn was playing up. She looked down at the pink shoes peeping from below the blue velvet hem. The leather was soft; it shouldn't be hurting like this, but they were a bit too narrow. She had told her she couldn't wear narrow shoes.

She went out, found her way along the corridors and so into the hall. There were two men standing waiting, but Rodney wasn't there. She looked about her. The hall, she considered, was very disappointing; it was ugly. The floor, that at first she thought was stone, she recognised now was marble. Opposite the door was a big fireplace and huge black dogs holding fire-irons but, incongruously, the fireplace itself was blocked up and in front of it now stood an imitation fire basket holding imitation electric logs. At each side of the fireplace were white pedestals on which stood white marble busts. All the wall space was covered with pictures. Very dingy they looked to her, and she couldn't even see what the higher ones were supposed to depict. There was a deep long sofa against one wall and a few leather chairs. She thought to herself that it looked like a club room, and a dingy one at that. She had expected something different, something like she had seen in the stately homes on the telly.

Where was Rod? What was keeping him? People were coming and going all about her now, and the women, she noticed, were in various kinds of get-up. She had even seen two in mini skirts, and they weren't young lasses either, well into their thirties she would say. She felt a little piqued when she realised it was only the really old women who were wearing long dresses.

Where was Rod? She had been standing here over ten minutes; it was after seven and the thing was supposed to start at seven. What was he up to?

Her temper was rising to meet her nervousness when he appeared out of a corridor walking between two men, deep in conversation, serious conversation by the looks on their faces. He didn't come immediately towards her but went on talking, and she stared at him, willing him to break away and come to her because she was beginning to feel all fingers and thumbs. She saw him nod to the men now, then look around before making his way towards her. He didn't speak when he reached her side, and she said under her breath, 'Fine thing, leaving me here standing on me own all this time.'

He cast a glance at her and, equally low, he replied, 'Now don't start, don't start. They're important men, I had to have a word with them.'

'Important!' She choked back the word as they went towards a door at the far end of the hall, because, she warned herself, she mustn't get het up. NOW. NOW was the moment. Just put out your hand and say 'How-do-you-do?' That's it, just say 'How-do-you-do?' You can smile but not too broadly; be dignified, keep your neck up.

There were two couples in front of them. She couldn't see the Duke.

Then there was only one couple in front of them, and there he was, tall, fair, young, smooth-faced . . . but surely!

Her thoughts were cut off. She was standing in front of the man and he was shaking her by the hand while at the same time saying, 'How-do-you-do? I'm so sorry, the Duke hasn't arrived yet, he has been detained, but I'm sure he'll be here soon. I'm his secretary.'

'How-do-you-do?'

She was moving on with Rod by her side, weaving in and out of groups of people. She had a queer feeling as if she was suddenly very thin. She had never felt like this before. Deflated; that was the word, deflated. For a full month working up to this, and then . . . nothing, her hand shaken by his secretary.

'Hello there.' They had stopped before a couple. The man was short and thick-set; his wife, taller than him, had a palish face and was dressed in a very ordinary fashion, in a sort of dress-cum-suit affair, as Maggie put it. But Rod was introducing her.

'This is my wife, Councillor Redfern, Mrs Redfern.'

'How-do-you-do?'

'How-do-you-do?'

So this was Redfern. She had heard a lot about Redfern. He had power on the Council. As Rodney said, he could open or close doors but you had to supply the oil for the key whichever way it went.

'The Duke has been held up then.' Mrs Redfern was speaking to her, and Maggie was comforted to hear she sound no better than herself.

'Yes. Yes, so I understand.'

'It's his brother, he's ill.' The councillor nodded knowingly. 'The one next to him you know, very close, very close. But if he can possibly get back he will; he loves his music, ah yes, ah yes. He's got a scheme in mind, did you hear?'

'No.' Rodney's voice was casual sounding.

'Quartets in the villages and running competitions, you know on the lines of the brass bands. I think it's an excellent idea, don't you?'

'Yes, indeed, yes; the very thing. Get people culture-minded again.'

Maggie looked at her man. Rodney talking about culture, and he knew as much about music as she did herself, and that was damned all. In fact, if it came to the push she could give him a few points, for she did listen in to Mantovani and Eric Robinson, and she liked to watch the ballet an' all.

'Ah, excuse us a minute; there's the Beddinghams. I want a word with him.'

As they moved away a waiter came up with a tray and, holding it out to her, said, 'Sweet or dry, Madam?'

She paused before saying, 'Sweet,' and he took a glass from one side of the tray and handed it to her, then looking at Rodney, he said, 'Dry, Sir?'

'Please.'

They took their drinks and stood near an open window that led on to a terrace and steps down to the gardens below. She guessed this was the side of the house for, beyond the terrace, she could see the drive where the cars were parked. She sipped at the wine and kept her eyes focused outside. Although she was feeling deflated it had done nothing to ease her nervousness and tension. She wished she could sit down; this corn was giving her absolute gyp now.

'Ah; hello, Gallacher. Didn't think you were a musical man.'

'Oh, hello there.'

She turned to see a thin man and woman so alike that they could be twins. The woman was well dressed, a bit over-dressed Maggie considered, for she was weighed down with jewellery, four rings on one hand, a heavy necklace, matching earrings and an ornament in her hair. Flashy, she would say. Arlette would have condemned her out of hand for bad taste. She felt slightly comforted and smiled pleasantly as they were introduced.

'How-do-you-do?'

'How-do-you-do?'

Pearce. Another big pot. Pearce was rotten with money, he had his finger in every pie in the town, so Rodney said.

'Your daughter attends the convent, doesn't she?'

'Yes.' She nodded pleasantly at the woman, proud in this moment to have a daughter at the convent, proud even to be able to send a daughter to the convent, because the convent fees were the stiffest in the town.

'My niece goes there. She has mentioned her name, Elizabeth, isn't it?'

'Yes, yes, Elizabeth.'

'I understand she's going into the Church.'

'We're hoping so.' She sounded, she thought, quietly proud, dignified.

'Wonderful vocation; but then it must be a vocation, mustn't it, especially these days?'

'Oh yes, yes.' But now her mind had jumped back to Liz going out with that fellow. She'd have to get this cleared up tomorrow morning; there was more in this than met the eye, for the simple reason that Liz had kept it to herself. Wait till she got her tongue around her . . . Aw, but no; she must take a gentle hand with her. My God! If anything happened to stop her going in . . .

'Yes, yes, it is a beautiful evening, delightful.'

'Quite a number here; more than usual I should say.'

Mrs Pearce, whose gaze had swept round the room while she had been speaking, suddenly cried, 'Ah! there's Rosamund. We must have a word with Rosamund, Charles, before we go in. Will you excuse us?' They both made a motion with their heads, then moved away.

The room was packed now and buzzing with conversation, everybody chatting to everybody else. They seemed to be the only two people standing alone. No, there were two others along at the other end of the second window. She recognised them as the young couple she had seen in the sports car. They seemed much too young for this occasion, sort of out of place. She looked at Rod and was about to speak to him but he was moving his head slowly from side to side as if looking for someone; then when there was a general movement she saw he was looking at the Pearce couple and the people they were talking to. She noticed, too, that he was sweating round the mouth and that his face was red, like when he was angry or upset, or nervous about something. But he couldn't be nervous; he was used to these dos. Still, he didn't meet a duke every day, but he did get out and about. Anybody, she considered, who was a member of Ransome's couldn't be nervous.

The woman whom Mrs Pearce had called Rosamund now turned and looked towards them. She looked at Rodney first; then Maggie found that her eyes were covering her, going down as far as they could. It was like someone playing a torch over her. Then she watched her leave the group and make her way towards them.

'How-do-you-do, Mr Gallacher?'

There seemed to be a very long pause before Rodney said, 'How-do-you-do, Mrs de Ferrier?' Then, his head bent slightly, his left hand extended forward, his elbow tight to his side, he indicated Maggie and said, 'My wife.'

'Oh.' The thin hand was held out to Maggie, and she took it.

'How-do-you-do?'

'How-do-you-do?'

Maggie looked back into the wide grey eyes. They were looking directly into hers, yet at the same time seemed to be taking in every aspect of her from her feet to her hair.

'Delightful evening isn't it?'

'Yes, very nice.'

'Who do you think we're going to hear tonight, Mr Gallacher?' Mrs de Ferrier was looking at Rodney now.

'Your guess is as good as mine.' He sounded nervous, ill at ease. Maggie couldn't understand it.

'Well, we won't have to wait long, shall we?' Mrs de Ferrier turned her eyes again on Maggie. 'His Grace always supplies programmes; they're on the seats awaiting you, just like church you know.' She laughed here, a high, soft laugh, and turning to Rodney said, 'He's got a new man at the piano tonight, a young protégé, Flynn. Have you heard him before?'

There was a pause again before Rodney said briefly, 'No.'

'Bernstein's playing the cello and, of course, Dorothea Craig is singing.' She made a slight face; then, her voice dropping, she added, 'And I wish she wasn't. Whom do you favour?' She had turned abruptly to Maggie, and Maggie, nonplussed, said, 'Who . . . what . . . I don't understand?'

'Oh! What I mean is are you a Bach or a Beethoven fan?'

'I think I prefer Mozart or Liszt.' Thank God for Arlette.

'Ah, you're a romantic.'

Maggie stared at this woman. She didn't like her; there was something about her that made her uneasy. She seemed to be laughing at her, at them both. But that was her imagination; she was likely used to talking about music and asking people what they liked, it was her own ignorance that was at fault.

'Ah, there you are, Gallacher.' Apparently, this was Mr de Ferrier, for he had put his hand through the woman's arm. She had never seen a man with such a white pasty face, it was so smooth as to be almost sickly. He was well into his fifties, she thought, but he hadn't a line or a wrinkle on his face, which made him look odd, characterless.

'Nice to see you. Nice to see you.' He was now shaking her hand. 'How-do-you-do? How-do-you-do?' He repeated everything. 'The troubadour hasn't turned up yet.' He was speaking to Rodney, and she deduced that by the troubadour he meant the Duke.

'I understand,' said Rodney, 'that his brother is ill and that he had to go to him?'

Mr de Ferrier leant his full white face forward and, his eyes darting from Rodney to Maggie and back again, he muttered on a smothered laugh, 'He's back all right, saw him in Newcastle early this afternoon. Enthusiasm waning; bet your life that's what it is. He starts these things on the top of a wave, gets everybody going then leaves it to them and wonders why the tide recedes. Ha! Ha! Oh, but I'm not saying he won't turn up; he'll turn up, but when all the palaver's over and he can just sit down and enjoy it. I've never known him miss anything he's organised yet, but I've never known him to be there at the start either.' He nodded knowingly, then laughed before exclaiming, 'Ah look. Ah look; they're making their way in.' He turned back to Rodney again, saying, 'We all have our allotted seats, I suppose. Be seeing you then. Be seeing you.'

'Yes, yes.' Rodney nodded to him, then towards Mrs de Ferrier, who in turn inclined her head deeply towards him.

As they, too, made to move towards the music room door there was a stir at the far end of the room, a hush, then a murmur, and everybody stopped and turned and looked in the direction of the man who was threading his way between the groups, shaking a hand here, having a word there.

Here he was then . . . the Duke.

Maggie's heart began to race; the feeling of excitement returned. She watched him coming nearer and nearer. He wasn't very tall, in fact he was short and nothing to look at, sandy hair, a small thin face, and weak looking eyes, but he was the Duke of Moorshire and he was coming to greet them. He was talking to the couple in front of them, he was even patting the man's arm; he had just to come round them to the right and then it would happen.

But the Duke didn't come round to the right, he went to the left and stretched out his hand towards a man who gripped it and smiled broadly and said something to him; then he was going ahead of them into the music room.

Again her body seemed to sink inwards. Rod had hold of her arm, pressing her forward. They were in a sort of disorderly queue now; then they were in the music room and being directed to their seats. The room was large and bare, nothing in it but chairs and, on a dais at the end, a grand piano.

Maggie found herself sitting to the extreme right of the dais with one side of her chair against the wall. Below the dais, sitting apart, were two men and a woman and she saw the Duke shaking each by the hand. Then he sat down and was lost to her sight and the two men and the woman went up on to the platform.

She looked at her programme. The man, Flynn, was to start. He was playing . . . what! Suite fü Klavier Op. 25 – Schoenberg. And the woman? Lieder! What the devil was Lieder? Anecreon's Grab – Hugo Wolf. Lord! Knees up Mother Brown.

Her attention was again drawn towards the dais.

The cellist and Miss Dorothea Craig had taken seats to the side of the piano and the pianist had seated himself; then the Duke's secretary, standing just below the dais, said, 'Ladies and Gentlemen, Mr Flynn.' He extended his arm backwards, then walked to the end of the first row and sat down.

A hushed waiting silence fell on the room; then Mr Flynn fell upon the piano. That's how Maggie put it to herself. He bent low over it and the sounds he brought forth appeared to her like a lot of bairns banging away for fun.

She sat still, watching him, fascinated for a moment by his antics. She could only see part of the keyboard and one of his hands, but that was enough. Before he'd been playing two minutes she wished to God he'd stop. She'd never heard anything so untuneful in her life. If this is what they called real music they could keep it. Why, when she thought of Mantovani and those lovely violins!

She was hot; it was airless in here. Her corn was going mad and she couldn't keep her neck stretched up like this, yet she couldn't slump altogether, her foundation wouldn't let her. How long was this bloke going on? If this was a sample of the things they were going to hear all evening she didn't know how she was going to sit through it.

When finally the pianist finished what she now thought of as his contortionist act, the applause was loud and prolonged, in which she herself joined, all the while calling herself a bloomin' hypocrite.

Mr Flynn bowed and bowed; then wiping his hands and brow, he walked to a seat at the side of the piano, and Miss Dorothea Craig took the centre of the dais and her accompanist took Mr Flynn's place.

Dorothea Craig began. Her mouth wide, her breast swelling, she went into Anecreon's Grab . . . So this was . . . what did the programme say? Lieder. Well! Well!

Maggie had no knowledge of this kind of singing, nor had any groping taste towards it. If she saw such work billed in the *Radio Times* she passed it over, thinking, Oh, that stuff! Yet she told herself, she liked Moira Anderson and that nice woman who died, Kathleen Ferrier, but she couldn't stand this.

Oh! her corn. If she could only ease her shoe off. She moved her left big toe towards her right heel and slowly began to lever the shoe off. This action caused her right knee to move up and down, but ever so gently, but gently as it was, it attracted Rodney's attention. She saw him turn his head slightly towards her, then slant his eye towards her knees. The next second she almost jumped out of her chair for his cautionary pressure with the heel of his shoe found its target on the very spot she was trying to ease. She only just stopped herself from yelling out, and she covered up her reaction to the assault by crossing her legs.

She was breathing as heavily as the singer now. Oh God! Wait till she got him home. What a bloody silly thing to do. He knew that that corn was as tender as a boil; he knew that it had troubled her all her life. She had gone to a chiropodist with it once but he had poked and poked it so much that the cure became worse than the disease. He had advised her to go to the hospital and get the root out, but she hadn't gone to the hospital and she hadn't seen him again. She had tended to it herself with a safety razor blade. She'd had a go at it only last night, but as the man had said, it was the root that caused the trouble not the hard skin on top.

Oh! Would that woman never stop bawling.

Didn't they have any windows open in this place? She was running with sweat, she would ruin her dress. That was another thing; nobody had taken any notice of her get-up, the biggest sensation she had caused was when she came down into the drawing-room. She'd like to bet she was better dressed than anybody in the room, and that went for that Mrs de Ferrier an' all, although she too got her clothes at Madam Hevell's. But she had no figure, she was as flat as a pancake.

Lord! How long was this going on? The man now was sawing away at the cello and attacking it as the previous one had the piano.

Maggie was experiencing real boredom for the first time in her life. She had never, up till now, had time to be bored. If there appeared nothing further for her to do in the house she made it her business to find something. She would go into the kitchen and knock up a cake or two; she would take up a piece of embroidery – she had been a dab hand at it once; it was her only talent, she considered, besides running a home. Then she knitted for them all; she couldn't sit looking at the television, her hands idle. And when she got her nose in a book, a real good book with a story, she became lost in it. No, she had never experienced boredom until this present minute and the forty-three minutes preceding it.

When at last the cellist ceased battling with the blown-up fiddle – that's all it was, and she couldn't help it if the Prince of Wales did favour it, every man to his taste – she let out a long drawn breath, just as, had she but known it, did more than half the company. When the clapping had died down there was no immediate rising; no-one left his seat until the Duke, accompanied by Dorothea Craig, Mr Flynn, and Mr Bernstein walked towards the ante-room, then the secretary indicated it was in order to follow him.

There was now a slow dignified concerted movement. Rodney, glancing at her, rose to his feet and when she, with a smothered sigh, stood on hers, she wished for a moment she hadn't, for although she considered anything better than sitting there, she found to her consternation that not only was her corn playing her up, but that the heel of her other foot now was feeling the pressure of the back of the shoe. She was subject to skinned heels with ordinary shoes, but these were very soft – and so they should be she thought, they had cost enough. It must be the seam of her stocking directly over the pressure point. Once out of here she'd go to the ladies' room and fix it.

This intention was baulked as soon as she entered the ante-room again for it seemed more packed than ever, and Rodney, after glancing quickly around, took her by the arm and led her along the wall to a corner. There they stood side by side, not uttering a word. Three minutes of this and it began to seem like three hours. She glanced at him. What was up with him anyway? He couldn't fault her; she had done nothing, she wasn't letting him down.

A waiter, threading his way between the groups, offered them their choice from the tray and again she had a sweet sherry, but when she was about to sip it Rodney muttered under his breath, 'Don't drink that unless you have something with it. Stay here and I'll get something to eat . . . Hold that.' He handed her his glass, then he left her. And she watched him, not without indignation, winding his way between the groups towards a long table set against the far wall.

Well! She looked nice didn't she holding two glasses! What would people think? She drank half her sherry, but when she was about to empty the glass she hesitated. He had said wait until she had something to eat with it. He was frightened it would affect her.

Another three minutes passed and she was demanding

of herself, where had he got to? Surely it didn't take this long to get a sandwich.

At this point a man moving from one group to another nudged her with his elbow, and as he turned to excuse himself his gaze dropped to the two glasses she was holding away from her dress now, and he said on a laugh, 'I'm sorry.' Then he added, 'But that's what I always say, be prepared, keep one in stock,' and before she had time to get out the words 'It's my husband's,' he had joined another group.

Everyone was laughing and talking; they all seemed to know each other. She was the only woman standing alone. No; there was one along there. She looked to her extreme right. The woman was standing near the window but she managed to catch her eye and half smile at her as much as to say 'We're both in the same boat.' But they weren't in the same boat for long, for the woman's husband came up with a plate in each hand, and once more she felt alone.

Where on earth was he? She'd have to get to the ladies' and see to her feet. If she could only sit down again.

Then she saw him. She couldn't mistake his head; he was making his way back across the room excusing himself as he circled round the couples. She was letting out a long breath of relief when it was checked, for he had stopped. He was talking to somebody. Oh, no! No! It was a woman, it was that Mrs de Ferrier. 'Come on. Come on,' she willed him, but he remained talking.

Her irritation, touching on anger, was suddenly soothed when she caught sight of the Duke. He had moved from behind a group and was not more than four yards from her . . . And here she was standing with two glasses in her hand! Oh, Rod Gallacher! Rod Gallacher! Wait till I get you home.

Well, she wasn't going to meet the Duke like this with no free hand to shake. With an unladylike gulp she finished her sherry; then almost in the manner of a curtsy she bent her knee and put the glass down on the floor near the wall. Upright again, she stretched her neck and brought a smile to her face, ignoring in this moment the pain of her corn and heel, as she watched him walk to the next group.

Her stomach churned when he moved to the right to join another couple; his next move would be the left and to the four people standing at arm's length from her; then there would be only her.

Her heart seemed to move upwards towards her throat when she saw her host make his last move. At the same time she thought she saw Rodney leave Mrs de Ferrier then turn to her again, but she took her eyes from him for here was the Duke not a yard from her. She heard him greeting a plain looking, dowdy woman, calling her by her christian name, Ida. 'Ah, Ida,' he said, 'it's so nice to see you again.' He was shaking hands all round now. She stopped herself from thinking again that he was ordinary looking, not a bit like she imagined a duke to be, not like the Duke of Edinburgh for instance. But he WAS a duke, and in a few minutes, even seconds, he'd be shaking her by the hand. They were all talking about the performers. The plain woman was enthusing about the singer. 'Wasn't she magnificent!' she was saying. Magnificent! Well, everybody to their taste, like the woman who kissed the cow, as her grannie used to say.

'Your Grace.' The secretary seemed to have materialised out of thin air; he was standing to the side of the Duke, bending towards him, and the Duke, turning and looking up at him, said, 'Oh, yes, yes, mustn't hold things up.' He laughed from one to the other, then turned about and walked away with his secretary.

Her body wasn't deflating this time, but every part of it was pouring out its disappointment in perspiration. What was the matter with her the night? Was there a jinx on her or something? And to add seeming insult to injury she now saw the de Ferrier woman put her hand out towards the Duke, and he stopped in front of her and Rodney. She could see, too, there was laughter because Rodney hadn't a free hand to proffer the Duke until Mrs de Ferrier took one of the plates from him, and there he was shaking hands with the Duke, smiling and, she thought grimly, putting on his best manner.

Now her body did begin to deflate and, strange for her, she had a desire to cry.

The stir in the room changed; like an ebb tide on shingle she saw the groups breaking up and moving back towards the music room again, and as Rodney now made his way directly towards her there arose against him an anger that would have found vent in a bellow if she had been in any other place. Instead, she lifted his glass of sherry to her lips and drained it, and she was just finishing it when he came to her side.

When he was foolish enough not to start with an apology but with a reprimand, saying under his breath, 'I told you not to . . . ' she hissed at him, 'Don't you talk to me!' Then to his consternation she was pushing past him and walking on her own into the music room.

He stood for a moment nonplussed with two plates of food in his hands; then sighting a waiter with a tray of empty glasses he pushed the plates on top of one another on to the tray before joining the slowly moving throng.

When he took his seat beside her there was no-one as yet seated near them, and he muttered, 'I was held up, it wasn't my fault.'

She turned and looked at him, her blue eyes the colour of a stormy sea now, and her voice cold but controlled, she said, 'I've been out there twenty minutes if a minute. You left me standing like a nobody; I was the only woman in that room by meself.'

His eyes were as hard as hers as he retorted in a thick whisper, 'I told you in the beginning you shouldn't have come.'

Oo . . . h God! If only she was at home; in more senses than one, if only she was at home. But if she had been there at this moment he would have got more than the length of her tongue, for she wouldn't have been able to keep her hands off him.

There was a rustle of gowns behind her. She sat straight as a ramrod watching the entertainers once more mounting the platform. The movement and chatter in the room subsided. Mr Flynn again went to battle stations at the piano, and then the whole boring business was repeated.

By the time the cellist gave his second recital she was so hot and tired, so bored to extinction, she could have fallen asleep; at one point she did feel her eyelids drooping. It was the same feeling that at times she experienced at Mass.

. . . Then it was over, and this very fact brought her wide awake. If that was a musical concert they could keep them; the only thing that she was going to get that was worth while out of all the money that had been spent on her, not counting the worry and anxiety of the past four weeks, was meeting His Grace.

When she made to rise the pressure from Rodney's knee warned her not to. She looked past him to where in front of the dais the Duke was standing with Mr Flynn, Dorothea Craig, and Mr Bernstein, and people were coming up to congratulate them. For what, she thought? This went on for four or five minutes; then gradually, the Duke and the performers leading the way, everyone once more returned to the ante-room.

As if it was a place that had been reserved for them Rodney went to lead her along the wall to the same corner that she had occupied earlier. But no; she wasn't having that. When she caught at his sleeve and brought him to a stop, he looked at her and asked, 'What is it?'

'This'll do, thank you very much.'

He seemed puzzled for a moment; then staring back into her eyes he let out a long, slow breath.

Again a waiter came up with a tray of drinks, and again she took one, just pipping Rodney from saying, 'No, thanks, we won't bother.' With the drink in her hand she stared at him and he himself was forced to pick one up from the tray, and as he lifted it to his lips he muttered, 'I warned you.'

'What did you say?'

He sipped at the wine, gulped in his throat, glanced round him, then bending his head he muttered, 'Give over.'

She bent towards him now, a tight smile on her lips, and again she asked, tantalisingly, 'Pardon. What's that you say?'

He looked at her apprehensively now; this attitude was part of her battle tactics, the prelude to a blow-up. He glanced about him almost furiously for some aid with which to damp down the fire. He found it as a man passed him, and he said in an overloud voice, 'Oh, hello there.'

'Oh, hello!' The man turned. It was evident he was making his way to join another group but he stopped and smiled at Maggie as Rodney said, 'My wife . . . Mr Bailey.'

'How-do-you-do?'

'How-do-you-do?'

'Have you enjoyed the concert?'

She stared at this man; she stared into his long thin face, the deep set eyes under the bushy brows, and in the seconds it took her to bring the lie on to her tongue, he read her thoughts, and glancing like a conspirator from side to side, he bent towards her and whispered, 'I agree with you,' then laughed, and added, 'Nearly went to sleep. Not my cup of tea at all.'

Maggie smiled now, her mouth wide. She liked this man; he appeared at this moment to be the only human being in the room.

He now nodded at her, then at Rodney, and said in his terse style, 'Seeing you. Must have a word with Jamieson. Goodbye.'

'Goodbye,' she said. She was laughing, until she looked at Rodney. His face was dark with temper. She took a sip from her glass, then airily she said, 'Glad to know I'm not the only one. If you'd had any spunk you would have agreed an' all, then that would have made a trio . . . we'd have had our own trio.' She laughed at her own wit. And her laugh startled him. He knew that laugh of old. She was always about to get jolly when she laughed like that.

His lips scarcely moving, he said now, 'I thought you wanted to go to the ladies' room?'

'Oh yes, I did; but that was a long time ago. I've stuck it out so far I can stick it out to the end.'

Go to the ladies' room, he said. Yes, and it would be just her luck that the Duke would make a round while she was away. She wasn't moving from this room until they said their goodbyes. Arlette said the Duke might stand at the door and they would shake hands when they were leaving. It would be hail and farewell for her, but at least she would have shaken hands with him. Go to the ladies' room indeed! She took another sip from her glass, then said, 'There's that Mrs de Ferrier over there. Why don't you go and have another natter to her?' She wasn't looking at him as she spoke, but she felt his body jerk round towards her.

In the old days when he jerked round like that it meant the flat of his hand across her ear-hole and a bloody great row to follow; but it was funny, after every row the making up was better. They hadn't had a real big row for over two years now. Things had changed in the last two years. She felt a sudden sadness swamp her as she again asked herself the question, What was it? What had happened? Were they getting like the married people she read about in the weekly magazines, them that wrote asking for advice? Aw, what was she thinking, and in a place like this an' all?

She turned her eyes over the heads of the crowds and high up through the open french windows. The moon was shining, it was a lovely night. Some people were walking on the terrace. She would like to walk outside. She wished she could go out now for a breath of air, but she had gauged from those women in the ladies' room that the procedure was to say goodbye to the Duke then wander down the garden before going off, and the procedure, she saw, had already begun, for some people near the french windows were already saying their goodbyes.

This fact hadn't escaped Rodney and so, clasping her almost roughly by the arm, he led her forward, twisting and turning in and out of groups until they came within a few yards of the open french windows and the Duke, who was shaking hands with a couple.

They could be next. At least Rodney surmised this, but it was she who noticed the concerted gaze on them from a line of couples that stretched back into the room. With an embarrassed laugh she nudged him and, motioning towards the row of faces with her gloved hand, she said, 'We'll have to take our turn, there's a queue.'

'Oh, I'm sorry. I'm sorry.' Rodney's best manner was again to the fore; and the faces were laughing with them now, and one man murmured, 'You're not the only ones, we did it too.' They were both smiling when they took up their positions at the end of the queue.

The procession towards the door was slow, the Duke seemed to be holding a long conversation with each couple. Well, she didn't mind that; they would get the same measure when their turn came. She ignored the pressure of the corn and her skinned heel, these would soon be eased.

There was more laughter when another couple was directed to the end of the queue. There were only five couples in front of them now, then four. He spent quite a long time talking to this couple, but at last they moved on to the terrace; then there were only three couples, then two.

Between the heads of the couple in front of her she could see the Duke's face and it was no longer smiling. He was talking very seriously, and he went on talking and talking and talking . . . And then it happened. Before her widening eyes and drooping mouth he took the arm of the woman and turning his back on the company, he walked between her and the man across the terrace and towards the sunken garden.

Maggie was dimly aware that the couple in front of her were looking at each other. They stood uncertain what to do, wondering perhaps if he meant to return. The woman rocked slightly as if she were balancing herself. They turned and looked at Maggie and Rodney, then along the faces behind them, after which they walked stiffly over the step and on to the terrace. And Maggie followed them, her eyes not on them but on the slight figure still walking between the two people and close to the stone steps now that led to the sunken garden, and the only thing she could say at this moment was, 'Well! What do you make of that?' And it came out on a loud wave of indignation. It startled the couple in front of her, and the woman, turning quickly, said in a polite hiss, 'Ssh! The Duke will hear you.'

Maggie glared from the woman to where she saw her host's head bobbing as it went down the first two steps into the garden and no power she possessed, no power on earth could have stopped her at the moment from expressing her feelings:

'BUGGER THE DUKE!'

The head of His Grace stopped bobbing. His face was turned towards her. All faces were turned towards her. If the announcement had just been made of a great national tragedy the hush that precedes the expression of deep emotion could not have been more full; for a long second it hung over the assembly, and when it broke into indignation from some quarters and smothered laughter from others, and amused astonishment from the main party concerned, she knew nothing of it, for she was being whipped along the terrace as if in the hands of a giant.

Not even when he reached the car and found he had left his keys in his overcoat pocket did he immediately loosen his steel hold on her. Still gripping her he glared at her in an almost maniacal way. His face in the moonlight looked like a devil's. His eyes bloodshot, his teeth grinding, he looked in this instant as if he were about to murder her, and she didn't care. When, with a rejecting thrust of his hand, he threw her against the car bonnet she fell on to her elbow and remained there for a moment watching him now running to the front of the house.

She didn't care, she didn't give a damn. She'd had enough, more than enough. She'd been ignored all night, put down by her own in the first place. Aye, no-one had ignored her like he had, her own man. And then that bloody little Duke. Who did he think he was anyway? Christ Almighty! To turn at the last minute and walk away like that!

It would have been no comfort to her to know that she wasn't the only one who had suffered from the Duke's bad manners which went under the name of absent-mindedness. Nor was it any comfort to know that he hadn't walked away deliberately from her but from the couple in front of her. She only knew that she wasn't sorry for what she had said, not yet anyway; tomorrow morning was a long way off.

At the present moment she could comfort herself that she was in the right; but also she realised that tonight was the end of something, that things would never be the same again. Well, it didn't matter, it didn't matter, it was about time they changed. She had stood on the sideline long enough, waving on the one-man team. But she had shown him; yes, begod she had shown him. She now straightened her body. She had shown him all right . . . she had shown him up as no man had been shown up before.

He came back at something between a walk and a run and rammed the key into the car door, and after flinging himself into the seat he did not lean across and open the door for her but, reaching to the back door he rammed down the lock and banged the door back.

She stood looking into the back of the car for a moment. So that was it, he couldn't bear her anywhere near him. Well, it suited her; they were both of a like mind.

She had hardly seated herself when the car bounded away. At another time she would have cried out at him because of the speed he was going, but not tonight. She had said enough, enough to last a lifetime . . .

Almost before the car had stopped the front door opened and there they all were. But she remained seated, she remained seated until she saw Rod going in among them, pushing his way like a bulldozer through them, their startled glances following him. Lifting one leg heavily after the other she pulled herself out of the car and walked slowly towards them, and they surrounded her, all saying the same thing in different ways, 'What is it? What's happened? Where's your coat?'

She, too, pushed her way silently between them. And then they were in the hall, and there he was standing, waiting for her, glaring at her, and the hate in his eyes pierced the armour of her defiance and hurt her like no hurt she had yet received in her life.

'Will you tell us what's happened?' Paul was standing in front of her. Without answering him she pressed him

153

gently to one side and walked towards the stairs, but when she was on the second step she turned and looked at him and said, 'You'd better ask your dad.'

As if a valve had been opened to allow boiling steam to erupt, Rodney took a step towards her. His shoulders hunched up round his ears, his chin thrust out, he looked like a gorilla about to spring as he cried at her, 'You big, fat, ignorant slob you! Talk of trying to make a silk purse out of a sow's ear . . .'

'Dad! Dad! What's this? Let up!' It was Willie shouting now, and Rodney turned on him and cried, 'Let up, you say! Do you know what she's done the night? She's ruined me. She's ruined us all, our business. You Sam, you Willie and you Dave, you'll soon be out of work because of that ignorant numskull. Tomorrow we won't be able to lift up our heads in the town, not even in Bog's End never mind in Ransome's or such places.'

They were all staring at Maggie now, a woman dressed in blue velvet and pink slippers, and they said almost in a whisper to her, 'What happened?' But it was Rodney who replied, 'She buggered the Duke, that's what happened. Your dear mother buggered the Duke of Moorshire because he didn't shake hands with her; because he dared to walk away from her with two of his friends she buggered him, an' for everybody to hear. A bomb couldn't have caused a bigger sensation.' His voice a deep bellowing roar, he finished, 'Can you believe it, she buggered the Duke!'

They all gaped at her, speechless, and they knew, each one of them, that their mother had in some strange way this night altered their lives.

Part Four

THE DISINTEGRATION

Rodney paced the long narrow lounge of the flat. 'It's the finish, I'm leaving her.'

'No!'

He stopped in his stride. 'What do you mean, no?'

'Just that, no. You're taking the whole matter too seriously. It's a joke; everyone's laughing at it. There's never been so much laughter on the phones as there has been today . . . '

'Stop it! Stop it!' He bent his head deeply and thrust his hand out towards her; then looking at her again he said, 'I'm a laughing stock, all right I'm a laughing stock.'

'I wouldn't say that at all; it wasn't you who buggered him.'

He stared at her. It was odd, she could say the word and it even sounded musical, but coming from Maggie it sounded coarse and low, depicting what she was. The word was bandied like 'God bless you' the whole length and breadth of the Tyne, but in the main by men; women who used it were considered common, and she was that, by God! She was that.

He said now bitterly, 'No, but I'm her husband, and do you think all the toadies and suckers in this town are going to let me off with this? There are those who voted me on to committees only because they thought I was well in with Pearce and Bailey and their like.'

'You may be surprised.' She reached out and brought a brandy glass to her lips and sipped at the neat spirit before she said, 'I wouldn't mind having a pound for all those in this town who themselves would like to bugger His Grace. I really think your wife has done something.'

'By God she has!' He dropped down beside her on the narrow couch and, his voice quiet now, he said, 'Stop trying to smooth things over; I know the reactions of the town, I've experienced them already. I purposely went into the Club this lunch time and two men actually walked past me and didn't see me.'

She raised her brows. 'Friends?'

He tossed his head. 'Not exactly, but I've spoken to them.'

'You could be imagining it.'

'Look, Rosamund, this is serious, something's got to be done. I'll never live this down, not unless I do something definite, cut adrift from her. It would at least show what I think about the whole business.'

With a swift, easy movement she rose to her feet and looked down at him. 'You know what I think, Rodney . . . ? You're an upstart of the first water. To put it as your wife might have done, you're a bloody upstart.' She pronounced it bleedy, and she laughed at him as she said it and he didn't take it as an offence.

When, holding out her hand, she said, 'Are you coming?' like a child he allowed himself to be drawn up from the couch and into the bedroom.

As she stood lazily taking off her clothes she looked at him through the mirror and said, 'If ever you wanted soothing that time is now, don't you think?'

He didn't answer. Continuing to look at him through the mirror she picked up the conversation where it had been dropped some moments before. 'Whatever you do you mustn't leave her; that would do you much more harm than good.'

His fingers became still on the last button of his shirt

and, returning her gaze, he said, 'You know, I can't really understand you. I thought you would have wanted me to break . . . get a divorce, and you to do the same. Wouldn't . . . wouldn't you want that?' He waited while her eyes looked into his, the cynical playful expression no longer in them. Then turning from the mirror and wriggling out of her last garment she stared unsmiling into his face and said, 'Don't be childish, Rodney. Really!'

He watched her go to the bed and lower herself on to it, lie down and stretch her legs, then raise her arms and put them behind her head, and he looked at her like a small boy might look at his teacher who had slapped him for saying something silly.

As he stared at her lying there stark naked waiting for him to take her the anger in his body was replaced by fear, the fear turned itself into a thought, and the thought was unbearable. If she ever left him, went out of his life. The thought was sapping him; he was undressing like an aged man, not like a man in his prime, and an ardent lover at that. With a sudden spurt he ripped off the remainder of his clothes and flung himself down beside her.

Willie, Paul, Dave Walton and Helen were in the drawing-room. Paul had just come in, and Willie who was pacing up and down, very much like his father had done last night in the lounge of the flat said, 'Something will have to be done with her. She can't stay up there for ever, and she's got to eat some time.'

'Has she not been out at all?' asked Paul.

'No, not that we know of. You go on up again,' he nodded at Paul, 'and have another try.'

'Where's Elizabeth?' asked Paul now.

'At Mass.'

Paul went out and up the stairs and, knocking on his mother's bedroom door, he said softly, as he had done numbers of times yesterday, 'Mam, it's me, Paul.'

There was no reply. Again he knocked, and speaking louder this time he called, 'Mam! Look, if you don't open this door I'll burst it open. Come on now. This has gone on long enough.'

There was silence for a moment, then he heard the soft padding of her feet across the carpet and her voice, strange sounding to him, said, 'I'm all right, Paul; just leave me alone. I'll be down presently. I'm all right.'

He stood looking helplessly about him before turning slowly and going down the stairs. Just as he reached the hall Arlette came in through the front door and made straight towards him. 'Is she down?' she asked.

He shook his head.

'Is Dad in?' she whispered softly now.

'No; I understand he came back late last night, slept in Willie's room and went out again early this morning.'

Arlette now looked about her, then said quickly, 'Come here a minute,' and hurried towards the breakfast-room at the end of a short corridor, and he followed her.

She closed the door behind him, then stood with her back to it looking at him, and he at her, while he asked, 'What's the matter? Something else?'

She blinked her eyes and gulped deeply in her throat before saying, 'It's Sam. I . . . I think he's going mad, really mad; he's hardly stopped laughing since he started on Friday night. All day yesterday it went on, and he keeps saying things like—' she bit on her lip '—B— the Duke. My mam said B— the Duke. Clever woman my mam . . . Paul—' she stepped nearer to him— 'He's . . . he's revelling in it. He hates her . . . Why?'

Paul shook his head, then looked down towards the floor; but after a moment he was looking at her again and he stared hard into her eyes for some time before he asked, 'What about you?'

She lifted one shoulder, then turned her head towards it as if wanting to hide her face in its hunched hollow. 'It doesn't matter, it won't be long now.'

'You're going tomorrow then?' The question was soft.

'Yes.'

'Arlette.' He caught her hand and gripped it but seemed unable to speak. 'Will . . . will you let me know where you are when . . . when you're settled?'

She still did not look at him as she made an almost imperceptible consenting movement, and at this he drew her hand tight against his breast and whispered, 'Arlette! Oh Arlette!' But now she tugged it gently from his hold and, shaking her head as if throwing off her own worries, she said, 'There's something else. Do you know anything about Dad? I mean, has he been up to anything that Mam wouldn't know of?'

'In what way?' he asked.

'I . . . I don't really know.' She bit on her lip. 'Don't mind me saying this, but he . . . he wouldn't have another woman, would he?'

'Dad!' His face screwed up in disbelief. 'Dad! No, no. However much they go for each other they're close, they always have been; they've fought all their married life but they've made it up immediately. Laughter and tears was my childhood. I cried when they were fighting and joyed with them when it was over. Another woman? No. What makes you ask that?'

'Well.' She moved from him and walked towards the window and looked out for a moment before turning to him again and saying, 'He, Sam, he keeps hinting that he can blow her sky high, and . . . and, Paul.'

'Yes?'

'You too . . . He . . . he knows about you . . . and . . . ' She dropped her head.

He didn't move from where he was when he said grimly,

'He can't; nobody knows that, only Father Armstrong, you and me.'

'He does, Paul.'

'Is it because he knew you came to the flat that Saturday morning?'

'No, no, something else . . . photographs that you've kept. I don't really know, but something in that line.'

'My God!' He drew his chin into his neck and gritted his teeth; then raising his eyes to hers, he said, 'He's been through my room. Well—' his chin came up '—let him do his worst. If he confronts me with it I'll tell him. And, you know—' he smiled sadly at her now '—it'll be wonderful to bring it into the open, to say . . . '

'No, no! Please, Paul, don't.' She came towards him. 'He's quite capable of . . . ' She stopped, then went on, 'Please don't say anything. Whatever he says or does please, please don't say anything.'

After a moment he replied, 'Very well.' Then his voice thick and low he added, 'I won't see you after today, not for some time then?'

'Not for some time, Paul; it'll be best that way.'

'Arlette.'

'Yes, Paul?'

'I'm used to waiting. I've been waiting all my life. I'll wait, no matter how long.'

She pressed the tears back into her eyes with her tightly closed lids, then she walked past him – close to him and he didn't touch her.

Frances had just entered the hall accompanied by her two children, and her greeting was typical. Almost glaring at Arlette she hissed under her breath, 'It's all round the town. They all know at church, there were giggles as I came out. We're getting out of this as quick as possible; we've had enough. This is the end.'

Arlette said nothing. What could she say? But Helen,

standing in the drawing-room doorway cried angrily, 'You'd better take Trevor with you, our Frances, for all I've heard since yesterday is "What will Mr Pattenden say?" What I say is, "Damn, Mr Pattenden!" Lord, you'd think it was the end of the world.'

Frances slowly turned towards Helen. Her voice flat and ominous, she said, 'You've said it, the end of the world. And it's the end of our world in this town, you mark my words. God! If only one could pick one's parents.'

CHAPTER TWO

THE WHIP

Maggie didn't feel hungry. It was strange; she hadn't eaten since Friday tea-time and now here it was Monday morning, and she didn't feel hungry. She had let Annie in last night with a tray of tea. There were some sandwiches and things on the plate but she hadn't eaten them; she felt she never wanted to eat again. She guessed she had enough fat on her to keep her alive for a week or so without eating, but she knew if she were to keep alive, then she must face up to life and leave this room.

Monday morning and they were all at work. There was nobody in the house only Annie, and Annie, strangely enough, had said no word of censure to her. Then, neither had any of the others; none of them had said anything. No, but their thoughts had been plain to read in their eyes on Friday night as she had looked down on them from the stairs. And they were right, they were all right to censure her, condemn her. She had done a terrible thing. She no longer defended her action. She no longer recalled, as she had done all day long on Saturday, a whole month of worrying, fittings, trying on clothes, repeating over and over the right procedure, sick with excitement and anticipation every hour of every day of that month, then at the last minute waiting for him coming in, and him late, and hearing about Lizzie, and finally, those two long sessions of boredom, and the heat, and her corn and her skinned heel, and nobody bothering with her, not even him. No, he could stand and talk to another woman for over ten minutes while she stood in a corner lost and alone . . . And then the Duke. Within an arm's length of her, and her thinking the moment had come to shake him by the hand, and him being called off. But that was nothing, no, nothing, nothing, until that very last moment and the slight, unintentional perhaps, but nevertheless a slight. Still, she might have covered it up if her tongue hadn't been loosened by the four sherries.

But since yesterday she hadn't used this way of think-ing in her defence, for she had seen herself as Rod had seen her, an ignorant, fat, big-mouthed slob. A pig in a drawing-room! That's what he had shouted up the stairs after her. And that was how she now saw herself, a pig in a drawing-room. And what could you expect from a pig in a drawing-room, he had said, but grunts and muck.

He had said she had ruined him, ruined them all, and she knew she had. In different ways that one night out in her life had ruined them all; an invitation from a duke had changed all their lives. What was going to happen from now on? She wouldn't blame him if he wanted to leave her. No, she wouldn't blame him, but deep in the soul of her she prayed that he wouldn't go to that length, for, with him she didn't amount to much but, without him she'd be nothing, muck indeed.

But she must get herself out of this room, she must go downstairs. And tonight she must talk to Liz. She had been thinking a lot about Liz these past few hours, but whatever she said she must say it quietly. Anyway she couldn't ever see herself raising her voice in her life again.

She walked out of the bedroom and crossed the landing as if she was in a strange house, and when she reached the foot of the stairs she stood looking about her. When the telephone bell rang it startled her, and as Annie came out of the kitchen to answer it she saw her, and they looked at each other. Then Maggie turned and went to the side table and picked up the phone.

'This is Arlette.'

'Yes, Arlette?'

'Oh! Oh, hello, Mam. Oh, how are you dear?'

'Well, lass—' Maggie let out a quiet sigh '—just as you would expect, repentant, flat, wanting to die.'

'Oh, Mam, don't . . . Mam.'

'Yes, dear?'

'I want to see you. I . . . I'm going away.'

'What did you say?'

'I said I'm going away, Mam.'

'That's what I thought you said, lass. Where are you going?'

'I . . . I can't tell you but . . . but I want to see you before I go.'

'What is this?'

'I'm . . . I know it will come as a shock to you but I wanted to tell you some time ago, but I didn't want to trouble you until—' There was a pause. 'Anyway, Mam, I'm telling you now. I'm getting a divorce from Sam; it's all arranged.'

Maggie held the phone from her face and stared at it and she heard Arlette's voice saying, 'Are you there? Are you there, Mam?'

'Yes, I'm here, lass. When . . . when did you decide on this?'

'Oh . . . oh a long time ago, Mam. May . . . may I come round and have a word with you? I don't want to go without seeing you.'

'Yes, lass; yes, of course.'

'I'll be there within fifteen minutes.'

'All right, lass, all right.' Maggie slowly put the phone down. What was happening to everybody? Arlette going to get a divorce from Sam. He'd go mad, he thought the world of her. Well, there was only one consolation in all this, they couldn't blame her for it, could they? Yet, coming as it did at this time, they would in a way link it with her.

But if Arlette went away that would mean . . . it would mean she wouldn't see her any more. Her body seemed to be coming into life again, there was pain in it, pain in her mind, protest. No, no, this shouldn't be, not Arlette and Sam. But, face up to it, she had known that there was something amiss for a long time, and Friday night in the room when she had turned on him, she'd never seen her look like that before. Dear, dear, God. A divorce . . . Father Armstrong! But worse still, Father Stillwell.

She went into the kitchen, and like a stranger she said, 'Have you got any tea in the pot, Annie?' and Annie said, 'Sit yourself down and I'll get you some breakfast.'

'No, no, I don't want anything to eat, just a cup of tea.'

'You've got to eat; if you don't want to land up in that room permanently you've got to have something in your stomach. Now I've just made that toast fresh. There—' she slapped the plate on to the table '—sit yourself down and eat it. Now go on, do as you're bid for once in your life.'

It was comforting to be ordered about. You belonged when you were ordered about. She sat down and took a bite from the toast but she had difficulty in swallowing it. Nevertheless she ate a slice and she drank two cups of tea.

She looked at Annie flitting back and forth about the kitchen for some time before she said, 'Arlette's coming round, she'll be here any minute. She's going away . . . she's going to get a divorce from Sam.'

Annie stopped in her bustling and looked at Maggie. Then raising her eyebrows and drawing in a sharp breath she said, 'Well, that doesn't surprise me; in a way it doesn't, for that lass has never been happy. She was too good for him. If you remember rightly I said that afore they were married. And if I also remember rightly you said something very like it yourself. But a divorce! We've never had one of those in the family. But there's always a first time. I wonder what will happen next?' She took a jug from the cupboard, poured a bottle of milk into it and ended, 'Everything goes in threes. Let it come soon whatever it is and we'll get it over with.'

It came soon, soon in Annie's reckoning, but long in Maggie's.

Arlette didn't come within fifteen minutes, she didn't come within an hour or two, or three. Maggie got on the phone to the house but couldn't get a reply. At twelve o'clock, only because she was extremely worried, she phoned the office to find out if Sam had been in. Miss Whitaker answered and said no, he had phoned from the house early that morning to say he was going straight into Newcastle and not to expect him.

She felt uneasy. She said so to Annie, and when Annie suggested her going round to Arlette's to see if she was still there she said, 'Oh, no, no, I couldn't do that.'

But when Annie said, 'It's fishy to me. Arlette isn't one to break her word; perhaps there's been an accident and she's landed up in hospital,' Maggie said, 'If she had we would have known before now. But all right, I'll go round.'

'Will you phone for a taxi?'

'No, I'll walk down to the hill and get the bus from there, it stops just beyond the bye-road.'

'Do that,' said Annie soothingly; 'it'll do you good to get out.' She didn't say '. . . take your mind off your own trouble,' but that's what she meant . . .

It was a quarter to one when the bus put her down on the main road, and she walked the few yards to where a lane turned off leading to the bungalow.

The bungalow was situated in a good position, being set well back from the main road and surrounded on two sides by open fields, and on the third side by a riding stable. The next bungalow was beyond the riding stable, a hundred yards away. She went up the lane and let herself in by the main gate, walked up the path between the rose beds – all in full bloom now – and to the front door, and there she rang the bell.

When there was no answer to her ringing the first, second or third time, she went and looked in the sitting-room window. But the blinds were drawn. The blinds were drawn too in the dining section. She walked all around the house. All the blinds were drawn. Why had Arlette drawn the blinds before she left knowing Sam would be coming home?

When she passed the bedroom window she thought she heard a noise and she walked back to it and put her ear to the glass and listened. The curtains were lined and padded. Cost the earth those curtains, and they muffled the sound. She stared at the blank window for a moment, then walked to the kitchen door. It was locked. She went to the front door again and she stood there, not ringing now, just waiting and listening. Then she heard a sound inside that she recognised. It was a door being quietly opened, and a moment later she knew there was something standing within an arm's length from her.

She felt herself sweating with an unknown dread. Sam was in there. Their Sam was in the house and all the curtains were drawn. And Arlette was in there, Arlette was in there an' all. Of that she was sure now.

She moved her feet on the stones of the porch, then purposely pushed the foot scraper into place near the step before walking away down the path. She let herself out of the gate and clicked it shut, then went down the lane again, but only a little way beyond the back gate.

The back gate led between a wall and a high privet hedge to the side of the house and the loggia, at the end of which were the outhouses and the garage. Inside the garage was a private door leading into the house, and a spare key for the garage, she knew, was kept on the flange near the top of the drainpipe – that's if her son, in his planning, hadn't already removed it.

She went noiselessly up the path, tip-toed across the loggia, reached up and felt for the key. And there it was. Gently she unlocked the garage door but opened it only wide enough to allow herself to squeeze through. Then she was walking between the two cars, Arlette's and his. She paused and looked in the back of Arlette's car. Two suitcases were lying on the seat.

Gently now she turned the knob of the door and went through into the narrow hallway, which led to the kitchen and bathroom. She had to cross here and go through the dining end of the lounge before she could reach the bedroom. She was walking stealthily towards the bedroom door when she heard Sam's voice, low, thick, laughter-filled as if he was drunk, saying, 'She's gone. Your dear, dear friend's gone. The ignorant old sow's gone, your last hope. Now what you going to do about it, eh? Are you ready for another dose or are we coming to some arrangement? You've only got to nod your head.' There followed a silence, then the voice changed. 'You stinking, scheming bitch you! A divorce is it? You would have gone and left me without a word, not giving a damn, leaving me in hell, leaving me to my own devices.' His voice was rising; it seemed to be screaming, yelling, yet it was eerily low.

When she heard the unmistakable crack of a whip and a smothered yelp and moan, her own body jerked and cringed. It came again, and yet again, before she sprang forward and burst open the door, only to come to a petrified stop when she saw her son, a whip in his hand, flaying his wife, who was tied naked to the bed, a gag in her mouth. For a full moment she thought she must be dreaming or she had gone mad, that the business of Friday night had turned her brain. Only when Arlette's head lifted towards her and her eyes beseeched her for help did she know that this was no dream bordering on madness. But she wished to God it was, for that maniac was her son, her own flesh and blood with a whip in his hand!

Now they were gaping at each other and both standing as if looking for an opening to the other's throat.

'You devil in hell!' The words were wrenched up from her stomach, deep, ominous. She cast a quick glance to each side of her for something to grasp, to throw. To the right of her on the window sill was a pair of vases, but they were too far away. But on the dressing table to her side was a tall glass candlestick. She thrust out her hand and grabbed it and the next second it was hurtling across the room.

It wasn't the first time she had thrown things at a man and with practice her aim had become good. The bottom of the candlestick caught Sam on the temple, and when he staggered back, stunned for the moment, his hands to his head, she was on him. Tearing the whip from him she slashed at him, beating him about the head and face and uttering sounds that could not be translated. But the very blows themselves brought him alert again, and she found herself flung backwards on to a chair, with his hands on her throat and his wide hate-filled face hanging over hers.

'YOU! YOU!' This was the only word he seemed capable of uttering through his tightly clenched teeth and he went on repeating it while his fingers tightened on her throat. With a strength born of desperation she brought her knee up and caught him hard in the groin, and he sprang back from her like a stone from a catapult. His body doubling up, he held himself as he groaned.

Slowly now she dragged herself to her feet, and rubbed at her neck while she stumbled towards the bed. Her eyes hard on him, she tugged at the knots in the pieces of torn sheeting that bound Arlette. When she had freed her she stared down in horror at the blue and red wealed body of her daughter-in-law; then gently she drew the eiderdown round her and brought her upwards on to the side of the bed, still keeping her eyes on her son who was standing upright now, or almost so. As they glared at each other she knew she was looking into the face of a maniac, not a maniac whom the law could pin down, say was mad and so lock up, but a clever, sly, scheming maniac, and she knew that she'd always been aware of this.

'Get out! Get out before I do for you.'

He moved sideways towards the door, his eyes unblinking, but there he stopped. The knob gripped in his hand, he licked at the froth round his lips before saying, 'There's more ways of killing a cat than drowning it. You're finished, you're as good as dead, Mother Gallacher, and I knew I'd see this day with you. Do you hear? I've been waiting for this day . . .'

'Get out, you dirty, filthy scum. Get out!'

For a moment she thought that he was going to spring across the room at her again; and so did Arlette, for her body shrank against Maggie's. But he only bent forwards, almost double now as he cried at her, 'You to call anybody dirty, you, you who begot me in a cupboard! You were determined to have me dad, weren't you? And that was the only way you could hook him. But he nearly slipped through your fingers even then. A shotgun wedding at the last with a priest on either side of him so that I wouldn't be a bastard. YOU, to talk about anybody being dirty! I was seven when I learned what you were, you fat loose piece, and I've hated you ever since.'

She stared at him, her face lengthening with her surprise. Like looking through old snaps she picked up in her mind the very night she and Rod had gone for each other, and the one and only time he had thrown it up at her that he'd had to marry her. And that lad had been listening, and all these years it had been fomenting in his mind. It didn't seem possible. But it was possible. You read about these things but you never thought they happened to you or yours. But dear God, all these years! How many? He was almost twenty-seven; twenty years he had been holding that against her. Dear, dear God! For the moment she felt a spasm of pity for him and an overwhelming sense of guilt against herself. The sins of the fathers. Aw yes, indeed, the sins of the fathers shall be visited on the children.

But what was he saying now? His words seemed to make her face contract, her eyes narrow, screwed up against their meaning.

'So Dad got his own back; he's played you for a sucker. These last two years he's played you for a sucker. He's got another woman. D'you hear? And not just any woman. No, a lady, by the name of . . . Mrs de Ferrier. And they've got a love nest in the flat behind the office. A Mrs Morland lives there. Eight pounds a week she's supposed to pay. It's cheap at that. She's a friend of Mrs de Ferrier; one good turn deserves another. Mrs Morland leaves every Friday night and Dad and his lady take up residence. Now what d'you think of that . . .? Even before you made yourself the big-mouthed scab of the town you were a laughing stock, for everybody's known that you were being duped. Friday night Rod goes to Ransomes.' Now he was mimicking. 'Saturday night Rod goes to a club in Newcastle, or a dinner or some such doesn't he?' He waited while he glared at her; then his tone changing and his face taking on an even deeper hatred, he spat at her, 'You're finished, finished. You've got nothing. They're all leaving you, all except perhaps your dear son, Paul. And here's something else I'll tell you afore I go. Do you know why he didn't become your blue-eyed priest? . . . Because of her.' He stretched out his arm, his finger stabbing towards Arlette. 'He fell for her, and they've been having a go together ever since. Now what do you think about that, Mam? And another thing. Did you know he was a poet, eh? It's him who writes that piffle for the paper. God help him when I tell our Willie. Fell off a lorry! He'll look as if the lorry had gone over him when Willie's finished with him . . . Well now.' He went to straighten himself, then put his hand to his groin again and it was evident that he was still in pain. 'There's a nice little lot for you to go on with, eh? . . . And as for you, Mrs Gallacher Junior. Give you a divorce? I will that, over my dead body. You try to get one and they'll hear my side of it. What I've done to you is because I found out you were carrying on with my brother; after egging him on to leave the priesthood. That's my case. Go on, try an' see who'll get sympathy in court. Go on.'

They stared at him now as if they were stupefied, and both saw him as something less than human, something epitomising evil.

Even after he was gone they didn't move. They heard him go into the garage, but the car didn't start up right away. It wasn't until it did that Maggie sat down on the bed beside Arlette, and they both looked at each other, with wells of pity in their eyes for the other's plight.

Maggie's brain was in a whirl. Mrs de Ferrier. That Mrs de Ferrier. She didn't question the truth of Sam's words; she seemed to have known it for a long time. There had been just a thin curtain in her mind that had hidden the knowledge from her. This then was the difference in Rod; all these months, all these week-ends he had been going with another woman, and all this time she had been sitting at home . . . like a fool; a great, fat slob with no brains to work things out, a trusting, great fat slob; a blind, ignorant, great, fat slob. But no! No! Her mind was protesting now. Rod wouldn't do that to her. He couldn't, not to her. She had borne him six children; she had worked like a slave for years. She had worked almost up to the last minutes before Sam, Willie and Paul were born. She had kept her job on in the factory so that they'd get a home together; and even when they started to get on and make money hand over fist, she had still continued to work and do for him and all of them, saving on this and that, not spending a penny on herself. What was more, she had been content to sit at home at nights with Annie and mend and sew and see to the bairns while he gallivanted – making contacts he called it. My God! And he had made contacts, hadn't he? De Ferrier; the woman who had looked her up and down as if she was something the cat had brought in, and all the while he had stood there knowing; and he had left her standing against that wall while he talked and talked . . . to his mistress. As if he didn't get enough of her, he had to stand in the middle of that room, a plate in each hand looking at her, while she had stood alone. It was an act of scorn, rejection. All his acts lately had been acts of scorn and rejection. All the while he must have been comparing her with that woman, that society piece, that flat shapeless piece, but a piece who had class written all over her. Aye, there was the answer.

She felt her size diminishing; the feeling on her now was not only one of deflation but also of extinction. She was nothing, nobody, not even fit to be treated as a pet rabbit, fit only for breeding. He had finished with his breeding spell and had moved on to higher things.

She stared before her dry-eyed, but she was crying with every pore of her body. There was no fight left in her; she had nothing more to fight with, nothing more to fight for.

When Arlette shivered in her arms she forgot her own misery for the moment. This lass, this lass. She looked into Arlette's face. It was like a piece of alabaster. Her eyes were half closed and, strangely, there were no signs of tears on her cheeks. How had she suffered this without crying, how? She bent down and muttered, 'Sit still, lass. Now don't move; I'll phone for a taxi.'

When she came back it was obvious Arlette hadn't moved. Everything about her was the same; she looked like a mummy.

'Do you think you can get into your clothes?' she asked her softly. She glanced round the room, at the scattered garments lying on the floor and the chairs; then she went and picked up a blue dress and, bringing it to the bed, said, 'If you could just slip into this, that would be enough.'

Still Arlette didn't move, and when she went to take the eiderdown from around her she had to force her fingers open. As she slipped the dress over her head she felt the shudder of her body and she closed her own eyes tight for a moment as if her skin too had been seared. She put on her shoes and helped her to her feet, then led her gently to a chair, saying, 'Sit there, and I'll get your things from the car.'

When she entered the garage again she stood aghast. The whole place was littered with the contents of the cases from the back seat of the car. There were petticoats, brassières, suits all scattered about as if a hurricane had whirled them into the air. He was mad, mad, but in his madness he still remained petty and small. She gathered up what she could and pushed them back into the cases, then re-entered the hall and as she did so the front door bell rang.

When she went into the bedroom again Arlette was sitting just as she had left her, and she put her arms about her, saying, 'It's all right, lass. It's all right. We'll soon be home.'

The taxi driver looked enquiringly but asked no questions. But when he put his hand on Arlette's shoulder to help her into the back of the car and she winced audibly he glanced at Maggie, and she, looking at him, said, 'Savile House on The Rise.'

Ten minutes later she helped Arlette gently into the house, calling as she opened the door, 'Annie! You there, Annie?'

Annie appeared at the head of the stairs, and after staring at them for a moment she ran down, saying, 'Good God! What's happened to her?' and Maggie said, 'Let's get her to bed; then ring for the doctor, her own doctor. I think it's Bentley. You'll find his number . . .' Her voice trailed away in the effort she had to exert to get Arlette to lift one foot after the other up the stairs . . .

It was an hour and a half later before the doctor arrived, and when Maggie drew down the sheet the man stared for a number of seconds at the criss-cross pattern of blue and red weals, some showing dots of dried blood now. Then, without lifting his head, he lifted his eyes upwards and looked at Maggie, and she could not return the look because shame was weighing her down. That flesh of her flesh could have perpetrated a deed like this! She could have understood a killing; she could have forgiven him in a way if he had shot or strangled her; but to do this!

Ten minutes later, out on the landing, the doctor walked slowly to the head of the stairs, Maggie by his side, and said quietly, 'The state of trauma, shock—' he inclined his head towards her '—may last. Keep her quiet, let no-one see her; but don't leave her, for when this passes off the reaction . . . well, it could be anything.'

He was half-way down the stairs when he said, 'If she had taken my advice and that of her solicitor she could have avoided this. I warned her.'

She waited until they reached the hall, then, standing in front of him, she asked quietly, 'You . . . you knew? About it going on?'

'Yes.' He nodded at her. 'For some time now. But not to this severity . . .'

'Then . . . then why did she put up with it?'

He shrugged his shoulders and moved his head. 'She's a very thoughtful, considerate person, she . . . she didn't want to cause trouble. She was to leave him five weeks ago and then because of some happening, some occasion in the family—' he paused for a second, his look questioning '—which she didn't want to disrupt by starting a divorce, she put it off.'

'Dear God!' Maggie hung her head and the doctor said, 'Well, it's no use worrying, it's done. But . . . but I'd better warn you that your son could be in trouble over this. This is not a case of mere flagellation which he demanded that she should practise on him and he on her, but an attack, a criminal assault and we have yet to see what the result will be. I think that you should get in touch with her solicitor. He's a relation of hers I understand, and it will be up to him to advise what steps should be taken.'

She nodded dumbly and he left her; and slowly she mounted the stairs again. Flagellation, assault, divorce, mistresses; her world was indeed exploding about her ears.

In the afternoon John Fenton called and Maggie told him that Arlette was asleep under the sedation the doctor had prescribed and no-one could see her.

She had heard about Arlette's cousin but had never before met him. He was a young-looking fellow, like one of her own lads, too young, she felt, to fight people's tragedies in law courts, that was until he started to talk. Had she any inkling, he asked, of what her daughter-in-law had been going through these past few years?

178

No, she hadn't.

Had Arlette mentioned nothing to her at all?

No, she hadn't.

Then he thought it was better she should know the facts of the case before it went into court, because he doubted if Arlette would give her the details, seeing that the man concerned was her son, and remembering, as he said, that Arlette had a deep esteem for herself.

As Maggie listened to the brief, short sentences which showed her son as a sexual pervert she wanted to be sick, to vomit out the knowledge which was being forced into her. You read about these people in the *News of the World*, but they were the kind of people you yourself would never have any truck with. They didn't live in your world.

When he left she went into the bathroom and stood over the basin for a time; she even put her fingers down her throat but she could get no release, the feeling of abhorrence was too deep.

In the bedroom, she took over from Annie and sat down by the bed, and while she sat she wondered at her own feelings. There was a strange calmness on her now. It wasn't like the old feeling, that calmness before the storm when she would remain speechless for a time before bursting into battle with Rod. This calmness was the calmness of despair, weighed heavily with guilt. But guilt for what? She didn't know, she hadn't done anything really bad in her life. Was what she had manoeuvred at her party all those years ago bad? Was that the reason why she was suffering now? One thing was sure, it was that act that had turned Sam against her, twisted his mind; in that moment of joy when she had started his being she had also fermented the seeds of hate. And had she lost Rod then, at that moment when she had trapped him? Or was it just because she was loud-mouthed at times, given to bawling her head off that she was sitting here now under this dragging, damning pressure of guilt?

If she hadn't bawled at Rod that night all those years ago he would have never thrown the truth up in her face and Sam would never have heard, but would that have made any difference to Sam's nature? Was the knowledge that he'd been got on the side enough to turn him into a queer? Because that's what he was, and not just an ordinary queer, a man who went after men; that was a quirk of nature and she pitied all such, but a queer that was so twisted in his mind that only the unnatural was natural to him, that only the unspeakable could bring him pleasure. Was she responsible for such a man? No! No! She denied it loudly in her head, for then she would be responsible for the lass there, lying in this state.

But she was responsible for Rod's defection. Deep, deep down in herself she shouldered the blame for this, for she realised now that as he had moved upwards she hadn't had the sense to follow him. But this admission did not stop her from hating him for doing the dirty on her; she would hate him until the day she died. She was consumed with the pain of her hate. She moved her buttocks back and forwards on the chair as if the pain were physical and she knew that if she let her mind escape this outer case of calmness and dwell on him she would throw herself on the floor this minute and beat her fists against it as an opiate to the agony. But there were other things she must deal with before she allowed herself to come to the main issue.

First there was Paul. Sam had said that he had been carrying on with Arlette, that she was the reason why he hadn't gone into the church. Was this true? She'd have to know.

And Liz? She had been so stunned over the week-end by her own actions that she had forgotten about Liz; but now she must see to her, and quick. She herself hadn't pressed her to go into the church. It had come as a surprise when Liz had first voiced her intention; but once she had known she had hugged the idea to herself and wallowed in the aroma of sanctity that the vocation presented for her daughter. It seemed then, in her naïvety, that God was making up to her for the disappointment she had experienced over Paul.

But she told herself she'd settle one thing at a time, she couldn't tackle them otherwise, and by this time tomorrow it would all be over.

Annie came up at half-past four. Tip-toeing into the room, she said, 'Liz is in; she's asking for you. I didn't tell her anything about—' she nodded towards the bed '—I thought I'd leave it to you.'

Maggie nodded back at her, then rose from the chair, and automatically Annie took her place.

When she entered the kitchen Elizabeth was sitting at the corner of the table drinking a glass of lemonade. She got to her feet immediately and, coming towards Maggie, put her arms around her and asked, 'Are you feeling better, Mam?'

Maggie answered, 'Aye, lass, aye. I'm all right.' Then looking straight into her daughter's face, she said, 'I want to talk to you.' When she saw a look like a dark veil pass over Liz's eyes and her head droop slightly, she said flatly, 'Come into the drawing-room, it's cooler there.'

In the drawing-room Maggie seated herself by the window, and when Elizabeth went and stood near the head of the couch she said to her gently, 'Come here and sit down . . . Bring that chair.'

Elizabeth obeyed her and sat down. She still had her head bowed and Maggie said to her, 'Before I get on to you I'd better tell you something, you'll have to know it sooner or later. Arlette's upstairs, she's pretty bad.

181

Sam—' she wet her lips and swallowed '—Sam's beaten her up . . .'

'O . . . ur S-Sam?'

'Our Sam.'

'Arlette?'

'Arlette. And—' Maggie pushed her lips outwards '—you're a bairn no longer, you've likely read about these things and now you'd better hear them. He . . . he did it with a whip. And not only the day, it's been going on for a long time.' As she watched Elizabeth put her hand across her mouth and grip her face she said, 'There'll be a divorce.' And now when Elizabeth's eyes stretched on the word divorce she thought, Aye, lass, you can open your eyes but there's no priest on God's earth, counting Father Stillwell, that'll be able to stop it in this case. She squared her shoulders and stretched her neck upwards, as if she were practising Arlette's trick of pulling her stomach in, as she went on, 'And now we come to you . . . Are you going to tell me, lass, or have I to ask you questions?'

When she saw the pitiful look in the young girl's eyes she wanted to thrust out her arms and pull her into the shelter of them, saying, 'There now, there now. Go whichever way you want.' But no, no, she warned herself, her road was already mapped out for her, there mustn't be a second farce.

When Elizabeth didn't speak she asked, 'This fellow, this taxi driver, you've been seeing him?'

Elizabeth shook her head, gulped, then pressed her fingers tightly across her mouth before taking her hand away and muttering low, 'Not really. Not really, Mam.'

'What do you mean, not really? Either you've been seeing him or you've not been seeing him.'

'It wasn't . . . it wasn't intentional, not planned, not planned or anything like that.'

'No?'

'No.'

'That's the truth?'

'Yes. Yes, Mam.'

'Go on then, tell me how it happened. Remember, you don't know what I know so be careful of your words.'

Elizabeth shook her head from side to side, then began haltingly, 'It was . . . it was after that night he brought me home. I . . . I was coming from school. I was just at the end of the grounds; his car was drawn up at the kerb; he was asking a woman how . . . how to get to the Convent House. She didn't know, she was a stranger, and I stopped and told him. I told him to gò round the block into Woodward Road and down the lane. He told me he was to pick up someone to take to the station, it was Sister Anna Maria; the jallopy, I mean the road car, had broken down.' She stared at her mother, gulped again, then went on more slowly now, 'The second time was in the Market. You had left me to go into Grimes's and I went to the chemist. He . . . he was in there. We just said hello, and had a word. That was all . . . I told you about it. But, but . . .'

'Yes, all right, go on.' Maggie's voice was quiet.

'The next Tuesday I was crossing over by the lights in Fulham Road to get the bus and he saw me and pulled up and . . . and asked if I was going home. I said yes, and he said he had to pick up a fare on The Rise, and to jump in . . . and—' she moved her head in a wide sweep now '—it seemed silly not to, and so he brought me home.'

They stared at each other, the silence like a wall between them until Maggie asked the question, 'Is that all?'

Elizabeth's eyes were wide now, unblinking. She said very slowly, 'The next time I saw him he was talking to Father Armstrong outside the Club. He was going to show the boys judo. We all stood talking and Father Armstrong, well, he joked and said if Peter—' she screwed her eyes up

183

tightly and bowed her head, and Maggie's voice cut in on her. 'Peter? He's Peter, is he?'

'Well—' the head was still bowed but there was a note of defiance in the voice '—Father Armstrong calls him Peter.'

'And you call him Peter?'

'No, I don't.' Her head came up; her chin was bobbing. 'But that's his name.'

'Go on.'

Some seconds passed before Elizabeth muttered, 'Father Armstrong said that . . . that God worked in strange ways, that I had to be rescued before he could get anyone to teach the boys judo.'

Father Armstrong! That simple-minded, big nit of a man, he would say things like that. But she must keep calm. She was calm; yes, she was calmer than she'd ever been in her life before. She said, 'Tell me the rest.'

'There's nothing more to tell only that he gave me a ride twice more from school. It wasn't planned or anything because, well, one night we were doing the rehearsal for the play and I didn't come back till six, remember? And last Wednesday afternoon; well, it was games day and I was home early, before four.'

Maggie looked at the crumpled face, the dry, bright eyes. It was all so innocent sounding. And perhaps it was innocent, but nevertheless she had been with that man five times in the car and she wasn't unaffected by it. No, she wasn't unaffected by it. She asked her quietly now, 'Did you tell him what you intended doing with your life?'

The answer was some time in coming. 'No.'

'Why?'

'It . . . I . . . it . . . I didn't think it concerned him.'

Again they were staring at each other, and Maggie wanted to ask the one question that mattered now, 'Are

184

you in love with this fellow?' But no, no, that was taking things too far. What she said was, 'I think you had better tell him, don't you?'

Again there was a pause before Elizabeth answered, and then she said softly, 'Yes, Mam.'

'When will you be seeing him again?' It was a trick question but Elizabeth did not fall into it. She said, 'I don't . . . I don't know, Mam. I told you, they just happen, the meetings.'

'Well promise me something, promise me something now girl, will you?'

'I'll . . . I'll try, Mam.' Elizabeth's voice was breaking.

'When next you see him you'll tell him of the decision you made at the beginning of the year, promise me?'

'I promise, Mam.'

Maggie got to her feet and went and stood by Elizabeth's side; then taking her head in her two hands she pressed it against her waist for a moment before going out.

Elizabeth sat staring in front of her. She was trembling from head to foot, weighed down with the enormity of her guilt. Within her mind's eye she gazed upwards, looking for the face of the Blessed Virgin, and when she found it the head was bent in sorrow, bowed low with grief, and near her stood Joseph with the infant child in his arms and their faces were turned from her. She looked from them down a long, long corridor. It was lined on each side with nuns. At the far end stood the Mother Superior, and next to her Father Armstrong, and behind them and above, overshadowing them all, stood Jesus, the bridegroom, who in her mind she knew she was betraying. His face was not turned from her but was full of pain and sadness for the rejection he read in her thoughts.

She dropped her head forward and cried into her hands.

*   *   *

Maggie phoned Paul at five o'clock. He said, 'Oh, is that you, Mam? How are you?' and she answered, 'I'll never feel any worse than I do at this moment. You'd better come round, there's things I have to see to.'

There was a pause before he said, 'Right, Mam.' And she put the phone down . . .

Twenty-five minutes later he came hurrying through the front door, and she was waiting for him. He went straight to her and kissed her and held her at arm's length, and as he looked into her face he thought, It's done something to her, she'll never be the same again.

They walked into the drawing-room, his arm around her shoulders, but there she disengaged herself from him and said in a voice that was strange to him, 'Sit down, Paul.' He did as she bade him as if he were a small boy again.

Sitting opposite to him, as she had to Elizabeth, she came straight to the point. 'Things have happened, Paul,' she said, 'and I'm not referring now to Friday night's business. Arlette's upstairs in bed; she's pretty bad.'

His body jerked to the edge of the chair. Then he became still. 'What's happened?'

'I'll tell you after you tell me something. Have you and her been carrying on?'

'NO! NO!'

Her head began to nod now as if it were on wires, and then she asked, 'Was it because of her you didn't go into the Church?'

He was still sitting taut on the edge of the chair and he held her eyes for a moment before he said, 'Yes; yes, it was.'

'Did she know?'

'NO! *No!* Well—' his cheek jerked with a movement like a tick '—not till recently. A few weeks ago she told me something, what she intended to do. It was then she knew, although I . . . I didn't say anything.'

'She told you she was going to get a divorce, didn't she?'

There was a short period of silence before he moved his head once.

She said now below her breath, 'Sam found out she was leaving him this morning. Perhaps he heard her phoning me to say she was coming to see me before she left. I don't know, she hasn't spoken. But anyway, he tied her to the bed and then—' she bit tight on her lip before she ended, 'he took a whip to her. Three hours of it she must have had before I got there.'

From under lowered lids she saw him rise from the chair and when she lifted her head and looked at him she looked quickly away again. She said now softly, as if stating an ordinary fact, 'Sam's a sex maniac. I had her cousin here this afternoon. He told me what she's had to put up with for a long time now.'

When Paul still made no comment she straightened her shoulders, lifted her head and looked at him again. His face was drained of every vestige of colour, making his red hair look like a flame on top of a wax candle; his eyes were black and staring, wild looking. The anger and the rage that should have been tearing through her she saw in him, and she wished in this moment that she could feel some of it instead of this deadness that had taken possession of her.

She watched him turn away and walk out of the room. It wasn't until he was in the hall that she realised he was making for upstairs, and she hurried after him. She caught him on the bottom step and held his arms and said, 'It's no use, she won't speak; she's in shock, the doctor said.'

He looked at her until she released the hold on his arm; then he turned and mounted the stairs. When he reached the landing her voice came after him, saying quietly, 'Willie's room.'

When he opened the bedroom door Annie turned in her seat and looked at him in surprise. Then she rose, and when he reached the foot of the bed she whispered, 'Nice state of affairs, isn't it?'

Slowly he took his eyes from her and gazed at the form lying under the sheet, the face above it looking like that of a corpse; and when Annie said, 'If you'll stay a minute I'll go down and make you a cup of tea, I'm sure nobody else'll think of it with the state of things,' he moved past her and took the seat she had vacated.

When he heard the door close he bent forward and lifted the hand that was lying limply on the sheet. Bringing it up to his cheek he pressed it there as he uttered deep thick unintelligible sounds. As they made way for his thoughts he wanted to get his brother by the throat and choke the last vestige of life out of him. Pray God they didn't meet up for some time.

A whip! He had used a whip on her? That was what she wouldn't tell him. Cruelty, she had said. 'Oh Arlette, my love, my love.' He laid her hand back on the bed and his fingers wavered over the edge of the sheet, which was all that covered his brother's handiwork for her shoulders were bare of straps, indicating no night attire. He held the sheet gently, lifted it from her breasts upwards but couldn't pull it back. He brought his hands together so that his nails dug into the backs of each, and oblivious of the pain his mind raced into the future. He'd give in his notice; he'd get a job elsewhere; he'd take her away. When the divorce was through they'd be married. They had everything in common. She liked him, he knew that she liked him. Did she love him? He didn't know. But the love he had, and could give to her, couldn't help but find its echo in her.

He heard the door opening behind him. He didn't turn round but he knew it was his mother standing near him. When he got to his feet, she said in an odd tone, 'Come back in the morning, an' by that time I'll have something else to tell you.'

He looked into her face and the change he saw in her hurt him; he had never seen her like this, she was quiet, controlled. Yet controlled wasn't the word, sort of lost. He whispered now, 'What is it?' and she said, 'I can't tell you till later. Come in the morning, as I said . . . And Paul—' she had half-turned from him and now she glanced at him over her shoulder '—Don't tell the others, not till the morning, not anything. Then—' she sighed '—and then you can give them all the news together.'

When she sat down it was like a dismissal, and he stared at her averted face for a moment, then looked again at Arlette before slowly turning and going out of the room.

It was quarter to twelve when Rodney came in. It had been quarter past eleven the other two nights. Although she had been locked away in her room she had known the exact minute that he entered the house, and she had followed his movements. He had locked the front door, then gone into the cloakroom, taken off his hat and coat, after which he had made straight for the stairs and the spare room. Tonight the procedure tended to be the same.

She had been waiting in the darkened drawing-room and when she heard his key in the lock she got to her feet and stood within the doorway while he locked up, then went into the cloakroom. At this point she switched on the drawing-room lights and when, a minute or so later, he crossed the hall he was brought to a standstill by seeing her standing in the framework of the doorway.

Stopping, he looked at her, then, dropping his head, he made to go towards the stairs but her voice checked him, and in a strange way, for it was flat and quiet. The words too were strange, coming from her, for she said, 'Don't go up there just yet, please. Come in here a minute, will you?'

When he looked at her again she had her back to him walking slowly into the room, and he paused before following her. Just within the doorway he stopped and stood watching her still walking towards the far end of the big chesterfield couch, where she turned and faced him. And again when she spoke her words were strange, not in keeping with the situation, for there was nothing repentant about her, no spate of words coming from her trying to explain her mad act, no abject apology, no calling herself a bloody fool. What she said was, 'Have you anything to tell me?'

'Tell you?' There was a slight sneer on his lips now. 'I thought I told you enough on Friday night.'

'We're not talking about the same thing.'

His face straightened out, stretched a little. 'What do you mean? What are you getting at?'

'The trifling matter of another woman called . . . Mrs de Ferrier?'

His mouth was dropping into a gape when he brought it shut with a snap. So it had come, had it? Well, it was time for it; nevertheless it was going to be damned awkward, bloody awkward, and noisy if he knew anything. He glanced swiftly round the room. She would likely pelt everything movable at him. There was the heavy cut glass ash tray on the side table within arm's reach of her; there was that set of vases on the mantelpiece, not to mention the alabaster figure in the middle. It was well he was standing with his back to the open door.

'It's true isn't it that you've been living with her over the past year in the flat behind the office?'

She waited, but he just stared at her.

'I want an answer.'

He squared his shoulders, moved his neck up out of his collar, then said, 'If you know it all why bother to ask?'

'Yes or no?'

Her voice should have sounded like the crack of a whip but it still held that strange off-putting flat sound.

He breathed in deeply; then as he let the breath out the words floated on it. 'Yes. Aye.'

The clock in the hall became audible, the seconds ticking away. What she said next was, 'You called me a big, fat, ignorant slob the other night, didn't you? You took me to that do and compared me with your fancy wife and found me wanting, badly wanting, didn't you? And you said you couldn't make a silk purse out of a sow's ear, didn't you? Well, perhaps you're right about that, but neither can you make one out of a hog's ear. I can see now why you've been breaking your neck this while back to play the gentleman. Naturally you wanted to match up to her style. Huh! I'm sorry for you, Rodney Gallacher, for that's one thing you'll never be, either in looks or manners. The fifty guinea suit you're wearing at this minute doesn't cover what you are, what you were, what you sprung from. You're built like a navvy, you come from a line of dockers at best; it's in your face, and you only have to open your mouth to give yourself away. Nobody's ever pointed this out to you afore, have they? No, it's me that's been the gobskite. You've never let me forget I've got a big mouth; but there were at least some times when I opened it when something else came out besides wind . . . What do you talk about, you and your fancy wife, music, painting, science?'

'Have you finished?'

'No, not quite.'

'Well, whatever you've got to say make it slippy, because I'm tired, and if you want to bring this up again I'll go into it the morrow.'

'OH NO YOU WON'T.'

For the first time her tone was one he recognised, but when she went on her voice was level again. 'This business is going to be finished the night . . . now. You're going

191

upstairs, and you're going to pack your things and you're going out of this house and you're . . . NEVER COMING BACK.' Again her natural self had broken through.

He was stretching upwards now, his chest out, his voice coming from his bull neck. 'I'll go out of this house when I damn well please. This is my house and I . . .'

Her voice, although controlled again, was belied by the expression on her face. Her lower jaw worked from one side to the other as she broke in, 'You'll go out of this house now. If you don't I'll get on the phone . . . Look at the clock.' She pointed. 'It's near twelve. Well, twelve or no twelve, I'll get on the phone, first to her man – I've got all the numbers here.' She pulled from her pocket a sheet of paper and read, 'Mr Roger de Ferrier, Brixton Manor, Felburn 27789 . . .' She held his staring gaze. 'And after him there's Mr Norman Pearce, and Mr Arthur Redfern . . . Councillor Mr Redfern. Then there's Mr Talbot on the Housing Committee and Mr Grey. They might all think I've gone mad after last Friday night's do, but if you're not out of this house within half-an-hour I'll phone every one of them an' chance it.' Her tone changing completely now, she cried at him, 'Every bloody one of them, Mr Gallacher! And I'll do a bit of twisting on me own; I'll tell them that the exhibition I made of meself the other night was due to me learning about you and her, and for the moment I lost control . . . An' it could be true at that, couldn't it?'

He was glaring at her now, very like Sam had done earlier in the day, and she thought for a moment he was coming at her, as he had done so many times before, to let out with the flat of his hand, if not his fist. But he didn't; he stood swaying slightly backwards and forwards as if he were drunk, and after a silence filled with their mutual hate she went on, 'You know this town even better than me, and you know that the aforementioned gentlemen are all very good-living citizens. You remember what happened to that Mr Price some years ago, him that had the business on the corner of the market and was going to expand to the next shop? The leases were up along Talbot Place; and then it came out. He was carrying on on the side, and him a Chapel man. And remember what happened? You told me the story yourself. They wouldn't renew the lease, not even on his own shop; they gave it to Woolworths after having refused it to them in the first place . . . and all because he was keeping a woman on the side. And it wasn't all that long ago, only four or five years. They're still the same men, those who are running this town, now.'

He wetted his lips, then dug his teeth tight into the flesh of the lower one, and the action seemed to drag his head down and his shoulders with it. Then he said in a tone that made her sick because it held a fawning quality, 'Look, Maggie; let's . . . let's be sensible about this. I . . . I know I haven't played it straight but I can explain, an' I'll promise . . .'

'You'll promise me nothing, so you can save your trousers and get yourself off your knees. For twenty-seven years I've been a doormat, a big, fat slob of a doormat, and a dim-witted bugger into the bargain, but no more, no more. As for you turning your coat at the last minute, even if I wanted to believe you I wouldn't. An' I'll tell you another thing. I wouldn't let you within a mile of me ever again. Do you hear? The very thought of you touching me makes me bowels rive . . . Now, as I said, you've got your choice, get packed and get out, back to your nice little nest, or listen to me phoning your pals.'

Again there was the silence, and when she broke it her voice held a tremor. 'Two more things I've got to say to you and then that'll be the end. First, I'm going to a solicitor the morrow about a legal separation. I'll see that you provide for me; I've worked for that at least. The other thing is, I would say to you, go and collect your eldest son and take him with you because it's a shame to waste two houses between you. His wife's lying upstairs. She's been beaten up, not in a natural way, but with a whip. He's flayed her nearly to death, and it isn't the first time. He found out she was leaving him and that's what he did.'

She watched his face stretch as he muttered, 'Sam! our Sam?'

'You can call him your Sam if you like, but he's not my Sam, he's a maniac, a sexual maniac. Like father like son, I would say.'

'Well don't!' he bawled at her now, his shoulders hunched. 'Don't you say that to me. Anyway you know it isn't true; I've . . . I've had one woman on the side, that's all, one woman.'

'Oh! Just one?' She nodded at him. 'Well, you should have known that just one would be one too many for me.'

He was glaring at her again, anger turning his face to a turkey red. His lips moved; he mouthed words that were soundless; and then he swung round and went out. From where she stood she saw his hand gripping the banister as he ascended the stairs.

Slowly she sat down on the couch. It was over. Her life was split in two. Why hadn't she battled with him? Why hadn't she thrown the things? She looked to the side of her, at the glass ash tray, then at the ornaments on the mantelpiece, at the two wine tables flanking the fireplace. She had thought when she came into the room earlier on that she would move all these small things in case she were tempted; then she had said to herself, 'No, leave them as they are; get through this last with a bit of dignity; take the wind out of his sails. He'll expect you to fly at him, swear, and throw things about. Don't let him see how deep the cut is, don't give him that satisfaction.'

Well, she had got it over with a certain amount of

dignity; but what satisfaction had she? God in heaven! What did satisfaction matter? She would have felt better if she had bawled him down, thrown every movable object in the room at him, marked him so that he'd have something to remember her by; but it was done now, done . . . quite done.

In less than half-an-hour he came downstairs again. She heard him slam the cases down outside the cloakroom door. When the front door banged the noise reverberated through the house. A few minutes later she heard the car start up and the revving was like that of a roaring motor cycle. She followed it round the drive, and down to the gate, then down the lane and on to the main road.

She was about to bow her head into her hands when she saw Elizabeth standing in the doorway in her dressing-gown looking piteously towards her. And now, a yell spiralling up from the depths of her, she screamed at her daughter, 'Get yourself away, out of me sight!' And Elizabeth, after one startled glance, turned and ran across the hall and up the stairs, whilst Maggie, her head and shoulders slowly drooping, fell forward on to the couch, and pressing her face into a cushion, let her pain flow from her like a torrent from a burst dam. All her past life, now in wreckage, was tossed and flung here and there, right back down the years to that day when she had come alive the day she had first set eyes on Rodney Gallacher.

CHAPTER THREE

THE CHASE

The following morning Elizabeth didn't go to school. Her eyes were red and she couldn't hide the fact that she had been crying; she had cried most of the night for her world, too, was shattered into fragments. The main catastrophe at the moment was the fact that her father had left her mother for another woman. She had stood on the stairs and heard all that had passed between them. She had known she shouldn't have been listening, but she had been unable to turn and fly to her room and bang the door on reality.

She couldn't believe that her dad had done this thing, because he was a lovely man, kind and generous. She loved her dad; she thought she loved her dad more than she did her mother. But no, no; at this moment her love for her mother was so deep, and the pain of it so awful as to be unbearable. Yet she knew that her pain was but a reflection of what her mother was suffering; she also knew she mustn't add to her sufferings, and so she must carry out her promise, she must see Peter today. She knew where he would be at a quarter-past six this evening, he would be going into the old school, where the boys' club was held.

She had passed the gates of the school twice and was on the point of retracing her steps for the third time when his car turned the corner and drew up to the kerb. Pushing his head out of the window, Peter called, 'Hello there.'

'Oh, hello.' She forced herself to smile at him, and she looked back into the eyes that were covering her face, her swollen lids, her puffed cheeks, and naïvely she said, 'I've got a cold.'

'Oh, that's bad; the summer ones are hard to get rid of. Been doing your rehearsal?'

'No, not today.'

'I'm just on me way to throwing me weight about again.' He laughed and nodded in the direction of the school, and she smiled and said, 'Oh yes, yes.' Then the smile slipping from her face, she bent down to him and asked softly, 'Can . . . can I come in for a minute?'

'Yes, yes, of course.' He leant over and opened the side door, then watched her walk round the bonnet of the car. His eyes were still on her when she took the seat beside him, but now her head was bowed and he asked, 'Is anything wrong?'

She raised her head slowly and looked at him. It was strange. She had known him for only a few weeks but she could talk to him freely, more than she could to anyone in the family, including her mother and Paul. 'Yes,' she said, 'things are very wrong at home. Everything . . . everything has happened at once.'

'I'm sorry to hear that.' He sounded sorry too.

And now for her piece. 'It . . . it appears.' She seemed to be searching for words. 'Well, the fact is my mother is going to be left alone. My dad, he's, he's gone . . . and it's worrying me because . . . well, you see I'm—' her head moved twice backwards and forwards '—I'm going into the convent . . . the Church, at the beginning of the year. I'm . . . I'm to be a nun, and she'll . . . she'll be left—' the last words trailed away '—alone, quite alone.'

She waited for him to say something: then her head still bowed she said, 'I should have told you before.'

'Oh.' His tone sounded airy, startlingly airy. 'I knew that's where you were for. Father Armstrong told me the first time I met him after that night.'

She was looking into his face, into his round kind face, into his round brown eyes, the eyes that she had looked into night and day for weeks past now, not being able to get their kindness out of her mind, and her chin wobbled slightly before she whispered, 'You knew?'

'Aye. Yes.'

She watched his adam's apple move up and down as he swallowed. His eyes held the same kindly expression, only deeper and more warm now. She wanted to hold her face in her hands, rock her body from side to side and cry and cry in an effort to erase not only the pain now, but the feeling of shame. He hadn't been thinking of her like that, it had all been in her own mind. He had just been acting kindly, you could say honourably, and she hadn't recognised it. After all, she didn't know many honourable men. Her father, Sam, they weren't honourable men; and Willie, with his pilfering, he wasn't an honourable man; perhaps Paul . . . she even had her doubts about Paul. But this man here, he had acted decently towards her, and all the while she had been reading something else into it, what her heart wanted her to read. She forced herself to mutter now, 'That's . . . that's all right then,' and he bent towards her and took her hand and asked quietly, 'It's what you want, isn't it?'

As she stared back into those eyes she couldn't bring herself to say 'Yes,' but she inclined her head, and at this he patted her hand gently and said, 'Fair enough.' Then he leant across her and opened the door and she swung slowly round on the seat and stepped out on to the road, and as she did so a car passed her. But she didn't notice the driver until it stopped a few yards ahead and the door burst open, and there stood Sam, looking as she had never seen him before, because their Sam always dressed smartly. But now he was wearing neither collar nor tie, his shirt neck was open, his black smooth hair was all tousled, his face was flushed like when he had been drinking a lot. However, it was his eyes that held the greatest difference; they were staring out of his head, thrusting forward, as were his head and shoulders.

As he made towards her, she sprang back into the car, shouting, 'Start up! Start up! Back it . . . back!'

'What!' Peter was answering her command automatically, at the same time repeating, 'What! What's up? Who's he?'

'Back quickly. It's my brother; he's, he's out of his mind.'

The car was moving swiftly backwards now towards the end of the road, and Sam was at the window running beside it, banging on it, shouting, 'Come out! Do you hear, Liz? Come out, you dirty young slut. Come out of that!'

When the car gathered speed he stopped, watched it for a moment, then raced back to his own car, by which time the taxi had turned about and was speeding down the main road.

'What's caused it?' Peter sounded as agitated as she was for from the glimpse he'd had of the fellow he could see he was wrong in the head, and though he wasn't afraid of any man, no matter how big he might be, maniacs were a different kettle of fish. What was more, she was scared to death.

He said now, 'Do you want to go home?'

'No! No!' She did not want to add fuel to the fires that were raging in the house by having him drive her up to the door, that was the last thing she wanted tonight, so she muttered as she looked through the back window, 'Drop me somewhere, a side road.'

They came to the traffic lights and, glancing through his mirror, he said, 'I don't think I'll be able to drop you without him coming up, he's only about four cars behind. What do you think I should do?'

So afraid was she now, she almost said, 'Go to a police station.' What she did say was 'Can you drive round by the docks? There are side streets there; you'll know your way better than him, you could dodge him.'

Yes, that was an idea. The lights changed and he spurted forward, overtook two cars, took a side turning to the High Street and went through the Market. Not being market day, there was little or no traffic in it at this time of night. Then he was making for the waterfront and the maze of small streets running off it. He knew what he would do; he'd turn down D'Arcy Street and on to the jetty that fronted Cowell's Warehouse – there'd be no boats unloading now and he'd have a straight run along the waterfront – and come up Ferry Street.

When he turned sharply into D'Arcy Street she cried out in alarm, 'Where are you going, the river's down there?' and he said, 'We can turn along the quay. I've been this way before.'

But when he came to the end of the street there, barring the entrance to the landing stage, was a great iron chain. It was attached at one end to a staple in the end wall of the warehouse and at the river edge was hooked to one of the timbers supporting the jetty. There were two boys sitting on the middle of it swinging back and forward and he wound down the window and yelled to them, 'Unhook the chain, lad, will you? I want to get along.'

'What do you say, mister?' They came to the window.

'Will you unhook that chain? I want to drive along there.'

'Along the quay, mister?'

'Aye. Yes.'

'The warehouses are all shut.'

'I know that. Here, do as you're bid.' He thrust his hand into his pocket, pulled out a shilling and handed it to the taller boy who was about twelve years old. 'Get going, quick.'

'Ta, mister. Ta.' They scampered across the jetty, but as they did so Sam turned the corner of the street.

Since the taxi was half slewed round it was Elizabeth who saw him first and she cried in deep agitation, 'Oh! Hurry, hurry; here's our Sam. Oh dear Lord! Oh dear Lord!'

Peter glanced to the side and saw the car bearing down on him and thought, if it's a show-down, it's a show-down. He had turned swiftly round again and had opened the car door when Elizabeth screamed, and his own loud cry joined with hers only a second later as he saw the bonnet of his car taking a nose dive over the end of the quay. Then he was falling forward with her clinging to him and her screams tearing through his head. As they plunged into the oily waters of the dock he thought, Why in God's name, why?

CHAPTER FOUR

REACTIONS

'It's as if we've been struck by lightning, everything's happened at once. I can't believe it, I can't take it in.' Helen looked around at them all gathered in the drawing-room, Willie and Nancy, Frances and Dave Walton, and her own husband, whom at this moment she was disliking wholeheartedly, and she finished, 'Where's it all going to end? That's what I'm asking meself, where's it all going to end?'

'I know where it's going to end for us.' Frances got to her feet; her face looked pinched and white. 'We're moving, we're getting out as soon as is humanly possible; I'm not going to go through this town with my head down to my knees for the rest of my life.'

'Well, if we all do that the boat will sink, won't it?' It was Nancy speaking, Nancy who was not supposed to have much up top.

Frances turned on her, her voice harsh. 'It's all right for you, Nancy, you're not of the family.'

'Well, I'll be damned!' Willie now reared upwards, pushing his hand through his hair. 'She's only me wife and she's not of the family!'

'You know what I mean, our Willie.'

'No, I don't. We're all in this, all concerned, every damned one of us.'

'I'll thank you not to say that I'm concerned with our Sam's goings on, nor with me dad's either, for that matter.'

'Sit down, sit down, and shut your mouth.' Dave Walton

tugged at his wife's arm, and Frances flopped down into a chair. But she would not be silenced and muttered now, 'And it caps all, our Paul and Arlette.'

'Now look.' Willie was pointing his finger at her. 'That was Sam's story. I know our Sam. He'll say anything at the best of times to put the onus on somebody else, but you're not going to tell me that our Paul didn't go into the Church because of Arlette. I tell you Sam was mad. He talked like a madman. And the night's business has proved it, hasn't it?'

'What about him writing the poetry then?'

'Oh that! Aye, well. By God! I'll have that out with him, see if I don't. "Fell off a lorry". The bloody nerve of him, spying. That's what it was, spying. And on his own folk at that. Aye by God! I don't know how I'll keep me hands off him . . . But the other business. No, I won't believe that. Why, he was all but a priest . . . An' don't tell me that priests are now campaigning to get married. I know all that. But they wouldn't be priests if they did, not to my mind they wouldn't.'

They were all silent now until Frances, her thoughts bursting from her again, cried, 'What was she doing in the taxi with that fellow anyway? She must have been up to something for Sam to chase them like that. Our Liz! I tell you it makes me mind boggle. If she doesn't go into the Church me mam will go mad.'

'If she dies she'll go madder.' They looked at Helen.

'Well, she's got a chance.' Willie's voice was quiet now. 'And it's thanks to that fellow, because if he hadn't dragged her out and held her up, an' that must have taken some doing in the condition he was in with her dead to the world, she'd have been a gonner in no time. And if those kids hadn't been there they'd both have been gonners.'

Helen began to walk about the floor now, shaking her head as she said, 'I wonder where he is?'

'We'll know soon enough; the police'll nab him.' Dave Walton stared towards the ceiling. 'Those kids were cute to take the number of the car.'

'What do you think they'll do to him?'

Dave Walton glanced at Helen who had stopped near the table, her joined hands pressed together between her breasts; then he lifted one shoulder and said, 'What do you think? Likely charge him with attempted murder?'

'My God!' Frances got up from her seat, and looking down on her husband she said, 'Come on, we'd better get back; I can't expect Mrs Denton to sit up all night with the children. Are you staying?' She turned to her sister, but before Helen had time to answer, Trevor Gillespie, his features more pinched, his manner more pedantic, his voice thinner than ever, said, 'We really must be making our way back too; I have to be at business tomorrow morning . . . '

Helen's voice now cut into his as she cried at him, 'Oh, for God's sake, Trevor!' She stared at him; then cried, 'Damn your business and Mr Pattenden! Tell him to go and stick it.'

'Hel-en!' The small thin body was straining upwards as he rose to his feet, and Helen cried back at him, 'Don't Hel-en me, not at this time. Go on home if you like, but I'm staying until Mam gets back from the hospital, if it's two o'clock in the morning, so there!'

'Very well, please yourself.' He walked out of the room, trying to keep his step steady. He would talk to her when he got her home. Yes, indeed he would talk to her. Damn Mr Pattenden she had said; and how he, in the depths of his being, damned him too! But Mr Pattenden had him trapped like a wild rabbit. The shop had been like a torture chamber yesterday and today. Helen's mother's affair – he didn't think of her now as Mam – was a joke being enjoyed by everyone in the town, and particularly by

Mr Pattenden. That piece in the *Saturday Evening Herald* headed 'Pygmalion Episode at Duke's Musical Evening' had set everyone in the town asking why and what, for the reporter hadn't gone into details such as names or described with any accuracy what had taken place, he had merely referred to a certain lady becoming disgruntled with His Grace and voicing her displeasure.

Who was she? and, what had she said? were the questions everybody was asking. And they soon got the answer. Gallacher, the contractor; it was his wife and she hadn't only bloodied the Duke, she had buggered him.

'No!'

'Yes!'

'What a lark!'

And those were the words Mr Pattenden had said to him. 'What a lark, Gillespie! So much for your folks consorting with the gentry, eh?'

He, like Frances, wouldn't be able to stand it, he'd have to get away from this town. He had had similar thoughts before, but Helen wouldn't leave the proximity of her family. That was the trouble with families like this one; when a bomb exploded under the parents everybody got splinters.

He was pleased with his simile. He shrugged himself into his coat and went out into the wet night thinking, I'll get away. We'll get away. I'll put my foot down, she'll have to come . . .

Frances said almost the same thing to her husband when she got into the car five minutes later; iterating her earlier statement, she said, 'We're getting out of this.'

'I've got a business don't forget,' he answered flatly; and to this she replied, 'You can travel to your business; we're getting out of this if it's only into Newcastle.'

He said spitefully now, 'I thought you had plans for taking over Savile House some time; and by the looks of things it'll soon be to let.'

'Don't be bitchy, Dave Walton,' she said.

He let out a deep sarcastic laugh. 'Bitchy, she says.' Then he set the car going . . .

Back in the room, Willie said to Helen, 'Look, I'll just slip Nancy home to see to the bairns, then I'll be back, I won't be twenty minutes.'

'All right,' she said dully. 'All right.'

So, ten minutes later when Maggie and Paul returned from the hospital, there was only Helen of all the family to greet them, and as she helped her mother off with her coat, she asked quietly, 'How is she?'

Maggie let out a long slow breath before she said, 'She'll survive.'

'And him?'

'He'll pull through an' all, with a bit of help.' As she went across the hall she asked, 'Where's Annie?' and Helen replied, 'She's in the kitchen, she was asleep. She's dead beat, she's never been off her feet.'

Maggie nodded, but when she entered the drawing-room she stopped and looked around her, then looked at Paul, for he too was surveying the empty room.

Sensing their feelings, particularly her mother's, Helen said apologetically, 'They had to go because of the bairns . . . and things, but Willie'll be back, he's just dropping Nancy. And . . . and I sent Trevor off because he's got to get up in the morning.'

Maggie moved her head twice up and down, then went heavily towards a chair and sat down.

'Can I get you something? A strong coffee?'

'No, a cup of tea, lass.'

When Helen had gone Maggie looked at Paul, who was standing now, his elbow on the mantelpiece, looking down on the bowl of flowers that filled the empty fireplace, and she said, 'What's hit us, lad?'

He turned his head slowly towards her. 'These things

happen, Mam. You can go on for years plain sailing, and then you run into a storm. These things happen.'

She shook her head slowly, took a handkerchief from her pocket and, wiping her mouth with it, said sadly, 'It's funny, but it all seemed to start with that invitation, and the climax came on the night, Friday night, and it's still going on. Arlette—' she paused '—your . . . your dad, and now Liz. And it isn't finished yet; when they catch him there'll be worse to come.' As quietly he replied, 'These things haven't just happened over the past days, or months. You know yourself, in . . . in all cases they've been brewing for a long time.'

'Aye, aye, you're right,' she said. 'We've all been blind, at least I have, as blind as a bat, stupid, gullible and blind.' Bitterness was in her voice now.

'This fellow,' said Paul, 'the taxi driver. Why was he with Liz? Or why was she with him?'

Maggie spread her handkerchief across her knees, pulling the edges straight, smoothing it as if it was important that all the creases should be levelled out, and then she said, 'She had promised me to tell him that she was going into the Church. He . . . Sam, he had seen them together. You heard him the other night, Friday night, afore I went out. I tackled her last night. She was upset, so upset that I thought there was more in it than she made out, and the irony of it is—' she closed her eyes and shook her head before ending – 'Father Armstrong told me the night that the young fellow knew all along she was for the Church, and that he was a good fellow and he had no intentions that way towards her. "Honoured her", was the term Father Armstrong used. But she, she had her own ideas about him, I'm sure of that.'

The door bell ringing startled them and Paul said, 'That'll be Willie back,' and she answered him, 'Willie wouldn't ring.'

'No, no, he wouldn't.'

She was on her feet now walking towards the hall and he followed her. Annie was coming from the kitchen, heavy-eyed as if she had just woken up, with Helen behind her, a tray of tea things in her hands.

It was Paul who opened the door and stared at the policeman and the plain-clothed man with him.

'Mr Gallacher?'

Paul inclined his head, then said, 'One of them. This is my mother.' He extended his hand towards Maggie, then said, 'Come in.'

When they entered the hall he did not ask what had happened, he left that to his mother, who, looking from the policeman to the plain-clothed man, said, 'Yes?' and the policeman moved his hat round between his hands before he spoke. 'We've bad news for you, Mrs Gallacher,' he said. 'We've found the car . . . and your son.'

She made two small assenting movements with her head then waited, and the policeman went on, 'We had been to the house, to the garage. It was empty. Then just half-an-hour ago a patrol car looked in. The garage was then locked where before it had been open; the car was inside, the engine still running, and . . . and I'm afraid your son is dead, Mrs Gallacher.'

For years afterwards, she denied to herself that the feeling she felt at that exact moment was one of deep pleasure, almost joy. As time went on she made herself look upon it as relief, but here and now there was this feeling that was telling her that the badness had gone out of her life, the wickedness, the perversion, the evil. When she trembled it was with remorse and fear of the feeling itself.

When Helen and Annie, one on each side of her, turned her about and helped her into the drawing-room, she really needed help for her legs were giving way beneath her. The feeling was still on her and her mind was gabbling, there would be no trial, her Elizabeth wouldn't have to go into court and face all that, and the business of her going to be a nun in the headlines . . . Then there was Arlette. She knew nothing about what had happened this night; she had slept most of the time since yesterday. Now she was free, no divorce court, no reporters, no muck spreading.

The feeling of release was so great that she felt it lifting her from the floor, and she heard Helen's voice from a distance saying, 'Look out! She's going to faint.' She had never fainted in her life before but she understood that when you did you were enveloped in an awful blackness. But this wasn't blackness, this was a peculiar kind of light, and gratefully she went into it.

CHAPTER FIVE

THE BRUSH OFF

Rodney sat facing Willie across the desk in his office, facing him but not looking at him. He had always been fond of Willie, more so than of Sam, perhaps because Willie's coming hadn't held a pistol to his head. But now his son's eyes were cold, condemning.

During the past two weeks or so when they had met Willie had hardly opened his mouth to him, and he had longed to explain and tell him how things were, that he hadn't wanted this to happen, that it just had and he couldn't do anything about it. He wanted to say to him that he was sorry for Maggie, deeply sorry, and that she had a case, oh yes, she had a case. He wanted to say that he knew he should have been back in the house shouldering the responsibilities for all that had happened. But he could say nothing of this because Willie's face wouldn't let him.

But he wanted to talk. Oh God! How he wanted to talk to someone, for not only was his home life shattered, but also there was something happening in his other life, the life in which his love was, that he couldn't understand, or, more to the point, didn't want to understand. And there was another thing, the firm. It seemed to be sliding away like quicksands beneath his feet.

He had imagined that, after that Friday night's business at the Duke's, his reaction in leaving home – they weren't to know he was ordered out – would have met with sympathy in some quarters, those that mattered anyway. But without anyone speaking about the affair openly to him he gauged that, instead of the episode being taken seriously, it was being treated as a huge joke; and there was even sly admiration for the perpetrator. Apparently Mrs Gallacher had voiced the opinion of many with regards to His Grace, and even His Grace himself, Rosamund had informed him, had laughed heartily over the matter. He had, she said, a rare sense of humour.

Public opinion might, he knew now, have kept to the level set by the Duke if it hadn't been for him giving Mrs Morland her notice from the flat.

After an uncomfortable night on the office floor and four lonely ones in an hotel he didn't see why this state of affairs should continue when there was the flat attached to his office.

But he reckoned without Mrs Morland's reactions. She was a dear friend of Rosamund de Ferrier and therefore, he thought, she would understand. But Mrs Morland didn't understand anything except the fact that because of the inconvenience she put up with in being turfed out every week-end she felt she more than earned her rent-free residence.

He hadn't realised the seriousness of his action until Rosamund had stormed in on him. And that was the word, for he had never seen her anything but calm before. On this occasion, however, she had gone for him in a way not far removed from that which Maggie would have used under the circumstances. Did he, she asked him, not know that Adelaide Morland was a spiteful bitch! Now their association would be passed on from one to another – as a deep secret of course. He was a fool! Did he not realise what a free flat meant to a widow with no means and expensive tastes?

There had been no sporting on the bed during that visit, and Friday night and Saturday night had both passed and she hadn't come. That was ten days ago. It felt like ten years. And the knowledge that the world of his business was being sucked away from under his feet seemed linked with her absence.

Willie was saying in a clipped, cold way, 'The Ratepayers Association have taken it up. There's another twenty-three houses affected on the Morley Estate, and they're in Bewlar Avenue now, not going straight across, but branching off. That could mean all that section, more than a third of the estate. The Chairman of the Association tells me that Redfern's coming out the day with the committee.'

His cheeks pushed up, bringing deep lines to the corners of his eyes. 'Redfern?'

Redfern was his friend, or had been. Redfern had pushed a lot of things through for him on the Council; if Redfern turned against him he could say goodbye to the Marina contract.

'There's something else you should know, you'll find it out sooner or later.'

'Well?'

'Sam had been fiddling on his own.'

'Sam!'

When, at the funeral, he had knelt in the chapel and watched the coffin disappearing through those curtains to meet total extinction he still couldn't believe that his son was capable of all the things that had finally brought him to his death. Sam who was always for a laugh. Sam who had always acted the goat and who, as Annie would say, was full of antrimartans. He himself didn't laugh easily, but at times Sam had caused him to double up with mirth; and all the time Sam had been odd, queer. It made you squirm deep inside to know you'd given birth to something like that.

'Well, go on,' he said.

'Riley came to me yesterday and asked if it would be the same arrangement as he had with Sam. I asked what that was, and he told me. For every ten lorry loads of sand and cement that were booked in only nine were delivered and they split the difference.'

On this Rodney bounced to his feet. 'What! Sam and Riley. You mean that they'd been doing me for . . . ?' His mind boggled as it groped at the amount that his son and the subcontractor had made out of him over the past years. He stood gripping the edge of the table. Sam, his own flesh and blood, who received twenty-five per cent of the profits of the whole concern, as did Willie. Most of his own profits were ploughed back, except the money needed to keep the house going and what was necessary for himself to keep up his position.

'Sam? The swine! But wait a minute.' He looked at Willie; then said slowly, 'But he'd be cutting his own throat in the end.'

'Aye, you might think so on the surface, but if you work it out you'll see different. He was getting his cut from the firm, yes, but you take the price of the load of one lorry in every ten and count that up for a week, just one week, and remember Riley was contracted for both sites, then divide it in half.' He paused. He was laughing. 'Talk about falling off a lorry!'

'What?'

'I said talk about falling off a lorry.'

Falling off a lorry? It went on all the time, high and low. He knew it went on among the sub-contractors; you had to keep your eyes on them, and that had been Sam's job. He had delegated more and more of that side of the work to him over the past years while he himself had supervised from the top level, thinking his main job now was to go out and mix, meet the men who would stand you in good stead when the votes were running thin on a wavering contract.

'Another thing.' Willie's tone was still chill. 'Just a small thing, but it might be the thin edge of the wedge. I passed

Bailey on my way here. He's always been very pleasant. We were on waving terms a fortnight ago, but the day he pretended he didn't see me . . . That's enough to be going on with I think.' He rose from his chair, looked hard at his father for a moment longer, then walked out without a so-long, a ta-rah, or a goodbye.

Rodney stood gripping the end of the desk. Bailey was a friend of Pearce, and they were both thick with de Ferrier, in fact they were the trio who, from behind cover, ran the town. He hadn't seen de Ferrier since the night of the Duke's party. Prior to this he had never minded meeting him, in fact inwardly he had enjoyed it, laughing to himself about making a monkey out of the white-faced, superior-acting nowt, as he termed him in his own mind. But now, although he hardly admitted it to himself, he was afraid of meeting him. De Ferrier, he knew, could break him; they, Bailey, Pearce and he together could break him into small pieces, strip him clean. If he didn't get the Marina contract, and if the Council stuck its heels in about the subsidence on the Morley Estate, and it became front page news – up till now the trouble had been given only brief notices near the back page – it would mean that the rest of the houses on the new estate adjoining Morley would stick. People weren't fools, they weren't going to buy houses where the walls were apt to split and the door joists come apart within weeks.

He sat down and groaned, and again he thought, God! If I had only someone to talk to, someone to go to; if only she would come . . . He couldn't go on like this, he couldn't, he'd have to phone her; if anybody could straighten things out she could. But he couldn't phone from here; there were those two back in the outer office who had ears like cuddies' lugs; he'd have to go into the flat.

He let himself out by a side door, went down the court-yard and unlocked the door of the flat. It was odd about the flat. Since he had lived in it he had come to dislike it heartily, even the sight of the bed did something to him. He sat down and picked up the phone and when he got through a polite voice with practised ease repeated the number, and he said, 'I would like to speak to Mrs de Ferrier.'

'Who's speaking please?'

'Oh.' His pause was accompanied by a jerk of his head. 'It's just a friend. I . . . I just want a word with her.'

'A moment, please.'

The minute sped to three minutes and then the same voice said, 'I'm sorry, Sir, Mrs de Ferrier is not at home.'

Again his chin jerked upwards. 'When will she be at home?'

'I . . . I couldn't say, Sir.'

He felt a blind anger rising in him. He could see her standing within arm's length of the phone, he could feel her, almost smell her; that scent she wore, that was like nobody else's. His voice was high when he answered, 'Tell Mrs de Ferrier that I will ring back in ten minutes' time,' and on this he banged down the phone, then sat punching one hand hard into the palm of the other.

Was she brushing him off? Was she telling him something? No, no; he would not, he could not allow himself to believe that. She was a bit scared about all the talk, that was all. Her scared! The thought brought him to his feet and he moved his body from side to side against the suggestion. The devil in hell couldn't scare her; she was the type that could freeze an opponent with a look. He stopped in his pacing. Was she freezing him? NO! NO! He brought out the words loud and definite. She was just angry with him for phoning the house. But didn't she realise that he would phone if she didn't come to him? Didn't she realise that he'd have to see her? It was ten days now since he had looked on her face, spoken to her, touched her, and although he told himself that he would want her all his life, he would never want her more than he had done during these past days.

Ten minutes later almost to the second he rang the house again, and her voice came immediately to him, 'Yes?'

'Oh, there you are.' He aimed to appear cool. 'I thought you'd taken a holiday.' He did not realise he was using the same tactics with her as Maggie had done with him.

'What is it you want?'

What did he want? He looked into the mouthpiece of the phone. What did he want? Then he said softly but grimly, 'That's a daft question isn't it, what do I want? I want to see you of course. Do you know it's over a week?'

She made no reply to this. Then her voice came to him just above a whisper, saying, 'I think it would be better for the time being if we leave things as they are.'

Again he was looking into the mouthpiece of the phone; and then he was bellowing. 'Now look here!' He gulped and his voice changed as if some of his vocal chords had been cut. Slowly and quietly now he said, 'Rosamund, look. I've got to see you, I'm . . .'

'I'm, I'm sorry but we are going away.'

'We are what!'

'It's . . . it's holiday time you know.'

He detected a lightness in her tone now as if she were discussing the weather.

'People do go away at this time of the year. We're going . . .'

'Look! Do you hear? Stop it, and listen to me! You're not going away, at least not before I see you. I'm coming over there.'

'Rodney!' The lightness was gone. 'I forbid you to come near the house.'

'You can forbid me nowt, nothing; I intend to see you.'

There was a blankness on the line and for a moment he thought she had cut him off; then her voice, as if it was coming through a thin reed pipe, said, 'I'll be there at seven o'clock.'

'You'd better.'

Just before he heard the phone click he thought he heard her say, 'How dare you!' but he wasn't sure. Yet, 'You'd better' must have sounded like a threat to her. He had forgotten he wasn't dealing with Maggie.

She arrived at seven. He opened the door of the flat as she stepped out of her car, and he held it wide as she passed him and went into the sitting-room. Then they were facing each other, three arms' length apart. No grabbing her to him now, no sudden pressure of her body against his, exciting him to a point of delicious delirium. Her face was whiter than usual, the grey of her eyes almost blue.

'Well? You wanted to see me?'

He remained quiet, staring at her. Some section of his mind was registering an odd thought; she was speaking to him like an upstart mistress would to a servant. She reminded him for a moment of that woman on Brampton Hill years ago. They were building an extension to her garage and she came and looked up at him and said, 'Kindly stop that whistling, it's irritating.' And he remembered he had stood with the trowel in his hand and watched her walk across the garden and into an arbour, and it was all he could do to restrain himself from sending a full-blooded mouthful after her.

There was a sickening sensation churning in his bowels now. He said slowly, 'Yes, I wanted to see you; we've met before, remember me?'

'Oh Rodney!' She turned her head to the side but remained standing where she was. 'Don't be childish. Must one spell things out for you?'

'Spell things out?'

'Yes, spell things out.' She was looking at him again, her eyelids blinking rapidly now, some of her coolness gone, her thin chin wobbling slightly. 'We've . . . we've been very happy, but all good things must come to an end. That's a platitude, but it's true. And when all's said and done you've only got yourself to blame for the abrupt termination of our friendship. You should never have turfed Adelaide Morland out of here the way you did; she can be a very good friend but an equally bad enemy.'

The sick feeling in his stomach was increasing; added to this he suddenly felt gauche, as if the veneer he had laid on himself over the past few years was rapidly slipping off him, as if his body had been covered with an extra strong paint remover, and he was back where he was at the beginning of things, a big brash young fellow who talked loudly, acted quickly, pushed, and greased palms, but a big young fellow who never grovelled. He had never grovelled in his life to man or woman, and what he should be saying to himself now was he wasn't going to start at his age. But this woman was in his blood as Maggie had never been. Maggie had been forced on him, but this woman here had burst into his life like a meteor and he had reached out and caught her and held her, and lost himself in her dazzling brightness. And she had loved him, she still loved him . . . Loved him? Could he remember her ever saying she loved him? That was beside the point. Her every reaction to him had translated her love. You could say in a way that she had translated it through many different languages; she had even taught him things he didn't know, and he'd thought he was wide in that way. But you lived and learned. Aye, you lived and learned.

But there was one thing he didn't want to learn at this moment, in fact he refused to recognise what was staring him in the face.

He went towards her, holding out his hands as if in supplication, and said, 'Rosamund, look I'm free, we're separated. I . . . I've fixed her up. She's all right. I've got nothing on me conscience, she'll give me a divorce presently, I know she will. You can have it any way you like.'

'Oh, please! Please!' She was stepping back from him, her head bowed but swinging from shoulder to shoulder. If he had been a strange man and was exposing himself to her she couldn't have shown more distaste, and this got through to him and he yelled, 'Look! Stop playing games with me. We've been at it for the last eighteen months, remember? You've been my mistress. And when I took you up I wasn't just some second-rate citizen, I was Rodney Gallacher, the contractor, the big contractor, working over two counties. True, you fiddled for me and I was grateful.' He paused before saying, 'In more ways than one.' But he didn't add 'You saw you had it in cash and not in cheques.' A lightning thought at this moment sweeping through his tormented brain yelled in an aside, 'Aye, a hundred pounds at a time for her nicknacks, and if you managed to remember a card on Maggie's birthday you thought that was enough.'

The look on her face cut off his tirade. He watched her hitch her handbag further up on her arm before she said, 'We're leaving tomorrow for France. After that we're going on to Spain and Portugal. We may be away six weeks to two months. When . . . when we return you'll likely be in a different frame of mind, and by that time also you'll no doubt have seen that what I am doing now is the most sensible thing for both of us.'

When she went to walk past him he thrust his arm out and grabbed her wrist and she became still; and once again he was pleading, 'You can't drop me like this, I need you; I need you in all ways, in all ways. Don't you understand?'

She was looking at him almost pityingly now and for the first time her voice held a tender note as she said, 'I'm doing everything for the best, Rodney, believe me. Taking Roger out of the way you'll have one less to contend with. He's a power behind the scenes is Roger, you know that. He's already seen to it that you won't get the Marina contract. I would suggest that you go quietly for a time, put the houses right on the Morley Estate, and keep your eyes open for Redfern, Pearce and Bailey.' She now looked down at his hand that had become limp on her wrist, and when it dropped away she said quietly, 'Goodbye, Rodney.'

He made no reply, he just stood there with an agony in him as if he had been disembowelled.

CHAPTER SIX

THE GIVING OF A DAUGHTER

She sold the house as it stood for twenty-two thousand pounds because, she said to Annie, she was taking nothing out of this old life into the new.

She had more money now than she had ever had in her life before, or ever thought to have. When Rodney had made money her share of it had been new carpets, curtains and furniture, but he had never given her any money for herself besides the housekeeping. He hadn't been stingy with that, but she wasn't one to skimp here and there in order to line her own pockets. When she needed clothes she would tell him so, and he would say, 'Well, go and get what you want,' which she did, but it was always third-rate stuff, at least compared with the other wives of big business men in the town. But now she hadn't only the twenty-two thousand pounds for the house, she had the rent from the flats in the two houses in Milden Place, and the rents came to close on thirty pounds a week.

He had been generous at the last, giving her the three houses. She supposed she had Paul to thank for that, for he had done the bargaining: for an empty life – payment, three houses.

The day after tomorrow they'd all be gone, separated for good. Arlette, Paul and Lizzie were going out of her life as irrevocably as Rod and Sam had gone. Aye, and Frances and Dave, because her snooty daughter had moved into Newcastle only last week, Helen and Trevor had been gone this past month to Hexham. It had all been too much for that little upstart, Trevor. Now there were only Willie and Nancy left, and in the bungalow where she was going to live she would be at one end of the town and they at the other.

But these last separations had all been quiet, without heartbreak, unlike the one this afternoon when Liz went in. But in a way she'd be glad when Liz was safely tucked away, locked away, for she weighed heavy on her conscience. If she hadn't made her promise to tell that young fellow her intentions none of this would have happened, at least they wouldn't have been thrown into the river and Sam wouldn't have died . . . But there, God's ways were strange.

Elizabeth's presence had tormented her since she had come out of hospital for she neither smiled nor laughed any more. Of course one didn't expect her to laugh under the circumstances, though a smile now and again would have been in order, but her face was set like a marble statue in a church. Indeed sometimes she put her in mind of such an effigy for she looked like someone already dead.

She had said to Father Armstrong, 'Ask her if she is sure, if her mind's still that way,' and he replied, 'She's sure.'

She shouldn't have been going in until the beginning of next year but she had asked to be taken in earlier. She had not returned to school after the holidays and her days were spent in helping Annie, or sitting in her room reading, reading the lives of the saints, the gospels, the tortures that the martyrs underwent. When Maggie looked at these books she shook her head and said to herself, Oh my God! But didn't know exactly why she was saying it, only that she thought, She's so young for all this.

Then tomorrow, Arlette was leaving. She was going off with Paul, and it didn't seem right. It was right that she should marry again, but she wasn't going to marry Paul, at least not yet she said; the very thought of marriage terrified her. At first she was going off on her own just as she had intended doing on that fateful Monday morning, but Paul had apparently worn her down. He was persistent was Paul; if he had been as persistent in his vocation he would have been a priest by now. That's what she thought was wrong about it, about them, for in her mind he was a priest, he simply hadn't taken the vows that's all. She had said as much to him just the other day, and he had come back with arguments that baffled her. He had wanted her to believe that his leanings towards the Church had come about because he was fascinated by the paraphernalia of the services, drugged by the incense, the Latin, and the holiness he attributed to all priests. He had said that if he'd had a real vocation the love of a woman would have appeared as merely a temptation set by the devil, and he would have had the strength to conquer it.

She looked round the room at the open cases and the blue velvet dress and coat lying on top of the largest one. She had never thought to see the coat again, and she had never wanted to see it again, but it had arrived the morning following the night when Rod had left the house, or, as she reminded herself when her ego was at its lowest, the night she had thrown him out. Anyway, the coat had arrived neatly packed, addressed to Mrs Gallacher, Savile House, The Rise, Felburn, nothing else. She had thought, I'll give it away. But who would she give it to? It would fit no-one in her family and she knew no-one outside that it would be of any use to either. Who did she know who would wear a thing like that unless they were going to a fancy dress ball or . . . a duke's musical evening?

She went out of the room and was crossing the landing to the bathroom when she saw Arlette and Paul in the hall below. They had just come in and they looked up towards her and Paul said, 'We're back.'

She nodded at them, then went on to the bathroom.

In the hall Arlette looked at Paul, then bowed her head and walked down the short passage to the morning-room, and there she turned swiftly to him and said under her breath, 'Paul, she's upset. I think you should stay with her, at least for a time. I've told you I'll be all right.'

Gently now he took her by the shoulders and he stared into her face for some seconds before he spoke. Then, his tone low and urgent, he said, 'Arlette, Arlette, we've been over this. I'm not staying with her. Anyway, there are only two bedrooms in the bungalow.' He closed his eyes and shook his head. 'I know I could get a flat, but I'm not going to. It's arranged, isn't it? It's arranged the way we want it. Anyway, darling, darling, don't you realise that nothing or no-one can keep us apart now? If—' he just prevented himself from saying, 'If I gave up God for you then I can give up my mother' '—if you never marry me,' he went on, 'it won't matter as long as I can be with you. And—' he moved his head slowly – 'you don't want anyone else.'

She stared lovingly back into his face. Then she said, 'She's shocked in so many ways. She's shocked because . . . because you love me, but more so I think because I . . . we're going to live together. She can't understand why, if I care for you, I can't marry you, at least, not . . . not yet.' This fact also shocked some part of herself and once more she asked the question why, if she loved him, she wouldn't agree to marry him. And although the answer was in her mind she would not let it have voice, she would not say, 'In him runs the same blood as in Sam.' Sam was loving and tender once, but marriage, like the breaking of a spell, had ripped the outer skin off him and showed the wild beast. She couldn't risk that again. If, she reasoned, she found after living with Paul they weren't suited – she used this term to replace the one that spelled out 'unnatural traits' – then he had no power to hold her, she would not have to endure torture a second time. She knew now her brain would never withstand another Sam, she'd become demented. She had thought amid the long silence following that terrible morning that she was going into madness and the horror of it was still on her. No, she could not risk a second Sam and only time would prove what her heart kept telling her, that Paul was no Sam.

Anyway, living with Paul or marrying him, staying in Felburn or leaving it, the family was no more, for from Willie down to Lizzie they were condemning her. At first, each of them had had difficulty in accepting the fact that Sam had been abnormal. Even when he had tried to kill Lizzie and Mr Portman, not one of them would totally accept that anyone in their family could be capable of behaviour that stemmed from madness.

But as she had struggled back from that terrible borderland over which Sam had tried to thrust her, their concern for her seemed to prove that they did believe what their brother had done, and had been doing for years before their mother had witnessed it. But this attitude lasted only until they knew for a certainty that Paul, their reserved brother, their aloof brother, their brother who wouldn't soil his hands accepting nicked goods, was proposing to go off with her, live with her. The very fact that he had always been in love with her seemed to them to be something more dirty than any act Sam had ever perpetrated. In fact their sympathy swung back to Sam, and she knew they were now saying among themselves that perhaps Sam had had cause after all for the way he had acted. Lesser things than that had turned a man's brain.

Of them all, she knew that Willie was the most bitter against Paul, and she guessed it wasn't simply because Paul was going away with her but because, as Willie had said, Paul had downed his own, he had gone behind their backs and shown them up in the paper.

The lines, 'They fell off a lorry', had stung him and the fact that Paul was the writer, Lacker, had roused his hatred and he wouldn't come near the house if he thought Paul was in.

Truly the family had broken up, but what hurt her most was the break between herself and Maggie.

She leant her head against Paul and relaxed in the gentle pressure of his arms. The die was cast; she was about to start a new life; as Paul was . . . as Lizzie was . . . as Mam was.

And Dad? No-one mentioned Dad; it was as if he too had died and was buried.

Two o'clock that afternoon Maggie went with Elizabeth to the convent. She had been in the convent a number of times before, at least in the school side of it. She had laughed with the nuns, even joked with them, but had always sat mute before the Mother Superior.

Today she went across a courtyard, down a long stone corridor to a part that she had never seen. A smiling nun opened a door to them and welcomed them, then led the way to a sparsely furnished room and asked them to wait, and they were left sitting looking at each other.

There was an indescribable pain in Maggie's heart. She had experienced all kinds of pain during the last three months but this was like nothing she had experienced before. She put her hand out and gripped her child's, because that's all she was, this tall, thin wisp of a girl, she was a child, but seventeen, she mightn't know her own mind. She said in a low rush, 'Liz, listen to me. There's still time. I . . . I won't mind, honest to God I won't mind if you don't want to go through with it. I'm telling you . . .'

Elizabeth looked back at her mother with dry eyes. That was another strange thing about her, since the accident she hadn't cried, she who was given to tears; any hurt, any sadness penetrated the thin skin to the sensitiveness below, and the tear ducts responded. That was until she awakened in hospital to find herself still alive. It was in the middle of the night when a nurse came to her and she had asked her, 'Is he dead?' and the nurse had tucked the sheet around her chin and answered, 'No, dear, he's all right.' And she had gone to sleep knowing that there was nothing more to cry for.

She said now to Maggie, 'It's all right, Mam, don't worry, this is what I've got to do.' Her face was straight, unsmiling, not sad, not happy, a neutral look, an unreal look.

Maggie sat back in her seat and said, 'Oh, lass! Oh lass!'

The nun came back into the room and led them down another corridor and into another room, and there was the Mother Superior, who took Elizabeth's hand and smiled at her and drew her to her side, drew her into another world, leaving Maggie in this one, staring dumbly at her daughter and regretting with every fibre in her that she had let the last comfort in her life go, for she knew that if she had pressed her earlier Elizabeth would have stayed with her. She could have convinced her that her own need at this time was greater than God's.

She was never to remember what the Mother Superior said to her, she only knew that Elizabeth kissed her and clung to her. Then she was walking blindly back down the corridor, out of the grey stone house, across the courtyard, through the school and into the street; and she was alone as she had never been in her life before.

Part Five

CHAPTER ONE

THE NEW LIFE

She had been in the bungalow six weeks. After the house it appeared to her like a little box, but this she didn't mind, she wanted to be enclosed. She wished a dozen times a day, and most of the long nights, that she were enclosed for ever in a box, not feeling, not thinking, not remembering.

Willie and Nancy came to see her, as they had always done, on a Friday night, but things weren't the same because she wasn't the same. And they weren't the same, at least Willie wasn't. Willie was solemn now, quiet, different.

Frances had been over from Newcastle to see her twice. Dave hadn't come with her. Frances had made her uneasy, especially on her last visit ten days ago, for then she had hinted at more trouble to come. But what more trouble could befall them? They could die, each and every one of them, but at this time she didn't look upon dying as trouble, only as release.

Helen had written every week from Hexham. Both Trevor and she had got work, but Trevor wasn't happy . . . Trevor would never be happy, Maggie thought, unless he won the pools. Then he would go headlong to hell.

She'd had one letter from Paul and one from Arlette. They had obtained a flat in Kingston and Paul had started teaching in a secondary modern school, and Arlette was taking languages at a college of further education. Both the letters said they were thinking about her and would like to see her; would she consider coming down to see them for a holiday, there was a spare room?

Such was her make-up that she would as soon have thought of taking a holiday in a brothel as she would of staying in a house where her son was living with a woman he wasn't married to. She told herself she wasn't narrow, but she couldn't face that. Yet, at the same time, she asked herself, would she have thought it so wrong if Willie, Dave Walton, or Trevor Gillespie were in a similar situation? Her answer to this was that her Paul was none of the others, he had been and still was somebody different, special – he had almost been a priest.

She had dreaded New Year's Eve because New Year's Eve was a time when they had all been together. There had never been a New Year since she was married when she had been separated from one of her children . . . or her man. Even during the war. He could have been called up in '43 when he was eighteen, but he had been working in munitions. And then he had got out of his National Service too.

No, they had never been separated until now, and she didn't know how she was going to get over this day, particularly the night. But yes she did. That's why she had got the hard stuff in. Two or three glasses of hard stuff, a bottle of beer or so, a glass of wine, she'd be out like a light, the mixture would see to that. Tomorrow she'd have a head like nobody's business; but tomorrow would take care of itself, she had to take care of tonight.

She was expecting Willie, Nancy and the children this afternoon. They were coming for tea after they had done their shopping. There had been no mention of their staying to see the New Year in.

But it was around eleven in the morning when Willie came in the back door. She was standing in the little kitchen with Annie, and Annie was saying for the hundredth time since they had come to the bungalow, 'Talk about swinging a cat! Take a deep breath and you'll bounce off the walls.' They both turned and looked at Willie, and after a moment's pause Maggie said quickly, 'What's the matter, you under the weather?'

'Aye, I suppose you could say that.'

'I've just made some tea,' said Annie; 'it's bitter out. Or would you rather have coffee?'

'Anything, anything,' he said walking past her and into the eighteen by twelve foot room, which served as both dining- and sitting-room.

When Willie stood with his back to the fire, his hands on his buttocks, his palms outwards to the flames, his eyes cast down looking at the hearth-rug, she said, 'What is it now?'

'You might ask!' He raised his eyes to hers. His face looked drawn, old, like that of a man over forty and he'd only had his twenty-sixth birthday last week. He said now slowly, 'I should have told you afore. If I'd had my way I would have, but he said no. Well, now he can hide it no longer.' He paused. 'We're going bankrupt.'

She lowered her chin downwards and to the side while still keeping her eyes tight on his. She didn't repeat, 'Bankrupt? Is that what you said, bankrupt?' She had heard aright, he was going bankrupt. She didn't think either of Willie standing there miserable or of Dave Walton – who, although not a partner, had his livelihood tied up with theirs – but at this particular moment she thought of Rodney, and being Maggie, Mam, the mother, no matter what her previous attitude had been, she should have become overwhelmed by compassion for this terrible misfortune. That it was a terrible misfortune, she was fully aware, if not totally for Willie, then for his father, the man who had put that long ladder up against the towering battlements of Felburn society and, rung after rung, had grappled his way up it, until when he reached the top he had picked from that society a woman . . . a lady, and kicked aside the one still holding the bottom of the ladder steady for him.

'MAM!'

When her head went back and there issued from her lips a rumbling chuckle like an echo coming up from a deep well and, her mouth wide, her tongue wagging, she laughed, Willie again exclaimed, as if in horror, 'Mam!' But she continued to laugh, and the sound closed her ears to something Annie was saying as she stood within the doorway, the tea tray in her hand. She laughed until Willie's voice penetrated her unholy joy as he bawled, 'FOR GOD'S SAKE, MAM!'

As her laughter subsided she passed her hand over each cheek and wiped the tears away, and Willie said in a trembling voice, ' 'Tisn't like you; you were never the one to hold spite, or be vindictive.'

'No.' She was still shaking with her mirth as she sat down by the side of the table and supported her head in the palm of her hand, and she repeated, 'No, I was never the one to be vindictive, but times have changed, lad, times have changed.' She took out her handkerchief and wiped her face, then said, 'Well, go on; I'm listening.'

'If this is going to be your attitude I want no more of it.'

'Don't worry, I've had me fun. When did it happen?'

He took the cup of tea from Annie's hand and helped himself to four teaspoonfuls of sugar before he said, 'These things don't just happen, they cover time, a long time. It was the Morley Estate that was the final blow. But we've been having trouble on the Rollingdon one for the past year or more, slacking, thieving, stuff being nicked. It was the ganger there who was the trouble, but the men were for him and we couldn't do much about it. But . . . but we would have weathered the lot if Dad could have extended his loan. He went to three banks; they all said no.'

He now banged the cup down on to the corner of the table and the tea splashed upwards and into the saucer and on to the fancy cloth. He did not apologise but turned away and marched to the window and back again, his fist clenched and wagging before his face as if threatening himself. Then he ground out between his teeth, 'That bloody woman! That bloody bitch!'

On this Annie turned and walked into the kitchen, and Maggie waited for him to go on. When he didn't, she forced herself to ask, 'What's she got to do with this?'

'What's she got to do with it?' He looked at her over his shoulder. 'What hasn't she got to do with it! Everything, every damn thing; or at least her man has. There's different ways of killing a cat besides drowning it. You can choke it for instance, and that's what he's done to us; he's choked every avenue that would have been of help. And the others are like a lot of sheep. No—' he made a spitting movement with his mouth '—rats! When she showed she wasn't having anything more to do with Dad now that things had come into the open they scuttled from him just like rats from a sinking ship.'

She was staring at the back of his head as he stood looking down into the fire and she made herself ask, 'When did she leave him?'

He turned and looked at her, then said quietly, 'Almost straight after he left home; she was one of those who didn't mind an affair on the side, but nothing must sully the name of de Ferrier. I know Dad's acted like a swine, and I was for killin' him meself, but she was a clever woman. She's been clever for years along that line. One of the things he's had to suffer is the knowledge that Pearce and Bailey were his predecessors; the difference was, they were sensible, they didn't want to make an honest woman of her, so to speak, and so everything was cushy and comfortable, and they got positions where they could call the tune. Second fiddles to her man perhaps, but nevertheless they were kept in the orchestra . . . and what they play this town dances to. My God! the things I've learned recently . . . And then our Paul. That bloody snot writing to the papers about falling off a lorry. A few pairs of stockings, socks, a jumper, he would have exposed me and all of us for that, while at the same time there were things going on in this town on the council and in every blooming tin-pot industry you could mention, trickery and wangling, thousands changing hands, and them getting medals pinned on them for it . . . God Almighty! And they say the tax men are cute. Blind, bloody blind the lot of them.'

She now made another laughing sound but kept it in her throat. It was funny how her mind was working these days. She was thinking that here was their Willie yelling about the tricksters yet it wasn't only the day or yesterday that he had been aware of this, for he and his Dad and the firm had done their share of it, thrived on it in fact. She remembered the presents, the money presents. Fifty pounds. One time it was a hundred that Rod had forked out, and you didn't give presents like that if you didn't expect something in return, and not little things at that . . . And then that bit he had said earlier on about the men thieving on the Rollingdon Estate. When he did it himself it was fiddling, when other people did it it was stealing.

She, too, had learned a lot lately, perhaps because she'd had time to think. And now she had something to think about, he had gone bust. Well, well! The big fellow had gone bust, and here was she with more money than she knew what to do with. After she had paid for the bungalow she had put eighteen thousand into building societies at five per cent, and this was to bring her in nine hundred pounds a year. Just think of it!

As if Willie had gauged her thoughts, he said, 'You must give him credit for one thing, he saw you all right first.'

'So he should.' She was on the defensive now.

'I'm not saying he shouldn't, but I'll tell you this. He hung on until the two houses were fixed for you. I mean the deeds through and everything settled because if he hadn't they would have been swallowed up an' all.' He could have added, ' . . . but they'd have cut down his losses.'

She asked now, 'What's he down?'

'A hundred thousand or so.'

'My God! A hundred thousand.'

'It's nothing, it's not much, taking everything into consideration. If we'd had a break he'd have weathered it. There's forty houses almost completed on the Rollingdon end, and they would have been done if it hadn't been for those blasted lazy swine. Yet they're not the stumbling block, it's de Ferrier, the pasty-faced bastard!' He was marching up and down again. 'Can't keep his wife so he . . . ' He stopped suddenly and swung his head downwards. Then, after remaining silent for a moment or so, he looked at her again and said, 'Some New Year.'

She wet her lips, one over the other, before she asked, 'What are you going to do?'

'Oh.' His body slumped, and he answered, 'Start again, I suppose.'

She went up to him now and said softly, 'There's eighteen thousand in the building societies, you could get going on that.'

'What!' He drew his head away from her as if she was aiming to strike him. 'Ah, Mam.' He gave a shaky laugh. 'Do you know what you're saying? Do you want him to lay me out? Because that is what would happen if I touched a penny of it. But . . . but thanks all the same.' He put his hand out and took hers, and said again, 'Thanks. I won't forget that you offered it, but knowing the struggle he's had to keep them at bay until the deeds of those flats came back, aw my! And you know something else? I think the fact of you knowing about this has affected him more than the town's reaction.'

'It would, wouldn't it?' she said with bitterness in her voice now. 'The big fella. The big head gone bust. He wouldn't want me to know that. He wouldn't want to give me the chance to gloat.'

'You're not gloating, are you, Mam?' It was a soft enquiry and she lowered her eyes and stared at the floor before saying, 'I don't know.' Then, 'Yes, I do,' she said. 'I'll tell no damned lie about it. I'm shoutin' inside meself, "Serve him damned well right, it's justice." One doesn't often live to see justice done, but in this case I have.'

He took his hand from hers now and, walking from her, said, 'Aye, I suppose so; but if we all got our deserts I wonder where we'd land up?'

'Willie.' He turned to her again.

'I . . . I can't help being bitter. He . . . he brought me low; he made me feel like nothing; scum; he said I was a big fat ignorant slob. I never felt a big fat ignorant slob until then, and since . . . well, I haven't seen meself as anything else.'

He came swiftly back to her and, putting his arm around her, kissed her, and his voice was thick as he said, 'You're my mother, and I've always thought you one of the best. Happy New Year, Mam.' He kissed her again, then turned quickly away and left her with the tears pouring down her face.

The church bells were ringing in the New Year, the hooters were blowing; in the town there would be people dancing round the old Memorial all singing and cheering, but here, in the living-room of the end bungalow, in The Crest, Balham Road, there was no sound except when they put their glasses back on the table. As the last echo of the church bells died away they looked at each other but didn't wish a Happy New Year.

When Maggie began to cry she pushed the tears from her cheeks with the side of her thumb, and the whimpering sound in the back of her throat changed to laughter and she said, 'Drink up, Annie. Drink up.'

They had been drinking more or less steadily since eleven o'clock. Maggie had had two glasses of whisky, a pint bottle of Guinness and two glasses of wine, and now as she sipped at her third glass of whisky her laughter mounted. Swaying forward, she leant across the little table towards Annie to where, glassy-eyed, she sat lost in the armchair, and said, 'You know what I'm thinkin', Annie? You know what I'm thinkin' about at this minute? . . . The party, the musical soirée.'

'No! Maggie.'

'Aye. Aye, I am, Annie. I'm right back there, an' I can even feel me damn corn givin' me gyp.' She sagged downwards and pressed the top of her slipper. 'And remember the way I was got up, Annie? Did you ever see anybody got up like me?'

'Never, Maggie, never.'

'And think what I spent, think of that money. A hundred and seventy-five pounds!' She drained her glass, then half filled it again from the bottle to her hand. 'And those creeps on the platform. He played like this, Annie. Look; look, this is how he played.' She pushed some of the bottles aside, almost upsetting them; then using the table as an imitation piano she bent her body over it and waved her hands wildly up and down. 'Tha's . . . tha's how he played, Annie . . . just like that.' Again she gave a demonstration. Then leaning back in her chair, she now cried, 'And the fellow with the cello, the blown up fiddle. Squawk, squawk, squawk.' Her knees wide apart, she was

239

now imitating the cellist. Then staggering to her feet, she struck a pose and on a high and full throated note she burst into song. But what she sang in imitation of Madam Craig was O Salutaris.

'O Salutaris Hostia, quae coeli panis ostium; Bella premunt hostilia. Da robur, fer auxilium.'

Her Latin was pronounced as she had learnt it at school. It would have made a Latin master cringe, and the fact that she was caricaturing the singer yet using the hymn that opens the Benediction, would, at any other time, have appeared as sacrilege to them both. But now Annie was rolling in her chair.

Following this, she started a perilous parade up and down the room. Strutting between the furniture, she demonstrated how different people she could remember from that evening had walked and talked. Then bending over Annie's chair, she laughed down at her as she cried, 'There was one snotty-nosed piece – you know the type, you see them in the magazines – when she opened her mouth you'd think she had a lump of paste in it. Honest, honest to God. And him, him the Duke, weak-kneed little squirt, he talked to her an' called her Ida.' She now did a jig, singing, 'Ida, Ida, aren't you a little snider.' Then stopping abruptly, the laughter leaving her she said, 'You know what, Annie? The mornin', I'm goin' to sit down an' I'm goin' to write to him. Duke or no Duke . . . I am, I am.'

Annie flapped her hand at her and spluttered, 'You'll have to learn to spell, Maggie.'

'I can spell when I want. Don't you forget it. Oh—' she backed away and flopped into her seat, '—if ever there was a snobby snot, he was one. But I told him, didn't I, Annie? I told him. I told him what he was. By God! I did.' She now became quiet and, her head moving slowly from side to side and her voice changing, she muttered thickly, 'But . . . but I should never have done it, Annie, should I?

I should never have done it. I let meself down a ton. An' not only me, but Rod. He's no good is Rod, he's a nowt, a nowt; but I let him down, an' I let meself down. Aye . . . ' She pulled herself forward on to the edge of the chair and, putting her elbows on her knees, she dropped her face into her hands and now her whole body gave one great heave before the tears burst from her eyes and an agonised sound was wrenched up from the tormented depths of her being, and came out through her mouth in a prolonged wail, which finally broke itself up in disjointed words. 'Liz. Our Liz. In there, for life. Loved that bloke, she did, she did. Liz. Aw Liz.'

'Don't, Maggie.' Annie was standing wavering in front of her. 'Come on to bed, lass. Come on to bed. Forget about it. Come on an' sleep it off. You can't better none of it. Come on, come on, lass.'

It was a good five minutes later when Annie got her up out of the chair, and erratically they made their way to their rooms, Annie to fall into a dead sleep almost straightaway, Maggie to lie fully dressed on the bed alternately crying and dozing until the early morning.

The drinking bout on New Year's Eve began a pattern for Maggie. The hangover Annie had on New Year's Day deterred her from further indulgence; she might have a glass of gin or a bottle of beer in the evening but that was as far as she would go. Not so Maggie; each evening now she would sit late by herself drinking, drinking and thinking. But she no longer cried. Sometimes she would not rise in the morning until eleven o'clock, and as the weeks went on she was no sooner out of bed than she was longing for the night to come when she could have a drink.

She did not drink during the early evening in case anybody should drop in, though few dropped in now. Willie and Nancy brought the children every Saturday.

241

They were now living in Gateshead where Willie had been fortunate enough to get a start as a costing clerk with a building firm. Some weeks he would drive over of an evening by himself. It could be any evening, and so she never started to indulge until about nine o'clock. But one evening he came at half-past nine, by which time she was starting on her third whisky. She hadn't time to hide the evidence before he was in the room, and he looked hard at her for a moment. She made an effort to pull herself together and talk about the things they usually talked about, the bairns, their school, Nancy coping in a small flat, and the awful weather. But this night the whisky had brought down her guard and all of a sudden she said, 'Where is he?'

'Dad?'

She didn't answer but continued to stare at him; and then he said, 'I don't know. After the business of the Official Receiver was over he said he was moving out. He wouldn't tell me where he was making for. They would likely know, he'd have to leave an address, but I didn't pry. He . . . he wants to be left alone . . . Why do you ask?'

'Why do I ask?' Her voice was thick. 'Well, you'd ask after a mangy dog wouldn't you, if you'd once fed that mangy dog? Stands to reason.'

'Would you have him back?'

She almost sprang out of her chair and her voice was loud. 'No, begod! No, not if he was dying. Have him back after having her on the side for years! What do you think I am? I might be a big fat ignorant slob but somewhere in all this bulk—' she thumped her stomach '—is a little bit of pride, just a little bit, and I'm going to hang on to it. Have him back you say!'

He had left almost immediately after this but before leaving the room he had looked at the bottle and said,

'I'd go careful on that if I were you, it leads nowhere but downwards.'

Two days later Frances had come to see her. She had not remarked upon her changed appearance but her look had been plain enough. It said, 'You have let yourself go, haven't you?' She didn't like their Frances, that was another thing she had learnt . . .

It was a bitter snowy night towards the end of February. She was sitting before a blazing fire that could not warm her, for she was shivering inside, waiting for the moment when Annie would go to bed and she could take a drop. Not that Annie didn't know that she was indulging, but somehow she didn't like drinking in front of her.

Annie was sitting at the opposite side of the hearth reading the paper. Suddenly she said, 'Well I never! Here's that Madam Hevell that you went to, advertising.'

'Oh yes?'

'She wants a model.'

'A model?'

'Aye, it says here: Wanted, a person of smart appearance, to model outsize exclusive gowns.' Annie laughed now and looking over the paper, said in a tone that was slightly derisive, 'If you hadn't put on so much lately you could have had a shot at it.'

'Aye, I could, couldn't I?'

Maggie looked straight back at Annie and their eyes held. She saw that Annie was looking at her with the same expression as had been on Frances's face, pity and scorn mixed, though in Annie's look there was more of the former.

Shortly after Annie went to bed, she got up and brought the bottle from the sideboard and poured herself out a good measure. She shuddered as it burnt its way down into her stomach. With her hand on the bottle about to pour a second measure she stopped, then looked down at herself. Her breasts were hanging slack, her stomach was bulging, she was wearing an old pair of corselettes. She must have put on a stone during the last few weeks. She went to the mirror over the mantelpiece and peered at her face. She'd always had a good skin, clear and cream-tinted; now it was blotchy and there were bags under her eyes. She stuck out her tongue. It was coated white to the tip, and the sight made her feel sick.

Helplessly, she sat down again and, resting her elbow on the table, laid her head on her hand. As she sat thus, she looked down on the paper that Annie had left there. On the front page was a picture of the Mayor and Mayoress and their guests at the Annual Ball. Standing next to the Mayor was Mrs de Ferrier, slim, elegant, smiling with a thin superior smile. The eyes seemed to come out of the page and appraise her with a combination of the expressions she had seen on the faces of Willie, Frances and Annie, only intensified a thousandfold. She took her fist and banged it down on to the paper; then as if she had been prodded out of the chair she got up swiftly and went into her room.

Standing before the long mirror, she looked at herself. She was a big, fat hulk. She was forty-four and she had a body on her like some old trollop from Bog's End. Swiftly now she tore off her clothes and, going to the bottom drawer, she took out the foundation that had been made for her eight months ago. With an effort she got into it, but struggle as she might she couldn't get the zip to fasten over her stomach. Her flesh sticking out through the gap was an embarrassment to her; it looked indecent. She tore off the garment, then got into her nightdress and into bed and lay with her face half buried in the pillow. But she did not cry; nor, when she could not sleep, did she get up and help herself to the bottle . . .

During the following week she hardly ate anything, so little in fact that she began to worry Annie, but each night she helped herself to one glass of whisky. She had to have that she told herself, no more, no less. The second week she endeavoured to make the measure less each night.

It was on the Friday night of this week when Annie was once again reading the weekly paper that she exclaimed, 'It's still in! That Madam Hevell's still got her advert in for a model. She must be finding it a job to get suited. You would have thought with all the fat lasses around the Tyne she'd have had somebody by now.' She stopped and looked half apologetically at Maggie, who said, 'It's all right, me skin's thick.'

'I wasn't meaning anything.'

'I know, I know; don't be so touchy.'

'Well, don't you think it's funny she hasn't been suited?'

'No, because I reckon you want more than a big figure to be a model, outsize or otherwise.'

'Yes, I suppose you're right.'

Later the same evening she tried the foundation on again and for the first time in weeks she smiled at herself in the mirror as the zip slipped over her stomach, perhaps not with the same ease it did when she had first worn it, but it fastened. Well, that was a start, she told herself; she was coming up out of the bog.

On the following Monday morning, when the wild idea came into her head, she looked at the Friday night's paper and for the first time read Madam Hevell's advertisement and knew that the idea was no spontaneous thing bred of the moment, the seed had been set a fortnight ago when Annie first read it out to her. But she was saying nothing to nobody, she wasn't going to make a fool of herself again, she would just see what came of it.

She didn't really expect anything to come of it but the fact that she was willing to have a shot at it meant something. She looked at her face in the mirror. If she could only get a start in a line like that, wouldn't it show them, the lot of them, every damned one of her family . . . but most of all, aw yes, most of all, HIM. Wherever he was at this moment, she wanted to give the lie back to him, to ram his words back down his throat, not in the old way by bawling and shouting but in a kind of refined way that would in itself prove that she was no big, fat ignorant slob.

'Where you off to?' Annie asked, when she saw her dressed for outdoors, and in her best coat and hat at that.

'I thought—' She turned her back and swallowed. 'I thought I would look in on Frances; I feel I want a trip of some sort. I haven't been out of the house for ages.'

'Aye.' Annie nodded at her. 'That's what you should do, go and see Frances. Take a trip, that's right. Will you be back for dinner?'

'I shouldn't think so.' She smiled. 'If she doesn't offer me any I'll go to a café.'

'Do that. Enjoy yourself, go on. Ta-rah then.'

'Ta-rah, Annie.'

Her legs trembled as she went down the path and into the road for she knew Annie was watching her. They trembled when she got on the bus; they trembled when she got on the train to Newcastle. They trembled all the way up Northumberland Street and down various side streets and the trembling had taken possession of her whole body when she stopped outside the small window of Madam Hevell's that showed one suit, a pair of shoes, a handbag and a hat. She gulped deeply, put her shoulders back, then opened the door and stepped on to the deep pile carpet.

A slim, elegant young assistant came towards her smiling. 'Good morning, Madam; can I help you?'

'I . . . I'd like to see Madam Hevell.'

'Oh yes. What name will I say?'

'Mrs Gallacher.'

The girl was new to her, she hadn't been here when she was in the shop before. She waited, looking nervously around the rose and gilt room. Then through the curtains at the far end Madam Hevell came towards her, her plump hand extended. 'Ah, Mrs Gallacher. How nice to see you. Come this way. Come this way.'

She wanted to say, 'Now look I'm not going to buy anything.' She wanted to explain why she was here, but Madam Hevell was talking rapidly. 'I have thought a lot about you, Mrs Gallacher; you did not return to tell me how you enjoyed the soirée.' As if she would. Madam Hevell knew all about the soirée and at this moment she was really amazed to see Mrs Gallacher for she also knew, through her ladies in Felburn, that Mrs de Ferrier had played the dirty on this woman's husband, shooting off like an astronaut for the moon when things on the Felburn planet got too hot for her. She thrived on intrigue did Mrs Rosamund de Ferrier. She wondered what kind of wear Mrs Gallacher had come for. From the look of her, outdoor, she thought, for her coat had peg written all over it. She must have money, but from where? She had heard they were separated and that he was in difficulties. She said now, 'A cup of coffee? I am sure you could do with a cup of coffee. Have you come straight from Felburn?'

'Yes; and thank you, a cup of coffee would be very acceptable.'

'Justine, ask Marianne to bring coffee for two.'

The girl bent her head almost obsequiously, saying, 'Yes, Madam.'

'Ah now!' Madam Hevell sat her short body down on the edge of a gilt chair. 'You are well?'

'Yes, yes, thank you.' Maggie smiled nervously. She had liked this woman; during the fittings she had found her very amusing. She liked to hear her talk; although she spoke English well, her French-Belgian extraction gave a quaintness to her speech. But she thought, I shouldn't have accepted her coffee, she thinks I've come to buy; I'd better get it over.

'Madam Hevell.'

'Yes, Mrs Gallacher?'

'I feel I'd better tell you right away. I . . . I haven't come to buy anything.'

'No? Perhaps then just to look? Very well, very well, we don't charge for looking. We like that you should look. Look all you want . . . '

'Nor to look, Madam Hevell. You see, I'm . . . well, it's this way. You had an advert in the paper, you wanted . . . ' She stopped when she saw the smile slip from Madam Hevell's face and the black eyebrows move upwards and the lips form themselves into a silent whistle.

'Ah! Ah! The model for the outsize. Ah yes! Ah yes! Well, well.' The smile was creeping back to her face. 'No harm done, no harm done, Mrs Gallacher.'

'Have . . . have you been suited?'

Madam Hevell rose from her chair, joined her hands together, wagged them in front of her and looked about her sumptuous fitting-room as if someone else were going to supply the answer to this. Then her small body became still. Her face solemn now, she looked down at Maggie and said, 'No, no, I have not become satisfied because, you see, there are special requirements for such as this.'

'Yes, yes, I understand.' Maggie nodded apologetically and made to rise, and at this moment Justine came through the curtain bearing a tray on which were a silver coffee jug, matching milk jug and sugar basin, together with two cups. Madam turned to her as if with relief and said, 'Ah. Ah, this is nice. Just there, Justine, just there.' Then, going to the tray, she cocked her head on one side and asked of Maggie, 'You have it black or white?'

'White . . . er white, please.'

After she had poured the coffee Madam Hevell sat down again and asked, 'You're in need of employment?'

'Well . . . well no, not really.' Maggie put her head first to one side, then to the other. 'I have plenty of money . . . what I mean is—' she closed her eyes for a moment '—I've got more than enough for my needs.'

'Oh, that is good, good.' Madam Hevell smiled widely.

'It's only . . . well, I need a job . . . occupation, and I haven't been trained for anything. Oh—' she put out her hand apologetically '—I know you need training to be a model, but I thought, well perhaps I could go in for it. I wouldn't mind paying to be shown . . . ' She broke off lamely here and they looked at each other.

Madam Hevell's mind was wont to work rapidly; it was doing so at the moment, even perhaps working overtime. She was badly in need of a model, and one of about this woman's size, for unhappily she had come to know that by the time the men made money, real money, their wives seemed to have expanded. There seemed to be a majority of careless ones, and they would pay the earth to appear a stone lighter without sacrificing their cakes and sweets and titbits. But there, you needed more than bulk to fashion clothes. Yet this woman here had herself suggested that she would pay to be trained; none of the applicants who had so far applied had made such a suggestion. Moreover, she couldn't start her Flout Street branch until she had a suitable person, who, besides modelling, could act as a representative for the . . . she would not even think the term, second-hand garments . . . off-models.

'Stand up.'

'Wha . . . Oh!' Maggie put the cup down so quickly that it rattled in the saucer; then she stood up.

'Walk to the curtain.'

Maggie walked to the curtain.

'Relax. Walk up and down the room.'

She willed herself to relax and move her arms as she had seen the models doing on the telly, but at one point her two arms went forward simultaneously and she stopped. Madam Hevell laughed and said, 'It's all right, it's all right, don't worry. Sit down.'

Maggie sat down.

'Stand up.'

Maggie stood up.

'You're light on your feet, that is something, exceptionally light.'

Maggie smiled.

'If I consented to train you myself personally, would you work for six months inclusive, I mean with the training, without a salary?'

'Oh yes, yes.' Maggie beamed as if Madam Hevell was bestowing some great favour on her, as indeed she was, though to no-one else would she have dared to suggest six months without pay.

'Well now, I think we may come to some arrangement.'

'Oh! Madam Hevell.' Maggie's body folded up, only to be brought stiff and upright again by Madam Hevell saying sharply, 'Now, now, no matter what the emotions, do not become a concertina. You know . . . ' She now demonstrated with her hands going in and out and up and down, and Maggie laughed nervously as she said, 'Yes, Madam. No, Madam.' She felt like a young girl going after a first job. It was strange but she had never been interviewed for a job in her life; her mother had gone to see about her being set on at the factory.

Madam Hevell was talking rapidly now. 'I am opening another business in Flout Street. It is not in the form of a shop, but an apartment, and it is for, well slightly used garments . . . we refer to them as off-models, you understand?'

Maggie nodded at this. It was a definite motion.

'The entire stock are garments from the upper . . . very wealthy people . . . you know. And not from this part of the country . . . no, no. But they're all models; quite a number of them are on the large size. What will be required of you will be to wear these models, interest my clients in them; these are the ones who cannot pay the price asked here.' She hunched her shoulders and spread her hands wide and looked about her. 'But they are clients with taste and who want to look well dressed and yet have no fear that the garments will be recognised in this part of the country. You understand?'

All Maggie did was to nod again.

'I may say that some of these garments originally cost . . . oh——' again she shrugged her shoulders '——twice as much as anything I have in my establishment. But my agent buys them reasonable, very reasonable, and I sell them reasonable, reasonable for the quality they are. But Flout Street will not only be a model agency it will also be a service; the stock sizes will sell themselves but the outsizes are best demonstrated. The model may sometimes have to be taken to the house of a client. In this way many sales can be effected and a personal relationship brought about between the client and me . . . us. You understand?'

'Yes! Yes! It sounds very interesting.'

'Stand up.'

Maggie was already an employee, she stood up smartly.

'Turn round. Ah yes!' Madam Hevell now placed her hands on both Maggie's hips and pressed them tightly, then said, 'You could do with at least seven pounds off here, and more off the stomach. Your legs, your legs are perfect. If you will learn to use them right then there'll be nothing to worry about there.' She now placed her hands under Maggie's breasts, saying, 'These will do; they're very fashionable at the moment. Make up your mind to lose at least half a stone in the next two weeks, then gradually get it down to a stone. I should say then you will be just right . . . Now, Mrs Gallacher, when can you begin?'

Maggie drew in a long breath and let it out again before she said, 'Oh, anytime, Madam Hevell; my time's me own.'

'Well then.' Madam Hevell was all business now. 'Well then, I think you should come here and stay in the background. Those are work-rooms and cutting-rooms.' She pointed to the wall to the right of her. 'There is also another large fitting room. There I can put you through . . . well, through your paces as they say; that is in between times when I'm not busy with a client. Other times you can watch Annette. You remember Annette? Ah yes; she helped to dress you. Well then, you can watch her at work with a client. You will pick up a great deal from Annette. It may take a month, two, or even longer before you are ready in any way. It all depends on your adaptability, you understand?'

'Yes, Madam, and . . . and I'll try my very best.'

Now Madam Hevell smiled. 'I am sure you will, Mrs Gallacher.' Then abruptly the smile went and she said, 'Be here tomorrow at nine-thirty.'

'Oh!' Maggie gathered her bag and her gloves into her hand, then said, 'I . . . I don't know about trains. I live on the far side of Felburn now; if I'm a little late . . . '

'You haven't a car?'

'No.'

'Do you drive?'

'No; I'm sorry, I don't.'

Madam Hevell now brought her small hands to her waist and poked her chin forward as she asked, 'Could you afford a car, Mrs Gallacher?'

Maggie hesitated a moment before saying with a shaky laugh, 'Oh yes; two for that matter.'

'Indeed! Indeed. Then I should suggest that you buy a car and take lessons. In the meantime we'll say that you'll be here . . . what? Ten o'clock?'

'Yes.' Maggie was slightly dumbfounded now, and as she went towards the curtain Madam Hevell said, 'Why I suggest the car is, it will be an asset when you go to visit your clients.' Again she smiled. She was bending towards Maggie from the waist and she patted her on the shoulder as she would a child as she ended, 'Go along; you could have a very interesting time before you.'

Maggie went out into the street, but she had nearly reached the station before she came to herself. She was breathing heavily as if she had been running. She knew she was smiling. She wanted a drink, oh she did want a drink. But no, that was finished. Tea or coffee. She'd just had coffee. There was a café opposite the station; she went in and ordered a pot of tea.

She, Maggie Gallacher, the big, fat, ignorant slob, was going to be a model. Not one of them would believe it; no-one on God's earth would believe it. She couldn't believe it herself. How would she break it to them? How would she tell Annie, and Willie, and Frances? Eeh! What would their Frances say? She was nodding to herself now. What would their Frances say? Frances who had always looked down her nose at her. She would write and tell Paul and Arlette. They wouldn't believe it either, but Arlette would understand. She had a longing to see Arlette. If Arlette were here she would put her arms around her and say, 'Oh, Mam, you're just cut out for it.' That was Arlette. And Paul, too; he would be glad for her. There's nothing like a dame! That had warmed her heart. There's nothing like a dame. If only they weren't living together, if only they'd get married. And Liz. What would Liz think? She shut her mind as to what Liz would think and asked herself how she was going to break it to Annie.

What would be her response? Would she laugh her head off . . . ?

Annie didn't laugh her head off. She just sat down on the kitchen chair and stared up at her. What she said was, 'You're kiddin', aren't you?' and Maggie replied, 'No, I'm not kiddin'; I'm going to model for Madam Hevell. What's more, I'm going out tomorrow to buy a car, and I'm taking lessons, as many as I can get in in a week. You see, as Madam Hevell said, in a position like mine I'll need a car.'

'God Almighty!' said Annie, but there was no disparagement in her tone, only sheer unadulterated amazement.

Part Six

CHAPTER ONE

THE MODEL

It was the first Monday in March. The morning was bright; there was a nip in the air that made you bustle and step out just that little bit faster. It was the kind of day that portended good for everyone.

Margaret Gallacher looked up into the clear blue sky as she finished her grapefruit and started on her toast, and she remarked to Annie, 'This is just the morning for it; this is the kind of light Arthur likes.'

'Have another piece of toast,' said Annie; 'you can't go out on that.'

'All right, just one . . . No, no, I'd better not.' She wagged her head, then added, 'Why do you keep pressing me when you know that I mustn't have it?'

'You're getting like a lath.'

'I'd better not—' Maggie laughed up at Annie now '—or I'll lose my clients. And that would never do, would it?' She poked her face mischievously towards Annie.

'Where are you going this mornin'?'

'Along the quay in Newcastle first, to take in the bridges, and then the Scotswood Road end of all places, where they're pulling down the houses.'

Annie stopped with the teapot in her hand. 'Along there?' Her face screwed up. 'What do they want to photo-graph models along there for?'

'Don't ask me,' Maggie shook her head, wiped her mouth, then got to her feet. 'But he hopes to take me just at the moment one of the houses is coming down . . .

257

It's artistic.' She pushed Annie, and Annie laughed and said, 'We live and learn.'

'Aye, we do that.'

Maggie hurried out of the little kitchen, through the living-room and into her bedroom, and having taken off her dressing-gown she made up her face, then sat back and examined her reflection before going to a rack that stood along one wall and took up about a quarter of the room. From it she selected a russet coloured two-piece suit, and from a tray standing on top of a low chest of drawers she chose a pair of tan leather court shoes, and a bag and gloves to match.

Having dressed, she draped over her shining lacquered hair a scarf of the colour termed seared leaf yellow, then she went back into the living-room, and Annie, coming from the kitchen, stopped and said, 'Oh aye! That looks grand, but that's not an off is it?'

'An off! No, this is a Hevell, sixty-five guineas.' She walked in an exaggeratedly sedate manner down the room, then looking over her shoulder she grinned and said, 'No patter with a Hevell; now if it was an off—' She assumed a higher tone and strutting slightly, said, 'Twenty-five guineas, Madam, and very reasonable, very reasonable. It's a model by . . . Spifflico. The original price was a hundred guineas. Yes, indeed, Madam, a hundred, and it's as new, Madam, as you can see.'

'Go on with you! What time will you be back?'

'Oh, let me see.' Maggie lifted her head and thought. 'He'll take a couple of hours over the quay shooting; then we'll go to the Station Hotel for lunch . . . '

'He'll take you to the Station?'

'Oh yes, he's generous is Arthur. Anyway, he should be. He doesn't pay half here what he does in London, I understand, and he gets better pictures. Still, I'm not grumbling. Oh.' She paused. 'What time will I be back?

If things go smoothly, say four o'clock. No, half-past.'

'Frances and Dave should be coming over the night don't forget.'

'No, I won't forget. Ta-rah.' As she went out she thought, And I wish they weren't.

She always chided herself for feeling cynical when she thought of Frances but she couldn't help it, for the fact was that since her status had changed Frances had hardly been off the doorstep. Yet it was she who had laughed loudest when she had been told that her mother was going to model for Madam Hevell, and her reply had been, 'When I see pigs fly I'll believe that.' She hadn't said it to her face. She had said it to Annie, who had given her the news in the kitchen. Frances had forgotten that they weren't in Savile House any more but in a little bungalow where her voice carried.

Willie and Nancy, too, had taken a lot of convincing. Not so Helen. But then Helen had had time to get over the shock before she phoned her from Hexham. She said, 'Good for you.' And now Trevor condescended to visit her, at least once a month. Of them all, it was Trevor, she felt, who thought her changed status a flash in the pan. She always detected in his eyes the awaiting of midnight, when she would change back into Mam, and Maggie Gallacher.

If any of them had joyed with her, it had been Paul and Arlette. But then she would have expected them to, though not to make a journey from London just to congratulate her. She had loved seeing them that time. She had been less embarrassed and condemning within herself towards them than she had expected, but their happiness in each other had made her sad, for it had emphasised her own aloneness.

Now, eighteen months later, she still couldn't understand why, loving each other as they did, Arlette wouldn't consent to be married; surely she knew Paul by now. Still it was their affair and she left it at that.

And Liz. She was the one now for whom she was concerned, and only her. Although it was three months since she had last seen her, her face still haunted her. This was at the time when she was about to take her second step towards her vows. When she had asked her, 'Are you happy, lass?' she had answered, 'Yes, thank you, Mother,' like a child repeating a phrase, but her eyes had seemed steeped in sadness. And there was an expression on her daughter's face that she didn't see on the faces of the other nuns; most of them looked smiling and happy. Some of the older ones had that look of settled serenity as if they had already been given a glimpse into their future home, the home for which they had spent a lifetime preparing to enter. She had said to Father Armstrong, 'I'm worried about her,' but his reply had been in the form of a reprimand. 'Then you should come to Mass and pray for her,' he said.

She was on the pathway to the garage when the phone rang, and she went back and saw Annie at the side table with the phone in her hand. 'It's Arlette,' she said.

She took the phone from Annie and said, 'Hello there, dear.'

'Hello, Mam.'

'Hello, lass.'

'Mam.'

'Yes?'

'I've got news for you. I'm going to have a baby.'

Maggie's mouth opened, then closed. She nipped at her lip, then said, 'Oh, that's fine, lass.'

'And Mam.'

'Yes?'

'We're . . . we're going to be married.'

Maggie was now smiling down at the phone and the

smile came over in her voice as she said, 'That's even better news, lass. Oh, I'm glad.' She swallowed deeply, then asked, 'When?'

'Thursday.'

There was a long pause now before she asked, 'Where's it to be?'

'In church.'

'Thank God!'

She was Margaret Gallacher, the model. She was known all over Felburn now. She was a big fish in a little pool, yet not such a little pool. No; it was a pool big enough to drown people in. Yet under her new skin, under her poise, she was still Maggie Gallacher, narrow in her views where they touched on morality. She told herself she couldn't help it, she was made that way. If she hadn't been, Rod might still be with her now, but if he had been – and she reminded herself often of this fact – she certainly wouldn't be Margaret Gallacher the model going out at this minute dressed as she was, to be photographed for a magazine.

'Are you there, Mam?'

'Yes, yes, lass, I'm here.'

'I never asked how you are?'

'I'm fine, on top of the world. I'm on me way to be photographed on the quay in Newcastle. It's for a magazine.'

'You're not!'

'Yes, I am.'

'Oh, Mam, it's wonderful.'

'Yes, isn't it? Funny the things that can happen in two years. You remember when you told me how I should walk and stretch me neck?' Arlette's laugh came to her now, and she went on, 'Well, Madam endorses all that. But she adds to it. Lift your rib cage, she keeps saying; lift your rib cage. And you know, she's right. See to your neck and your rib cage and the rest of your carcass takes care of itself. Aye, the things you learn.'

'I wish I were near you, Mam.'

'I wish you were at that.'

'Would you like us to come that way again, Mam?' Her voice was soft, enquiring.

'Would I? Aw, lass, I would love it.'

'We were talking about it last night. Paul wants to be near you, and it goes without saying I do. We'll slip down next week and talk about it, eh?'

'Do that. Oh, that would be lovely. Wait a minute, wait a minute, I must look at my diary . . . Margaret Gallacher must consult her diary.' She laughed derisively at herself, then said, 'Tuesday and Friday I could finish early, around three; the rest of the week I'll be full up.'

'All right, dear, we'll make it Tuesday or Friday. Bye-bye, Mam. Bye-bye.'

'Bye-bye, lass. And tell Paul I'm happy for you, happy for you both. Bye-bye.'

'Annie!' She turned around. 'They're going to have a baby.'

Annie stood at the kitchen door nodding her head. 'I gathered as much. Well, you can't say they've rushed into it. And they're going to be married an' all?'

'Yes, they're going to be married.'

'Well, that'll be another weight off your mind.'

'You've said something there. But now I must fly. Ta-rah!'

'Ta-rah,' said Annie.

She felt happy, happy as she hadn't been for a long, long time. Her new job had brought into her life a feeling of excitement and pride that she had never experienced before. It hadn't brought her happiness, not as she thought of happiness, but a certain contentment, yes, and a strange fulfilment. There were times when she felt there was nothing of the old Maggie Gallacher left in her until, as a while ago, the issue had arisen of her son marrying in a church or in a registry office. It was at these times she knew that there were large remnants of herself still left, old-fashioned, environmental remnants.

Because of the parking problem in Newcastle she had arranged to meet Arthur Leonard on the quay itself, and as she turned down a side street towards the river she saw his car, and him standing beside it already waiting.

When she drew up alongside him he came and greeted her effusively in his quick-fire way. 'Ah, Margaret, had a time getting through, did you? But you're only five minutes out. Let me have a look.' He held her away with one arm. 'Ah! Yes. That's it, that's it. And it's the light for it.' He looked up into the sky, then across the river. 'There's a boat at the quay discharging into a warehouse. We're lucky, I'll get you at the warehouse doors with one or two of the fellows looking at you. Then I'll see the skipper; might get you on the gangway. Come on.'

He took her arm and led her on to the quay. As he approached the opening to the warehouse through which the men were trundling trolleys piled high with boxes, he called to a distant man, 'All right, mate?' and the man turned and looked from him to Maggie, and smiling broadly said, 'I don't see why not.' Looking back at him, Maggie returned his smile and said, 'Good morning.'

'Morning, Miss.'

Miss! On forty-six and being called Miss! The man could give her twenty years, but still to be called Miss. Her eyes twinkled at him and she said, 'Your eyesight's bad,' at which he let out a loud guffaw, then answered gallantly, 'Don't you believe it.'

The session on the quay went well and as they were leaving one bright spark called out to her, 'Doing anything the night, lass?' and she called back, 'Yes, washing the bairns,' and at this there was a great howl of laughter.

Arthur Leonard, leading her along the quay now over

the uneven planks, squeezed her arm and said, 'Margaret, my love, you know if you would come up to town you'd go like a bomb. Still, you do all right here, don't you?' She gave him a sidelong glance and with mock seriousness answered, 'And it's cheaper, Arthur, isn't it?'

He laughed and chided, 'Naughty. Naughty.'

They now did some takes outside the civic centre and in front of the gates of the college, and it was turned one o'clock when they went into the Royal Station Hotel for lunch.

After lunch she went back to Flout Street and changed into another model, not an off, but a three-piece she had brought from Madam's yesterday. The coat and skirt were autumn yellow, not unlike the colour of her head scarf. With the suit went a fine wool sweater in chocolate brown and a large matching hat with a floppy brim. She wore the same shoes, but her gloves and bag were of a darker tan. She looked back in the mirror and surveyed herself. She liked this rig-out; she had thought of buying it herself, all except the hat. You couldn't go round Felburn in a thing like this. Madam might let her have it near cost; she wasn't bad that way.

When the door bell rang she opened it to Arthur Leonard. He had been along to see Madam Hevell, and in high approval he now exclaimed, 'Aw yes, yes. This is it, glamorous autumn. Ah yes, now there's a title, glamorous autumn, what do you think?'

'Very good.'

'And you're very good, dear.' He patted her. 'Except the hat. Just a little more to the side.' He adjusted it. 'That's it. By the way, do you know you're high up on her list, Madam's? Do you know that? She calls you her swan. Not that you were ever an ugly duckling, dear, never could have been—' he touched her cheek '—not with that skin, and those eyes.' He jerked his head at her, then bent closer and whispered, 'You could go places with Madam, you know. She's no family, no ties. Anyway, dear, you keep your eye on the main chance and you could work towards a partnership, at least at this end. Very nice little business here, ve-ry nice. Do you know what she makes on these?' He touched the lapel of a coat hanging on a rail.

She said somewhat stiffly now, 'No, I don't, but I know she gives me a generous bonus on the sales, and that's all that matters.'

'Well!' He shrugged his shoulders and his tone became light. 'If you're satisfied, dear, we're all satisfied. Come on. Come on.' He looked at his watch and cried, 'What are we standing here for when those houses are coming down like nine pins? I want to get you just as that great ball hits a wall, you know, the second before it disintegrates and the dust starts. Come on.' He almost hustled her from the room now and she had to pull him to a stop outside, saying, 'Wait a minute! Wait a minute; I must lock up . . .'

The demolition squad looked as if it had almost finished its work, at least on this section, for only two warehouses, at the end of a long open rubble-strewn space, were still to be disposed of. Grabs were biting into the rubble and filling lorries, while a crane with a great iron ball swinging from its cable stood to the side of the building. In front of it, the dust was settling on the rubble of a side wall against which the ball had just crashed. Most of the front wall of the building, too, had gone, exposing the inner sections like the combs of a beehive.

Maggie drew her car up on the opposite side of the road. Getting out, she stared for a moment in amazement at the men clambering about on the battered walls, and she said to Arthur Leonard, 'Surely that thing doesn't work with them inside there?' He laughed, saying, 'They're all right, they know when to jump.'

'They'll need to,' she said; then pausing in the middle of

the road, she added quickly, 'Now, Arthur, I'm not going too near that lot, no matter what you say.'

'I don't want you to, dear; you're much too precious.' He put his arm around her shoulder and as she pushed him off he laughed again and, leading her tentatively forward, said, 'Just here, near the edge of the pavement on the corner, so I can get the interior in.' He pointed upwards to the honeycomb shell. 'And a bit of the crane.'

As she posed herself on the edge of the gutter she slanted her eyes at him and said, 'This get-up and that!' She jerked her head backwards. 'I can't see it meself.'

'Art, love, art. Circular staircases, marble halls and woodland glades are out; reality, reality, that's what they want. And—' he moved back from her, talking all the time, '—if I get this as I want it, it will be reality.'

He put his eye to the camera, then came hurriedly towards her again and took her by the arm and led her further towards the corner of the building. They had now attracted the attention of some of the men who were knocking the loose interior walls down by hand, but it was the crane man himself who shouted, 'I hope you know what you're doing, mate. You'd better look out, there'll be a hell of a dust in a minute.'

'All right, pal.' Arthur Leonard shouted up at him, a wide grin on his face. 'Fire away, that's what I want.'

'Look,' said Maggie, posed with one foot in the gutter, one foot on the kerb, her head well back and looking in the direction of the crane; 'I don't like this. What happens when it hits that wall?'

'Nothing will happen, dear, nothing.' He was backing from her. 'If you're uneasy, as soon as you see it contact give yourself one, two, three, and then dash back. But it won't fall your way . . . can't.'

'That's what you think.' She saw the great ball swing backwards, then forwards, and she didn't hear the click of the camera but as soon as the iron weight came in contact with the brickwork she dived back across the road, then clung to Arthur, laughing all the while.

Most of the wall settled into a great pile of rubble, and when the dust subsided he said, 'I'd like one or two more of those. All right, all right, dear—' he placed his fingers across his lips '—I'll settle for you in the front.'

'I should say so.'

He was walking away from her now, still talking. 'Yes, that's it, dear. Yes, all right, love. Put your head to the side this time. Look upwards to the men swarming about.' He dashed back to her and tilted her hat. 'Like that. Lovely. Lovely. You know,' he grinned at her as he said under his breath, 'you're a good looking lass, as they say around here, Margaret. But as I said to Madam, Maggie would have been much better on the bills. Maggie Gallacher, much more character than Margaret Gallacher.'

She suppressed a grin but said nothing. She liked Arthur Leonard, he had a way with him. Anyway, he could make her laugh and make her forget everything but the job in hand. She looked upwards and into the eyes of three men who were standing perilously balanced on a narrow ledge of wall. Their only support seemed to be the huge iron hammers in their hands. Then her gaze became focused on one, and although he was covered in dust there was no mistaking Ralphy Holland. She held her pose, a half smile on her face now, staring up at him and he down at her. During the time she waited for Arthur's voice to say 'Right!' she watched Ralphy's mouth drop into a great gape. She saw his tongue curl over his lower lip, licking at the grey dust that covered his face. She noted that his tongue looked grey, too, not pink. Before Arthur shouted, 'Right!' she saw Ralphy drop from the wall as though he had fallen. But when Arthur's voice came to her saying 'Good enough,' and she straightened up and moved towards him, Ralphy Holland came running from the floor of the building towards her. About a yard away he stopped and stared at her.

'Hello, Ralphy.' Her voice was quiet, ordinary, and at the sound of it he let out a high whoop like a cowboy, riding a broncho, and the next minute he was holding her immaculately gloved hand between his grime-covered ones. 'Why! Maggie. Maggie, I thought it was you, but I wasn't sure, I couldn't be sure. Even a second ago I couldn't be sure.' He was shaking his head. 'But I said to meself there couldn't be two of her, there couldn't be two Maggies. Aye, lass. What you up to? What's come over you? God above!' He stood back from her, still holding on to her hand. 'Like a million dollars. Who would believe it?' He turned for confirmation to the man at her side, and Arthur Leonard, his face prim now, said, 'She should add to that million dollars by claiming a new pair of gloves.'

'It's all right, Arthur, it's all right. This is, this is . . . Mr Holland, an old friend of mine.'

'Oh yes?' Arthur Leonard didn't show any enthusiasm, but he couldn't quench Ralphy's pleasure and excitement.

'Known her since she was that big.' He relinquished her hands and measured a distance three feet from the ground. Then looking at his hands and dusting them quickly, he said, 'Sorry, Maggie, sorry; I should have known.'

'That's all right, Ralphy. How are you?'

'Oh, I'm all right, Maggie. You know me; beer and a bed and I'm satisfied.'

'Oh, Ralphy!' She shook her head at him sadly, and on this he became quiet and the expression on his face changed. The excitement went out of it and he looked about him as if he had just remembered something. He looked towards the crane behind them, then to the far side of the warehouses where one wall was still intact; then his gaze became still and she followed it.

A bulky figure was standing half hidden by the side of a naked chimney breast on the second floor. He was, like the rest of the men, covered from head to foot in grey dust, and like them he was holding an iron hammer. She could see only half his face and half his body, but it was more than enough. Across the road and over the space of the bottomless floor their eyes met, the eyes of the elegantly dressed woman and those of the demolition labourer.

The weakness attacked her first in the throat, flowed down her arms, then to her legs. She turned away, then half turned towards Ralphy again, saying, 'Goodbye, Ralphy.'

'Ta-rah, Maggie, ta-rah. Nice seeing you.' His voice was quiet, apologetic now.

As she went towards the car Arthur muttered, 'Look, come on. He won't trouble you any more. Just another few.'

'No, Arthur, not here.'

'Oh! Look, Margaret.' He spread out one arm with the elbow bent, the fingers stretched in his characteristic manner, saying, 'Have a heart, have a heart; I won't get another chance like this, it's a marvellous set-up.'

'NO!'

'What is it?' His voice was quiet, enquiring now.

She kept her back to the buildings and speaking down to the car door she said, 'I want to get away from here . . . now.'

He glanced slowly over his shoulder, then said, 'OK, Margaret. OK. There are other places.'

When she took her seat in the car he said, 'Drive to the church, just beyond the station; we should get parked there.'

Ten minutes later he was looking at her again, and he asked quietly, 'That fellow upset you?'

'No.' She shook her head.

'What then?'

It was some time before she answered, 'I saw my husband.'

'Oh.' He nodded twice, then said, 'Oh, I get it.' And after a moment he exclaimed, 'That's life, that's life, Margaret. At least that's what they said to me when they put me along the line for bigamy.'

She wanted to laugh, but there was no laughter in her. Yet there should be, for was she not Margaret Gallacher, the model? Model for the larger woman, photographed for magazines, in demand for store lunch parades, not only because she modelled well but because she drew the customers. She was a character, for was she not also the woman who had buggered the Duke of Moorshire?

Oh, she knew what they said, and thought. She knew that her mercurial rise in this cut-throat profession owed as much to her raw outspokenness on that particular Friday night as to her ability to wear clothes and suggest to the onlooker that they only had to possess them for their fat to fade.

But there was one other thing to which she owed her success and this was the urge, the desire in the early days that had almost become an obsession with her, the desire to show him, and the hope that some time or other they would meet and her very appearance would ram his words down his throat: 'You big, fat, ignorant slob, you!' But she had never dreamed it would be like this. There was that old saying in the Bible, 'How are the mighty fallen,' and begod! it was true in this case. If ever justice had been done it had been done today, for now, not only were their places reversed, but he was lower than she ever imagined he could be, a labourer in a demolition squad.

She should be crowing, but she felt sick.

She said, 'I'm going to change and go home, Arthur.' And he said, 'Yes Margaret. Yes Margaret . . .'

When she reached home she put the car in the garage and

entered the house by the kitchen door. Annie was mashing a pot of tea at the stove and she turned quickly and said, 'Oh, hello there. You're before your time . . . You've got a visitor.' Then putting the lid quickly on the pot and bringing it to the tray on the table, she narrowed her eyes at Maggie and said, 'What's up, something happened?'

For answer Maggie said, 'Who is it?'

'Father Armstrong.' Her voice dropped low. 'But what's the matter? You look like death; you feeling under the weather?'

'I'm all right, I'll tell you later. What does he want?'

'I don't know, he didn't tell me, but he asked when you'd be in. He said he'd wait.'

They were still whispering when Annie, lifting the tray from the table, said, 'How did the quay session go?' and Maggie stared at her for a moment before saying, 'Oh, that went all right.' Then she opened the door and walked ahead of Annie into the sitting-room.

Father Armstrong rose from his seat by the window. 'Ah! There you are, Maggie. My! You are looking well.'

'How are you, Father? I suppose you could do with a cup of tea?'

'I wouldn't refuse one, I never refuse tea.' His words were light, but his manner wasn't jocular, and she knew instinctively that this visit wasn't one of his parishional calls.

When the kitchen door had closed on Annie and she had poured out the tea they both sat drinking it for a moment before he said, 'I'm coming straight to the point, Maggie; I'm the bearer of bad news.'

Her eyes tight on him, she put out her hand and placed the cup back on the table, feeling against the edge so that it wouldn't drop off.

'Bad news you say . . . Elizabeth?'

'Elizabeth.'

271

She waited, and the waiting she knew wasn't something born of the moment, a silence created in her by his shock tactics, but went back weeks, months, back in fact to the day she had left Liz in that grey room. Part of its substance had been a dim apprehension, an alertness whenever Father Armstrong called and brought up her name; and now the waiting was over.

'Now you must not take this too badly, Maggie, for she has tried, we all know she has tried. There's no-one to blame. She thought she had the vocation . . . so did we all.'

She brought her joined hands up to her mouth and bit hard on her thumb nail. 'It's that fellow, isn't it?'

There was a pause before Father Armstrong said, 'It may have been in the beginning, but it isn't so now. She isn't coming out to go to him, I can assure you of that. And you mustn't blame him. Peter Portman is a good man, a really good man. I only wish some of my own flock were as good . . . Ah yes, you can look like that, Maggie, but I happen to know him. He has done some very good work for the boys over the past two years. He doesn't believe in God but he believes in his fellow men, and that is something to start on.'

Maggie got up and walked to the fireplace and leant her elbow on the mantelpiece. There was another saying. It never rains but it pours. It was odd but everything seemed to happen to her in dollops. She could go on for years as she had done, with life mundane, uneventful, and then the explosion had taken place under her home and had blown it sky high. She had picked herself up and made another life for herself, a different life, an exciting, rewarding life, a life that she never imagined she could live, not a big, fat, ignorant slob like her. Her life over the past eighteen months had acted like a salve on the pain of her heart, at least during the daytime hours, and lately it had promised her, some time in the future, total freedom, forgetfulness. This morning its promise had been great. The morning had been bright, it was a day on which no bad thing could happen, and it had been given a good start with that telephone call from Arlette . . . And then she had to see him. In the most unlikely place in the world, she had to see him.

It was over a year now since she had heard of him. Willie had said he understood he was working for a firm in Doncaster, and she had imagined him in a managerial position. Never for a moment did she think he would go for anything less, nothing less than assistant works manager to a contractor. But there he was, not only back where he had started, working with Ralphy on the buildings, but knocking old ones down. Yet somehow, in a way, it seemed symbolical that he should be tearing things down.

'What did you say, Father?'

'I said, Maggie, that she doesn't want to come home.'

She turned about sharply now, her voice high. 'Why?'

'Well, I've been trying to explain, Maggie. As I said, she doesn't think she could bear to witness your pain in this. This is the second time you've been hurt in this way; she knows it only too well and it's worrying her. I . . . I think she would have made the break in the first year of her noviciate if it hadn't been for the thought of letting you down. She has tried, God knows she has tried, but it's not to be.'

'Well—' Maggie's voice was high and rough sounding now '—if she's not coming home, where does she think she's going? To that fel—?'

The priest closed his eyes and lifted his hand in protest. 'Maggie, she is not going to that fellow. Nor would that fellow want her to. Get that into your head: that man had no designs on her. What might have happened if she hadn't been going into the Church I don't know, but he respected the fact that she was. He doesn't know she's coming out, no-one outside knows this, until this moment.'

Her voice was low now as she asked, 'Well, what is she going to do, Father? Go into a home of sorts, or what?'

'No.' He stood up, placed his cup on the table, and said briefly, 'She wants to go to Paul.'

'Paul!'

'Yes, Paul.'

'Huh! Well, birds of a feather.'

'Now, Maggie, you mustn't take it like that, that's bitter.'

'Bitter? Huh! How do you expect me to take it? Does Paul know of this?'

'I've told you nobody but yourself outside the convent knows of this.'

'Would you consent to her going to Paul and him living with another woman?'

'Well, the fact is, Maggie, once she leaves the convent she can please herself. For myself, I think it's a very wise decision.'

'You mean I wouldn't be good for her?'

'I'm not meaning anything of the sort. I only mean that if I were in her place I wouldn't like to live with you and see the disappointment in your eyes every minute of the day.'

'Oh, Father, Father.' She sat down suddenly in the chair and her head drooped on to her chest, and he came and put his hand on her shoulder and said, 'There now. There now. This is life.'

Again she said, 'Huh!' This was the second time she had heard that within an hour.

'I must be off now, Maggie.' He patted her shoulder twice. 'I'll look in again at the end of the week; things should be finally settled by then.'

'By the end of the week?' She looked up at him.

'Yes, she could be leaving by Friday.'

She moved her head slowly from side to side, then bit hard down on her lip, and when she felt him walking from her she turned her head to the side, but didn't look at him, as she said, 'You might as well know that they are to be married, Paul and Arlette. She phoned me this morning.'

. . . 'In church?'

'In church.'

'Thanks be to God for that. Goodbye, Maggie.'

'Goodbye, Father.'

She didn't rise to let him out.

What had life against her? What had she done that every wish of hers should be bogged? She wouldn't care if they were selfish wishes. She had never wanted anything for herself.

When Annie came in their eyes held. 'You heard?'

'Yes,' said Annie, 'I heard. And . . . well, it's not news to me, I'm sure you must have been expecting it yourself. Anyway, it's nature.' She went to the table and picked up the tray, and as she walked towards the kitchen with it she ended, 'She's pleasing herself now and her instincts, not God or you.'

'What did you say?'

Annie disappeared into the kitchen, then came back to answer the question, and she stood with her hands joined at the front of her waist and said flatly, 'You heard what I said, an' you know as well as I do she only went in there to please you, at the end I mean.'

'She did nothing of the sort.' Maggie was on her feet now, her voice loud. 'Don't put the blame for that on me an' all.'

'It isn't blame, it's just the plain fact. It was the case of Paul all over again, only in her case, poor lass, she hadn't a chance, not right from the beginning, because she was partly brought up within the walls of the convent, being there from when she was seven, the nuns hovering around her all day like plastic angels, though some of them were far from angels. That Sister Martha had a tongue on her like a navvy's ganger. Remember that day we went to see them playing hockey? I was never more shocked in me life, running with her gown tucked up to her knees and bawling her head off. It wouldn't have surprised me if she had come out with a mouthful an' all. But there was Liz, in that atmosphere, Holy Marys two a penny; she hadn't a chance. Then she was just at an impressionable age when Paul did his bunk, and she saw how it affected you, so sacrifice, sacrifice, she offered herself, and you let her. I'm going to say this, though I shouldn't at this time, but if you had faced up to Paul's desertion and not gone on as if he'd just missed being made Pope that lass would have got over her fancy, and it's two to one she'd have been married by now. So there! That's flat.'

'Shut up! What's come over you, what you getting at? You out to get me mad or something?' Maggie was leaning over the table. 'I'm warning you, Annie Fawcett, be careful of that tongue of yours else you'll be sorry.'

'I'm never sorry for telling the truth.' Annie flounced round and went into the kitchen, and Maggie remained bent over the table, her hands gripping the edge now. The truth, the truth. What was the truth? Had she pressed Liz into the convent? Had she in some unspoken way let her see that's what she wanted for her, a life between four walls, a life of restriction, of denial of natural desire? . . . Oh, my God! What was the matter with her now thinking like this? She began to pace the floor. Yes, yes she had wanted her to go in, because nuns were happy. You had only to look at their faces, you had only to hear them talking; did you ever hear them grumbling? And what's more, inside there they escaped most of the torments of life, and deep down that's what she had wanted for Elizabeth, a life free from emotional torments, of battles and reconciliation, and aye, even of the joys the questionable joys of love, the rending of the body in a moment's ecstasy. And for what? Pregnancy after pregnancy. The distortion of the body wasn't beautiful. When she had carried Sam she had carried him high, seemingly under her breasts – Sam. Oh my God! Sam. – But her grannie had looked at her on her weekly visits and explained the position by saying, 'Young cows carry high, old cows carry low.'

Cows, yes; that's what she had tried to shelter Elizabeth from, the indignity of being a cow.

Looking back on her life at this moment she recognised with some surprise that for years there had been a private war raging inside her. Buried in her bulk, there had been another and quite separate individual who had been striving for life, a life of its own, but it had been smothered by her early environment, then by routine . . . and love, blind, adoring, unquestioning love for a big young fellow with short cropped hair, deep set eyes, puggish nose and bull neck, and everything had become subordinate to that love, principally the struggling self.

And now Lizzie wanted to go to Paul, and if Paul agreed it would mean they wouldn't come this way to live. How could they, Liz feeling like that? She couldn't win, not with her family she couldn't.

Annie had come into the room again, with another tray in her hand. She put it down on the table, picked up a cup of tea and handed it to her, saying, 'I've made a fresh one.' It was the usual form of apology.

Maggie didn't want more tea but she took it and sat down by the side of the fireplace, and Annie sat opposite to her and as she stirred the spoon round in her cup she said, 'You'll get over it; it's a small mountain to the others you've climbed.' Then having put the spoon in her mouth and licked it, she placed it on the saucer before asking, 'What upset you outside?'

277

There was a long pause. The words were there but she couldn't get them out, not until Annie, impatient now, said, 'Well?'

'I've seen him,' she said.

'Rod? Where?' Annie bent quickly forward and put her cup down on the tiled hearth. 'Did he speak to you?'

Maggie shook her head.

'You didn't pass him?'

Again Maggie shook her head. 'It . . . it wasn't like that. I . . . I was down the Scotswood Road. Arthur was taking me against some buildings they were pulling down, big warehouses. I was looking up and . . . and I saw Ralphy.' She stopped for a moment and they stared at each other, and then she went on, 'He . . . he came dashing down and spoke to me, and . . . and then I happened to look up and there he was, on one of the walls with the gang.'

'Labouring?'

'Labouring.'

Again they were staring at each other.

'And you were all rigged out special like?' Annie's voice was low.

'Very special like. The yellow rig-out I was telling you about, and the big floppy hat, very special like.' She shook her head.

'Poor Rod.'

Maggie blinked her eyes as if coming out of a dream and demanded, 'Poor Rod? Whose side are you on anyway?' She was on her feet now staring down at Annie. 'Blaming me for Liz, and now taking his side.'

'I'm not taking his side, you know I'm not, but . . . but did you get any satisfaction out of seeing him labouring? I ask you, did you?'

She walked to the window and stood looking out. The little garden showed faint signs of spring. There were yellow crocuses in the border and the buds of the daffodils were fattening. She began to wonder where he was living, in lodgings somewhere, perhaps with a landlady. Aye, her thoughts hardened, very little doubt about it, there'd be a landlady.

'He'll feel like hell the night.'

Again she turned swiftly on Annie. 'You're sorry for him, aren't you? Would you still be sorry for him if he was with her and in a white collar job?'

'No, I wouldn't; but he's not with her an' in a white collar job.' Annie too was on her feet. 'He's, as you say, labouring, and if he's with Ralphy Holland, it's a poor kind of labouring he's at.' There was a personal bitterness in her voice now. Against this Maggie bowed her head, and under her lowered lids she watched Annie grab up the two cups and march into the kitchen.

Later that night, having had her bath, creamed her face, set her hair in preparation for the activities of the following day, Maggie came into the living-room to say good night to Annie.

Annie was sitting staring into the fire. Usually she had her nose in a book at this time, some love story she'd got from the library, or following a serial in any one of the three women's magazines she took each week.

'Good night,' said Maggie quietly.

Annie turned sharply round and said, 'Oh, good night.' Then, as Maggie was going into her bedroom, she said, 'Maggie.'

'Yes?'

'Would you have him back?'

It was like the old days when some incident caused the cork to fly and, her voice seeming to spiral out of the top of her head, she would bawl her opponent down whether it be one of the lads, one of the girls, Rod, or Annie herself. 'What! Have him back? You've lived with me all these years and you're stupid enough to ask me that!

Have him back, did you say? I wouldn't let that man come near me if he was to crawl on his hands and knees. If I was dead and he came and looked at me I would know an' spit in his eye. HAVE HIM BACK!'

The bedroom door banged and Annie stood looking at it for a moment, then raised her eyebrows, sat down and continued to stare into the fire.

CHAPTER TWO

THE LEOPARD'S SPOTS

During the summer months the picture of Margaret Gallacher appeared on the front pages of the *Messenger* at least three times.

On two occasions the demonstrations had taken place in private restaurants. The third had been in the dining room of an ultra-modern hotel on the outskirts of the town and had been given star billing.

Naturally Maggie didn't appear alone at these dress parades, but nearly always it was her picture which appeared in the papers. There had been good models in Felburn before, but if once during her career one of them had had her photograph in the paper she had felt flattered, and very lucky. Madam Hevell attributed the generosity of the press first to the quality of her models and secondly to the ability of a big woman like Maggie to carry them, and to this she added unself-effacingly the fact that Maggie owed her present success entirely to her coaching.

What Madam didn't realise was that reporters were very observant people; also there were those among them who were patient and given to hunches, although the hunch they had with regards to Margaret Gallacher relied more on fact than feeling. A leopard didn't change its spots; under her finery Margaret Gallacher was the woman who had buggered a duke; wait long enough and anything could happen.

Maggie was not insensible to all that was going on around her. She realised that she was lucky to get her billings in the paper. She realised that she was very lucky to know a photographer like Arthur Leonard; she realised that she had fallen on her feet, so to speak, the day she went to Madam Hevell's, and she was now interested, and not a little excited, at the prospect of a partnership in the Flout Street business.

Her salary was double what it had been this time last year and her bank balance was rising rapidly. She was financially on top of the world. She was envied, not only by others in the profession, but also by the members of her own family, and not by Frances alone now, but by Nancy, pregnant once more, and struggling on housekeeping one third of what she had been used to. Indeed, she was not the easygoing, laughing girl of three years ago but a peevish woman who questioned the right, and not always in private, of a mother-in-law who had all the breaks.

Helen was pretty much the same, except when Trevor came visiting with her. Trevor's innuendoes, like his face, were sharp and Maggie gauged that he thought it highly unfair that she, who, to his mind, had been the instigator of all their troubles, should not only benefit from them but come away out on top.

Elizabeth's reactions to her were puzzling. She had seen her only twice in the six months since she had left the convent, and on each occasion she had been filled with embarrassment and not a little guilt.

It was six weeks after Elizabeth had gone to live with Paul and Arlette that she journeyed to London to see her. She had expected to be confronted by a subdued, pale, reticent creature, someone nulled; what she found was a highly excitable, rakishly-dressed, loud talking girl. She made Maggie think of an animal that had been trapped and suddenly let out, dashing here and there, and it was this that engendered the guilt in her. She felt responsible for robbing her of two years of life. Her daughter had greeted her as if she had just left her yesterday, and she had talked and talked, she had never stopped talking. She had wanted to yell at her, 'Stop it, girl!' But this wasn't Liz, not the Liz she remembered, this was the girl who had been hidden under the surface of Liz, Liz of the vocation.

Three months later, when they met again, Liz had a post as secretary in a firm in the City. She had been learning typing since she was sixteen while at the convent, and apparently she was very good at shorthand. Her conversation on this visit had, in itself, been embarrassing for she had talked of her boss and the men in the office with cheap familiarity.

She had asked Arlette, 'Is this just put on for me?' and Arlette had shaken her head and said, 'No, Mam; she's like this all the time.'

Maggie looked at her daughter-in-law and said, 'It must be wearing for you.'

Arlette had smiled at her but made no comment except to say, 'I think she'll get married soon. There's a boy in the office; they're seeing a lot of each other.'

She had turned her gaze away from Arlette as she muttered, 'I seem to have a lot to answer for.' And Arlette had put her arms about her and kissed her and said, 'You mustn't blame yourself for anything.' Arlette was still a comfort.

Last week Paul had phoned to say that they had had a daughter. She was happy for him, happy for them. He had also said he thought he had better tell her that Elizabeth had moved out; she was sharing a flat with another girl. But she hadn't to worry, he was keeping an eye on her. Anyway, he thought she would be married soon; she was going strong with a young fellow.

Was he a Catholic?

283

No.

Well, it didn't matter, did it?

No, he said; it didn't matter, not these days.

'It's October again,' Annie said as she brought the post in. 'If you were blind you could tell by the mornings, the air hits you. You've got a nice lot this morning, eight. And look.' She sorted one out. 'There's one from the television people. Tyne-Tees, it's got on it.'

Maggie pulled a face and took the envelope from Annie's hand. When she opened it and read the contents she gave a little laugh, looked at Annie, then handed her the letter.

After reading it Annie said, 'My! My! You've hit it now, haven't you? Them asking you to go on a programme and paying you for it . . . Television! What'll it be next I wonder? Eeh! Wait till this gets about.'

'They're not asking me to do a series.' Maggie slanted her gaze up at her. 'Nor giving me a half-hour to myself, they're just asking me to demonstrate while one of them is talking.'

'Oh yes.' Annie looked at the letter again. 'You won't have to open your mouth?'

'No, I won't have to open me mouth . . . Isn't that a good thing?'

'Aw you!' Annie threw the letter on the table; then seating herself, she said, 'Nevertheless, it's a start; it could lead to anything.'

'Yes, anything.'

'What's the matter with you, you sound as flat as a pancake this morning.'

'I've got a headache, didn't sleep much.'

'Well, you went to bed early enough.'

'Yes, I know I did, but as I said I didn't sleep.'

'Eat your breakfast.'

'I've had all I want.' She rose from the table now, taking her letters with her, and Annie said, 'You sickenin' for something?'

Maggie bowed her head, then turned round and looked at Annie, and in a childish voice she simpered, 'Yes, Ma, mumps.'

'Aw you! Go on with you,' said Annie, and they both laughed.

That morning, she had to visit a Mrs Penrose on the outskirts of Felburn and take half-a-dozen off-models. She had met the lady before and classed her as the huntin', fishin' and shootin' type, of which she now had a number on her books. But she wasn't prepared for Compton Place, and she was made to wonder as she drove her car up the long drive to the Tudor-style house why anyone living in this style should need to buy second-hand rig-outs. But inside the house, where there was an absence of staff, except for one indifferent looking maid, and a great deal of unpolished furniture and dust, she thought she had the reason. The off-models were one of the reasons for keeping up appearances like the two horses she had seen coming out of the stable yard. The Colonel, too, must keep up appearances. Well, she told herself, as she was shown upstairs, it was their life; but she wouldn't like to live it.

She came away from Compton Place quite satisfied with her own way of life, and her case lighter by an evening gown, two suits and a coat.

She had another call about two miles away in Burlington Terrace. This was breaking new ground. The Burlington Terrace district was an upper working class part of the town adjacent to Bog's End. One wag had said that the social aspirants jumped like fleas out of Bog's End into Burlington Terrace, then crawled like snails to the foot of Brampton Hill. The appointment was for twelve-thirty, an odd time she thought; perhaps the woman went out to work and was dashing back at dinner time. Muriel had thought this, too, when she had made the appointment, but she realised she was a new customer, so didn't haggle about the time being awkward.

Muriel was an acquisition of six months' standing in Flout Street. She took in the calls, made the appointments, pressed the gowns and did alterations. She was a find, was Muriel, because she was a widow who needed the money and never quibbled about staying half-an-hour late. Moreover, she was Maggie's size and they got on well together.

About a mile from Burlington Terrace the road was up for repairs, and joining a slow stream of cars she made the detour that wound into Bog's End. At the traffic lights she turned down Farley Road. Farley Road was a narrow road, always congested; it ran for about a quarter of a mile and was made up of odd shops, factories and small houses. Towards the end of the road, as if it had been stuck on by mistake, was a row of four-storey terraced houses which, in better days, had housed in grand isolation captains and their like, but which now from the top of their ornamental blackened chimneys to the rusted iron railings at their feet appeared like genteel ladies who, through no fault of their own, had been reduced to penury.

When she was almost half-way along the row she had to pull to a sharp stop; there was a hold-up in front of her. She leant back in her seat and relaxed; she had plenty of time, twenty minutes, and she was only five minutes away from Burlington Terrace. She turned her head casually and looked out of the window across the pavement to where a man was leaning against the stanchion of a door. He had his hands in his pockets, his eyes looked blank, he appeared a picture of dejection. Her shoulders came up sharply from the back of the seat and she brought her face to the open window, and perhaps it was this quick movement that drew the man's attention, for within a second his whole manner had changed, and with three strides he was at the car window.

'Why, hello, Maggie.'

'Hello, Ralphy. How are you?'

'Oh, you know.'

Yes, she knew. Twelve o'clock on a weekday leaning against a wall meant out of work. She stared up into his face. It was sad, as always when he was sober.

The traffic was beginning to move. She looked quickly through the windscreen, then back at him. She couldn't leave him like this, he was on his uppers; she'd have to give him something but she couldn't stop. She said quickly, 'I'll have to be moving; get in a minute.'

'What!'

She leant over and opened the back door of the car, and like a shot he was in.

She took the first turning up a side street, then drew the car to a stop. When she turned round and looked at him he was leaning forwards with his forearms resting on the top of the seat. She began in the usual way, 'Well, how are you, Ralphy?'

'Oh, alive and kickin', Maggie.'

'Are . . . are you living back here now?'

'Yes.' He jerked his head upwards. 'Along there, number seventeen. I've got a room.'

They stared at each other, and she waited for him to go on, but he just sat looking at her wide-eyed, a half smile on his face that gave it an expression of wonder.

'Are . . . are you working?'

'Well, not at the moment, not at the moment, Maggie; things are black. You wouldn't believe it, all this talk of new industries comin' in, and when you go they're full up . . . but—' he put his head on one side and grinned at her '—if you're a young lass you can get a job anywhere.'

They were silent again, and again she waited; then she asked, 'Haven't you tried the buildings?'

'Oh, they've got their regular chaps, you know how it is . . . You're looking bonny, Maggie. Aye, I can't believe it. Not that I didn't always know you had a fine figure.' He jerked his head to one side. 'By! Aye! You always had a fine figure; but I've never seen you dressed up to the eyes like this afore, I mean until I saw you that day havin' your picture took. Eeh! and it was a picture. You were a sight for sore eyes, an' I said that to Rod . . .'.

His chin dropped and his eyes followed suit, and she asked, her voice tight, 'And what did he say to that?'

He raised his eyes to hers. 'Nowt much, Maggie.'

'Nowt much!' She repeated his words.

'Oh,' he was quick to assure her, 'he wasn't nasty or owt like; he was just, well, taken aback, floored like. An' I'd never seen him floored like that afore, the wind was taken completely out of his sails. I might as well tell you, Maggie, I thought at the time, it serves him bloody well right, but I still couldn't help feelin' sorry for him. You know what I mean?'

'What did he say?' Her tone conveyed her persistence.

He looked down again; then said quietly, 'Well, it was nothin' really, just what you make out of it. What he said was, if you spit against the wind you always get your own back.'

It's what you make out of it. She stared at Ralphy, at his unshaven face and his bleary eyes. She wanted to say to him, 'Where is he now? Has he got a room in number seventeen an' all?' But she couldn't bring herself to ask such a question because there was always the possibility that Ralphy would go straight back and tell him. The next

288

minute, however, Ralphy gave her the answer without her asking.

'The job in Newcastle finished just after that, but the firm had a contract for here, lower Bog's End, Fenwick Street an' thereabouts, an' one way an' another he could have had another three weeks' work, but he went off, said he was goin' south.'

Her body was deflating again. It was a long time now since she had experienced this feeling; it was a strange sensation. Underneath her smart make-up and elegant clothes she was falling inwards to the core of herself, where the truth lay.

She stemmed the shrinkage by opening her bag and looking in her wallet. Her fingers were on a five-pound note when she thought, If I give him this much he'll blow the lot. The thing to do with Ralphy was to dole it out in small amounts. But then she might not see him again for months, if ever. She crumpled the note up and pushed it into his hand, saying, 'Now get yourself some food in.'

He did not look at what she had given him but attempted to push it back at her, saying, 'No, no, Maggie. Now look; now there's no call for that. And I wasn't after anythin'. Look, I get me dole the day after the morrow, I'm all right. But,' his fingers now closing over the note, he ended, 'thanks, lass. You've got a big heart, Maggie.' He moved his head slowly. 'Although it's been broken you've still got enough left for two.'

She half turned from him, her throat tight; then looking at her watch she said quickly, 'Ralphy, I'll have to be putting a move on, I've got an appointment with a client.'

'Oh aye. Yes, Maggie. OK.' He opened the door and got out. Then putting his head through the window, he said, 'It's been grand seeing you, lass. Things were lookin' black this mornin', but there's always a silver lining, isn't there? Always a silver lining.'

As she stared at him the smile went from his face and it became serious, as did his tone as he ended, softly, 'If it's any consolation to you, Maggie, he . . . he never bothers with women. I've worked alongside of him for nearly a year now, on and off like, one place and another. He's had a chance; but no, he wouldn't look the side they were on.'

She cleared her throat, took in a long breath and, her face tight now, she said, 'It's no consolation, Ralphy . . . Bye-bye.'

'Bye-bye, Maggie. Ta-rah, lass.' He straightened up, and she started the car and moved off.

If it's any consolation to you, he never bothers with women. No; perhaps he was still pining for his lost lady-love. She wondered what Mrs Rosamund de Ferrier would have thought if she had seen him, as she herself had seen him a few months ago; or how he would have re-acted if he had come face to face with the lady. Well, to hell! It made no odds, it didn't matter a damn to her how he reacted; as he had said, he had spat against the wind and had got his own back.

She left Burlington Terrace at quarter past one, after having sold a dress and a suit, knowing she had made another good contact. She went into a restaurant and had a hasty lunch. There was one more call to make at four o'clock, but before that she must get back to Flout Street and collect the appropriate models for the customer, and if time allowed she intended to drop in to Madam's and give her the details of the two sales she had already made and put a suggestion to her that they should add shoes to their list. Twice within the past week, she had been asked if they dealt in these. And last but not least, she must tell her about the television invitation . . .

It was just on three when she entered the shop and she noted at once that business was brisk. It was rarely that Madam had more than three customers in at a time, but now Annette was busy with a client at one end of the room, and Marianne was trying to interest another in a lamb's wool twin-set, while a third sat in one of the gold brocade chairs and waited, with seeming patience.

Leaving her client, Annette came swiftly to Maggie and said under her breath, 'Madam's in the dressing room with Lady Shaw.' She pulled a face. 'And there's another one waiting in the Blue Room.' She thumbed genteelly to where the blue velvet curtain hung down over the archway. 'Have you any time to spare . . . ?'

It was at this point that Madam opened the door of the fitting room. Evidently she had been going to give Annette a message, but seeing Maggie she exclaimed brightly, 'Ah! Margaret. You have come at an opportune time. You have a few minutes to spare? Come.' She took her by the arm, then whispered, 'Have a word with Madam, will you? I'll be with her shortly.' She led the way to the blue velvet curtain, pulled it aside and stepped beyond into the room, and Maggie followed her, at least as far as the archway for there she stopped and looked to where the client was sitting reading a magazine. The client looked up at her, and recognition was mutual.

At this moment Maggie was solid and sober. She had been solid and sober for two years now, so her reaction to the sight of the client could not be said to have been aided by drink. The only difference between her reactions now and on the night she swore at the Duke was that now there was nothing spontaneous about it, she took her time over it. Drawing herself up to her full height, her eyes cold, her tone icy, she proclaimed in a voice that carried, not only into the shop but into the fitting room, 'I don't wait on whores.'

She could have counted ten in the silence before she turned away from the white, shocked face of Rosamund de Ferrier, and she had walked down the shop and was going through the door before the indignation, coming solely from Madam, burst behind her.

CHAPTER THREE

POWER

Maggie did not see Madam Hevell until forty-eight hours later.

When she had arrived home after the incident, Annie, looking at her and noting that the barometer was down, asked quietly, 'What's happened now?' and Maggie, in a few precise words told her, after which Annie stared at her, then cupped her face with her hands, rocked herself gently and said, 'Woman! you're going to land yourself in trouble one of these days.'

'Doubtless,' said Maggie, and went into one of her long silences, which meant that she was either very angry or full of remorse; but Annie knew it wasn't the latter in this case.

The following day she kept to the house and there was no word from Madam, but at noon the next day the phone rang and Madam's voice giving nothing away said, 'Margaret?' and Maggie said briefly, 'Yes.' She didn't add Madam.

'What is the matter with you, why haven't you been in to your work?'

Is she joking? Maggie looked about her as if in search of eyes to answer the question. When she made no reply, Madam's voice came again, saying, 'You are ill, are you?'

'No, I'm not ill.'

'Then perhaps you'll oblige us by calling this afternoon?'

'Very well.'

At three o'clock Madam and Maggie faced each other across the table in the fitting room. At this time yesterday

Madam would have cried at her, 'Get out! I never want to see you again; you have ruined my business. You are a disgrace. Why did I ever think of taking on a person such as you.'

But since then she had gone over the whole scene yet again, with Annette, Marianne and Justine and, not least, Muriel from The Rooms, and all dropping their deferential manner for once, had said that although Margaret had laid it on a bit thick she was nevertheless right, for Mrs de Ferrier had had more men on the side than there were fingers on their hands.

Ah but, Madam had countered, her morals were of no concern of theirs but her custom was, she was a very good client.

'Well,' Annette had said, 'you'll lose her, so what! But I bet when this gets around you'll have more customers than ever; if they only come to see Margaret, someone who had the nerve to tell that piece what she was. She has a lot of enemies, has Mrs de Ferrier, and Lady Shaw is one of them. I bet her phone's been hot since she left here.'

And then there was Arthur.

'What!' he had cried. 'Sack Margaret?' All right, she had called a client a whore. A scene like that was good for business these days. Better still if Mrs de Ferrier sued her. Sack Margaret! She must be mad.

And lastly there was Muriel. Muriel had been very upset when she heard what had taken place because, she ended, 'This would put paid to the television do.'

'What television do?' Madam had demanded, and Muriel had told Madam of the letter Margaret had received from the Tyne-Tees people.

So Madam now looked at Maggie in great sorrow, and with her head on one side and her hands clasped together at the top of her bony breast she said, 'Ah, Margaret, Margaret, you are very naughty, very naughty indeed. I should be very angry with you, but there.' She now sprung her hands apart and held them out palm upwards as if in supplication to Maggie herself. 'What have you to say?'

'What can I say?'

'You called her a very bad name.'

'To my mind she's a very bad woman.'

'Ah yes. Ah yes.' Madam nodded her head sympathetically now. To give her her due, when she had ushered Maggie into the Blue Room she had forgotten completely that it was Mrs de Ferrier who had stolen Maggie's husband. But she wondered now that the two hadn't met before, for at certain times in the year Mrs de Ferrier would come at least twice a week for fittings. Again she shook her head at Maggie.

Far from finding Madam's attitude reassuring Maggie was finding it irritating. If she was going to fire her she didn't want it buttered up like this; anyway she had already fired herself, it didn't matter. She would get another job, her name was good . . . Good for what? Aye, good for what? This was the second time she had blotted her copy book in this town. It would seem that Rodney Gallacher was right, she was at rock bottom nothing but a big, fat ignorant slob. But she wasn't sorry for what she had said to that one. No, by God! She had often thought of how she would react if ever they met, and when it happened she'd had very little time to think. Nevertheless, her thinking had been straight and to the point. No, she wasn't sorry.

Her eyebrows moved slowly upwards as Madam, rising to her feet, said, 'Well now, it is over, done with, finished. I will, what you say, cut my losses. And—' she wagged her finger down into Maggie's face '—there will be losses. Ah, yes. Ah, yes. Her cheques were big and regular. But there, there; that is life.' Again she spread her hands; then when they were joined once more at her breast, she said, 'And now, have you replied to the Tyne-Tees people?'

Maggie stared at her, and after a moment she had the desire to burst out laughing. She wasn't being given the push; she must be more important than she realised, indeed, yes. Have you answered the Tyne-Tees people? She smiled at Madam. She was cute, was this little French-cum-Belgian woman; she wasn't keeping her on because she loved her, but because in her own way she had assumed some sort of power. Funny that, her, Maggie Gallacher, having power of any kind. She thought secretly to herself in an aside, 'I could start off on my own in this business now, and if I was to let that drop to Annette or Marianne, I'd like to bet a partnership in here would be forthcoming the morrow. Huh! Wheels within wheels. Rod used to call it legal blackmail.'

Rod? He had gone South then. She might never see him . . . Funny how things seemed to happen to her in batches.

'Well, I haven't answered it yet but I'll get it off tonight.'

'That's right. Margaret, that's right. Now along you go.' Madam patted her on the shoulder as if she were a child, and as if she were addressing a child she ended, 'And behave yourself. Do you hear, Margaret, behave yourself. And be grateful that I am so fond of you.'

On her way out she winked at the girls, and in the street she paused a moment to look up at the sky. Life was funny, and not always heartbreakingly funny, sometimes ha-ha-funny!

CHAPTER FOUR

RALPHY

Life went on, day after day, week after week, getting busier and busier; more clients, more bonuses, pictures in the local paper, her name, Margaret Gallacher, in heavy black print below. At one time it would have read: Margaret Gallacher modelling gowns for Madam Hevell. Now it merely said: Margaret Gallacher, the model. People noticed her when she walked through the town. Strange women stopped her and spoke to her. It was all very exciting, very gratifying; that is when she could give her whole mind to the job in hand, but as time went on she was finding this more difficult.

She could say that for perhaps two-thirds of the day and part of every night her mind was on other things, and not least the futility of her life. It was very strange, even disturbing when she recognised she was less fulfilled now than she had been during those long years when she was tied to the house, first with the bairns, and then as a waiting wife, waiting for her man coming in – the big, fat, ignorant slob sitting waiting for her man coming in.

She found that for long stretches at a time, mostly in the early part of the night, she would think of individual members of her family, taking them as it were from a box in her mind and standing them before her on the palm of her hand, very like the trick photography you saw on the television. And from the vantage point of distance, she would search for reasons for their behaviour; Paul's, Liz's, Frances's; but not Willie's or

Helen's, theirs seemed ordinary and predictable. Lastly, it would be Sam she would examine. She could do this unemotionally now, and she had come to think that Sam's trouble was that he had suffered a kind of rejection, too, by knowing that he was an accident in the first place and hadn't been wanted, at least not by his dad. Yet it was on her he had vented his spleen.

The more she thought the more she delved, and the more she found out about the members of her family the more she realised that they were mostly strangers to her, that they always had been. There was only one person who had been no stranger, and if she'd had him alone and had never conceived one of her six children she would still have felt satisfied, still have been fulfilled.

But strangely Rodney was the only one she didn't put on her hand and look at. She had no need, she knew all about him . . .

'Surely,' said Annie, 'you're not going photographing the day?'

'Surely, we are,' Maggie mimicked her as she shrugged herself into a Kolinsky coat which was to be sold as a mink.

'You'll freeze.'

'What! In this?' She did a few professional steps across the narrow hall, then turned and said, 'Original price, fifteen hundred, Madam; it's an utter bargain at three fifty.

'Yes, of course, Madam, I can leave it; I only have my vest and knickers on underneath, but anything for you . . . and business.'

'You're daft.' Annie had her head down trying to suppress her laughter. Then, her face straightening suddenly, she said, 'It's going to snow or come down in ice cubes by the feel of it. I bet you a shilling we'll be up to the eyes in it afore Christmas. It's bad enough when it starts in the New Year. Do you think you'll get home for a bite of dinner?'

Maggie considered for a moment, then said, 'Well, I might and I mightn't. I've got three calls to make this morning then I'm going back to Flout Street this afternoon to pick up Muriel. I'm taking her out with me. It's to an old customer; she wants fitting.' She considered again, then said, 'I'll try, but if I'm not in by one-thirty don't wait, have your own.'

'It's a casserole, it won't hurt. Get back if you can, no matter what time. You want something inside you, weather like this, not restaurant ket.'

'Ta-rah,' said Maggie; and Annie, coming to the door, called after her as she walked carefully down the frost-glistening path to the garage, 'Mind how you drive. If the roads are like this you'll be up a lamppost afore you know where you are.'

Maggie was still smiling when she brought the car out of the garage, and she waved her hand out of the window to Annie, not in farewell but to indicate that she should get inside out of the cold. As she drove into the road she thought, as she had often done of late, that life would indeed be stark if it wasn't for Annie. It was odd how God, the designer of fates, or whoever it was who traced out the map of your life, managed to leave you a little comfort. She never went to church now but her lack of religion didn't trouble her. She was fortunate in this way that she could question without fear.

She arrived in Newcastle about ten o'clock. Her first client's address was in the residential part of Gateshead. This was breaking new ground, and she wasn't quite sure how to get there. As she drove over the bridge across the river she decided that once she got clear of the main stream of traffic she would ask her way; and this she did a few minutes later.

'Oh, Steinbeck Crescent,' said the man on the pavement. 'Oh, no, missis, you're some way from that, you've come in at the wrong end. But look I tell you what.' And now, like all northerners when directing a stranger, he drew a map with his hands, his head, and his tongue. 'You go up there, you see, and you take the first turning on your left, what I mean, the big turning, not that little one, that leads to a cul-de-sac, the turning after the third lamppost, you see? Well now, that's Bourne Road. Now you go down there.' He paused and considered and stared slantwise up into the grey sky before he continued. 'Then you come to a crossroad. There's no traffic lights, just a sort of halt. Now you turn right there and you're in Delia Road. Now that's a long road; keep straight on.' He paused again. Then his arm extended to its fullest length, his finger pointing as if directing her destiny, as, unknown to them both, it was, he went on, 'At the end you come into a huddle of shops, some new, some old. They've built a supermarket there recently, that's 'cos of the new estate. But that's on your left. Now you cut through there until you come to a library. It's a branch library, you can't miss it; it's an old greystone building like a miniature town hall. Now you turn sharp left there and once you do that you're all right. Just keep on, and if I'm not mistaken you come plumb into Steinbeck Crescent. All right?'

She laughed up at him. 'All right, and thank you very much.'

'Now you've got it? First turning on your left, turning after the third lamppost, down Bourne Road till you come to a crossroad, turn right into Delia Road and then straight along and there you are.'

'Thanks,' said Maggie again.

'Ta-rah,' said the man.

'Ta-rah,' said Maggie. She was laughing as she repeated to herself: Left, right, then straight along. And he was right in his directing, for eventually she came to the huddle of shops, a baker's, a grocer's, a fish shop, newsagent's, a post office. It looked as if it had all once been part of a village. Then further on she spied the library. It was just as he said, like a miniature town hall, with an ornate façade and a flight of steps going up to double doors. She was actually passing the steps when she recognised the figure walking down them. It was Ralphy Holland, but what was more strange than the sight of Ralphy in this unexpected place was that he was carrying an armful of books.

She pulled to a stop at the side of the kerb and looked back. He was coming her way. When he was abreast of her she put her hand out of the window and said, 'Hello there.'

'Why, Maggie!' His face lighted up. 'Fancy seeing you.' He bent down to her and stared at her. 'By! You're looking well . . . bonny.'

'How's yourself?'

'Aw.' He moved his head stiffly. 'Not so bad, not so bad.'

As she stared up at him icy drops of rain began to fall and he said, 'Here it comes!' At the same time he pushed the books under his coat, saying, 'They go for you if you get them wet.'

'Far to go, Ralphy?'

'St Frances Road, Maggie; a step or two it is.'

She opened the door and, hopping in, he said, 'Oh ta, Maggie. Thanks. By!' He shivered. 'It's lovely in here, warm.'

She didn't start up the car but sat looking at him, willing herself to ask the question but unable to come straight to the point.

'You studying something, Ralphy?' She nodded at the books now stacked on his knees.

'Me?' He dug his thumb into his chest. 'Me studying, Maggie? Now you know me better than that. I've got

301

nowt in me head to study with, lass.' His tone was self-deprecating. 'No.' He paused while looking straight into her face. 'These are for Rod.'

'Oh!' She pursed her lips and moved her eyebrows, and Ralphy went on, 'He reads all the time, can't keep him supplied. Studying electricity now he is, electronics or some such, I don't know. Anyway, it gives him something to do 'cos you can't just lie in bed and think. 'Tisn't good for you thinking too much, is it, Maggie?'

'No, Ralphy. He's in bed then is he?'

'Oh aye; of course, you wouldn't know, but he's been bad, right bad, bit of bronchial trouble he had. Got wet; you know how it is. And you know what he's like, don't you? Won't change his shirt when he should an' dry off, and it turned to pneumonia. The doctor's warned him to stay put for another three weeks, but you might as well talk to yourself.'

Ralphy was staring at her now, not speaking, and she turned from him and started the car.

Bronchial; he had never had bronchial trouble, he was as strong as a horse. But then he had never gone out in wet things, she had seen to that. Oh yes, she had seen to that. He'd hardly got in the door before she had his things off him, even if his shoulders were just damp. She had even whipped off his socks in the winter when she had suspected his feet were wet, knowing he wouldn't go to the trouble to take them off himself. Knelt on the floor before him, she had, and unlaced his shoes and pulled off his socks and rubbed his feet between her hands. The things she had done! And now he was having bronchitis . . . Well, that wasn't going to make her fall on her face and weep.

Her eyes were fixed straight ahead when she asked casually, 'You living together then, Ralphy?'

'Aye Maggie, I brought him to my place. 'Tisn't much, God knows, but it's better than where he was. But you know of old, Maggie, you can't satisfy Rod; he hates kipping in with anybody. But he didn't know much about it the time I fetched him. Thought he was a gonner; so did the doctor; and they couldn't get him to the hospital, it was full. There was a flu do a few weeks back, spread like wild fire it did . . . You turn off here, Maggie.'

She braked sharply and turned the car into a side road, and he said, 'One-two-five, near the middle; it's a Mrs Bradshaw's place. She lives upstairs and she lets the bottom two rooms; we've got the front one.'

A few seconds later when he said, 'This is it, Maggie,' she drew the car up outside a dingy house that seemed to be but one of hundreds in the dingy road. She added dirty to the dingy, for as far as her eyes could see there was peeling paint everywhere, and on the window right opposite to her a piece of brown paper had been stuck over a crack.

'Maggie.' His voice brought her eyes to him. 'You wouldn't . . . ? What I mean is, you wouldn't come and . . . ?'

'No, Ralphy, I wouldn't.' She thrust her hand into her bag and, opening her purse, again took out a five pound note and pushed it towards him. This time he made no protest but muttered gratefully, 'Ta. Thanks; it'll come in handy, Maggie. Ta, lass.'

'It's for food, not the hard stuff, mind.'

'Aw, I know, Maggie, I know.' His eyes became suspiciously bright and he turned quickly from her and fumbled at the door handle. She had to lean across him to open it, and as he stepped on to the pavement her eyes passed him and went to the window, not more than four feet away, and to the face looking out through the dirty pane. Her gaze became riveted for a second. It was his face, yet not his face, only the eyes seemed recognisable; they had always been deep set, but now they looked like round black blobs lying in sickly white hollows. The face was unshaven and seemingly without flesh . . . Oh, Holy Mother!

When Ralphy turned and glanced at the window the head disappeared and he looked at Maggie again and said, 'I . . . I put his bed against the window so he could look out.' He stared down at her, waiting for her to say something. Then he watched her pull herself upright and take the wheel. Bending down again, he said, 'Thanks, Maggie, it's been grand seeing you. Take care of yourself.'

Still she didn't speak, just nodded her head once, then started up the car.

Annie said, 'Why didn't you then? Why didn't you go and have a word with him?'

'WHAT!'

'Never mind what; it would have been an act of charity, if nothing else. And I'll tell you something.' She stabbed her forefinger at Maggie. 'It wouldn't be, because you didn't want to. And don't bawl at me 'cos I know what I'm talking about.'

'You know damn all if you're such a numskull as to think I'd move a step out of me way even if he was pegging out.'

'You're hard, Maggie Gallacher.'

'Yes, I'm hard, Annie Fawcett; and I'm going to remain hard.'

'The way you go on you'd think you were the only woman who had been let down in her life. And I'd like to remind you that if you hadn't been let down you wouldn't be where you are the day, an' in the position you're in.'

Damn the position! She only prevented herself from saying it aloud, but of late she had kept damning it, yet she didn't really know why, for she liked the work and she didn't know what she would do without it. It not only filled her life but it was like a snowball growing larger with every move she made, for now she had connections that took her miles out of Felburn.

She went to bed early on this particular night . . .

During the following two weeks she had no need to go through Gateshead or to pass the library that looked like a town hall, nor was she likely to have a client in St Frances Road, but she drove down it, at speed, at least once.

But it was not in St Frances Road that she met him, it was in the street market in Newcastle. She had some business to do in Northumberland Street and had left the car at the nearest point of parking, which was a good five minutes' walk away. She liked the Market arranged as it was along the pavement. In the early days she and Rod had come here all the way from Felburn to do the week's shopping. They could have got the stuff as cheaply in Felburn Market but they looked on it as a trip, a day out. There was a particular stall that used to sell scallions, and he would make her laugh her loudest by buying a bunch, nipping the tops off and eating them as they were, and he always smelt like a poke of garlic devils afterwards.

She was side-stepping to let a woman with a pram pass, and there he was opposite her, as if he had been conjured up out of the past, or she had stepped back all those years. It was him, and yet it wasn't him.

They stared at each other, eyes unblinking, mouths closed. When she was pushed aside by two laughing couples larking on, his hand came out to steady her, but stopped before it touched her and dropped to his side again. They still stared, neither of them speaking. She had always told herself, mostly at night time when she lay thinking, that if ever she did meet up with him, if ever this moment did happen, she wouldn't be the first to speak. But now she was forced to. 'Well!' she said. 'How are you, then?' She kept her eyes on his lips in case they should stray over his suit, a cheap summer suit, shiny and worn.

'Oh, all right, Maggie.' His voice had a hoarse, hesitant sound; it seemed not only a chesty voice, but one not often used. 'You busy these days?'

'Yes.' She looked into his eyes now. 'Pretty busy. And you?'

'Oh.' He jerked his chin. 'I keep going.'

They were silent again. She watched his neck straining up out of his collar, a remembered sign of agitation, and then he said, 'Well, I mustn't be keeping you.'

She heard herself saying, 'That's all right; I don't work on a Saturday, although—' she gave a short laugh '—that's not their fault, they'd keep me at it all the time. You know how it is.'

He made a small movement with his head and said, 'Yes, yes.'

When someone dunched into him now she said, 'I think we're holding up the traffic, I'm—' She tried to prevent herself uttering her next words but they came out in spite of it. 'I'm making my way down Pilgrim Street. There's a little place off where I go for lunch.'

'Oh yes. Yes.' It seemed as if this was all he was capable of saying, and it came to her with pitying knowledge that it was about the sum total of what he would ever say to her, placid as they both were now.

When she turned, he turned with her. But when they had cleared the crowd he stopped; and he looked into her face, from one feature to another, before he said, 'It's been nice seeing you, Maggie.'

She swallowed but was unable to say anything.

'I'd just like to say I'm glad about . . . about all that's happened to you.'

He was glad about all that had happened to her. Dear God.

'Goodbye, Maggie.'

'Goodbye, Rod.'

He turned from her, and she turned too – she wasn't going to be left standing – and they went their separate ways.

'Why didn't you ask him to have a bite?'

'How could I . . . ?'

'Because he wasn't got up?'

'No, no. Use your head, woman. Could you imagine him sitting through a meal and me paying the bill at the end? Talk about coals of fire on his head.'

'You know what you are? You're a fool. Look inside yourself. Who are you hurting? You're a fool.'

'Then there are two of us, aren't there?' Maggie's voice was flat sounding.

And on this Annie turned away, saying, 'Our cases are different. Ralphy was a soak, he was born with the taste for liquor, and he'll die of it. I was sensible, an' you know I was. Look where I'd be the day if I'd taken him. And don't say—' she flung round and stretched out her arm, her finger pointing '—don't say that I would have made a man of him; Ralphy Holland's not the kind of man any woman could alter. There are some made like that.'

'He's got his good points.'

'But they aren't good enough.' Annie's voice was flat too now, and she turned away and went into the kitchen, but reappeared in a moment and, standing with her hands on the stanchion of the door, she said, 'Have you made up your mind about Christmas yet? I want to know what to do. Here it is, only a fortnight off, and neither a puddin' nor a cake made.'

Maggie looked at her, then into the fire. Paul and Arlette were anxious for her to go to London. Willie wanted her to spend Christmas with them. Even her daughter Frances had extended a warm welcome to her. She shook her head. Frances was cunning. A sprat to catch a mackerel, that was Frances. And Helen; she'd had no word from Helen for the last few weeks. Helen hadn't asked to come here, or her to go there. Helen was having trouble with Trevor; she'd always have trouble with Trevor. She wouldn't be at all surprised, or upset for that matter, if one day she walked in and said she had left him, or indeed said she wanted a divorce. No, nothing would surprise her any more.

And Liz? Liz, of all of them, had seemed to drop away beyond her horizon. Liz was leading a life of her own, having a good time, she called it, still not married. It was strange, but Liz was as dead to her as was Sam. Sam in a way had succeeded in killing her.

She looked up at Annie and said quietly, 'I think we'll stay put.'

At this Annie jerked her head once, then turned about and went into the kitchen.

CHAPTER FIVE

CHRISTMAS EVE

It snowed on Christmas Eve, as it had done on the four days previously. The main roads were being kept clear but the drifts at each side were four feet high, and more against the doors of the houses. The town was hushed as if under siege.

Willie had made his way over early in the day and brought her and Annie their Christmas boxes, and she had piled him high with parcels for the children. To him and Nancy her present had been a substantial cheque, which he had received gratefully with a muttered, 'Thanks, Mam.'

She had sent a cheque, too, to Frances, and one to Helen.

With one exception they had all sent her presents, mostly household things of more use to Annie than to her now. The only present that would be of any use to her had come from Arlette and Paul; this was a gold wristlet watch. The exception was Liz; Liz had sent her a Christmas card, a cheap, gaudy Christmas card, nothing else. Liz was indeed an enigma. Paul had said on the phone earlier in the day she hadn't to worry about Liz, she was finding herself, and one of these days, he said, she would open the door and there Liz would be standing, a new Liz, even better than the old one. But in the meantime she was to have patience. Liz was now attending an art school and her work was surprisingly good; this might be the answer.

So, on Christmas Eve she was alone. She did not count Annie. Although there was hardly a day went by now that she didn't thank God for her, Annie wasn't her family. She had six children and a husband; yes, she still had a husband, legally, and she was alone.

It was turned seven o'clock and they were sitting looking at the television when the phone rang. Annie went to answer it. A moment later she was back in the room. Standing looking down at Maggie, she said, 'It's Ralphy; he . . . he says . . . he says Rod's in a bad way, very bad way. Thinks his number's up. He thought you should know.'

Her head was back, her mouth was hanging open. There was a feeling between her breast bones as if an icicle had pierced her ribs.

'What'll I tell him, he's waiting?'

She got to her feet and stared at Annie. Then like a child seeking advice, yet knowing what she had to do, she said, 'I'd better go, hadn't I?'

'Yes, you had. I'll tell him.'

When Annie came back from the phone, Maggie was pulling on her high-legged boots, and she said, 'I wonder if I'll get through.'

'They'll have kept the main roads clear. You'd better wrap up well . . . Do you want me to come with you?'

'No.'

'Well, let me know how things are.'

'Yes.'

A few minutes later she eased the car on to the icy side road, and cautiously drove to the main road. Twice the car skidded, and as she hadn't experienced this before it scared her.

It was an hour-and-a-half later when she reached St Frances Road, and when she knocked on the door Ralphy opened it to her.

'Hello, Maggie.' His voice was a whisper.

She stepped into the hallway, and she not only saw the dirt, even in the dim light, but smelt it.

Silently now Ralphy led the way down a short passage and opened a door, and she went past him and into the room. And there he was lying on the bed fighting for his breath. He had changed so much, even from the time she had last seen him in the market, that he was almost unrecognisable.

When she stood by the bed his eyes met hers, no look of stubbornness in them now, no remnants of pride, just the knowledge that he was dying . . . and something else, something standing out from the sorrow. A plea.

His lips moved, but only a breath-heaving croak came from them. She sat down on the wooden chair that Ralphy had pushed forward and she lifted the sweaty hand from the dirty rumpled candlewick bedspread. Rod! Rod! The name was filling her, swilling clean her body with pity and remorse. He had been lying in this stinking, dirty room for God knows how long, and she could have prevented it. She could even have prevented his condition at this moment if on that Saturday in the market just those few weeks ago she had said, 'Rod, let's talk; let's go somewhere and talk.' For only she could have made the first move. Their positions were so reversed. He was lying flat at the bottom of his ladder and had no hope of climbing back to where she was, not even to where he had left her three years ago. All he'd possessed on that day in the market was a fragment of his self-respect, and he had hung on to that – it had been up to her.

She turned to Ralphy and whispered, 'The doctor. Has he had the doctor the day?'

'No, Maggie; I . . . I phoned him yesterday. He said he was full up, he'd be in the day. An' we've waited, an' he hasn't come . . . it being Christmas like.'

She released the hand that was holding hers with a weak grip and got to her feet; and now said to Ralphy, 'Does he live far?'

'Oh aye, quite a way, Maggie.'

'Do you know his number?'

He went to a table in the corner on which stood a gas ring and some old cooking utensils; above it was a shelf with a row of hooks holding a few cups and a jug. From one hook he took a piece of paper and, coming back, he handed it to her.

'Where's the nearest telephone box?'

'Oh, just at the top of the street. Will I go, Maggie?'

'No, I will.'

When she reached the telephone box she was sweating although the air was cutting at her throat.

A female voice answered her ring and to her enquiry said immediately, 'Oh, I'm sorry, Doctor Fine is out.'

'This is Doctor Fine's private address, isn't it? Well, you tell him to come to the phone.'

'I've told you—' the voice took on a haughty tone '—the doctor has been called out.'

'And I'm telling you, whoever you are, I don't believe you. Now look; the doctor had a message to come to this patient two days ago. He's got bronchial pneumonia and he's dying. Do you hear? Dying!' She was bawling in to the phone now. 'He won't last the night. If your man isn't at number one-two-five St Frances Road within the next hour or so you can tell him from me somebody's going to hear about this.'

'Who's speaking?' The voice was quiet but stiff now.

She was for saying Mrs Gallacher, and then she said, 'Margaret Gallacher,' and repeated, 'Margaret Gallacher. And it's my husband I'm talking about.' She didn't know whether her small fame had spread as far as this, but it just might have, and names counted for something with some people. 'If a doctor, and I don't care which doctor it is, but if a doctor isn't here as I said within

312

an hour then I'm phoning a hospital, and if they won't take him in without a doctor's note then I'm phoning the police. If this man dies through lack of attention, by God! I'll make somebody pay.'

She rammed the phone down, then leant against the partition and closed her eyes. Maggie Gallacher was back, blaring, shouting, bludgeoning her way through. She only hoped it worked. But she had meant what she said. If he didn't come within the hour or so she would phone the hospital.

When she opened the door of the room again Rodney's eyes were waiting for her. She went quietly up to the bed and, once more taking his hand, she bent over him and said, 'It's all right. You're going to be all right, the doctor's on his way.'

He moved his head slightly, tried to say something, then was racked with a fit of coughing.

When her arm went under his shoulders and supported him it was as natural as if she had done it yesterday, as if they had never been separated. When she withdrew her hand it was wringing with sweat; his whole body was bathed in sweat, the bed was wet with it, the sheets were wet. She walked from the bed and beckoned to Ralphy. 'Have you any other bedding, sheets?'

He shook his head, then said, 'She only supplies three altogether and they're not much cop. That one there.' He pointed to where a worn grey flannelette sheet was lying over a chair in front of the gas fire. It was sopping. 'I keep drying them and puttin' them back.'

She bit on her lip, then asked, 'Has he had anything, I mean a drink, milk, or brandy?'

His lips moved into a quirk. 'No, Maggie. Anyway, he couldn't take it, he couldn't swallow.'

'Have you any milk?'

'There's half a bottle in the cupboard.'

'I don't suppose—' she moved her head as she whispered '—you have any brandy?'

Again his mouth went into a quirk.

'Here.' She went to her bag and, taking from it a pound note, said, 'Get a miniature brandy, a double, and have a glass of hard stuff yourself. Just one mind, because I want the change.'

'Yes, Maggie, yes.'

'Go on then, quick!'

'Yes, Maggie.'

She now took an old towel from a line hung up over the shallow sink next to the table, and went to the bed and began to wipe his face and hands with it. All the while his eyes stayed on her, but she could not meet them in case she broke down. Now and again she spoke, saying, 'You're going to be all right. Once the doctor gets here you're going to be all right . . .'

It was almost two hours later when she heard the car draw up outside and Ralphy whispered, 'That'll be him.' And she said, 'Leave it to me, I'll open the door.'

She was still wearing her coat because it was cold in the room, but she hadn't a hat on, and when the doctor stepped into the passage he recognised her as someone alien to these surroundings. He stared at her coldly as he said, 'Are you the person who threatened my wife?'

'No, I am not the person who threatened your wife, doctor, I'm the person who threatened you, or any other doctor, who would leave a man in the state my husband is in.' She jerked her head towards the door. 'You were phoned two days ago.'

'I'm a busy man.'

She stopped herself from saying, 'Not too busy to get bottled,' for his breath wafted of spirits. Christmas Eve; he had likely been having a party or some such. And why not? Why not? But then, he hadn't been at a party for two days.

They stared at each other, hostility between them, and he said now, 'I left a prescription for your husband, and if he had followed my instructions over the past two weeks he wouldn't have needed even that.'

He marched from her and into the room and put his bag down on the table with a thump, then went to the bed. Bending over Rodney, he stared down at him. He had no need to examine this man's chest; he put his hand down under the bedclothes and over his heart. Then he held his wrist, and as he stood with it in his hand he looked across at Maggie at the other side of the bed. His eyes met hers for only a moment before travelling upwards, downwards, then around the room, and she knew that he was concerned.

When he put the hand back on the bed he went to his bag and took out a syringe, knocked the end off a glass tube and sucked up its contents into the valve, then he pushed up the loose shirt sleeve on Rodney's arm. When the needle went in Rodney made no sign.

He was at the bag again when he looked at Ralphy and said, 'The pills I gave you for him?'

'Aye, doctor.' Ralphy went to the iron mantelpiece and took down a bottle, which he handed to the doctor. It was three-quarters full and the doctor, shaking it, said, 'I told you he had to take them every four hours; it was imperative he took them every four hours.'

'He's stubborn, doctor. And then his throat got so sore he didn't want to swallow.'

The bottle on the palm of his hand, the doctor turned to Maggie and said grimly, 'If he had taken these he would have never reached this state.'

She was silent for a moment; then she said, 'But he has, and what's got to be done about it?'

He stared at her as if he hated her with a personal hate; then he looked towards the bed again and, his eyes on

315

her once more, he said, 'He's allergic to drugs, heavy drugs. These are mild; they would have taken time but they would have been effective. Well now I will have to put him on something that will act more quickly. It will be drastic, and there might be side effects. There undoubtedly will in his case, but we'll have to deal with them as they come. There's an all-night chemist open somewhere.' He now fumbled in his pocket and brought out a diary. Flicking over the pages he passed his fingers down a list of names and said, 'Crowley's, Fowler Street; they're open for service. Ring the bell.' As he ended he turned and looked at Ralphy, but Maggie put in, 'I'll go; my car's outside.'

He was looking her up and down now, from her high black leather boots to the green open coat, with the fur collar showing the red quilted lining and the dress beneath that matched the coat. Then his eyes slid from her to the bed. She saw that he was trying to work it out.

He said to her now as he wrote out the prescription, 'One every three hours for the next twelve hours, then one every four hours for the next forty-eight hours.' After a moment, as he snapped his bag closed, he added, 'I'll look in in the morning.'

She wanted to thank him, but she didn't. She'd wait till the morning when they'd both be in a better frame of mind.

As he went towards the door he said over his shoulder, 'I've put down a linctus and a rub. He should be changed frequently. Keep him dry if you can.' Now he turned his head right round and looked fully at her. 'But I can leave that to you, I suppose?'

'Yes.' She inclined her head stiffly towards him. 'You can leave that to me.'

When she let him out a church clock struck twelve, but neither of them remarked it was midnight on Christmas Eve; they didn't even exchange a goodnight . . .

By six o'clock the next morning she had changed the bed completely four times.

Annie had come in a taxi with a stock of sheets, pillow cases, blankets and towels and between them they had changed him and sponged his fevered body, and got a trickle of warm milk down his throat. Now at six o'clock on Christmas morning they were both weary and tired, but wide-eyed, because whatever was going to happen they knew would happen within the next two hours. He had seemed, for most of the night, to be only partly conscious but now his breathing was so painful that Maggie's shoulders were permanently hunched against the sound of it, and against the sound of Ralphy's snores, too, from where he was lying in the corner of the room. At three o'clock she had persuaded him to go to bed, telling him that he would be needed later on and that he must get some rest.

As she sat now watching the bedclothes rise and fall, as if they were being pumped by automatic bellows, she wished she were alone with him, for she wanted to put her face down to his and answer the question that had been in his eyes and say that she forgave him, even say that the blame was hers because she had been a stupid woman, a fat, easygoing – no, not a slob; no, never a slob – just a fat, easygoing stupid woman. To tell him that it was her fault in letting him climb up the ladder by himself; she should have known that there were all kinds of dangers on the way. But she hadn't been worldly enough, smart enough. You read your weekly magazines and the philosophy they put over, all about people like her and Rod, but you didn't take it in; it was never going to happen to you, it was just fiction.

She was startled when she heard him croak, 'Maggie!' His eyes were open and she bent above him and looked into them and said softly, 'Yes, Rod?'

317

'Maggie.'

'Yes, I'm here.'

He made an effort to say something, but when his heaving chest blocked the words she said, 'There now, don't try.' He was sweating again. The water was actually standing in blobs on his short hair before running down his brow and the sides of his face, and they changed him yet again and into, of all things, one of her own soft brushed nylon nightdresses, for she had long since got rid of any clothes he had left behind.

When he was settled again, Annie gathered up the wet sheets and, standing with them in her arms, she looked at Maggie and said under her breath, 'It would be easier, wouldn't it, if he was back home.'

Maggie's eyes did not flinch from hers and she answered, 'I know that; I'm going to put it to the doctor when he comes . . . '

The doctor came as he had promised. His face still looked grim. He gave Maggie no greeting, he did not even knock when he came in, but after looking down at Rodney for some minutes, then taking his pulse, he turned to her and said, 'Well, you're lucky . . . he's lucky; it's done the trick, but he's not out of the wood yet not by a long way. One of the off-shoots now will be diarrhoea. He's in a very weak state; that'll need a fight all on its own.'

She drew in a long breath. She would deal with whatever had to come. She said, 'It's difficult nursing him here, how . . . how soon could he be moved?'

'Oh.' He made a sound in his throat and looked at her as if she was an idiot and, his voice filled with sarcasm, he said, 'If you want to bury him, move him any time within the next week.'

She stiffened. 'I was thinking about an ambulance,' she said.

He lifted his bag. 'I wasn't thinking about a push bike.'

How was it, she thought, that you could hate a man you'd only seen twice?

He went out of the door and into the passage; then he turned and looked at her standing in the middle of the room. She was a fine looking woman, even tired as she was, and a battler. With a quick drooping movement of his head, he said, 'I'm sorry. I'm sorry.'

As she looked back at him she wondered now how it was that two words of apology could sweep away all bitterness. Her own voice was quiet as she replied, 'Me, too, doctor.'

He turned from her and went to the front door and, without looking at her again, he said, 'I'll be along later.' And now she said, 'Thanks. Thank you.'

When she had closed the door she stood for a moment staring along the grimy passage, and all of a sudden she felt weak, slightly sick, and had a great desire to cry. It was Christmas morning; the bairns were all playing with their toys, the mothers were getting the dinners ready, the dads were seeing to the drinks. Christmas day, Christ was born.

She had prayed intermittently all night; she had promised to go to Mass and her duties, if only he was spared. Well, she would keep her promise, and not only that, she would try to be better. She wasn't, she considered, a good woman, she was too big-mouthed, too quick with her tongue, saying things first and thinking after, but from now on she'd be different, not only outwardly like Miss Margaret Gallacher, but inwardly where a change was needed most.

CHAPTER SIX

THE CHOICE

After weeks of a repeated pattern of snow-storms and thaws the streets were now clear of sludge and the sun was shining; but as people prophesied, that wouldn't last long as it was only the beginning of February.

Maggie had made a point of not visiting clients on a Saturday; Saturday she took as a day off, except on the occasions when she was asked to join in a dress show at one of the leading restaurants, and on this particular day she had just finished one in Newcastle. She had shown three garments, one consisting of a two-piece ensemble, a woollen dress in turquoise, and a three-quarter length coat with a collar of turquoise that could be manipulated into a hood. This brought a great deal of applause, and Madam Hevell, who was sitting at a reserved table, patted her hand and gave her the smile of approval.

The business of the day over for her, Maggie didn't bother changing but went home as she was. She'd be modelling this again on Monday in any case. She was pretty sure she had a customer for it.

She drove the car to its limit and was home within half an hour. Annie was in the kitchen making some coffee, and she turned and looked at her and said spontaneously, 'Oh! I like that.'

'Yes, so did they.'

'Everything go off all right?'

'Fine, fine . . . How is he?'

'Oh, just as you left him.' Annie's voice was light and airy.

'Did he eat all his dinner?'

'No, but he got through a good bit.'

She went across the sitting room and into the bedroom, her bedroom, and started talking as she opened the door. 'Well, that's over. It's lovely out, lovely to see the sun.' She looked at him propped up in the bed, a little more flesh on his bones than there had been a few weeks ago, but he still remained a shadow of the man she knew, the big fella.

Unlike other times, he did not speak and say, 'Hello, Maggie.' He never just said, 'Hello', or 'Hello there,' as one would to someone close, but 'Hello, Maggie,' and the use of her name indicated a courteous diffidence, a polite barrier. Not that he wasn't grateful for all that had been done for him; the gratitude was in his eyes, but even so his look was always veiled. But now she watched his eyes covering her from head to foot; then she laughed with embarrassment, saying, 'Oh, this! I didn't change; the dressing rooms are always crammed in those places, and it's warm. The collar's a hood, look.' She twisted the collar up and the blue hood framed her face, and when he closed his eyes she let it drop back on to her shoulders and, standing at the foot of the bed, she stared at him until he opened his eyes again, then she turned from him and went out and into the room she shared with Annie.

Sitting on the edge of the bed, she looked at herself in the wardrobe mirror opposite. The blue velvet get-up the night of the do; it must have reminded him, for this too was all blue . . . and dressy. She was too dressy altogether. Everything she had in her wardrobe was dressy, everything.

All the years she had been married to him he had never seen her look like she did now. He likely could have if he had spent money on her, and that's what he must be

321

thinking. Her success was a reproach to him, everything he saw in her must be like a thorn in his flesh, that's why he couldn't talk to her. She was nobody he recognised. He had been in this house a month now and they had never talked. It had been 'Yes, Maggie,' and 'No, Maggie,' and 'Thanks, Maggie.' The politeness was wearing. Oh dear God, she never thought she'd know the day again when she would welcome a crack across her lug. But never again as long as they lived, and if they should live together, would he raise his hand to her, she knew this.

If they should live together? As soon as he was well he would go. She knew this too in her heart, because he could never be the husband of Margaret Gallacher.

There was only one way to stop him, to hold him.

She stared at her reflection until her face seemed to take up the whole space of the mirror and when it spoke to her and voiced her thoughts she cried at it 'No!' in loud protest. But when she uttered it for the third time the protest was much weaker, and her reflection said, 'Well, it's either one thing or the other, it's up to you to choose, you can't have it both ways. That's life, you can't have it both ways.'

CHAPTER SEVEN

MAGGIE GALLACHER

From the Monday of the following week she went out early in the mornings and returned home late each night, and on the Thursday night Annie said, 'Look, what's up? Have you taken to working overtime?' and her answer to this was, 'Something like that.'

'There's something up with you, what is it?'

'I'll tell you tomorrow,' said Maggie.

'That Madam Hevell been on at you?'

Madam Hevell been on at her? And how! Yes, and how.

On the Thursday night too Rodney said, 'I'm getting up the morrow, Maggie,' and she answered, 'I wouldn't hurry, there's plenty of time. You know what the doctor said, go careful.'

'I've gone careful for weeks,' he said quietly; 'I've got to make a start.'

'Well, just as you wish,' she said, and he looked at her, puzzled by a certain sadness that was in her manner, but a sadness that didn't seem connected with himself.

And then came Saturday. She was working this Saturday she said, but she should be home around five.

She wasn't home at seven, she wasn't home at eight. At half-past eight Annie said to Rodney, 'Something's up, something's been up all the week. Has she said anything to you?'

'No, Annie.' He shook his head. 'But then she wouldn't, would she?'

She looked at him where he was sitting by the side of the bed in pyjamas and dressing gown and she said, 'Maggie's changed you know, Rod,' and he answered, 'Yes. Yes, I know that, Annie.'

'Nobody ever realised what she was capable of.'

'No, they never did.' His head was bowed.

'I'm not blaming you, Rod.'

He raised his eyes to hers. 'Then you should.'

Yes, Annie should blame him, everybody should blame him, but even then their combined censure would not match the blame he took upon himself. Why had a man to go through hell before he could see things clearly, see himself for what he was? But then he always thought he had known himself. He was Rod Gallacher, the big fellow, knowing where he was bound for, and what road he was going to take, and the more short cuts he made the quicker he would arrive. Maggie had been an obstacle laid across that road. The day he had stood at the altar rails with her he had cursed her and the whole bang shoot of them, Father Stillwell and Father Armstrong included for saddling him with a big-mouthed, brainless, laughing lump. Still, the outcome had been better than he had expected. She was a worker both inside and outside the house, and she had satisfied his needs more than a little because she was crazy about him. Then as the years went by he had been pleasantly surprised when she became a sort of comfort to him. After going at it hell for leather all day she was there for him to go back to, to coddle him like a mother, feed him like a wife, and love him like a mistress. Things were all right, he had told himself as time went on, he hadn't made such a bad bargain after all; and what was more she didn't want much, not for herself. She wasn't demanding in that way, what she wanted was a home and the bairns. He could leave her at night and no questions asked, except perhaps a jibe when he got in late with a load on. But she never fought with him about this. He couldn't remember now what they had fought about, but they had fought, God, like tigers they had fought. That's one thing that had surprised him in the early days, her temper. Plump, easygoing people hadn't got tempers, at least that's what he had thought, but she had shown him differently, and it was odd but he had respected her more when she went for him. The times he had swiped her across the mouth! He bent his head against the memory.

Yet during all those years living with her he had never grown to love her; he hadn't loved anybody until he had met Rosamund de Ferrier. And the feeling he'd had for her? Was that love? He had asked himself this question countless times over the past few years. What was it anyway, love? Fascination? That had been the core of his feeling for Rosamund de Ferrier; he had been like a rabbit before a snake. But does a rabbit know the thing writhing before him is called a snake? A rabbit couldn't put any name to it, it could only feel powerless, drained of will, drained of the desire to turn and flee, capable of only one thing, waiting to be devoured. He had been devoured, then spewed up again. He saw her face now like the snake, her tongue licking away the taste of him. Could humiliation kill love, kill fascination? If that was possible then his love for her had died quickly, drowned in the well of self-denigration.

In those early days of agony he had not let himself think of Maggie, because when his thoughts touched on her it showed him up as a fool, someone who had never been able to see farther than his own nose, his own desires. Yet the estrangement from the rest of his family had brought him no pain at this time; he felt no sense of loss with regard to them. When he was really alone and at bottom, there had been only one person he thought of, she who had been a trinity to him; and added to his self-knowledge was a picture of a man, an ignorant man, a nowt, a man who had been capable of achieving only one thing in his life, building up a business. And then not even capable of doing that properly. On the sideroads he had to take on the way to his objective there had been toll gates, and as he advanced farther up the road so the rates of entry had become higher. But you did not always have to pay in money, you paid in kind; scratched a back here and there, turned a Nelson eye, lifted your hand in a vote. One thing apparently wasn't allowed, setting your sights on the toll-keeper's wife.

It was hard now for him to believe that he had reached as far as he had in the big business world with such little sense, for real sense lay in judging people, judging their worth. He had judged Rosamund de Ferrier and found her a gift of the gods; he had judged Maggie and found her wanting. But let him be fair to himself on this point; any man would have reacted as he had done the night she buggered the Duke.

Nevertheless, he hadn't proved to himself how much he had changed until, having reached rock bottom, he knew he would rather come face to face with Rosamund de Ferrier than with Maggie. And then he had seen her. He had gazed down on her from that half-wrecked building, and his amazement couldn't have been greater had he witnessed the resurrection.

After that, he had flown from the north, swearing never to return, but in six months he was back, at least in the county. Why? He wasn't even big enough yet to give himself the answer.

He had seen her three times before the night when he thought he was finished, but he had never seen her as Maggie, the Maggie that had been familiar to him; not even since he had been in her house during all these weeks had he glimpsed her. There was just a faint memory of Christmas Eve when she came to him and she had held him, and vaguely he remembered her arguing with the doctor. That had been Maggie.

He had told himself for days he'd have to pull himself together and get away. He couldn't go on much longer living on her charity, and seeing the pity in the eyes of his family. One thing he had to face up to and squarely: if he had changed, so had she. The irony of it was that the feeling he had for her now must, he thought, be something akin to what she'd felt for him in the early days. But also he felt that her feelings towards him were now as lukewarm as his had once been. She was still kind, compassionate. That was her nature, she couldn't be otherwise. And perhaps underneath there remained the old Maggie. If so, it was well coated with a veneer, a fashionable veneer. And it wasn't just a veneer, more like an armour, and he knew that he could never hope to penetrate it, not as he was now. Anyway, he wouldn't want to as he was now. If he could only get on his feet again . . .

'What's that you say now, Annie?'

'I said I'm going to phone The Rooms.'

'Won't they be closed?'

'Not if she's there.'

He sat waiting for her coming back. When she stood in the doorway and said, 'No reply . . . Do you think I should phone Willie?' he answered slowly, 'Give her another few minutes.'

It was a quarter of an hour later when, pulling himself to his feet, he said, 'She could have had an accident.'

'They would have let us know, wouldn't they? She's . . . she's got papers on her.'

He bowed his head; there were some accidents that left no papers. He felt sick, frightened, weak, terribly weak. He sat down again. 'You'd better phone Willie.'

'You think so?'

He nodded at her.

'If she comes in, she'll go mad if she thinks I've made a fuss. I'll . . . I'll go down to the gate for one last look.'

It was as Annie reached the gate that the car came along the road, and she stood aside as it turned in at the driveway. But almost before it had stopped she was at the window demanding, 'Where do you think you've been?'

'Now don't start.'

'Start! You've had us nearly round the bend. Do you know what time it is, after ten.'

'I've been busy.' She went to push the door open, saying, 'Let me out.'

Annie let her out, then started again, 'Why didn't you phone?'

'I couldn't, I was held up.'

'Held up be damned! Surely you haven't been held up all that much that you couldn't pick up a phone.'

'I was at Muriel's place; she doesn't have a phone . . . not yet.'

'Then there are call boxes, aren't there?'

'Stop shouting, I'm tired.'

'You're tired, what about us? Him in there—' Annie thumbed back towards the house – 'he's nearly been round the bend.'

'Really!' Maggie's tone was cold and brought Annie's voice rasping at her low and angrily. 'Now don't start that again, time's past for make-believe. You know, and I know, and he knows there's got to be a showdown, or a clearing of the air, at least. He's got to know where he stands.'

'ANNIE!'

They were standing by the side of the car, their faces reflecting the light from within as Maggie hadn't yet closed the door. Her voice dropping, she said, 'I'm tired. I've been in a showdown all day, all week . . . And that's over now, it's ended.'

328

'What do you mean?'

'I'm finished with the business.'

'My God! No! Never!'

'Yes, that's what it's all about.'

'But why?'

'Aw, Annie.' Maggie made an unusual gesture by putting out her hand and gripping Annie's shoulder and, her voice soft and weary, she said, 'You know me, but you also know him. Would he settle for the set-up as it is?' She shook her head. 'Not Rod.'

Annie's lips were quivering now, her eyes were blinking. 'But . . . but to give it up after you've worked so hard and . . . and made a name.'

'What's a name, Annie?'

They stared at each other a moment longer; then Maggie said, 'I want a drink, something hot. Make me a coffee will you, put a dash of brandy in it?'

They walked side by side along the path, through the back door and into the kitchen, and Annie said, 'Go on in and relieve his mind; I'll bring it in to you.'

'Aye, Maggie.'

She took off her hat and coat as she crossed the sitting room, and when she opened the bedroom door he was standing at the foot of the bed. He looked thin and gaunt, his short black hair, greying in parts, accentuating the pallor of his skin. He was breathing heavily, as if he had trouble drawing the air down into his chest. He went to speak, but his lower jaw dropped, and his lips moved and he swallowed his spittle before he said, 'You were held up?'

She noticed that he didn't say Maggie. For the first time since their lives had come together again he hadn't used her name when speaking to her.

'You should be in bed,' she said. 'Go on, get back into bed.'

He shook his head with an impatient movement. 'I'm all right, I'm all right. What kept you?'

'Sit down,' she said. She went towards him but didn't touch him. He turned and walked unsteadily back towards the chair and she, looking round, went to bring a chair up to him but changed her mind and sat on the edge of the bed opposite to him.

She looked at his hands gripping each other on his knees, those big hands patterned like his face, square and bulky, but like his face now pale and washed-out looking. By the working of his fingers she could tell he was agitated.

She went to let her body slump but checked it. No, no more of that; that was one thing she wasn't going to let go. And she was going to keep dressed, and well dressed; she'd got a taste for dress and she'd promised Madam she'd always be a customer, at least at The Rooms.

'Something wrong?'

'No, nothing wrong, Rod; it's just that I've given up me job.'

'What!' The word was a muttered whisper.

'Yes, that's what's kept me busy all week, that and something else.'

'But why? You've made such a success of it.'

'Oh, I don't know, Rod.' Her head drooped and she shook it from side to side. 'It's tiring. And the people you've got to meet, they're not all that you would wish.' She gave a half laugh. 'Wanting the best clothes, but wanting them cheap and ashamed of buying them second-hand . . . Oh—' she closed her eyes and laughed softly '—you mustn't use that word, second-hand. God! The snobbery that you meet up with. Paying fifteen pounds for a sixty-guinea suit, then demanding to know which part of the country it came from, and are they likely to meet up with the previous owner? Then you waffle and give them the old talk: "I doubt it, Madam, unless you are going into

330

society." Oh, that always does it. They try to get names out of you then, and you have to stop yourself from letting your imagination run riot and start throwing titles about.'

She was smiling, but his face was straight, tense. 'Won't you miss it?' he asked.

'I suppose so, a bit; but then I need a rest. I'm not a girl any more.' She spread her hands and let her smile widen and watched his eyes move over her.

When he asked, 'What will you do with yourself?' she looked down on his joined hands, and when her answer came, 'I've got another job,' she watched them move slowly apart as he repeated, 'Another job?'

'Aye, a bit different though.' She pulled a face at him. 'And I'll need help, somebody in the know.'

As he waited for her to go on, Annie came in with the coffee on a tray. 'Get that down you,' she said, 'then come and have a bite, it's ready.'

'Thanks.' She took the cup of coffee and drank deeply from it, then she sighed and said, 'Ah, that's better.' And when she looked at him again, he asked, 'Where?'

'Oh well now, it's difficult to describe. It's past Denton. You know the estate on the right-hand side as you come out of Newcastle? Well, on the left there's the west road to Corbridge and Hexham. It's along there, it's a house.' She paused, and he screwed up his face and said, 'A house? You're going to work in a house?'

'Aye.' She nodded at him. 'You could say that, in a kind of way.'

'A big house?'

'Yes, biggish, fourteen rooms all told.'

'. . . What . . . what are you going to do there?'

'Well, for a start re-decorate I should say.'

He made a slight movement with his head.

'That's what I'm going in for, sort of re-decorating. I've been round some houses in the last few years and

331

I've always thought to meself if I had this I would do so-and-so. And now that's what I'm going to do. There's four acres of land attached.' Her face was straight now. She was looking into his eyes. 'There's building permission for two houses. They must have not less than half an acre each. It's that kind of district you know. I thought it would be sort of a good idea . . . When the big place is re-decorated it'll be worth two or three times what it's going for now. Well, then the other two houses could be built in easy stages, no hurry you know, and a nice little profit at the end. And in the meantime look round for other plots. You hear it said that all these places have been bought up, but that isn't so, I've been to three this week similar. But I picked on this because I, well, I thought the country air would do you good, and—' She could not go on to say, 'it's well away from Felburn,' but said softly, 'You could practically build them yourself with help from Ralphy . . . you always said you could build a house on your . . .'

'Maggie, for God's sake, don't!'

His head was deep on his chest, his shoulders were hunched, and she muttered, 'Rod, we've . . . we've got to talk.' She bent forward and put her hand on his and he groaned, 'You don't know what you're doing to me.'

'I do, Rod, I do. Believe me I do, but I was never very good at being subtle.'

'Oh, Maggie, Maggie.' Her name was wrenched up from the depths of him and his hands came away from hers and covered his face, and as the sobs racked his body she pleaded, 'Rod, don't, don't take on. Don't.' She went to put her arms about him but couldn't. This was one step she couldn't take, not on her own.

When he slipped from the chair and on to his knees and buried his head in her lap she closed her eyes tight before she gathered him to her, and like a mother now she held him and listened to him sobbing out his deprecation of himself.

'Maggie, Maggie, as long as I live I'll never forgive meself.'

'It's all right, it's all right. There, there, give over now.' Her own tears were washing her face, her own voice was broken.

'Maggie . . . Maggie, I want to say something to you.'

'Aye, yes, I'm listening, Rod.'

'I . . . I love you, Maggie. I love you, I do. Believe me, I do. Aw, Maggie, Maggie.'

She made no answer to this. She had been married to this man for almost thirty years and this was the very first time she had heard these words from his lips. Unbelievable when she came to think of it; she had borne him six children, and there had been times when they had frolicked and made love but never, never, had he said the words, 'I love you, Maggie.'

This was what it was all about. For this she had endured hell. For this she had thrown away the ladder that would have taken her to the heights, albeit the small heights where Margaret Gallacher would have reigned. She would be forgotten, except perhaps as that woman Maggie Gallacher who had buggered the Duke.

But it was to Maggie Gallacher he had said, 'I love you, Maggie.'

She pressed him fiercely to her.

THE END

JUSTICE IS A WOMAN
by Catherine Cookson

The day Joe Remington brought his new bride to Fell Rise, he had already sensed she might not settle easily into the big house just outside the Tyneside town of Fellburn. For Joe this had always been his home, but for Elaine it was virtually another country whose manners and customs she was by no means eager to accept.

Making plain her disapproval of Joe's familiarity with the servants, demanding to see accounts Joe had always trusted to their care, questioning the donation of food to striking miners' families – all these objections and more soon rubbed Joe and the local people up the wrong way, a problem he could easily have done without, for this was 1926, the year of the General Strike, the effects of which would nowhere be felt more acutely than in this heartland of the North-East.

Then when Elaine became pregnant, she saw it as a disaster and only the willingness of her unmarried sister Betty to come and see her through her confinement made it bearable. But in the long run, would Betty's presence only serve to widen the rift between husband and wife, or would she help to bring about a reconciliation?

0 552 13622 0

THE GOLDEN STRAW
by Catherine Cookson

The Golden Straw, as it would be named, was a large, broad-brimmed hat presented to Emily Pearson by her long-time friend and employer Mabel Arkwright, milliner and modiste. And before long it was to her employer that Emily owed the gift of the business itself, for Mabel was in poor health and had come to rely more and more on Emily before her untimely death in 1880.

While on holiday in France, Emily and the Golden Straw attracted the eye of Paul Steerman, a guest at the hotel, and throughout his stay he paid her unceasing attention. But Paul Steerman was not all he seemed to be and he was to bring nothing but disgrace and tragedy to Emily, precipitating a series of events that would influence the destiny of not only her children but her grandchildren too.

The Golden Straw, conceived on a panoramic scale, brilliantly portrays a whole rich vein of English life from the heyday of the Victorian era to the stormy middle years of the present century. It represents a fresh triumph for this great storyteller whose work is deservedly loved and enjoyed throughout the world.

0 552 13685 9

A SELECTION OF OTHER CATHERINE COOKSON TITLES AVAILABLE FROM CORGI BOOKS

THE PRICES SHOWN BELOW WERE CORRECT AT THE TIME OF GOING TO PRESS. HOWEVER TRANSWORLD PUBLISHERS RESERVE THE RIGHT TO SHOW NEW RETAIL PRICES ON COVERS WHICH MAY DIFFER FROM THOSE PREVIOUSLY ADVERTISED IN THE TEXT OR ELSEWHERE.

☐	13576 3	THE BLACK CANDLE	£5.99
☐	12473 7	THE BLACK VELVET GOWN	£5.99
☐	14063 5	COLOUR BLIND	£4.99
☐	12551 2	A DINNER OF HERBS	£5.99
☐	14066 x	THE DWELLING PLACE	£5.99
☐	14068 6	FEATHERS IN THE FIRE	£5.99
☐	14089 9	THE FEN TIGER	£4.99
☐	14069 4	FENWICK HOUSES	£4.99
☐	10450 7	THE GAMBLING MAN	£4.99
☐	13716 2	THE GARMENT	£4.99
☐	13621 2	THE GILLYVORS	£5.99
☐	10916 9	THE GIRL	£4.99
☐	14071 6	THE GLASS VIRGIN	£4.99
☐	13685 9	THE GOLDEN STRAW	£5.99
☐	13300 0	THE HARROGATE SECRET	£4.99
☐	14087 2	HERITAGE OF FOLLY	£4.99
☐	13303 5	THE HOUSE OF WOMEN	£4.99
☐	10780 8	THE IRON FAÇADE	£4.99
☐	14091 0	JUSTICE IS A WOMAN	£4.99
☐	14091 0	KATE HANNIGAN	£4.99
☐	14092 9	KATIE MULHOLLAND	£5.99
☐	14081 3	MAGGIE ROWAN	£4.99
☐	13684 0	THE MALTESE ANGEL	£5.99
☐	10321 7	MISS MARTHA MARY CRAWFORD	£5.99
☐	12524 5	THE MOTH	£5.99
☐	13302 7	MY BELOVED SON	£5.99
☐	13088 5	THE PARSON'S DAUGHTER	£5.99
☐	14073 2	PURE AS THE LILY	£5.99
☐	13683 2	THE RAG NYMPH	£5.99
☐	14075 9	THE ROUND TOWER	£4.99
☐	13714 6	SLINKY JANE	£4.99
☐	10541 4	THE SLOW AWAKENING	£4.99
☐	10630 5	THE TIDE OF LIFE	£5.99
☐	12368 4	THE WHIP	£5.99
☐	13577 1	THE WINGLESS BIRD	£5.99
☐	13247 0	THE YEAR OF THE VIRGINS	£4.99

All Transworld titles are available by post from:

Book Service By Post, P.O. Box 29, Douglas, Isle of Man IM99 1BQ

Credit cards accepted. Please telephone 01624 675137, fax 01624 670923, Internet http://www.bookpost.co.uk or e-mail: bookshop@enterprise.net for details.

Free postage and packing in the UK. Overseas customers allow £1 per book (paperbacks) and £3 per book (hardbacks).